"MISS DARLINGTON, DO YOU KNOW HOW BEAUTIFUL YOU ARE?"

"Am . . . I . . . beautiful?" she said haltingly.

He slid his hand under her satin-soft chin and tilted her face, urging her to look at him. Shyly, she met his gaze. He smiled. "Oh, yes," he assured her. "You're very beautiful. And standing so close to you like this is playing havoc with my self-control and making me wish I weren't a gentleman. You are the sweetest, the most delectable temptation to come my way."

Her hands had remained on his chest, and now her fingers were splayed and were lightly—unconsciously?—caressing him. He could tell she was a sensuous woman underneath her prim exterior.

"Miss Darlington, have you ever been kissed?"

Her eyes lifted to stare into his. "Yes," she replied in a tremulous whisper. "But . . . not by you."

Praise for *REMEMBER ME*

"Ms. Allen is an author whose writing has 'star quality' written all over it."

Affaire de Coeur

REMEMBER ME

DANICE ALLEN

AVON BOOKS ◆ NEW YORK

REMEMBER ME is an original publication of Avon Books. This work has never before appeared in book form. This work is a novel. Any similarity to actual persons or events is purely coincidental.

AVON BOOKS
A division of
The Hearst Corporation
1350 Avenue of the Americas
New York, New York 10019

Dedicated with heartfelt gratitude to my sister-in-law, Debbie Ford. Deb, I can never thank you enough for taking care of my mom. May the angels watch over you and yours forever.

Chapter 1

Darlington Hall, village of Edenbridge
Surrey, England
October 1816

"**M**r. Tibble, can you possibly be saying that you've had this letter in your office since my father and mother died six months ago?"

The harried solicitor gripped the rim of his hat as he held it against his chest and peered anxiously at Amanda over the top of his spectacles. "Yes, Miss Darlington," he admitted meekly. "It was a grievous mistake made by one of our less experienced clerks. The letter had been misfiled under Darling*scott*, a client of ours in ... er ... Warwick, I think. Or is it Wart Hill?"

Amanda raised a brow. "Indeed, Mr. Tibble, it appears that everyone in your office has difficulty with names."

Mr. Tibble bowed his head, and Amanda was immediately sorry she'd spoken with such cool disdain. She did not like to see timid Mr. Tibble quake, but she was having a hard time controlling her displeasure. The envelope she'd let fall to her lap, standing out so glaringly white against the skirt of her black

1

bombazine gown, might contain a letter from her deceased parents using just the sort of tender words she'd longed to hear from them when they were alive.

It had been difficult mourning them, for they had been reserved and sparing with their affections. This posthumous letter gave her hope that unexpressed warmth had been hidden beneath her parents' staid exteriors.

"When was the letter delivered to your office, Mr. Tibble?" asked Amanda in a purposely softened voice.

Mr. Tibble dared to look up. "According to our records, it was three years ago, Miss Darlington. The instructions attached to it stated that the letter was to be delivered unopened to you on the advent of both your parents' death, whether they died separately and years apart, or together . . . as they did."

"Yes, as they did," murmured Amanda, remembering anew the horrible night she learned of the carriage accident that had instantly killed her father and mother. As an only child, Amanda had had to deal with all the arrangements for the funeral with only her two aunts, Nan and Prissy, to assist.

Mr. Tibble stood up. "I want to apologize again, Miss Darlington, most profusely," he said with respectful fervor. "I do hope you'll forgive me."

Amanda sighed. "It wasn't your fault, I daresay."

Mr. Tibble smiled tentatively and bowed, giving Amanda an eye-level view of his balding pate. "How gracious you are, Miss Darlington! Now I will leave you to your letter. That is, unless you wish me to be present in case . . ." His voice trailed off tactfully.

"I'm sure there's no need for you to stay," said Amanda, also standing, and towering over the diminutive Mr. Tibble. "As we covered everything that could possibly be related to the estate directly after the funeral, this can only be a private letter dealing with family matters."

Mr. Tibble smiled and bowed again, taking a backward step toward the door to the library. "Yes, of course. Excellent."

Amanda advanced and the solicitor took another backward step, still clutching his hat to his narrow chest. "I'll be going then. Do send word if you need me."

A few steps later and in a bracing tone, he said, "Tibble, Benchworth, and Cadbury have been unutterably honored to take care of your father's business for thirty years, Miss Darlington, and I do hope this little matter of misfiling won't offput you so much that you decide to—"

Amanda took Mr. Tibble's arm, gently turned him in the right direction, and hastened him to the door. She felt rather like a bully, as she had his advantage in height by at least four inches. "Never fear, Mr. Tibble," she assured him, showing him firmly out. "I don't intend to change solicitors. Henchpenny will show you to the door. Good day, Mr. Tibble."

Finally having got rid of the obsequious fellow, Amanda returned to her comfortable chair by the fire and sat down. She picked up the letter from the table on which she'd placed it and unsealed the envelope with a crested dagger. With trembling fingers she removed a single piece of parchment paper and carefully unfolded it.

She closed her eyes for an instant and took a deep breath. She was prepared to be moved by emotion. She was ready to shed a few tears.

She opened her eyes and fixed her gaze on her father's pinched, formal handwriting. Five minutes later, the letter fell from numb fingers and fluttered to the floor. She leaned back against the cushions of the wing chair and stared dry-eyed at the brightly colored autumn leaves as they drifted past the mullioned windows of the library.

"Dearest, you look positively ashen!" cried Nan.

"As pale as a ghost," concurred Prissy. Both of them hovered over Amanda like hens over a chick. "Whatever's the matter, Amanda Jane?"

Amanda stirred herself and sat up straight in the chair. "Dear aunts," she said sadly, "you had better sit down."

As well it might, this ominous pronouncement struck terror to the hearts of the two elderly spinsters and immediately compelled them to do exactly as they'd been advised. They sat down and, speechless for once, waited for their niece to explain.

"I received a letter today from the solicitor."

"Oh, dear," Nan said faintly. "Your father's will has been found to be null and void? You don't own the house after all?"

"No," said Amanda patiently, "the house is mine. The farm is mine. With no title in question and no male heir, Father could leave his money to whom he pleased. I am just as rich as ever, and you both are just as settled as my permanent houseguests. There is no question of our security."

"Then what was the letter about, pray tell?" prompted Prissy, twisting her hands in her lap. Aunt Prissy's hands were constantly in motion, the nervous habit as much a part of her as the mother-of pearl combs she always wore in her silver hair. Nan covered her own baby-soft thatch of white hair with a modest lace cap that tied under her plump chin. As befitted their period of mourning, they both wore severe black gowns.

Amanda shook her head. "I don't know if I believe it yet, even though I read it with my own eyes." She paused, then forced herself to press on to the crucial point as quickly as possible. "Father has more property, a cottage on Thorney Island in West Sussex."

The aunts exchanged glances. "But more property is good news, isn't it, Amanda Jane?" Nan's fading brown eyes were wide with puzzlement.

"Generally speaking—"

"I've never heard of Thorney Island," interrupted Prissy, "but if the cottage is livable, I daresay we could use a little holiday now and then on the coast. A cottage which is charmingly rustic is always pleasant, but I cannot abide damp walls, you know. How far is Thorney Island from here, I wonder? Brighton's so crowded lately, and it's harder than ever to get a bathing machine—"

"Oh, hush, Pris!" admonished Nan, swatting at her sister's skirt. "Amanda Jane's not finished speaking."

"Yes, do hear me out," said Amanda, with what she thought was admirable restraint. "This is not the time to rejoice in the possibility of dry stone cottages and bathing machines, Aunt Prissy. The house on Thorney Island is already occupied."

Nan, the more perceptive of the two, said, "And the occupant of this house is the thing that worries you most, Amanda Jane? Who is it? Good gracious, has your father got a mad uncle boarded up in the attic or some such French penny-novel nonsense? I never liked him, you know—God rest his soul—and I warned Clorinda not to marry him, but she wouldn't listen—"

"Now whose tongue is singing like a fiddlestick?" observed Prissy with a sniff.

"Don't argue, please," said Amanda, suddenly feeling very unequal to the task before her. She ran a shaky hand over her eyes and fell back in the chair.

"You are truly upset, Amanda Jane," said Nan with concern. She leaned forward and placed her hand on Amanda's knee. "Tell us, dear. Tell us what's wrong, and we promise to listen quietly."

Amanda rested her own hand on top of Nan's and forced herself to smile. "Thank you, dearest. Your quiet, undivided attention would be greatly appreciated."

Completely sobered and frightened by Amanda's unusual show of emotion, the aunts sat broomstick straight and listened. "The letter isn't from the solicitor; it's from Father and Mother."

"How is that possible?" asked Prissy in a quavering voice.

Amanda explained how the letter had been misfiled. "It was meant to be read directly after the funeral. It tells of another relation to us, but not an uncle ... mad or otherwise."

Prissy wrung her hands even more energetically than usual. "Then who?"

Amanda cleared her throat and dropped her gaze to her hands, which were resting in her lap. Now she clenched them till the knuckles were white. "I have a sibling."

This statement was met with silence. Without raising her head, Amanda hurried on. "Father had a child with a woman other than my mother. The letter doesn't say what sex or age the child is. It says only that the child has been kept at father's property, Thornfield Cottage on Thorney Island, since birth. Raised by a caretaker named Mrs. Grimshaw, the child has no knowledge of who its parents are. According to the letter, Father has been sending Mrs. Grimshaw fifty pounds every two months as a salary—to keep the house, buy food, etcetera. He does not mention any education for the child."

Amanda braved a look at her aunts and found them slack-jawed with shock.

"I don't wonder that you are surprised," said Amanda, adding bitterly, "Father and Mother were such models of respectability."

"I warned her not to marry him," murmured Nan.

"Men are such vile beasts!" added Prissy.

"What happened to the child's natural mother?" asked Nan.

"She died at childbirth."

"Oh," said the aunts together, silenced again.

Amanda stood and paced the hearth rug. She caught a glimpse of herself in the gilt-edged mirror over the mantel and was surprised to see her usual neat reflection staring back. Not a wisp of her pale blond hair was out of place. Her high-necked gown was as tidy and prim as her strict and proper mother could have possibly wished for. But inside Amanda was in turmoil, as torn apart as she'd ever been in the whole of her three-and-twenty years.

"My parents' entire life was a lie."

Nan rose naturally to the defense of her sister. "Don't blame Clorinda for something your father did."

"Mother knew of the child and must have condoned this secretive arrangement."

Prissy shrugged her narrow shoulders. "But what could she do about it? At least the child has been cared for."

"I find the handling of the whole situation deplorable," said Amanda with disgust. "Hiding the child away on some remote island, raised by a paid caretaker, was wrong. The child should have either been taken in by my parents when the natural mother died—even if Father had to claim him or her as an orphan he'd decided to sponsor—or arranged for the child to be adopted by a caring couple."

"There would have been speculations, whispered rumors," suggested Nan. "Your father would have found that sort of thing ... unpleasant."

"How pleasant has it been for my brother, or sister? Practically imprisoning the poor thing, with no idea who he is, with no one to love him but a servant who may or may not be kind!" Amanda shook her head vehemently. "I shudder to think my father's conscience was so easily mollified by sending off fifty pounds every other month, then never giving the poor little merry-begotten another thought!"

"Amanda Jane!" exclaimed the aunts in unison, surprised by her loose language.

Amanda stopped her furious pacing and turned to face her aunts. "Do you realize that no money has been sent to Thornfield Cottage since March and it is now the fifth of October?"

"Have there been no letters from Thornfield Cottage requesting money of your father?" asked Prissy.

"According to Father's letter, the caretaker was never told the family name or given the directions to this house. Father's instructions to me were to continue the same practice as long as I deemed it necessary—basing my decision on yearly visits in the spring to Mrs. Grimshaw at a prearranged spot away from Thornfield Cottage—or to simply quit sending the money if I chose to ignore the situation. It sounds like he never once clapped eyes on the child." She shook her head. "And he must have thought me as heartless as he if he thought I could act in a similarly cold and businesslike manner."

"What are you going to do, Amanda Jane?" asked Nan. "Obviously you are gravely concerned about the child."

Amanda felt a calmness wash over her even as she drummed up the courage to speak. "I'm going to fetch the child and bring it here."

"You're going to do *what*?" Once again the aunts were in fine voice and completely unified.

"Well, why shouldn't I? I've led a proper life, looking up to my parents as shining examples of how to behave. And look where's it's got me! I'm quite on the shelf, as stuffy and joyless as my parents ever were. Did you see them exchange one tender look, aunts? Did she ever straighten his cravat? Did he ever stroke her cheek or allow his hand to linger at her waist once he'd guided her through the door? Never!"

"They did not approve of public displays of affection, I daresay," offered Prissy, not very convincingly.

"Nor private, either, I'd wager," said Amanda. "Once Mother gave birth to me, they probably never again shared a warming pan. I shan't let my life be dictated any longer by my parents' notions of what's proper. I'm going to go immediately and find out what's happened to that child and then rescue it from Father and Mother's so-called charity."

"People might think the child is yours," suggested Nan in a quiet voice.

"I don't give a blessed fig what people think of me anymore," announced Amanda, moving to the bellpull by the fireplace and giving it a vigorous tug. "I only want to do what's right for the child, and the gossips be hanged."

Prissy wrung her hands with feverish intensity. "What's right for the child might not include bringing it here, Amanda Jane. Are you perhaps thinking of yourself a little? Have you wanted a brother or sister to care for?"

Amanda was brought up short. Was she being selfish? Did she want a brother or sister to share this massive house with her? Did she want a child to raise, since she apparently wasn't destined for marriage and children of her own? She loved her aunts, but they'd not be around forever. And even now, they couldn't fill a need in her that grew stronger every day.... Would a child, a sibling, fill that void?

"I'm not going to worry about my motives right now, aunts," she told them. "Time is of the essence. Who knows what's happened to that child since the money stopped coming. Once I've made sure of the child's well-being, I'll give considerable thought to the future."

The door opened, and the butler entered the room. "You rang, miss?"

"Yes, Henchpenny. I need you to make some arrangements for me. I'm going on a trip."

"To the village, miss?"

"No, Henchpenny, this will be a long trip. I may be gone several days."

He did not blink an eye, although Amanda hadn't ventured much beyond Edenbridge since her miserable season in London four years ago. "You'll need the traveling chaise then, miss. How many outriders will you require?"

"Only two. Harley and Joe will do nicely. If Theo complains, simply tell him I'll drive myself."

The butler's lips twitched. "Yes, miss. I make no doubt that such a threat will secure Mister Theo's immediate cooperation. And shall I tell your abigail to pack for the both of you?"

"No, Henchpenny," said Amanda, stooping to retrieve the letter from where it still reposed on the floor. When she stood up again her face felt flushed, but whether it was from dipping her head or from the exhilaration of the new sense of freedom that surged through her veins, she wasn't sure. And she didn't care. "No, Henchpenny," she began again. "Tell Iris to pack only for me."

The aunts gave a collective gasp.

Henchpenny was beginning to look baffled and disapproving. "Er . . . may I tell Iris to pack for Miss Nancy and Miss Priscilla, then?"

"No, you may not. I'm going alone."

"Amanda Jane, this is foolishness!" exclaimed Prissy.

Nan pushed herself up from the sofa. "It's too dangerous to go alone. If you insist on going, I'll go with you."

"I wouldn't dream of exposing you to such an arduous journey, Aunt. And, as the mission I'll be on is of a rather delicate nature, the less people involved the better." Amanda turned to Henchpenny. "I give permission to my aunts to explain to you where I'm going and why, but that's as far as I wish the story to spread. I'm counting on all three of you to be very discreet. Of course I must confide in Theo, too, but no one else. When I return from Thorney Island, hopefully with someone with me, we'll decide what the next best step should be. Does everyone understand?"

By now, Henchpenny was looking thoroughly perplexed. "I shall strive to, miss," he murmured.

"Now hurry along, Henchpenny," said Amanda as she breezed by him into the hall. "I want to leave before dark, and it's already half past four. There's a full moon tonight, and unless it rains, we'll be able to drive quite long after sunset. I'll stop at a roadside inn around midnight, then resume my journey on the morrow. And do get rid of that Friday face, Henchpenny. All will be well."

As Amanda's quick footsteps echoed down the hall, Henchpenny turned to the aunts. "Pardon me, ladies, but what the devil has come over the mistress?"

"You might well ask, Henchpenny," said Nan with a raised brow. "See to the mistress's traveling arrangements, and Miss Priscilla and I will be happy to explain."

Henchpenny stalked away, his heavy brow still furrowed in a deep frown. The aunts watched him go, then turned to each other and nodded their heads sagely.

"I was wondering when some of *our* side of the family would show up in the chit," said Nan. "I was beginning to fear that father of hers had completely ruined her, just as he ruined Clorinda."

"You know, Nan," said Prissy, her eyes taking on a dreamy quality, "now that I've given it some thought, I think I shall *like* having a child about the house."

"Yes," agreed Nan with a decided nod. "A child would be even better than a seaside holiday."

The tiny country pub called The Spotted Dog was filled with smoke and smelled of liquor, sweat, and cow manure. Jackson Montgomery, Viscount Durham, slumped in his chair and counted the empty tumblers on the table in front of him. It was becoming rather difficult to focus, and he greatly feared that he was counting some tumblers twice.

"Tha's one, tha's two, tha's three—"

"Fifteen. Thirty-four. Ninety-nine. What does it matter how many you drink, Jack?" was the devil-may-care question posed by his traveling companion and best friend, Robert Hamilton. "I say, eat, drink, and be merry, old chap, because tomorrow you . . . *marry*."

"You're so right," said Jack, squinting across the table and seeing two of his friend instead of one . . . two heads of blond curls styled à la cherubim, two choirboy faces with blue eyes and long lashes. "But why don't you join me, ol' chap. You've only had a couple, Robbie."

"*I'm* not getting married, Jack. You're the *lucky* one."

Jack frowned. "I do believe you're hoaxin' me, Rob."

"Drink up, Jack!" said Rob in a bracing tone. "Finish your brew and I'll call the barkeep for another."

Obediently, Jack took another long drink from his tumbler of Blue Ruin, then wiped his mouth with the back of his hand. "Bad form to *shtagger* down the aisle, don't ya know."

"Pooh, Jack," said Rob, waving a hand—or was

that two hands?—dismissively. "You've got Charlotte in your hip pocket, just like every other chit in
London. She'll be waiting for you at the altar whether
you dance, march or fly down the aisle. Wish't I had
your way with the ladies," he added with grudging
good humor.

Jack took another drink. "Charlotte likes you,
Rob."

"Not as well as she likes you."

"Only wish't I liked her as well as she likes *me*,"
observed Jack morosely.

"If you don't love her, Jack, why don't you leave
her to me?"

"Don't think I'll ever fall in love, Rob. Never have,
ya know, and I was two-and-thirty last June." He bit
his lip, concentrating hard. "Or was that *three*-and-
thirty? But never mind. Charlotte's a good 'un, ain't
she, Rob?"

"Rich, too," grumbled Rob.

"That don't signify," objected Jack.

"Not to you."

"Fun to hug, she is. Plump in all the right
places . . . if you know what I mean."

"Yes, and plump in the purse, too."

"A man'd be an idiot, a *shelfish* brute, a . . . a . . .
villain to want more, eh, Rob?"

"I couldn't agree with you more," concurred his
amiable friend, rising from his chair to stand over
Jack. "Stay here, old man; I'm going to see if they've
got any food in this godforsaken place. I'll send the
barkeep over to pour you another drink."

Jack didn't bother to reply but finished off the
dregs of his brew in anticipation of another full
tumbler.

"Milord? Are ye wantin' another?"

Jack carefully lifted his chin and peered at the
blurred figure of a man standing by the table. He
had to look up . . . and up . . . and up to finally fix

on the man's face. Eventually Jack's head was resting on the back of the chair. There was only one of them, but the face was merely a fuzzy oval with two dark slashes for eyebrows and tiny dark holes for eyes. Those slashes and holes were vaguely familiar.... Ah, yes. The barkeep.

"How kin' of you t'wask, my good man," said Jack, stretching his mouth into a friendly smile. "Rob sent you over, did he?"

"He did, milord. Only I wonder if'n ye really need another drink," he said doubtfully.

"If Rob says I need a drink, I need a drink," said Jack, sounding as firm as his slurred speech would allow. "He saved my life, ya know, in Oporto, fightin' that bloody bastard, Napoléon."

"He's got you as a friend fer life, then, don't he, milord?"

"Right as rain, my good fellow. Now pour the gin, *pleash.* I'm *thirshty,* y'know. So damned *thirshty* I could drink the North Sea."

The man's shape shifted, the broad part of him bobbing up and down. There was a sound like an owl hooting, only in fast succession. Then he realized the barkeep was laughing. Jack was glad he'd said something amusing, but he couldn't for the life of him remember what.

"Still thirsty, eh? Must have coated yer throat with dust good and proper on yer way up from Brighton," said the barkeep, pouring more gin into another tumbler. "Well, I'll give ye one more for the road. Ye're in yer altitudes, milord, and bound t' be shootin' the cat soon. I wouldn't let ye get so foxed if'n I didn't depend on yer friend ... what's raidin' my kitchen and chasin' the scullery wench ... t' get ye safely back to London t'night."

"Safely to London," repeated Jack, staring wide-eyed at the tumbler of gin. "Safely home to my blushing bride."

The barkeep whistled. The sound made Jack's head buzz, and he shook it to clear out the infernal hive of bees that must have entered through one ear or the other. "Ye're newly leg-shackled, then, milord?"

Jack dragged the tumbler to his side of the table. Then with considerable effort he lifted his head again to look at the fuzzy oval that was the barkeep's face. "No, my good man," he said with deliberate pronunciation. "I'm not shackled yet." He pointed to his chest with his forefinger. "Till tomorrow morning, I"—he poked his chest—"am"—another poke—"a free man." Poke, poke, poke.

"Ah, so's that's the reason we're in our cups, milord? Can't say I blame ye. Marriage is a drastic step for a chap."

"One *drashtic* step," agreed Jack. And one he'd avoided for years. But he wanted an heir. Legally there was only one way to accomplish that, and he was prepared to make the sacrifice.

"It's not that she's such a bad sort," he mumbled into his mug.

"What's that, milord?"

"My fansee—"

"Yer fancy, milord?"

Jack hiccupped, then furrowed his brow in serious concentration. "No. My fee-on-shay—"

The barkeep bent near. " 'Fraid I don't understand ye, milord," he apologized.

"My betrothed," said Jack, abandoning the French word for one less difficult to pronounce.

"Ah!"

"She's smart, pretty, and pleasant to kiss," he said, praising his bride-to-be to this total stranger, much in the same way he'd praised her to Rob. He suspected he was only trying to convince himself, and not them, that he was doing the right thing. "What else could a man want?" He looked to the barkeep for corroboration.

"Right ye are, milord," the barkeep said readily. "What else could a man want?"

What else indeed? thought Jack philosophically. A man could want to be truly in love for once in his life. But right now, after too many tumblers of gin to count, a man could want to relieve himself. He put both hands flat on the tabletop and pushed himself to his feet. Immediately his head began to spin.

"Hell and damnation."

"Do ye need some help, milord?" The barkeep had somehow skirted the table without Jack noticing and was standing at his elbow. Jack had no desire to be helped outside for the private purpose he intended. It was unmanly. And it proved he was too drunk to take care of the most basic of human functions.

"No thank you, my good man," he said, lifting his chin proudly even though his head was already pounding like a kettledrum. "Just direct me to the *nearesht* door, if you *pleash*."

The barkeep pointed to a dark archway that looked to Jack about a mile away. "That's the back entrance, milord."

"*Exshellent*," said Jack, and he weaved himself in that direction.

He got outside, wandered in a profusion of bushes for a while, took care of matters, then headed back toward the door of the pub. But after several minutes, he realized that he'd perhaps gone the wrong way. He stood still for a moment and looked around.

The trees were tall and blocked out the moonlight. The vegetation surrounding him was thick and he could observe no evidence anywhere of a footpath parting the shrubbery, but it was dark and foggy, and everything was spinning. "Hell and damnation," he said in salute to the wilds of the West Sussex countryside.

He was beginning to question the wisdom of pulling over at such a secluded, bump-in-the-road pub to wet his whistle. They could have gone on a while longer and stopped somewhere more civilized. But they'd stopped at his command, then the gin and the miserable anticipation of his wedding on the morrow had overcome him.

Jack strived to think. He must face facts; he was as fuddled as he'd ever been in his life and, judging by the ominous rumblings of his stomach, about to cast up his accounts. He staggered to what he hoped was a clearing in the brush and felt the cool rush of wind in his hair. For the first time since he'd left the pub, he noticed it was lightly raining. The cool water on his face was refreshing, so he stood there for a minute with his eyes closed as his stomach thankfully began to settle.

A noise was intruding on his serenity, though. A distant thunderous sound. He felt vibrations through the soles of his boots. But his brain was so muddled by booze, he couldn't remember where he'd heard that sound before.

The sound was getting louder, coming closer. He opened his eyes and realized he was standing in the middle of a highway. Terror struck him as he suddenly recognized the sound and anticipated his fate. Coming round a bend in the road was a coach-and-four being driven at a spanking pace.

As he lunged to the side in a desperate effort to avoid the imminent trampling of his sorry bones, he speculated wryly that death was certainly one way to avoid marriage but not the sort of escape he'd have willingly chosen. So awfully permanent, you know....

Chapter 2

The driver shouted a curse, the horses whinnied, and Amanda lurched forward as the coach rocked and shuddered to an abrupt stop.

"Good heavens!" she exclaimed as she righted herself in the seat and pushed the rim of her bonnet out of her eyes. "We must have hit a cow!" But when she scrambled out of the coach, she found Theo kneeling beside the prone figure of a man, the two outriders standing over him with lanterns.

Amanda's stomach twisted with empathy and apprehension, and for a moment she was unable to move. The man's long legs, clad in light gray breeches and tall black boots, were the only part of him she could see from where she stood; his face was entirely hidden from view behind Theo's broad back. The man did not lie directly in the path of the agitated horses but was sprawled just off the road to the side. He was very still. *Too* still.

"Good God, Theo, we haven't killed him, have we?" she asked her coachman in a tremulous whisper.

"We didn't trample 'im, if'n that's what ye're wonderin', miss," answered Theo, turning to look at her. As he was crouched directly under the lantern glow,

Amanda could see her coachman's distraught expression quite clearly.

"Then what happened, pray tell? You wouldn't look so milk-faced if there was no reason for concern. Why does he lie so still?"

"He was standin' dazed-like in the middle of the road, miss. He got out th' way just in time, but it appears he hit 'is head on a rock."

"Is he breathing?"

"Yes, miss."

"Is he . . . bleeding?"

"Like a faucet, miss."

"Then stem the flow!"

"Beggin' yer pardon, miss, but with what?"

"Good heavens, Theo, use your imagination!" Amanda said, exasperated. She watched Theo cast his eyes about the wet, leaf-strewn ground in a helpless manner for no more than thirty seconds before she lifted her skirt and tore a flounce from her petticoat. Theo and the two young outriders averted their gazes.

"Here, use this!" ordered Amanda, thrusting the length of muslin toward her embarrassed servant. "When a man's life is in jeopardy, 'tis ridiculous and *deadly*, I daresay, to be a prude!"

"Yes, miss," mumbled Theo, taking the delicate ruffle with shaky fingers and wadding it into a ball.

"No, Theo! Fold it!" admonished Amanda, advancing till she stood next to him. "Fold it several times, then press it to the wound!"

Theo tried to do as he was instructed, but he was as ham-handed as possible, even dropping the fabric twice on the sodden ground. "What's the matter with you, Theo?" Amanda demanded. "Your ability as a horse doctor is well known!"

"But this ain't no horse, miss," Theo complained miserably. "This here's a swell if ever I seen one!

Nursin' a nobleman ain't no joke! What if he turns up 'is toes and they string me up fer murder?"

"Nonsense!" scolded Amanda.

"It could happen, miss," Theo assured her. His round face, framed by muttonchop whiskers, was etched with worry.

"Don't be a peagoose, Theo! He's not going to die ... unless, of course, we let him bleed to death!" Amanda intensely disliked the sight of blood and was certainly not accustomed to touching strange gentlemen, but this was an emergency. She lifted her chin and demanded, "Step aside and let me have a go at 'im!"

Theo more than willingly relinquished his responsibility for the swell into his employer's only slightly steadier hands.

As Amanda got down on her knees beside the man, she sternly told herself to be calm and efficient. Now was not the time for her to get swoonish over a bit of blood, or to let her shy reluctance to touch a member of the opposite sex get in the way of saving a man's life.

Without looking directly at the unconscious gentleman, and disregarding the muddy ground and the rain that spotted her velvet cloak, she hastily folded the muslin. "Hold the lantern closer, please," she ordered.

In the bright glow of the lantern, Amanda finally looked at her patient. For a moment she was so arrested by the man's face, she froze. He was by far the handsomest man she'd clapped eyes on in an age. She winced when she saw the gash above his left brow, however, and immediately pressed the folded muslin against it for a couple of minutes, then dabbed away some of the blood.

She was relieved to see that the laceration was not very deep, but he did have a rather alarming lump beneath it. She supposed the swelling accounted, in part, for his continued unconsciousness. But Amanda smelled the strong odor of liquor on the man's person and concluded that he was inebriated, too. She wondered how much his unconsciousness could be attributed to his injury and how much was the result of too much brew-tipping!

While her servants once again averted their gazes, Amanda tore another length of muslin from her petticoat, then wrapped it around the man's head in a makeshift bandage. "There, that shall have to do till a physician can be consulted," she said, briskly whisking her hands together. "We'd better get him off that cold ground and out of the rain immediately or else he might catch an inflammation of the lung to add to his troubles. Lift him into the carriage, gentlemen."

"Where are we takin' 'im, miss?" was Theo's most reasonable question.

Amanda's brows furrowed. "I don't know." She scanned the area, seeing nothing but thick shrubbery and trees shrouded in mist. "I can't even imagine where he came from in the first place. I don't see any lights or smoke from a chimney."

"According to the map, the closest village is ten miles west of here, miss," said Theo. "They might have a doctor there to attend to the gent. And even if they don't, I'm thinkin' it'd be smart to rack up for the night at the first decent inn we see in town and take care of 'im as best we can."

"Yes, that would be the logical thing to do," Amanda agreed. "I had been thinking it was time to stop even before this unfortunate accident. We're nearer the coast here, and the fog is rolling in. Travel could become quite difficult. As for this gentleman, once he's regained consciousness, he'll be able to explain the whole incident and give us names and directions of relatives we can notify."

And hopefully they'd not be delayed too dreadfully long from pursuing the real purpose of the trip, thought Amanda. She felt sorry for the injured gentleman, as well as responsible, but getting to Thorney Island to rescue her half-sibling was uppermost in her thoughts.

"You take 'is feet, Harley," ordered Theo, speaking to the smaller of the two outriders. "I'll take 'is upper parts, and Joe, you keep 'is middle parts from saggin'. The bloke weighs at least fourteen stone, I'd wager!"

Amanda held both lanterns and watched as her servants lifted the man—with some considerable effort—off the ground. He was absolute dead weight and hadn't moved, nor even so much as twitched, since he'd hurtled himself out of harm's way and connected in such an unfortunate manner with a rock.

His inertia alarmed Amanda. After all, he looked to be in prime twig. He couldn't be much over thirty years old, and every bit of the fourteen stone he carried on his tall frame had to be either muscle or vital organs, as he appeared not to be the least encumbered by fat. He was dressed very smartly, too, and would no doubt be horrified to know how muddied he'd become.

Despite the labored breathing of her servants and their uncertain footing in the muddy road, the removal of the gentleman to the carriage was going along fairly well till Joe slipped and fell. Without his assistance, Theo and Harley staggered and looked ready to drop their burden had not Amanda set down her lanterns and come to their rescue by supporting the suddenly unsupported "middle parts."

Even as she exerted all her effort to do her fair share of the heaving and hoeing, Amanda thought with some amusement that for the first time in her life she had her hands quite firmly planted on a man's derriere. She also thought, with a rush of blood to her cheeks, that his derriere felt rather pleasantly . . . firm.

Not too soon for Amanda's deteriorating composure, they finally maneuvered the gentleman into the carriage and draped his large body on the forward-facing seat. The man was much too big to fit comfortably on the cushions; his legs dangled off the end and stretched across the foot space between the seats. But in his condition he could not be aware of how uncomfortably he was situated, so Amanda tried to disregard how awkward he looked crammed into the small space and stepped into the carriage to sit down opposite him.

As she was settling her damp skirts about her, Theo stuck his head in the door and said, "We'd best get Harley or Joe in here with ye, miss."

"Under the circumstances," said Amanda dryly, "I don't think a chaperon is necessary."

"He might wake up, miss, and be out of 'is head. He's in 'is cups, and who knows what he'd do once't he found hisself alone with a comely female . . . if ye don't mind my plain speakin', miss."

"If the goose egg on his forehead doesn't keep him sleeping like a babe till long after we reach the inn, the goodly amount of liquor he imbibed certainly will," Amanda calmly replied. "Besides, there's no room for another passenger."

"Harley's no wider than a lamppost, miss. He'd squeeze in nicely, I should think."

"No, thank you, Theo," she said firmly. "If I find myself in danger of being seduced or strangled, I shall certainly use my parasol to knock on the ceiling . . . or on the stranger's head if the situation is desperate."

Theo frowned doubtfully.

"Now, do hurry along, Theo, and drive us to that village you mentioned before I freeze to death or the gentleman actually *does* recover his senses."

"I don't know, miss," Theo said stubbornly, convinced it was an odd business allowing his mistress to be closeted with a stranger . . . swell or otherwise.

"He'll have the devil of a headache, you know, when he does come about," Amanda said pointedly. "He'll want some brandy and a warm, dry bed to collapse into. Remember, Theo, we're dealing with a gentleman who is accustomed to comfort, and who may perhaps be a little toplofty, as well. If he learns you delayed our departure out of concern for my safety while in his company, he might take umbrage!"

Theo needed no further inducement to climb atop the box and urge the horses to a gallop.

Amanda leaned back against the velvet squabs of the carriage and pulled off her wet and dirty gloves, her eyes fixed on the fashionable fellow sprawled on the seat across from her. The lantern inside her carriage was lighted, and she could observe him quite easily and, since he had no notion he was the object of her perusal . . . quite freely as well. Though considerably disheveled at the moment, he was a handsome one, all right. But what did that signify to an old maid like herself?

She sighed deeply. "How one's life can change in the twinkling of a bedpost," she commented aloud. "First I find out I have an illegitimate sibling I must rescue, then I am compelled to play nursemaid to a sinfully handsome, inebriated fellow who wandered—quite out of nowhere!—directly into the path of my galloping horses! I feel perfectly justified in complaining that I've not had a fortuitous day!" She shook her head and clicked her tongue at her unconscious companion. "And neither have you, my good man."

To Amanda's considerable consternation, the gentleman chose that moment to stir. He moaned and reached for his bandaged forehead, instinctively seeking to alleviate the source of his discomfort. Just as instinctively, Amanda leaned forward and grasped the man's wrists.

"No, you mustn't touch the wound, sir," she admonished him in a low but forceful tone. "The bleeding may start again."

His head moved fitfully on the cushion, but his eyes didn't open and he did not answer her. She glanced down at his hands and was astonished that she had managed to stop him from grabbing his bandage. Though finely shaped, with long fingers and neatly trimmed nails, it was obvious his hands were capable of great strength. They'd gone limp now, and she lowered them to his chest.

Bracing herself against the back of the seat as the carriage swayed and rocked over the country roads, she stood over him till he settled down and appeared to be sleeping again. Then, for good measure, she stood over him a few minutes longer. She tried to convince herself she was merely concerned that he may suddenly become restless again and reach for his bandage, but her inherent honesty forced her to admit otherwise.

She *liked* looking at him. Except for the dancing she'd shyly suffered through during her season four years ago, she had never been this close to a man. And certainly no man as attractive as this one.

His hair was a riotous tumble of black curls flattened here and there by a glob of mud, but she could well imagine how fine it would look clean and gleaming in candlelight or sunshine. A curling strand dangled over his brow, and her fingers itched to touch it, to examine its texture. But she hesitated, held back by the habits of her strict upbringing. She almost felt it would be a sin of sorts to indulge her curiosity, because she was quite sure she would find touching this strange man most pleasurable.

Then a rebellious thought came conveniently to her

rescue. Why should she allow the habits instilled in her by her parents to continue to dictate her actions when she had so recently received shocking proof that her mother and father's pious existence was nothing but a sham?

Amanda clenched her jaw. It was but a paltry act of rebellion, but it was a start. She bravely reached down and caught the dusky curl, gently pressing and rubbing it between thumb and forefinger. She smiled to herself, satisfied that her imagination had not exceeded reality in this case. The strand of hair was as silky soft as a kitten's ear, but thick and springy, too. She brushed it back from his forehead and looked critically at the man's face.

His brows were black and gracefully arched. Feeling quite brazen by now, she lightly followed the curve of his brow with the tip of her finger. She admired his thick lashes, which were lush enough to send a green girl into heart flutters. Luckily she was no green girl, or she might have misconstrued that odd sensation in her chest.

His nose was straight and slightly aquiline. His lips were boldly curved, and she would have traced their sensuous outline, too, if she hadn't been convinced that she'd already been rebellious enough for one day.

But then she noticed a scar on his upper right cheekbone, very thin and silvery white, and at least an inch long. It looked like a knife or saber wound. Instead of detracting from his looks, it seemed to add to them, making him appear brave, dangerous, mysterious. . . . She touched the scar. It was smooth and soft.

Then she found herself fascinated by the shadow of a beard on his jaw and chin, and she couldn't help but wonder how a man's skin felt when he needed a shave. She doubted she'd ever have the opportunity to find out during the sort of physical intimacies enjoyed between husbands and wives, so she decided that one last delicious act of rebellion was inevitable.

She ever-so-carefully laid her palm against his cheek, ready to pull back the instant he reacted to her touch. Feeling a strange flutter of excitement, she lightly moved her hand back and forth. The beard stubble tickled her tender palm like the soft bristles of a brush. She wondered how those bristles would feel against her cheek, her breasts. . . .

Alarmed and feeling flushed by such unusually provocative thoughts, Amanda was about to remove her hand when the man, who had been lying so peacefully an instant before, grabbed her wrist and pressed her palm to his lips. As Amanda stiffened with shock, he released her hand, and a faint, sly smile flickered over his lips.

"You minx," he murmured in a low, seductive voice. "Don't you ever get enough? Grant me a half-hour's sleep, then I'll—"

But what he would do remained a mystery because his words trailed off as he grimaced with pain and reached for his bandaged head again. Amanda shook free of the pleasant paralysis that had been induced by his warm mouth against her skin and prevented him from disturbing the bandage.

As before, he was surprisingly easy to control. But she suspected that his meekness was only a temporary condition, a product of his inebriated state and the easy, alarming way he slid in and out of consciousness, and not a usual facet of his personality.

Amanda sank into her seat, feeling as though she had been walking on the edge of a cliff, playing a dangerous game far beyond her power to control. She took one last look at the gentleman, who was again lying quite motionless, and closed her eyes. It had been wrong to touch the man without his knowledge or invitation, and it would be easier by far to abstain from further misbehavior if she ceased to gaze at him like a mooncalf.

Soon they would arrive at the inn, and despite the glib way she'd spoken to her coachman, she sincerely hoped the man would have regained consciousness by then. She greatly feared he had suffered a concussion. As well, he might already be missed by friends or relatives, and they'd be worried about him. She wanted him to give a lucid accounting of himself because it was puzzling how he could have ended up in the middle of a wilderness quite drunk and entirely alone. As soon as he could speak, he'd hopefully be able to clear up the mystery surrounding his odd appearance out of nowhere.

She wondered if he was married. She saw no wedding ring on his finger, but men were frequently indifferent about wearing a piece of jewelry that announced one's marital status. She wondered if the "minx" he'd dreamily referred to in his state of semiconsciousness was his wife . . . or some bit of fluff?

Amanda felt an unexpected stab of jealousy toward this unknown female. And despite her conviction that such thoughts were improper, Amanda couldn't help but indulge in a short but extremely pleasant daydream that involved her willing participation in minxlike behavior with the handsome stranger sharing her coach.

Moments later, Amanda pulled herself together and gave herself a stern mental shake. She was surprised by her instant attraction to this man and the risqué thoughts that had beset her ever since she'd first laid eyes . . . and hands . . . on him.

She wasn't sure if there was something so compelling about him that made her give in to urges, or if she was simply rebelling out of anger against her parents. It was too complicated, and she had too many other things to think about . . . namely the more important and pressing problems that awaited her on Thorney Island.

The horses slowed to a canter, and Amanda lifted the leather shade to peer out the carriage window. They were passing through a small village and, within moments, had pulled into the cobbled courtyard of an inn. Amanda could see a large lantern hanging from an awning over the front door, the glow from it illuminating a wooden sign declaring the name of the establishment to be the Inn of the Three Nuns. It was a modern structure of stucco and thatch but was rather small. She hoped there would be no trouble bespeaking at least two rooms, since she was fairly certain a small village in West Sussex could boast no more than one public inn.

When Harley opened the door and let down the steps for her, she instructed him to stay inside with the injured man till she made sure rooms were available, but she motioned for Joe to follow her as she hurried through the drizzle and up to the door. Once they stood inside the cozy hall, she glanced about for someone to assist her.

At last a sharp-faced, angular woman, with gray hair pulled into a tight coil at the nape of her neck, came through a narrow doorway. She was dressed in a plain gray dress and white apron and was wiping her hands on a dishcloth.

"What kin I do fer ye, miss?" she asked without a trace of hospitality in her manner. Her hard eyes flitted over Amanda's mud-spotted skirts, then over to where Joe stood near the door, his coat dripping water on the clean floor.

"I'd like to speak to the landlord, please," Amanda replied politely.

"M' husband's been dead nearly a year and a half," the woman informed her briskly. "I run the inn now and you'll have t' speak t' me."

"Oh, I see," said Amanda, not sure whether to

offer condolences or simply state her business as quickly as possible. By the continued unfriendly expression on the woman's face, Amanda decided on the latter. "I'd like a room," she said. "That is, I'd like three rooms if you have the vacancies. One for me, one for my . . . er . . . companion, who is waiting in the carriage, and the last for my servants, whom I should wish to see accommodated in the house rather than above the stables."

The woman scowled, giving the distinct impression that she'd rather Amanda had simply stopped to ask for directions and not troubled her with a request for rooms. She shook her head, saying, "Only got one room left, miss, and it might not suit ye. 'Tis the smallest of the lot."

Dismayed by this news, Amanda exclaimed, "Oh dear, what's to do? I don't suppose there's another inn for miles!"

"Not fer another fifteen, miss."

Amanda bit her lip and frowned. "Then we'll have to manage with the one room." She wasn't sure how, but she'd figure something out.

The woman shrugged. "Suit yerself, miss. Make's no never mind to me. If'n ye stay, the servants can bunk with the ostlers above the stables. 'Tis clean enough, and there's but a few fleas this time o' year. The room I told ye about is indeed quite small, but the bed's big enough fer two, if'n yer husband's reasonable sized."

"Oh, but he's not—" Amanda stopped herself before she uttered the words she was suddenly quite sure would land her in the suds. She very foolishly had not considered how improper it would appear to most people—and certainly to this crotchety old tough who had already narrowed her eyes suspiciously—to be traveling without a chaperon and in the company of a man who was not her husband. There were extenuating circumstances, of course, but

Amanda didn't have time to waste lengthy explanations on someone who would very likely be unmoved by them.

"Was you about to say he's not yer husband, miss?" the woman demanded to know. "We run a respectable establishment here, and I'll not have folks playin' fast and loose on my premises!"

The woman's ferret-like eyes took another more inclusive assessment of Amanda's person. As she was enveloped in a black velvet cloak and wore an unadorned bonnet on her head and plain black kid boots on her feet, Amanda couldn't imagine how she could look more respectable. She could perhaps be a bit more modishly rigged out, and she was a little muddy and travel-worn, but she was quite certain she didn't bear the slightest resemblance to a woman of easy virtue.

"My dear lady!" exclaimed Amanda, forcing a laugh. "You quite misunderstand! I did not say he *wasn't* my husband, I only meant to say he is not—as you so charmingly phrased it—of a reasonable size! And since he met with an accident en route here, I hadn't planned on ... er ... sharing his bed in the first place. I'll need a cot and a—"

"Met with an accident, did he?" the proprietress asked sharply. "What sort of an accident?"

"He fell and hit his head on a rock when we were compelled to stop the carriage and allow him to ... er ... step out for a few moments," said Amanda, blushing with embarrassment because she was forced to refer to private matters no lady had any business discussing.

"He's not bleeding, is he? I've just scrubbed the floor, and there's a new carpet in the room you'll be stayin' in," was the woman's most unsympathetic rejoinder.

Amanda was at the end of her tether. She perceived that no amount of patience and pleasantness

would be effective in dealing with such an ill-
tempered woman. Amanda lifted her chin and lev-
eled her a chilling, contemptuous gaze. "My good
woman, I have tried to be gracious despite your sin-
gular lack of concern toward my injured husband,
the *earl*." Amanda thought she heard Joe gasp and
sincerely hoped he wasn't staring with his mouth
agape. "It appears I have no choice but to—"

The woman's jaw dropped. "Your husband's an
earl? And you're a *countess*?" She gave Amanda's
well-made but unremarkable traveling apparel another once-over.

"The one usually goes with the other," sniffed
Amanda.

"I saw you coming from an upstairs window, and
I don't recall seeing a crest on the carriage," the
woman said doubtfully.

"As you can plainly see by my appearance, we're
in mourning, and in such times of grief my husband
prefers to travel as inconspicuously as possible. But
that is beside the point. He may have a severe concussion and is still lying in a cold carriage when he
should be properly put to bed and looked over by a
physician. But if you persist in lamenting the possibility of blood on your clean floor, we may certainly
travel farther on in search of a warmer welcome. I
daresay, however, that his lordship shan't have much
good to say of your hospitality, and if business suddenly drops off, you'll have no one to blame but
yourself!"

Amanda pulled a fat purse from a pocket hidden
in her skirt. " 'Twill be a shame, too, if you decide
not to accommodate the earl, as he is known for his
generosity and would be *most* grateful to you!"

"Oh, my *lady*!" exclaimed the woman, transfixed
by the size of Amanda's purse and convinced by her
haughty manners that she was indeed a member of
the peerage. "Don't mind me, if you please! I've had

the megrims all day and beg your pardon for takin' my troubles out on you!"

Amanda gave a slight nod as mute acceptance of the woman's apology, then inquired, "What is the name of this town, madam?"

" 'Tis Horsham, milady."

"And what is *your* name, if you please?"

The woman curtsied. " 'Tis Mrs. Beane, if you please, milady."

"Mrs. Beane, have you an available servant to send to the village for a doctor? I trust you have a doctor hereabouts?"

"Indeed, milady, we do. But first perhaps your servants will need assistance in carrying the earl to your room?"

Amanda disdainfully agreed that her men might indeed need some assistance in transporting the earl upstairs, as he was rather large.

Toplofty manners, money, and the mention of a grand title worked magic on Mrs. Beane, changing her in the wink of a jaundiced eye to a hostess who couldn't do enough to make her new tenants comfortable, even going so far as to suggest throwing out the guests who occupied the inn's largest room and giving it to the earl and his countess. With regal condescension, Amanda refused to allow Mrs. Beane to evict unsuspecting patrons.

When the gentleman was finally taken to a small, low-pitched room and laid out on the bed, Amanda stood over him and looked worriedly down at his pale face. He was still handsome but rather like a statue with his noble features carved from marble—cold and immobile. Lifeless. Amanda had a sudden sickening thought that he might actually die. After all, despite four men manhandling him up the steep, narrow stairs, he was still quite oblivious to his surroundings.

"Gracious, he looks fagged to death," commented

Mrs. Beane in a tone of forced sympathy. She turned to Amanda. "Where's your husband's manservant?"

"He was ... er ... not well when we left our home," Amanda improvised quickly. "He had a fever. My husband is very compassionate and chose to dress himself rather than inflict a journey on his ailing manservant."

"Well, I daresay that *does* show a great deal of solicitude for one's servant," Mrs. Beane agreed with scornful disbelief, as if to say she'd never be so solicitous of a mere underling. "But now that your husband is unable to dress or undress himself, *you* are left to do the job."

Amanda felt the blood drain from her head. She grasped the rounded top of a bedpost for support. "Me?"

"Well, milady," said Mrs. Beane with raised brows, "I don't think it will be wise to leave him in those damp clothes, do you? If you hurry, you'll be able to have him undressed and under the coverlets in three flicks of a lamb's tail."

Amanda stood in shocked silence as Mrs. Beane moved briskly past her to the door. "Meanwhile I'll make sure your servants get a hot supper in them before they retire to the room over the stables for the night." Theo, Joe, and Harley stood in the hallway and stared into the room with horrified expressions. "And I'll send a chambermaid up with more wood for the fire and a tray for you."

To reassure her servants, Amanda roused herself and attempted a composed appearance. "Yes, Mrs. Beane, that will do nicely." She turned to her servants. "Do go along with Mrs. Beane to the kitchen and have your supper," she told them, forcing a smile. "I shall be quite comfortable and *safe* here with my husband ... the *earl*."

They had immediately caught on to Amanda's charade and gone along with it grudgingly, but it appeared that Theo in particular was having difficulty leaving his mistress alone with a strange man whose clothing she was intending to remove.

"Well, *do* you want your supper or not?" Mrs. Beane shouted from the top of the stairs. "You'll eat it now or go without!"

This threat inspired Joe and Harley to scurry away, but Theo stood stubbornly in the hall, his face pulled with worry. "Miss," he said in an urgent whisper. "This ain't right! Let me stay and undress the gent."

Amanda was sorely tempted to allow him to do so. "No," she said at last. "It will look odd to Mrs. Beane if I hesitate to undress my own husband. And she must believe he's my husband, or she'll throw us out on our ears!"

"Not if ye pay her enough. She can be bought, that one!"

"But I already told her he's my husband, Theo. We'd better leave well enough alone!"

"Ye told her he's an earl, too, miss," said Theo, shaking his head disapprovingly.

"It was the only way to get the old harridan to treat us with respect!" she replied defensively. "Now *do* go away, Theo, or you'll miss your supper!"

"But miss—"

Amanda raised her chin. "That's an order, Theo!"

Theo finally skulked away, looking cross as crabs. Amanda closed the door, then turned and faced the bed, contemplating with considerable nervousness the task before her. The broad-shouldered, lean-flanked stranger was sprawled over the entire surface of the medium-size bed, his arms and legs thrown wide. His muscles were clearly defined beneath the smooth, fine fabric of his coat sleeves and trouser legs. Just looking at him gave Amanda a weak, warm feeling in the pit of her stomach.

She reminded herself that the man was injured and needed help. She had to get those wet clothes off before he took cold. And if she found the task of disrobing him a trifle embarrassing ... or a trifle too *titillating* ... she would just have to grit her teeth and carry on.

Taking a deep, shaky breath, she leaned over and took hold of the man's right boot.

Chapter 3

Amanda learned from firsthand experience why fashionable gentlemen required the assistance of a valet, or at the very least a bootjack, to pry off their boots. It was no easy task, and once she was done, she took off her velvet cloak and hung it on a hook by the door; she certainly didn't need it to keep warm!

Staring down at the man, Amanda dabbed at her damp forehead with a handkerchief and contemplated the best way to remove his coat. Of a rich burgundy color, the elegant cutaway jacket was tailored to fit exactly the man's wide shoulders and then to follow impeccably the lean lines of his torso. The renowned Weston, who was most probably the man's tailor, had given little thought as to how difficult it would be to remove such a close-fitting jacket from an inert body. However, beleaguered valets probably had to perform such miracles regularly, so Amanda decided to take courage and inspiration from them.

"I do wish you'd wake up," Amanda grumbled in a soft voice, leaning over to wedge both hands under his right shoulder. "Though when you do, I shall

37

probably have the devil of a time explaining how we came to be married, my lord."

She gave him a push, hoping to roll him onto his side. He didn't budge. "But all things considered, that might be easier than trying to undress you."

She climbed onto the bed and tried again, putting her whole weight into it. With a most unladylike grunt, she pushed him onto his side, then kept him there by bracing her knees against his back.

"I wonder," she said, pulling the coat off his shoulder and yanking the bottom of the sleeve over his hand, "if you actually *are* a lord of some kind. You look plump enough in the purse, and you have that sort of aristocratic air, even as drunk as you are. Maybe I didn't actually perjure my soul for lying when I told that old biddy you were an earl."

She'd got one sleeve off, and now she needed to get to the other side of him to duplicate her maneuvers and tug off the other sleeve. She eased him flat on his back again, and instead of climbing off the bed to approach the job from the other side, she decided to straddle him and thus get the business over with more quickly. It would only take a second.

Unfortunately, Amanda had not taken into consideration the encumbrance of her skirts and petticoats. Crawling about on her knees tugged at the fabric of her gown and seemed likely to tear it, so she lifted her skirts just far enough to free her legs to move.

With her bombazine skirts bunched around her, Amanda braced her hands on either side of the man's chest and lifted one leg over him. As he was lying with his own legs rather spread out, Amanda found she could only straddle one thigh at a time.

She had conquered the first thigh and was about to conquer the next when—alas—the door to the small room opened and a chambermaid with a bundle of wood appeared. When she saw Amanda more or less atop the stranger and with her skirts in a bunch, the chambermaid was forced to come to only one conclusion: that she had interrupted a conjugal moment.

"Oh, la, milady," she blurted, her cheeks aflame. "I'm sorry! I thought 'is lordship was knocked out from a bump to the noggin, or I'd not 'ave rushed in so—"

The mobcapped, plump, fair-haired maid stopped midsentence. Her gaze had strayed to the face of the prone nobleman, prepared to be cowed by the angry look in his eyes for having interrupted a passionate interlude, but any idiot could see that the gentleman was in no condition for hanky-panky. He was out cold.

The maid turned with a bewildered expression back to Amanda, frozen in the same precarious position she was in when the maid first entered the room. Amanda was sure her own complexion rivaled the chambermaid's for rosiness.

"This is not what it looks like—" Amanda began.

"Now that I see that 'is lordship is truly knocked out," said the maid, clearly confused, "I'm not sure *what* it looks like, milady."

"I need some help, you see—"

The maid backed away to the door. "I'm sure I can't help ye, milady."

Amanda gave a huff of exasperation, pushed herself up, and sat back on her heels. Still straddling one of the gentleman's thighs, she put her hands on her hips and said with asperity, "Don't be a ninny, girl. I was simply trying to take off the man's—*my husband's*—coat. I have to get him out of his wet clothes and into bed before the doctor arrives. I don't know if you've ever undressed an unconscious man—"

The maid's eyes widened. "I'm very sure I 'aven't, milady."

"—but it's extremely difficult. Especially when he's

as large as this—er, *my husband*. Come here and help me get his coat off. Don't worry, I shan't expect you to help me with his trousers."

The maid set down the bundle of wood and cautiously approached. Amanda climbed off the bed and shook her skirts into respectability, then directed the girl in helping her remove the stranger's coat, his cravat, and his dove-gray pinstriped vest with all its fobs and chains still attached. As it had been protected by the jacket and vest, his shirt was dry enough to leave on, and Amanda was grateful that she could in good conscience avoid stripping him down to his bare chest. His trousers were another matter, unfortunately. They were soaked through and had to come off.

At this point the chambermaid excused herself, built up the fire with extra wood, then scrambled out of the room.

"Coward," muttered Amanda under her breath as the door shut behind the hastily retreating servant. She turned back to the bed and pursed her lips.

"I daresay, my good man," Amanda began musingly, "that I shall be able to pull off your trousers without putting myself to the blush again if I cover you first with a blanket. You might be wearing drawers, but then again perhaps you aren't. I don't intend to find out." She paused, her brow wrinkling. "However I *will* have to unbutton your trousers before I can pull them off."

Hopeful that she was about to finish up what was proving to be the most awkward and unsettling experience of her life—ranking right up there with her terrifying introduction to Lady Jersey at Almacks—Amanda leaned over the bed and, with trembling fingers, proceeded to undo the man's trouser buttons. She averted her gaze from the obvious bulge behind the buttons, and she tried not to think about the part of his anatomy her fingers worked so closely to.

The shirt was still tucked in, so she was spared the embarrassment of seeing the man's exposed abdomen. Still, she'd never expected in a dozen lifetimes to be in such an odd position—unbuttoning the pants of a strange man! And such a handsome one, too. . . .

Her eyes strayed to his face. Fear twisted in her stomach. He was as white as the pillow case. Even his pale scar stood out more glaringly. And he still hadn't moved much or spoken at all since he'd called her a minx . . . mistakenly, of course. She was no more a minx than Aunt Nan or Aunt Prissy, but she liked the way he'd said it. She wished she could hear him say it again, if only to reassure herself that he was going to regain consciousness and be restored to his former vigorous self.

There was no chance of a full recovery, however, if she didn't hurry up and get his wet clothes off, she reminded herself. Picking up a multicolored quilt that had been thrown over the arm of a rocking chair, Amanda draped it over the man, leaving his stockinged feet to poke out at the bottom. Standing at the foot of the bed, she tugged on the man's breeches till she had them off.

"Thank goodness," she said aloud, folding the trousers and placing them on a chest of drawers with his other clothes, "*that's* finally done. I should hope that the worst of this unfortunate predicament is over!"

She had a few moments to tidy herself before the doctor arrived . . . a portly gentleman in a worn brown coat and trousers, sporting muttonchop whiskers, much like Theo's, and a pair of thick magnifying spectacles that made his eyes look owlish and wise. He came into the room without knocking—which habit seemed customary at the Inn of the Three Nuns—bade Amanda a gruff good day, introduced himself as Doctor Bledsoe, then bent over the patient. After prying open the man's eyes and peering into them, sniffing his breath, checking the gash beneath the makeshift bandage, determining his temperature with a palm held against his brow, then listening to his pulse, the doctor straightened and turned. "What is his name?" he inquired, looking gravely at Amanda.

"His name?" Amanda repeated stupidly.

"Yes," said the doctor, raising a shaggy brow. "What is your husband's name?"

Her brain searched for a title she could use without impersonating an existing earl, then decided impulsively to make one up. "He's the Earl of *Thornfield*," she informed the doctor loftily. At the doctor's scowling expression, she added nervously, "Have you never heard of him?"

"Never," he replied briskly. "But I don't care a fig what the butler announces when your husband arrives at a fancy ball. I want to know what *you* call him, m'dear. What is his Christian name?"

Surprised but not offended by the blunt, familiar way he addressed her, Amanda decided that it wasn't necessary to play the grand lady with the doctor. She sensed a compassionate nature beneath his rough exterior and immediately warmed to him. She was about to tell him that her husband's name was John, when a sudden playful quirk got hold of her. Her ideal romantic name for a man was Demetri, a hero from a novel she'd read.

"His name is Demetri," she said, repressing a smile. "Why do you ask, doctor?"

"Because he is more apt to respond to his Christian name than to Lord Thornfield. Don't you think so, m'dear?"

Amanda nodded meekly but knew full well that it was extremely unlikely that the unconscious fellow would respond to either of the unfamiliar forms of address.

The doctor cleaned and re-dressed the wound, then

stood over the man and said loudly, "Demetri? Demetri, can you hear me?" The gentleman did not stir. The doctor said Demetri three more times in a booming voice, then turned his penetrating gaze on Amanda again. "Are you aware, m'dear, that your husband is extremely inebriated?"

"Yes, I know he is," Amanda replied. "I wondered if that was the reason he's still unconscious."

"I'm not sure," the doctor answered seriously. "But it certainly doesn't help matters. Your husband has a concussion, and there may be complications."

A shiver of fear raced down Amanda's spine. "What sort of complications?"

"I will speak plainly. There might be pressure on the brain due to internal bleeding, which could cause him to sink into a coma."

"Good heavens!" exclaimed Amanda, horrified.

"I only said it might, m'dear. I want you to be prepared for the worst, though I am by no means convinced that such a calamity will befall your husband." The doctor scanned the man's reposing figure with a keen eye. "He seems in remarkably fine fettle. How old is he?"

"Er ... thirty, sir." Amanda hoped she was estimating close to the gentleman's actual age and watched for the doctor's reaction. He nodded, seeming to accept the calculated guess.

"Young. Still young. Indeed, I suspect he will recover very well, with the possibility of some short-term thought impairment. However, I suspect you are in for a tiring and very worrisome night, m'dear."

"What can you mean, doctor?" Amanda asked anxiously. "He does nothing but *lie* there!"

"He might spike a fever—get restless and delirious. If he does, you must sponge him off repeatedly with a cloth dipped in vinegar water. Strip him down to nothing, and don't encumber the poor fellow with bedclothes, not even a sheet. Fevers are best managed by lowering the temperature of the skin. Feed him barley water when you can get him to take it, and generally do whatever you can to make him comfortable."

"Yes, doctor." Amanda blushed as she thought about what she might have to do to save this stranger's life.

As the doctor bent to pick up his scuffed leather bag, more than embarrassment overcame Amanda. For the first time in her life, sheer terror and panic gripped her. Unable to stop herself, Amanda grabbed the doctor's coat sleeve and said beseechingly, "Must you go? I don't know if I can manage him alone. He's very strong and . . . and . . . *large*. What if I should do something wrong?"

The doctor smiled and patted Amanda's hand. "There's probably not another person on earth who can manage him as well as you, m'dear. Speak to him soothingly, affectionately. Your familiar voice and touch will calm him. And I've complete confidence in your nursing skills. There's nothing you can do wrong. Just keep his fever down as best you can, say your prayers, and I'll see you first thing in the morning."

It seemed too late to admit that she was not the injured gentleman's loving wife; explanations would be lengthy, confusing, and suspicious. And Amanda knew that though she wasn't the ideal nurse the doctor thought she was, there was probably no one in the house who could do a better job. Besides, though it was certainly an accident and the gentleman was partly to blame, Amanda felt responsible for his current state of injury. She truly didn't want him to die.

And beyond all these perfectly logical reasons to continue to masquerade as the stranger's wife, Amanda finally had to admit to herself that she . . . well . . . *enjoyed* the masquerade. She liked being thought of as this attractive man's better half . . .

someone whose voice and presence while he was sick would be his best medicine. She felt special, needed. She felt like a beloved wife, something she might never be. . . .

The doctor left and Amanda ate a dinner of cold meat, hot soup and crusty bread in the room, ordered a cot to sleep on, washed her face, and brushed out her hair, all the while waiting in dread for the man to suddenly start thrashing about and mumbling incoherently. But he did nothing of the sort; just as before, he simply lay there. She tested his temperature every few minutes but discovered no fever.

At nine o'clock there was a knock at the door, and Amanda opened it to Theo. "I thought you'd retired for the night, Theo," she said. "I'm sorry I couldn't get you a room inside the inn, but—"

"Thank you, miss, but I couldn't care less where I sleep," said Theo, glancing past Amanda into the room. His eyes fastened on the stranger in the bed, and he frowned. "But I'm troubled about yer sleepin' arrangements."

Amanda sighed and turned to look at the man, too, his dark head and broad, bare shoulders showing above the coverlets like an ancient bust of a Roman warrior. "It can't be helped, Theo. I feel responsible for him, and now that I've fibbed to Mrs. Beane and Dr. Bledsoe, I can't very well recant my story about being the gentleman's wife."

"But what will you do when he wakes up, miss?"

"I'll tell him the truth, then find out how I can contact some member of his family. I only hope he does wake up. The doctor said 'tis possible that he may fall into a coma ... if he hasn't already done so," she added glumly.

"Why don't you let me stay with the gent tonight, miss?"

"It would look so strange, Theo, I dare not. Besides, I want to stay with him. I'm worried about him. Since I got his clothes off"—Amanda paused as both she and Theo averted their eyes—"he's been very little trouble. The doctor said I might expect him to spike a fever and become restless, but I'm beginning to doubt that will ever happen. I'd be relieved if he *did* thrash about a bit. It would be a sign of life and spirit."

"It'd be a fine kettle of fish if'n he turned up 'is toes, wouldn't it, miss?" Theo said dourly. "He looks as though he's laid out fer burial already, bein' flat on 'is back like that and not movin' a muscle. What would we do with the body? We couldn't very well bury him without alertin' the constable 'bout the accident and seein' if they could identify the bloke."

Amanda felt ill at the mention of bodies and burials. "Don't talk so, Theo. Should the gentleman die, *our* troubles would be the least to be concerned about. He's too young to die!"

"Now, don't go gettin' sentimental 'bout the gent, miss," cautioned Theo. "You don't know 'im from Adam. And he looks like a rogue t' me!"

"And don't you go gettin' mother-hennish," Amanda returned with a raised brow. "I daresay rogues come in all shapes and sizes. For all we know, this fellow might be a bishop of the church on holiday."

"And pigs kin fly," Theo muttered, clearly disbelieving.

Amanda clicked her tongue. "Go to bed and get some sleep. Perhaps we'll be able to travel on the morrow, and I want you fresh for the trip."

Theo grudgingly obeyed, and Amanda watched him walk slowly down the hall, looking peevishly over his shoulder at her only three times. Despite her brave, calm front to Theo, Amanda felt more than a twinge of fear as she finally shut the door. She had just sent away her last hope of rescue from what could prove to be a dreadful night.

She walked to the bed and gazed down at the man. In repose, his features had an almost angelic, boyish aspect. She felt his forehead again and took his pulse. He felt cool, and his heartbeat was fast but only moderately so.

She sat down in the rocking chair near the fire, unfolded a warm quilt over her lap, and wrapped it around her feet. A single candle burned on a bedside table, softly illuminating the man's face in a golden glow as he rested against the pillows, his hair gleaming blue-black against the pale casing.

Amanda began to gently rock, her mind busily speculating about the stranger she'd nearly trampled with her coach-and-four. She wondered what his real name was, if he was indeed titled, where he lived, why he was alone and inebriated on that deserted stretch of highway, and—most of all—whether or not a woman waited and worried at his absence.

She shook her head and smiled wryly. Maybe Theo was right. Maybe he was a rogue, a womanizer, a charming wastrel with a checkered past that included a string of broken hearts he was ruthlessly responsible for.

However, even if he weren't a rogue or something similarly shocking, it wasn't difficult to imagine such a gentleman's disappearance causing a fair share of female histrionics.

"What do you *mean* he's disappeared? He *can't* have disappeared! What's a wedding without a groom! Well, I'll tell you ... it's a social disaster, that's what it is!"

Inside the drawing room of the great white mansion on Great Stanhope Street, a plentitude of candles illuminated the pale, pained, pinched faces of two handsomely attired females and two dashing gentlemen.

By the aspect of each player in what was apparently a tragedy of Greek proportions, a plump, middle-aged lady in puce silk, reclining on a chaise longue with a vinaigrette tucked under her nose, held center stage. But one of the players, a very tall gentleman, stood in the shadows near the door. He'd entered after declining to be announced and was secretly observing the play.

"Oh, this is just like Jackson Montgomery," Lady Batsford wailed, plaintively clutching a handkerchief sprinkled with a medicinal dose of lavender water to her ample bosom. "He's always been such a scapegrace, I wonder your papa allowed him to court you, Charlotte, dear!"

"Now see here, Theodora," blustered Sir Thomas Batsford, abandoning his usual spot near the fireplace where he could lean against the mantel and smoke to his heart's content. "Everyone in this room can testify to the fact the you've been pushing for this match since our little gel peeked her pert nose out of the schoolroom. She wasn't but thirteen when you ordered come-out gowns from Madame Simone and dancing lessons from that chitty-faced caper merchant André ... somebody-or-other! And it was all done with designs on Jackson Montgomery!"

Lady Batsford's eyes bulged and her chest heaved as she absorbed the blow of her husband's betrayal. "Thomas, how can you talk so to me? Have you no consideration for my shattered nerves?" she demanded in a voice quivering with indignation. "How dare you imply that this dreadful fiasco is *my* fault!"

"If it's anyone's fault, it's mine," said a contrite Robert Hamilton from his seat beside Charlotte on the striped damask sofa. He held her hand and chafed it gently between his two. "I should have kept my eyes clapped on 'im the whole night! But I only stepped into the kitchen for a bite, you see, and next thing I knew, he'd vanished! We scoured the area for miles but came up with nothing!"

"You mustn't blame yourself, Robbie," said Charlotte, looking pale and worried but showing more composure than the lot of them together. "You couldn't have expected him to wander away."

"If that's what he did," mumbled Lady Batsford under her breath.

Charlotte straightened her spine, and her eyes sparked as she faced her mother. "Mama, I certainly hope you are not implying that Jack is deliberately avoiding the wedding with some sort of ... cruel trick," she said quietly but with a thread of steel in her voice. "He's full of fun and mischief, I will allow, but he'd never do such a thing."

"Right you are, Char," Rob joined in bracingly. "No need to besmirch Jack's character. I know better than anyone what he's capable of. He's known for his rigs and rows, but he'd never jilt Charlotte ... even if he *were*—"

Everyone turned and stared expectantly at Rob. Seeming to realize that he'd said too much, he looked sheepish and clamped his lips tightly together.

"Even if he were *what*, Robbie?" asked Charlotte.

Julian decided it was time to make his presence known. Moving soundlessly, he positioned himself behind the sofa and spoke before anyone even knew he was there.

"I'm sure Robert is too embarrassed to finish the sentence," he began, enjoying the jerks of surprise occasioned by his phantomlike appearance. "No doubt his sentence would go thusly ... 'Jack would never jilt Charlotte even if he were as soused as a pickle.' I had understood that Jack was staying at the Royal Pavilion. After spending the day with Prinny and our regent's profligate court, I've no doubt my little brother was inebriated. Am I correct, Rob?"

"Dash it, Lord Serling, why are you always creeping up on a person?" Robert complained as he stood up and turned to face Julian.

"You sent for me, did you not?" Julian inquired with an assumption of mild surprise. "You left word at White's that I was to join you as soon as possible at the Batsford's."

"I'm astonished that you came, my lord," Rob admitted with a touch of surliness.

Julian raised a haughty brow. "I wouldn't have ... except that you mentioned my brother's name in connection with some sort of calamity, and since I have a familial partiality for the harem-scarem fellow, I couldn't very well ignore the summons, now could I?"

Julian lifted his quizzing glass and stared down from his great height till Rob was obliged to fidget and look away. Satisfied, Julian extracted a delicately worked snuff box from a coat pocket and took a sniff. He knew Jack owed his life to Robert Hamilton, and for that reason alone did Julian tolerate the encroaching mushroom.

Rob was a social climber, a rattle, and was addicted to every sort of intemperate wagering ... with disastrous results. He owed a small fortune to the duns, which his modest allowance from an obscure and mysterious "uncle" in Yorkshire couldn't even begin to touch. Naturally, none of these attributes recommended him to Julian's fastidious tastes. And he suspected that those weren't the worst of Rob's defects. He had an idea the man was basically corrupt. He just needed proof. The little sod had been imposing on his brother's good nature too long.

"I have ascertained a great deal already, but why don't you tell me what happened, Rob?" said Julian, folding his arms across his chest, standing with his feet slightly spread. "Bore me with every detail, if you please."

When Rob was finished, Charlotte said, "Oh, Lord Serling, isn't it a dreadful business?" She looked up at Julian with a sincerely despairing expression in her soft green eyes, which were a lovely complement to her auburn hair. "What can have happened to him? I'm so afraid he's met with ... *foul play!*" Her voice trembled on those last words, and her eyes grew misty.

Julian was touched. Though he disapproved of many of Jack's actions, his younger brother's engagement to Charlotte Batsford was a delightful surprise. Despite the appalling example her mother set her and the ineffective blusters of her father in trying to control his domineering wife, Charlotte Batsford was a female in possession of some fine qualities.

Before Charlotte, Julian had watched with tried patience as Jack lost his impetuous heart and squandered his money on a dozen ladybirds in half as many years. He refused to take a lesson from his older brother and conduct his *affaires d'amour* with dignity and discretion. Jack used to laugh and accuse Julian of being a block of English ice. Then he'd clap his brother on the back and offer to buy him a brew.

In the war, Jack had been a courageous officer, never asking the enlisted men he commanded to do anything he wouldn't do himself. He was sent home from the peninsula when he received a serious injury to his right knee. It took him several months to walk without a cane, and even now, he sometimes limped when he was tired or overtaxed.

Jack was generous to a fault, fond of practical jokes, and addicted to flirting. But above all, he was just and honorable.

In looks, as well as in many facets of their personalities, Julian and Jack were as proverbially different as night and day. Julian was as fair-haired as a Viking, and Jack was as swarthy and dark-haired as a gypsy. But they were as loyal to each other as two brothers could possibly be. Affection for Jack ran deep and powerful beneath the placid surface of Julian's elegant facade, and he resented Lady Batsford's insinuation that Jack was ducking his duty and putting them all in a fret just to avoid the nuptial knot.

Julian knew Rob had been about to imply—with that adroitly delivered unfinished sentence—that Jack was regretting his betrothal. Self-interest was involved here . . . he was sure of it. Rob wanted Charlotte for himself, though why he supposed she'd ever have him or her parents would ever allow her to marry such a worthless fellow was beyond Julian's comprehension,

Maybe Jack *did* regret his betrothal. Maybe he had admitted as much to Rob. But as Julian said himself, Jack wouldn't jilt Charlotte even if he were as soused as a pickle. Like Charlotte, Julian very much feared that Jack had met with foul play . . . or some sort of unforeseen misfortune. It was the only explanation for his strange disappearance.

"I won't trifle with your feelings and offend your intelligence, Miss Batsford, by telling you not to worry," said Julian. "We have every reason to worry."

Charlotte grew more pale, and a single tear escaped the corner of her eye. Embarrassed, she turned away and surreptitiously used her handkerchief to wipe away the evidence of her distress. Julian liked her better for trying to control her emotions. He detested female watering pots. It was plain that Charlotte's grief, though restrained, was absolutely genuine.

"Why frighten the girl, Serling?" said Rob through gritted teeth, throwing Julian an accusing glare as he sat down beside Charlotte and reclaimed her hand. "I'm sure Jack will turn up," he told her soothingly. "He's like a bad penny, you know," he added, in an attempt to lighten the mood.

Charlotte tried to smile at Rob's witticism, but her gaze lifted to Julian's face. "You say we have reason to worry, my lord ... but might I at least *hope* that all will be well in the end?"

Julian smiled, the warmth of his approval meant for Charlotte alone. "I'm counting on your hope *and* your prayers, Miss Batsford. I'm worried, but I'm by no means hopeless. In fact, I'm quite determined to find Jack no matter where the ramshackle fellow has disappeared to."

Her relief was visible. It was obvious Jack's little bride-to-be had confidence in Julian's determination. She slipped her hand out of Rob's grasp and offered it to Julian. Rob scowled as he watched Julian lift her hand to his lips and lightly kiss it.

"I'll leave first thing tomorrow morning, at cock's crow," said Julian, businesslike and brisk after he'd released Charlotte's hand. "Every nook and cranny of this great island shall be scoured, if need be, starting in West Sussex." He bowed. "I'll keep you informed, Miss Batsford," he promised her.

"Is there anything I can do, my lord?" asked Sir Thomas, stepping forward with an anxious expression.

"Nothing at present, Sir Thomas. Thank you for the offer," Julian returned, coolly polite. He bowed again, punctiliously including Lady Batsford in his departing salute. She merely sat there, silent and ashen-faced.

Julian was glad the shallow woman had held her slanderous tongue during his short visit, or he might not have been able to refrain from humbling her with one of his famous snubs. To Lady Batsford, Jack's disappearance meant a social embarrassment and the necessity of sending out hundreds of notes that night to announce the indefinite delay of the wedding. She didn't care whether or not Jack was lost, dead, or shanghaied to China.

But Julian cared. He cared very much indeed.

Chapter 4

"**B**ehind you, Evans! Blast it, man, look behind you! *Nooooo!*"

Amanda woke up with a start. She was disoriented at first, and her eyes darted anxiously about the room till everything came back to her in a rush: her spontaneous trip to Thorney Island, the accident, the handsome stranger, the doctor.

She sat up abruptly. The single candle she'd left burning beside the stranger's bed had extinguished, and the room was dark except for the embers of the fire. Around midnight, still fully clothed, she'd laid down on the cot to doze a little before rechecking the stranger's temperature and had fallen sound asleep!

She quickly snapped open the watch locket pinned to her bodice and leaned toward the dim glow of the fire to ascertain the time. It was three o'clock in the morning!

"You had too much faith in me, doctor," she muttered under her breath as she rose to her feet. "You said I couldn't do anything wrong. Well, I've just ignored my patient for three hours, and heaven knows what condition he's in!"

Amanda quickly crossed the cold floor to the stranger's bed. She could hear him moving about and hurriedly lighted another candle and set it on the bedside table. She was shocked at her first clear view of him; he'd changed from looking as pale and still as a marble effigy atop someone's tomb to looking flushed and restless.

His black hair was damp and wildly tumbled on the pillow from turning his head from side to side. His lips looked parched, and the front of his shirt was soaked through with sweat. He mumbled unintelligibly and shouted exclamations that plainly revealed that he was delirious and reliving horrific experiences of some battle.

Riddled with guilt and the fear that she may have neglected her duty just long enough to guarantee the stranger's death, Amanda set to work with a vengeance. She threw back the bedclothes, determined to follow the doctor's instructions down to the letter even if it made her blush crimson. He'd clearly said that if the stranger developed a fever, she was to strip him down to nothing.

Amanda bit her lip as the man's long, muscled legs were revealed below the hem of his long shirt, the tail of which barely covered his private parts. She knew now that the gentleman did not embrace the practice of wearing drawers. But soon it wouldn't matter, anyway. She had to take his shirt off, and then he'd be as naked as a babe ... but with the developed body of a mature man.

Swallowing nervously, trying to be as objective as a nurse might be in the same situation, she unbuttoned his shirt with trembling fingers. There were a great many small slippery buttons, and she had to lean close to his body to see what she was doing.

With his shirt half open and a glimpse of his chest impairing her concentration, his right arm suddenly lifted and curved around her shoulders, flattening her upper body against him. With her nose buried in crisp curling hair, and a hard nipple pushing into her cheek, Amanda braced her hands against the man's chest and tried to straighten up.

"No, Laura," said the man in a thick voice. "Don't go, love. I need you. I need you. . . ."

Then, just as suddenly as he'd grabbed her, he let her go. Amanda straightened immediately and worked faster on the buttons, worried that he might take another notion to pin her down to that hard, broad chest.

Chastising herself for being so unforgivably carnal as to admire his physique when she needed all her concentration to save his life, Amanda pulled off the shirt without stopping to think or look or register any sort of emotion. The shirt turned out to be much easier to take off than his jacket, particularly since he was constantly moving and lifting his arms instead of lying still.

The shirt was off and on the floor, and Amanda walked to a little chest of drawers where she had a basin of vinegar water and a cloth ready and waiting. She dropped the cloth in the water, carried the basin to the bedside table, then set it down.

She hesitated for a few seconds as she tried to convince herself that she could sponge the gentleman off without allowing her eyes to stray to "that part" of his anatomy. She wondered if perhaps singing a hymn would help her thoughts remain chaste while she worked to get his fever, as well as her own alarmingly warm thoughts, under control.

She wrung out the cloth and began by pressing it to the stranger's hot forehead. He immediately responded with a sort of grateful gasp. And when she began to sing in a breathless, barely audible voice, she sensed a general calm wash over him.

Could it be possible? she wondered, amazed and flattered. Could she really be a comforting influence to this strange man? Thinking that perhaps the words of the song were what comforted him, she sang a little louder. She decided that perhaps he was a respectable, religious man after all if he could be soothed by a hymn.

She slid the cloth over his face, along his jaw—scratchy with the beginnings of a black beard—over his dry lips and down his neck. It was a strong, tightly corded neck that curved into broad, brown shoulders. She dipped her cloth again and bathed his shoulders and chest, circling self-consciously around his small wine-colored nipples.

At this point, she had to stop singing for a moment to swallow hard. Then she resumed her song in a stronger, more determined voice. This time she was singing entirely for herself ... trying to bolster her own wavering courage as she approached that part of his body she'd been trying to pretend didn't exist.

But it did exist, and with a freshly dipped cloth making its way down his taut, flat abdomen, she was forced at last to face reality.

Amanda's song caught in her throat. Naturally she'd never seen a naked male body before, but once, when she was looking in her father's expansive library for a medical book that would explain some of Prissy's arthritic symptoms, she had run across a volume that diagrammed both male and female forms. So, while she was not entirely unprepared for what she saw, seeing it in the flesh, so to speak, was rather stunning. She looked ... fascinated and not the least bit properly repelled.

"Gretta?"

Amanda jerked guiltily when the stranger spoke.

"Why are you stopping, Gretta?" he asked in a weak, plaintive voice. "I like it when you bathe me, sweetheart."

In his delirium, he seemed to bounce from the battlefield to the bedchamber in the blink of an eye. Amanda wondered what had happened to Laura, whom he had mentioned only moments before, and decided that perhaps she'd been precipitate in bestowing him with a religious nature. Theo's conjecture, that he was a rogue, was probably much closer to the mark.

Amanda ran the cool cloth down both long legs. She discovered a thick, ugly scar on his right knee that made her wince. She could imagine how serious the wound had been when it was fresh. She thoroughly dampened down every inch of his body, then started at the top again and repeated the exercise several times. After an hour of these intimate ministrations, she noticed that his skin felt cooler and had returned to a more natural color. Glancing in a mirror near the bed, however, she observed that her own complexion was exceedingly rosy.

But how could it be otherwise? She had just attained a thorough knowledge of the physique of the male sex and a detailed familiarity with one very masculine body in particular. Every significant mole, every angle of bone and curve of lean muscle was etched on her memory forever. As long as she lived, she'd never be able to erase from her mind the image of this stranger stretched out naked on the bed.

Like a guilty pleasure, the sight of him was stirring and disturbing at the same time. She knew she had no choice but to look at him ... but she *enjoyed* looking.

It was a long night for Amanda. Once she got his fever down, however, she was grateful to be able to cover him up again. He continued to be restless and to talk in his sleep, naming several more females. In connection with these names, there was sometimes a fleeting smile on his lips, a bawdy suggestion, or a soft-spoken endearment. Amanda could no longer ignore the obvious; whether he was married or not, the stranger was definitely a lady's man.

Near dawn, the stranger seemed to fall into a more natural sleep. Instead of lying flat on his back in a funereal pose, he actually shifted onto his side, drew his knees up, and tucked his hands against his chest. Feeling much more at ease about his condition but still worried that he might have a relapse, Amanda drew the rocking chair near the bed and sat down.

She had been sitting only a very few minutes when she realized how cold the room was. She got up and threw kindling and a large log on the fire and stoked the embers. When she returned to the rocking chair, she drew her feet up under her skirt and wrapped herself in the quilt but she was still cold.

It occurred to her that now that the stranger's fever had abated, he might be cold also but was too soundly asleep to realize it. At the moment, he was covered only by a sheet and a thin blanket. She wasn't about to neglect her duties as nurse again, so she unfolded another quilt that was hanging over the footboard of the bed and drew it up and over the stranger's shoulders.

Tucking the blanket under his bewhiskered chin, resting her hands on his shoulders, and leaning close enough to admire the way his thick lashes feathered over his tan cheek, she couldn't help but linger and look. But she lingered too long. Out from under the covers came his left arm, reaching around her shoulders as he'd done before and drawing her to his chest.

"Lie with me, sweetheart," he murmured huskily.

"Indeed, I cannot," Amanda said breathlessly, trying to pull away.

"Don't play the tease with me, Angela," he said, a faint smile tugging at the corners of his mouth. "I know you want to. And I'm so cold. . . ."

Amanda thought that for an unconscious man his strength was quite amazing. Every time she wriggled in an attempt to free herself, his hold on her tightened.

At this point, after hours of tending and worrying

over the fellow, Amanda was bone weary. Caught in the stranger's embrace, she was experiencing some new and pleasant sensations as well. Amanda had never in her entire life been held in such a manner. And even though he thought she was "Angela," the circle of his arms warmed and comforted her.

Presently, tired of struggling and desperate for some sleep, she eased herself onto the bed, reached behind her for the extra quilt, snuggled her head into the hollow of the stranger's neck, and went to sleep.

Jack was dreaming. He was in church, and an angel in a diaphanous white dress was floating overhead, singing a single hymn over and over again to the accompaniment of a gilded harp. The angel's face was hidden behind a veil, but her voice had an ethereal quality that calmed and soothed him.

Then, suddenly, she was not an angel, but a bride ... a bride marching up the aisle, her train sweeping behind her like an anemic witch's cape, her head bobbing up and down in time to a militant tune.

He stood by the altar and waited . . . and sweated . . . the insides of his stomach sloshing like cream in a churn. He stuck his finger inside his tight collar and tried to breathe. But he couldn't. He'd never breathe again because, in less time than it took to pull the legs off a spider, he'd be married. Married. *Married!*

He fought hard to rise through the black, downy layers of unconsciousness. He needed to wake up before it was too late ... before he was well and surely caught in the parson's mousetrap.

The black turned to gray mist; then spots of light broke through, but his eyes were still closed and seemed determined to stay that way. His lids felt heavy and gritty, his mouth felt as dry as a bale of winter hay, and a dull ache pounded his temples with the mournful regularity of a drumbeat in a funeral march.

He must have been drinking last night, he reasoned . . . chirping merry till the crack of dawn, no doubt. And now he was paying for it. Would he ever learn?

With much effort, he opened his eyes. He blinked against the glare of sun spilling through a small, square window covered with a flimsy curtain. He had no trouble recognizing that he was in a rented room at a public inn.

As his eyes adjusted, his other senses kicked in. He could smell freshly laundered linen, and something sweeter and more fragrant. Something like . . . a woman.

His eyes suddenly focused, and literally right under his nose was the source of the teasing scent. Hair . . . pale blond, gloriously shiny hair just inches away.

Using his powers of deduction—which weren't completely obliterated by the effects of alcohol—he knew that below the hair there had to be a face, and below the face a body . . . both of which he hoped were fetching.

His brows furrowed. He liked to think he had consistently good taste in females, but for some reason, he couldn't remember. He shrugged, knowing his full faculties and capabilities would return in time. This certainly wasn't the first morning he'd awakened feeling decidedly cup-shot.

One ability of which he was rather fond seemed to need no recuperative time period. Below the blanket he was nude . . . and aroused.

That the lady he held in his arms was dressed and above the blankets seemed odd, but he was willing to wait for an explanation. For now he'd rather do again what they'd obviously done already and he'd forgotten.

He bent and kissed the top of the blond head, the slight angling of his neck bringing a surprising twinge of sharp pain. He winced. "Damn every potent potable on the face of the earth," he muttered thickly.

In time the pain abated, but he decided to move his hands for a while instead of his head. He began to explore the curves of the female in his arms, starting at the swell of her womanly hips, moving to the dip of her slim waist, then up to the firm roundness of her breasts. They were good breasts, healthy and resilient, not too big nor too small but just right. . . .

She gave a soft little moan and shifted in his arms, her face now tilted so that he could look at her. She was lovely. And she wasn't wearing a trace of cosmetics, which was highly unusual for a lightskirt of the sort that serviced public inns. He felt himself getting tighter, harder, and he decided that it was time to wake up Sleeping Beauty with the proverbial kiss.

But as he lowered his face to hers, her eyes suddenly opened. They were as blue as a robin's egg, lined all round with spiky brown lashes. And they were filled with terror.

"Merciful heavens!" she screeched, pushing frantically at his chest, rolling off the bed, and springing to her feet, her long, tangled hair flying in the air. "Whatever do you think you're *doing*?"

Confused and irritated, Jack sat up, his blanket falling to his waist . . . and his head *exploding*!

The sudden onslaught of excruciating pain struck him like a bolt of lightning. He squeezed his eyes shut and fought the encroaching darkness that threatened to consume him again. At all costs, he had to avoid the darkness . . . and the dream.

His head fell to the pillow, and he reached instinctively toward the pain, bursts of blinding white playing against the dark curtain of his throbbing eyelids.

Just as his hand came into contact with a strip of

padded cloth covering his forehead, he felt the woman's small cool fingers circle his wrists, restraining him. "Don't disturb the wound!" she beseeched. "Please, sir, you might start to bleed again!"

Jack's eyes flew open. "What the hell are you talking about?" he demanded to know.

Her eyes widened. "Don't you remember the accident?"

It was an effort to talk. Jack was nearly overcome by waves of nausea, and his tongue seemed stuck to the roof of his mouth.

"I need something to drink," he croaked, then clamped his jaw shut and ground his teeth together till they squeaked. He refused to throw up. He *hated* throwing up.

"Here, take some of this," said the woman in an urgent tone, placing the rim of a mug against his lips and gently tipping it.

As the liquid drenched his mouth and seared down his parched throat, Jack was aware at first only of the blessed quenching of his thirst. Then he tasted the stuff, and his stomach did another turn. He started choking and pushed the mug away.

"What the hell *is* that stuff?" he said, wiping his mouth with the back of his hand. "Water from the trough?"

The woman puckered her lips disapprovingly and stood with her fists on her hips. "I am not accustomed to gentlemen cursing in my presence, sir, and I'd thank you very much if you'd refrain from doing so while we are forced to keep company! For your information, the liquid you just imbibed is a nourishing beverage the doctor recommended last night. He said I was to give it to you as soon as you would take it."

"Well, I *won't* take it. I'd rather have—"

"I know what you'd rather have," the woman said tartly. "But you had far too much of *that* last night.

Perhaps if you hadn't been foxed, you'd have avoided the accident and neither of us would be in this predicament."

By now Jack had figured out that the woman was not a doxy. No doxy he'd ever consorted with dressed in simple, severe black. Nor had he ever met a doxy who talked like she did, spewing out prim indignation like a regular jaw-me-dead.

So, she didn't like his cursing, and she seemed miffed with him about something ... something that had to do with the accident that had left him with this blasted head injury. His mind was a muddle, and he had a million questions. He knew that if he wanted the woman to cooperate and answer his questions *nicely*, he'd have to ask them *nicely*.

With his head on the pillow and his eyes closed, the pain returned to a level he could tolerate. He was about to open his eyes again and make another go at requesting some tea—this time doing it like a gentleman would—when he felt the heavenly pressure of a cool, wet cloth on his brow. He looked up and saw the woman bending over him with a contrite expression.

"I'm very sorry I snapped at you," she said, dabbing the refreshing cloth here and there on his face, "but I'm *very* tired, you see. I was up half the night tending you through a fever. I'm extremely untidy this morning, too," she continued, self-consciously pushing back the tangled hair that fell in abundance over both shoulders. "And that *always* puts a lady out of sorts."

"You look fine to me," he murmured.

"Apparently so," she said, rosy spots appearing on both cheeks. "When I woke up, I noticed you were ... er ... *touching* me."

"I beg your pardon for that," he answered awkwardly. "I was confused. I thought you were ...

someone else." He couldn't very well tell her he'd mistaken her for a lightskirt.

She looked thoughtful as she redipped the cloth in a basin of water, wrung it out, and bathed his neck. "Considering your condition, I'm surprised you had the strength to attempt . . . well, *you know*," she commented shyly.

Jack smiled. "Men are surprisingly resourceful when it comes to finding strength for . . . well, *you know*."

The woman blushed again, then apparently decided that she'd had enough improper conversation and assumed a businesslike mien. She returned the cloth to the basin and stood up, elbows out, hands clasped loosely together at her waist. "You are doubtless thirsty and hungry, sir. Is there something you drink *besides* liquor?"

"I drink tea," he answered, amused by the contrast between her prissy language and her disheveled, almost wanton appearance. "And I'm famished. Have the proprietor of this establishment send me up a roasted chicken or something."

"You'll have weak tea and barley water, sir," said the woman, talking down her pert nose. "And nothing else till the doctor says otherwise."

"Damn the old sawbones," muttered Jack. "All doctors are quacks."

"Excuse me while I tidy up," said the woman, ignoring his surly comment as she stepped to a nearby mirror and picked up a brush. "I'll just make myself presentable, then order your tea. In the meantime, I suggest you rest."

"I don't want to rest," Jack said irritably. "I want some answers. I want to know how I got here and where I am."

"I have questions for you, too, sir," said the woman, brushing out her tangled hair. "But you'll feel much better after you've had a little nourishment. You might not wish to admit it, but you're in a rather weakened condition just now."

Jack wanted to argue, but he was too tired. So he simply lay in the bed and watched her rhythmically pull the soft bristles of the brush through the long wavy length of her hair. Watching was mesmerizing, comforting, relaxing. He thought he must have always enjoyed watching women brush their hair, but for some reason he couldn't recall a single experience doing so, nor even conjure up a single female face that was familiar.

It was all very odd, thought Jack, growing drowsy despite himself. His thoughts seemed so scrambled, and images that he should be able to easily grasp hovered just out of reach. Perhaps after he'd eaten something his thoughts would fall into a logical order and his memories would quit being so damned elusive. And perhaps if he closed his eyes for a moment . . .

While the stranger slept, Amanda stoked up the fire, gave herself a hasty sponge bath behind a folded screen, changed into a fresh black dress, fashioned her hair into a neat coil at the nape of her neck, then ordered tea and breakfast from the chambermaid who scratched on the door at the stroke of seven. It seemed that after interrupting Amanda while she was undressing the stranger yesterday, the maid was cured of entering without knocking first.

While Amanda waited for the tea and the breakfast tray, Theo showed up. Realizing that the stranger would need to take care of personal matters, Amanda asked Theo to wake the gent and help him with the chamber pot while she took a morning stroll. She felt she was already too intimate with the man, and she had no desire to embarrass either of them by taking on *all* the duties of a nurse.

When Amanda returned to the room, the maid had

arrived with the breakfast tray. As the maid prepared to leave, Amanda remembered that the stranger's shirt needed to be laundered, and she handed it over with instructions to make it fit to be worn as quickly as possible. She had no desire to be confronted with the stranger's bare chest any longer than necessary.

With Theo hovering at the end of the bed with a scowl that could scare off bears, Amanda simultaneously ate her own breakfast while helping the stranger manage his.

"It's very rude of you to eat that in front of me," the stranger said peevishly, swallowing the last dregs of his barley water.

"Eggs would only make you sick," said Amanda, dabbing a napkin to her mouth. "By this evening I daresay you'll be able to eat something solid."

"I certainly intend to," he said in a tone that implied he'd brook no opposition. He pushed himself to sit taller against the pillows, and as he scooted up the bedclothes fell away to expose a goodly portion of his chest. Amanda felt her color rising—remembering just how much of his body she'd seen last night—and she resolved to look him straight in the eye and nowhere else.

"You look as though you're feeling better," Amanda said bracingly. "There's color in your cheeks. Does your head still hurt?"

"Not as much. But I'm dizzy."

"I'm sure it will pass. The doctor will be here soon."

"I have some questions—"

"So do I. And I must insist that I ask at least one of mine first. I am on a rather urgent journey and cannot linger here any longer than necessary. So, if you'll just tell me who you are and how I can contact your nearest relative, we can send word immediately. I daresay there's a great many people—and perhaps someone in particular—who will be very glad to know you are safe—"

Amanda stopped speaking. The stranger had turned deathly pale, his expression a mixture of panic and astonishment.

"Good heavens! What's the matter?" she asked him, bending solicitously forward. "Are you going to be sick?" Theo rushed forward with an empty basin.

The stranger impatiently pushed aside the basin and ran a shaky hand through his disheveled hair. "I'm not sick," he said.

Amanda's brow wrinkled in puzzlement. "Then what is it?"

The stranger lifted his eyes to hers. They were brown eyes, dark as a gypsy's but with surprising flecks of gold. And the expression in them was one of startled disbelief. "You see," he began, giving a soft, slightly demented laugh, "I just realized that I can't tell you who to notify about my accident."

"Why not?" asked Amanda, on a rising note of panic.

"Because," said the stranger, a small, daft smile tilting his lips, "I don't *know* who my relatives and friends are."

"Good God!" Amanda's voice trembled. "You don't mean . . . ?"

"I'm afraid I do," he admitted wonderingly. "Damned if I don't have the slightest idea who I am!"

Chapter 5

❦

"This is terrible!" said Amanda, pacing the rag rug in front of the fire and wringing her hands in a frantic fashion that would rival Aunt Prissy's finest technique. "What are we going to *do* with you?"

"I'm very sorry that my amnesia interferes with your schedule, madam," the stranger said caustically. "But I can't help it." He crossed his muscled arms over his bare, broad chest and frowned, looking for all the world like a king of some uncivilized country with no one to behead.

Amanda stopped pacing and stood at the foot of the bed. "No, of course you can't help it," she said resignedly. "But *I* can't help being disappointed." Her tone turned imploring. "If you only knew how urgent it is that I leave soon to rescue my—"

Amanda bit her lip, almost wishing she could bite off her traitorous tongue! She was certainly not going to confide in this stranger about her illegitimate sibling. She had plans that she did not wish to be overset by a gossipmonger spreading rumors.

By his fashionable appearance—and all his other worldly recommendations—Amanda had no doubt that her disgruntled patient was a regular in the London set, and perhaps even an icon of the *ton*. If he found out why she was going to Thorney Island, he might later use it as an amusing *on-dit* at some social function, thereby ruining her sibling's chances of ever making a respectable marriage—particularly if the sibling turned out to be female. Everything was harder for a girl!

"So, you're off on some rescue mission, eh?" said the stranger, looking as though he thought she were foolish beyond description. Then his brows drew together in puzzlement. "But where is your escort, madam?"

"My escort?" she repeated stupidly, just as she had when the doctor inquired about her "husband's" name.

The stranger waved an elegant hand. "Are you traveling with your father?"

She shook her head.

"Your brother?"

She shook her head again.

He began to look incredulous. "Your ... *husband*, perhaps?"

"I can boast no such connections, sir," Amanda said loftily. "And even if I did, I shouldn't need them to mollycoddle me about the countryside as if I were a green girl! After all, I *am* three-and-twenty and perfectly able to take care of myself!"

The amnesiac, who had apparently not forgotten how to argue, opened his mouth to retort when there was a scratch at the door. Theo was walking over to open it when Mrs. Beane waltzed in without an invitation.

"Good morning, milady," she said courteously but with her habitual sour expression. At the mention of "milady," the stranger turned his gaze back to Amanda and raised a brow in inquiry. He had very expressive brows, that one.

"How does your husband fare this morning, pray?"

Now both black brows lifted, and a hint of wicked amusement glittered in his eyes.

"He ... he ... fares much better, thank you," Amanda stammered nervously. She moved to the side of the bed and took the stranger by surprise by grabbing hold of his hand and squeezing it very hard. "Lord *Thornfield* has a headache and—most regrettably—a memory lapse, which we naturally hope will be of short duration."

She smiled gamely at Mrs. Beane, then gazed down on the stranger with an expression she hoped would pass for fondness. However, it was hard maintaining her devoted pose when the stranger returned her look with one of pure devilish intent. Amanda sincerely hoped he'd not say or do anything to embarrass her or expose her lies to Mrs. Beane.

Mrs. Beane tsk-tsked about his lordship's loss of memory, but Amanda was quite sure the old hag wouldn't lose sleep over it as long as the earl didn't forget where he kept his purse when the time came to divvy up the ready. "What a shame," she said, then moved right on to business. "Will you be stayin' a few more days, then?"

"I don't—" Amanda began, but was interrupted by his lordship himself.

"My wife and I will be leaving tomorrow," said the stranger, smiling dulcetly at Mrs. Beane and lifting Amanda's hand to his lips to kiss it. The pleasant sensation that shot up her arm at the touch of his warm mouth kept Amanda speechless as the stranger continued. "Although I am unable to remember precisely what it is, we have urgent business to attend to ... do we not, my darling?"

"Well, yes, I ... that is ... we *do*," Amanda said weakly, surprised by the stranger's sudden participation in her charade and thoroughly unprepared for the effect it was having on her. To be called "my darling" by such a man, even in the most mocking tones, made her spinster's heart race like a thoroughbred.

"Are ye sure ye'll be well enough, milord?" asked Mrs. Beane, who had probably hoped to keep the well-heeled earl and his entourage under her roof for at least a week. "You've not yet seen the doctor today."

"Naturally I'll submit to the doctor's examination and consider all precautions he suggests. However, I'm absolutely certain that despite my indistinct memory of her more *tender* qualities, should we leave the inn this instant I have complete faith in my wife's abilities to take prodigious good care of *all* my needs." He squeezed Amanda's fingers nearly as hard as she'd squeezed his, then smiled up at her like a mooncalf.

If he was trying to pretend he was fond of her, Amanda was quite sure he was overdoing it and Mrs. Beane would see right through his exaggerated sentimentality.

"Well, stay as long as you like," said Mrs. Beane, backing toward the door with a disappointed expression. "Are there any special requests for luncheon?"

"Yes," the stranger said, sitting forward eagerly and wincing as if it made his head hurt to move even slightly. "I'd like a nice kidney pie, a roast chicken, cream cheese and bread, potatoes—" He stopped to ponder, then added, "Do you have beer, Mrs. Beane?"

"Dearest, you know you can't have beer," Amanda interrupted in a soft tone but with a look that spoke volumes. Then she turned to Mrs. Beane and asked, "Do you know how to make a nice beef broth?"

"I should say I do," said Mrs. Beane a little defensively.

"That's all the earl will be having for luncheon

today. Well, and perhaps some weak tea and a small crust of bread. By dinner he might be able to dine a little more heartily."

"I should hope so, or I'll bloody well starve," said the stranger under his breath, just loud enough for Amanda to hear him.

"What was that, milord?" inquired Mrs. Beane, only too ready cater to a rich earl's every whim.

"Nothing, Mrs. Beane," said Amanda, stepping forward to graciously hurry her out the door. "You have been extremely hospitable. Thank you, but that's all we'll be needing for now. Do send the doctor up as soon as he arrives, if you please."

When Mrs. Beane left, doubtless sorry that the earl's wants were so moderate, the stranger looked eager to take Amanda to task. Knowing how protective Theo was, Amanda asked her devoted servant to leave them alone. He pulled a mulish face and scowled as hard as he dared at the stranger, but he finally left.

"So, you don't need a husband or any such superfluous male presence as escort when you travel, eh, madam?" the stranger inquired with malicious enjoyment.

"No, I do not!" Amanda insisted.

"Then why did you tell Mrs. Beane that you and I are married?"

Amanda folded her arms over her chest and walked to the window, looking out on a wet courtyard and a gray, somber day. "Because she wouldn't give me a room till I told her you were my husband," she admitted grudgingly. "There, are you satisfied?"

"Not hardly," he said drily, as if just warming to his subject. "This is a small room, indeed . . . for an *earl*."

Amanda turned to face her interrogator. "It was the only room left and not easily acquired. Mrs. Beane is a grasping old witch much impressed by titles and even more so by money. Therefore, not only did I give you a prestigious title but I brandished a plump purse."

He raised an interested brow. "Is the purse mine?"

"No, it's mine. But you do have a rather heavy purse of your own, which we found in your coat pocket."

His eyes narrowed.

"Don't look at me like that," Amanda said huffily. "I don't ordinarily pilfer through gentlemen's coat pockets. My servants and I were trying to find something that would give us a clue as to your identity."

"I never supposed you were out to rob me," he said. "If that was your motive, you'd have left me to die instead of nursing me through the night."

Amanda lifted her chin. "A fact for which you've yet to thank me!"

The stranger shrugged his broad shoulders and managed to look contrite. "You're quite right, and I do thank you."

Amanda was a little flustered by his bluntly and sincerely expressed gratitude. "Well ... you're welcome. I'd have done it for anyone, you know," she disclaimed awkwardly. "And as I felt partially responsible for your injury—"

"Indeed?" said the stranger, raising those wicked brows again. "Please, madam, don't leave me in suspense. Explain why you feel responsible for this goose egg on my head!"

"I only said *partially* responsible," she amended.

"*Partially*, then," he said in a beleaguered tone. "But before you begin, perhaps you could tell me your name? I do not think it would be inappropriate to do so, as we are, after all, husband and wife ... or at least pretending to be! I'd introduce myself first, but as you know, that's quite impossible."

Amanda assumed a prim pose. "You may call me Miss Darlington."

The stranger's lips twitched. "That's a rather long form of address to have to attach to the end of every sentence. For example, 'Will you plump my pillow, Miss Darlington? Can I please have some real food before I faint, Miss Darlington? Do you think it shall rain, Miss Darlington?'" He grinned. "Do you see what I mean . . . Miss Darlington? I'd rather just keep on calling you darling."

Flustered, Amanda said, "But I'd rather you didn't."

His eyes gleamed with mischief. "But as long as I'm masquerading as your husband, I daresay you shan't refuse me the convenience of doing so . . . at least not in the presence of others."

Amanda's jaw tightened. She raised a haughty brow. "Then you won't object to me calling you *Demetri*."

"*Demetri?*" The stranger looked aghast. "Is that how you referred to me in front of the others? It sounds like something out of one of those gothic Radcliff novels!"

"Demetri was the only name I could think of at the time."

"I doubt that very much, *darling*, but I have no desire to argue about it. I'm sure I'll get my memory back by nightfall, and I'm counting on your sense of fair play to call me by my correct name when we . . . er . . . *both* know it."

"By nightfall there's no telling what names I might wish to call you," she murmured.

He laughed. "You're a saucy wench. I don't remember, of course, but I rather think I *like* females of your spirit."

Much against her will, Amanda was reluctantly pleased by his flirtatious compliment and turned away to hide her blush.

"Why don't we compromise?" he said to her back.

"Compromise?" She turned around. "What do you mean?"

"I'll call you Miss Darlington if you'll call me something ordinary . . . like John or Jack or Joe. Don't you think a plain name suits me much better than Demetri?"

Amanda didn't think there was anything plain about the stranger, but she did see the sense in calling him something simple. "I'll call you John," she said. "Will that make you happy?"

"John" smiled. He had a delightful smile that showed off straight white teeth and a single dimple in his left cheek. "It's a start," he said. "Now, before we get sidetracked again, please tell me how I got injured. Perhaps if you acquaint me with the circumstances surrounding the accident, I may remember something. We can then send word to my friends or relatives—"

"Your *wife*, perhaps."

The smile disappeared. "I'm quite sure I don't have one of *those*. I'd certainly remember that."

Amanda ignored the way her heart skipped a beat and continued on. "So, you *do* remember some things?"

"I seem to remember everyday things, like my preference for strong coffee and tea—two lumps of sugar, no cream—eggs over easy, sunshine instead of rain, gray horses instead of black, etcetera." He paused and threw her a teasing leer. "And since I like *you*, Miss Darlington, it goes without saying that I like beautiful women."

"My coachman thinks you're a rogue, and by the shameless way you flirt with a woman of my obvious maturity and respectability, I tend to agree," said Amanda, trying to sound severe.

"That plain black dress does not hide your beauty, Miss Darlington," said John. "And three-and-twenty is far from matronly."

"Do you know that you talk in your sleep?" she said, changing the subject. She wished she had a fan to cool her heated face. The dratted man seemed determined to discompose her.

"I don't *recall* that anyone has ever told me so, Miss Darlington, but my lamentable memory . . ." He smiled crookedly.

Amanda looked away, absently tracing a grooved pineapple design on the bedpost. "You mentioned several female names." She threw him a glance from under lowered lashes and observed that he had the audacity to look pleased.

"Will you repeat them?" he asked.

"If I can remember them all," said Amanda with a shrug, hoping he hadn't detected the peevish tone that had crept into her voice.

"Maybe the names will help restore my memory. But please, Miss Darlington, first tell me about the accident."

Amanda told him all about the accident: the location, the time, and his extremely inebriated condition. He sat forward and listened intently, then leaned back into the pillows with a thoughtful expression.

"When I awoke this morning," he said at last, "I assumed I was suffering the after-effects of too much brew-tipping, but I can't imagine being so fuddled that I'd actually wander into the path of a coach-and-four!"

"The fog was very thick last night in that particular area," Amanda offered as a partial explanation.

"But still, it's not my usual style to be so careless. Curious! Now, tell me the names I mumbled in my sleep."

Amanda sat down in the rocking chair and clasped her hands demurely in her lap. She was determined not to let the subject make her uncomfortable. After all, she was only trying to help John regain his memory; then they could both go their separate ways.

"Laura was the first name you mentioned."

"What did I say about the lovely lady?"

"Not much. Just that you ... er ... *needed* her."

He looked disappointed. "That's all? How *very* un-original. Who next?"

"The next name I heard you clearly say was Gretta." Amanda picked a piece of lint off her skirt and cleared her throat. "She used to ... er ... give you baths, apparently."

John's brows flew up. "Are you sure? How could I possibly forget a female who was so agreeable as to give me a bath!"

Amanda very properly made no comment but secretly thought that Gretta would certainly retain *her* memories of the bathing incident. The image of John's naked body would be singed into Amanda's brain till her dying day.

"Well, weren't there others?" John said, urging her on.

"There was Angela."

"A beautiful name," John said approvingly.

"Yes, I suppose it is," said Amanda. She hesitated, then suddenly blurted, "You thought I was Angela this morning when you pulled me onto the bed."

"So *that's* how you got there," he said in the delighted tone of one having just been given the answer to a riddle, then slyly added, "but why did you stay?"

Amanda abruptly stood. In a stiff voice, she said, "I only stayed because it seemed to comfort you and because I was cold and cross and tired. And since none of the names I've repeated seem to have jogged your memory, sir, I have no desire to continue a meaningless and distasteful conversation."

"I beg your pardon, Miss Darlington," said John, trying to repress an amused smile but failing miserably ... the wretch! "I promise not to beg you for more names, but you *will* tell me, won't you, if there were other things I mentioned in my dreams which might help identify who I am?"

Amanda hesitated. She knew John was just baiting her, just setting her up for more blushes and embarrassment. But there *was* something else she could tell him that might prod his memory. She could tell him that during his worst deliriums he thought he was fighting battles. It was a sobering revelation that might bring back the most hideous of all his recollections, but Amanda felt it was in his best interest— and hers—to help John get his memory back by any method available.

Gravely she said, "I think you were a soldier, John. Last night you were reliving battles. You cried out. . . ."

John's amusement faded away as uncertain, troubled emotions flitted across his face. Amanda was sure he was remembering something, or at least close to doing so. But presently he shook his head as if to clear it and locked eyes with Amanda again.

"If I was a soldier," he said with a shrug and the return of his rakish smile, "I don't remember it."

"Or maybe you don't *want* to remember it," suggested Amanda. "If I had fought in the war, I'd try to forget."

"I'd much rather remember Gretta and those baths," said John, obviously determined not to embrace a single serious subject.

"You're hopeless," said Amanda with a shaky sigh. "And I need some fresh air." She stood up and wrapped a black wool shawl around her shoulders. "I'm going to get that little chambermaid up here to sit with you while I take a walk." She moved to the door and threw the stranger a narrow look over her shoulder. "Please don't terrorize the poor girl by chasing her about the room."

"I promise to be good," said the irrepressible scoundrel, "because I simply don't have the energy to do otherwise. You're starving me to death! But before you go, Miss Darlington, might I suggest a possible way to determine if I was once a soldier?"

With her hand on the doorknob, Amanda turned. "Pray, what do you suggest?"

"If I were a soldier, it's likely I was wounded."

She knitted her brows, afraid of where he was going with his theorizing. "So?" she said unencouragingly.

He smiled like the devil himself. "Well . . . was I?"

"Were you what?" she asked cautiously but with a growing sense of dread.

"Was I wounded, Miss Darlington?"

She felt the warmth creep up her neck. "How could I possibly know?"

"I'm not unfamiliar with what is necessary to do when a person is feverish, Miss Darlington. Perhaps last night, when you took off my clothes and sponged me with a cool cloth to bring down my temperature, you might have noticed if I had any war wounds . . . ?"

Jack was having a capital time. His head ached a little harder after Miss Darlington slammed the door behind her as she made a hasty exit, but the pain was worth it. He loved watching the proper Miss Darlington blush. The silly girl probably thought that dressing like a Quaker camouflaged her pale beauty, but Jack thought the plain black frock only accentuated it.

He shifted against the pillows, his back stiff from lying too long abed, his stomach rumbling with a hunger that could not be appeased by beef broth and a crust of bread. He rubbed a hand over his jaw and wished he could shave, then brightened at the notion that he might be able to tease Miss Darlington into doing the task for him. She'd have to bend close to him, and those winsome breasts of hers would be just inches away.

Of course, now that he knew she was a lady, he'd never touch her or try to compromise her—it was a sure way to get leg-shackled and marriage was the last thing on Jack's mind—but he was going to flirt and be as provocative as possible. How better to while away the hours of his recuperation?

It wasn't just Miss Darlington's beauty and prim innocence that intrigued Jack. She was a bit of a mystery, too. After all, despite her obvious respectability, she was traveling without a chaperon or a male escort of any kind, she was a woman of independent means, and she was on some sort of secretive rescue mission. Although he would be denied a truly intimate knowledge of the fair lady, Jack felt it would be extremely entertaining to get to know as many of Miss Darlington's secrets as possible.

He might even be able to help her out of a fix ... if she should happen to be in one.

Jack grinned sheepishly. Perhaps he was an honorable sort, the gallant type that enjoyed being of assistance to damsels in distress. Then again, perhaps he was a rake, seducing women right and left. But for some reason, Jack wasn't too concerned about what sort of man he was yesterday or two years ago, or even ten years ago, but was rather more intrigued with enjoying the possibilities of *today*.

Jack's brow furrowed, and he absently rubbed his bare chest as he considered his situation. He'd lost his memory, and he should be gravely concerned about that fact. But he wasn't. He felt sure he'd get his memory back soon enough and completely intact. His loved ones and friends would be missing him by now, and while that was regrettable, there was nothing he could do to change things. He simply couldn't remember who he was.

To be completely honest with himself, for some reason Jack *liked* not knowing who he was. It was like living in a pleasant state of limbo. He felt *free*.

There was a sense of having escaped something
dreadful, but he couldn't imagine what.

Amanda had hit on an interesting point when
she'd remarked that if she had been a soldier, she'd
try to forget fighting in a war. Jack had a sneaking
suspicion that he wanted to forget something, too,
but he didn't think it had anything to do with a
possible military career or wartime experience. What
he wanted to forget was far more personal. . . .

Jack's eyes drifted shut. He was tired, and his head
was throbbing again. He'd sleep for a while till the
doctor came, then he'd spin a whisker and tell the
old sawbones he was feeling as spry as a spring
chicken. If he didn't remember who he was by the
next day, there was no way he was going to be left
in the care of that hatchet-faced old crone who ran
the inn. He'd rather take his chances with Miss Darlington, no matter what buffleheaded scheme she
was involved in. He'd prove he was travel-worthy,
then take to the road with his "wife."

Just as Jack drifted off he remembered the dream
about the wedding and fervently hoped it would not
return. He enjoyed pretending to be married, but the
real thing was another matter altogether.

Amanda pulled her shawl close about her shoulders. It was starting to sprinkle, and she knew she
ought to go back inside. She'd enjoyed looking at
the flowers planted against the wall of the inn—the
candytuft and forget-me-nots, the larkspur and clove
pinks—but now she was getting cold.

Yes, it was time to go in, but Amanda was less
afraid of catching her death than of facing John
again, especially now that he'd revealed that he knew
she'd seen him naked. He'd obviously deduced that
there was no other way she could have nursed him
through the fever than by stripping him down and

sponging him off. He'd doubtless seen the method used a thousand times during his service in the war.

Amanda looked up at the small, partitioned square that was the window to the room where the stranger lay on a narrow bed, tall, tan, *still* naked, and still disturbingly masculine. With the bandage slanted across his brow, a day's growth of black beard, and a bare chest as finely sculpted as Michelangelo's *David*, he looked as wicked and wild as a pirate. And when she woke up this morning, having slept for hours against the warm hardness of his body, he was touching her breasts.

At first she'd thought she was dreaming. She was married and being held by her husband, loved and treasured in a way she'd always privately yearned for. It was intoxicating, it was erotic, and it was . . . very improper. She'd very *properly* put a stop to such goings-on, but—dash it all!—she'd loved it while it lasted.

Amanda paced the cobbled yard, taking two or three agitated turns. She knew John was thoroughly enjoying teasing her and making her stutter and blush. It was a game with him, but she was so vulnerable, so stupidly flattered by his silly compliments! She just wished the dratted man would remember who he was so she could wash her hands of him and get on with her trip.

He seemed so unconcerned about his amnesia! If she suddenly woke up in a strange place with no memories beyond whether she took one or two lumps of sugar in her tea, she'd be quite hysterical. But John took it all in stride, seeming not the least worried. He was either a wise man, patiently awaiting the inevitable return of his memory, or a foolish man, too cocksure of himself to realize that he may have lost his past and his identity forever.

And the problem remained as to what she was going to do with the fellow. He had told Mrs. Beane that they were both leaving on the morrow, but Amanda couldn't allow that ... unless she took him only as far as the first populace town and left him in the care of the constabulary. They'd know how to advertise John's situation and find his family. A sketched likeness of him circulated round London would probably get immediate results.

Amanda stopped pacing and looked up again at the window. She supposed she could put up with the fellow long enough to get him to the authorities. And possibly she wouldn't even have to do that much. He could regain his memory any hour, any moment. And if he remembered who he was, it wouldn't hurt him a bit to stay with Mrs. Beane till some member of his family came to get him.

Thinking of family reminded Amanda of her brother or sister on Thorney Island. She clamped her lips tightly together as a protective instinct surged through her. She'd never tell her family secret to John. She'd never give him or anyone else an opportunity to hurt the child who was hopefully still living on at Thornfield Cottage. But each moment that passed was precious time wasted. No matter what happened, no matter what the doctor said, no matter whether or not John got his memory back, Amanda was leaving in the morning for the coast.

Just then a gig rattled into the courtyard, and Amanda turned to greet Doctor Bledsoe. Together they walked up the cinder path and into the inn to see the patient.

Chapter 6

"You're much better, my lord, but not well enough to travel on the morrow," was the doctor's opinion after examining his patient. "The wound won't bleed again, I daresay, but you'll have a scar."

"One more can't hurt," Jack commented.

"As for your memory ..." The doctor scrunched his time-weathered face into a thoughtful frown and pulled on his chin with short, blunt-tipped fingers.

"I'm sure it will return," said Jack, sitting up in bed with the sheet pushed down to his waist in order for the doctor to listen to his heart and lungs. He caught Miss Darlington staring at his chest and winked at her when she looked up. She pressed her lips together, jerked her chin up, and immediately shifted her gaze to the doctor.

"I think it will, too, my lord," the doctor agreed, "but I couldn't even begin to guess when that happy event might occur."

Jack watched the effect this vague pronouncement had on Miss Darlington's composure. She squeezed her hands together and held them at bosom-level, as if she were imploring or even praying, then stepped closer to the doctor. "You do think his memory will return *soon*, don't you, doctor?"

Jack suppressed a grin. The chit couldn't wait to get rid of him, but he had no place to go and was as happy as a fat cat to stay exactly where he was—with Miss Darlington.

"As I said, m'dear," said the doctor, stuffing his instruments into his leather bag, "I haven't the slightest idea when he'll regain his memory. It could happen today, it could happen tomorrow, or it might not come back for a month or more. 'Tis impossible to predict. And in the meantime, be aware that your husband might have occasional bouts of confusion. He's very lucid at the moment, but one never knows with these head injuries."

Miss Darlington's frustration was obvious. The doctor noticed, too, and laid a comforting hand on her shoulder. "Don't fret about it, m'dear," he advised. "Take an example from your husband, here." He gestured toward the bed, and Miss Darlington lifted her forlorn gaze to Jack's face. "His lordship is handling this unfortunate situation very well ... *very* well, indeed. He knows, as I do, that his memory can't be forced but will return naturally as he is reintroduced into his everyday life."

"You mean when I get back to my home in—" Jack turned to Amanda and widened his eyes in a pose of innocent inquiry. "Where *do* we live, my darling?"

Jack could almost see the cogs and wheels turning in Miss Darlington's brain as she scrambled for an answer. "Why, in Yorkshire, dear," she answered with a guilty twitch of her upper lip. He could tell she wasn't a seasoned liar, and Jack gave her credit for thinking of a county far enough away that no one would be familiar with the landed gentry who resided in that area.

"There, you see," said the doctor in a satisfied

tone. "All will be well. You are extremely lucky, my lord, that you were traveling with your excellent wife when this accident befell you. She's been a wonderful nurse. And I shudder to think what would have happened to you had you been off by yourself, so far from home, and with no one and nothing to connect you to your true identity."

"Yes, that *would* be a rather desperate situation," Jack agreed gravely. "In such a case, one would be entirely at the mercy of strangers."

He slid a pathetic look toward Miss Darlington. He watched as her small aristocratic nostrils flared and her jaw tightened in an effort to keep from making an unwise retort in front of the doctor. She doubtless understood that Jack was implying that it would be a heartless desertion if she left him behind with Mrs. Beane.

But if she thought he was going to try to delay her departure, she was wrong. Despite the doctor's advice to the contrary, Jack was going to insist that Miss Darlington resume her journey first thing in the morning . . . taking him with her.

"You are indeed far from home," said the doctor, moving toward the door. His eyes skimmed Miss Darlington's black dress, and he made an observation that Jack should have made hours ago. "You're in mourning, m'dear?"

Miss Darlington looked startled at first, then gave a slight nod, as if she did not wish to speak any further on the subject. But the well-meaning doctor did not take the hint. "Could you be on your way to a funeral, then?"

"Why, yes," said Miss Darlington. Her cheeks pinkened suspiciously, and Jack was sure she was lying again. "That's why we're so far from home, Doctor Bledsoe."

"No one hereabouts died, did they?" asked the

doctor with a look of professional interest. "I doctor them as far west as Shopwyke."

"No, the funeral's in quite another county," Miss Darlington briskly assured him. "Thank you for coming by, doctor. We shan't trouble you again unless my husband takes a turn for the worse. But as I intend to follow your instructions to the last detail, there's no fear of that."

Then, before the doctor could respond, Miss Darlington pulled out her purse, shook out a very fair amount of coin, and handed it to him. The doctor was sufficiently distracted to finally drop the subject of the funeral and forget any further repetitions of the instructions for Jack's care. She then adroitly maneuvered him out the door.

"A nice fellow," opined Jack as Miss Darlington shut the door behind the doctor and turned with a frosty look.

"I thought you disliked doctors," she answered in an equally frosty tone. She was apparently still angry with him for bringing up the war wound. "Not more than an hour ago I distinctly heard you say they were all quacks."

Jack shrugged. "I must admit that I don't remember any past experiences with doctors that would lead me to have such a low opinion of their abilities, but I have a feeling that compared to the others I've doubtless known, this fellow is superior. Dr. Bledsoe is blunt, practical, and experienced. I like him."

Miss Darlington's icy attitude seemed to thaw a little as she answered, "I like him, too."

Jack raised a brow. "I hope you don't like him so well that you are determined to—as you said just now—'follow his instructions to the last detail'?"

Miss Darlington crossed her arms and stood at the end of the bed. "What detail are you concerned about, John?"

"The detail about not allowing me to travel tomorrow."

Miss Darlington sighed and looked down, her arms falling to her sides.

Jack cocked his head and tried to peer up into her downcast face. "He's wrong, you know," he stated firmly. "I know you're itching to be off, and I wouldn't dream of delaying you another moment."

She lifted her head and asked cautiously, "You mean you're offering to stay here?"

"No," he answered firmly. "You've known my feelings all along about that. I mean to go with you."

"But you're not well enough," she argued, looking distressed.

"The alternative is to leave me in the care of Mrs. Beane till I recover my strength or my memory, whichever comes first. Could you do that in good conscience, Miss Darlington?" he demanded to know. "And how will you explain running off and leaving your husband in such a way?"

"I could tell the *truth*!" Miss Darlington crossed her arms again and took an agitated turn on the rug. " 'Tis a unique idea, I grant you, but it could be done! I *hate* lies. I've always hated lies, and most recently have had reason to hate them even more. But here I am spinning one whisker after another! I should be able to tell Mrs. Beane the truth, then go about my business as before without a single regret. You've got plenty of money to pay for your keep!"

"But your conscience won't let you go without me, Miss Darlington. Anything could happen if you left me here. *Anything*," he stressed.

Amanda stopped pacing and took her position at the end of the bed again. "Now you're being melodramatic," she accused. "But it would worry me if I left you here, though I wonder if being rattled to pieces in a carriage will do you more harm than a little hard nursing by Mrs. Beane."

"What if I prove I'm up to snuff, Miss Darlington?" said Jack, pushing up in the bed and shifting one leg to the edge of the mattress as if he were about to stand up.

Miss Darlington blanched and lifted both splayed hands in front of her. "Don't you *dare* get out of bed without your clothes, sir, or I shall scream!"

Having sincerely forgotten that he was naked, Jack resettled in bed and pulled the sheet up to his Adam's apple. "And an odd notion Mrs. Beane and the entire population of this inn should have about our marriage if you *screamed*, Miss Darlington. But I do beg your pardon! It's just that I've been sitting around like this for so long, and am so comfortable doing so, I forgot I was not"—he paused, fishing for the right words—"properly outfitted for presentation," he finished wryly.

"Your clothes should be ready by now," said Miss Darlington, unknowingly showing her maidenly agitation by fussing with the buttons that marched up the entire front of her bodice to her chin. "I'll speak to the chambermaid." She turned and moved to the door.

"I won't put my clothes on, you know, until I—"

Miss Darlington turned swiftly, her slim white hands, which he distinctly remembered being so cool and soft, curled into fists. Or had he just dreamed about her hands? "Until you *what*?" she said with ominous calm, as though her patience was at the end of its tether.

Jack gave her a look that implied that the answer was self-evident. "Until I get my bath, of course."

"Oh." She was clearly disconcerted. "I hadn't thought of that. I imagine you do rather—" She waved one hand ineffectually.

"Yes, I do rather *need* one," he finished for her.

"Yes . . . er . . . yes, well, I'll arrange for the water to be heated at once," she said, turning to go.

"I'll need assistance," he reminded her as she was halfway out the door.

She turned back, and he could see by her angry and implacable expression that he'd irked her into forgetting her embarrassment. "No matter what argument you put forth, sir," she said with steely calm, "I will not assist you in a bath. I am *not* your wife, nor am I Gretta, of whose charms and talents I've no doubt you will someday again fondly remember. *I*, however, will never be a fond memory of yours, John, nor will my name *ever* be murmured by you whilst in the throes of a delirium."

"Perhaps the chambermaid would be willing to lend me a hand," he suggested demurely. He was immensely amused by Miss Darlington's conversation and couldn't seem to stop himself from egging her on.

"One of my men can assist you," she said with finality. She stopped, pondered for a minute, then smiled maliciously. "I should think Theo would do nicely, since he's the largest of the lot and dislikes you the most."

"But I'll need a shave, too, Miss Darlington," Jack objected, laughing. "And by the looks Theo gives me, I must confess I'd fear for my life if he took a razor to my throat!"

"Then behave yourself, sir," Miss Darlington advised him with a triumphant sniff. "Behave yourself and do not vex me, or I'll tell Theo I wouldn't mind it very much if his hand slipped a *little* while he shaved you."

And with that last warning, she left.

The smile remained on Jack's face for several moments after Miss Darlington left the room. He couldn't remember the last time he'd been so well entertained . . . but then he couldn't remember much of anything, could he?

Jack ran his hand over his raspy jaw, and his smile

faded. He certainly hoped Theo had steady hands and no taste for murder. Then it occurred to him that he *could* shave himself. That the idea hadn't occurred to him before indicated that he wasn't accustomed to doing his own toilette and normally enjoyed the services of a valet.

Jack sighed and acknowledged to himself that there might be some advantages to getting back his memory, one of those advantages being the services of a valet, and another advantage being the chance of becoming reacquainted with the commendable Gretta. After all, Jack thought philosophically, there wasn't a friendlier thing a female could do for a fellow than *bathe* him.

He sank into his pillows, imagining mounds of frothy soap floating in a tub of steaming water. And there, so clear to his mind's eye as she bent near him, was Miss Darlington ... lovingly wielding a sponge.

Amanda was amazed at the progress John made in the next few hours. The fellow seemed absolutely dead set on proving he was travel-worthy. With Theo's help he took his first unsteady steps to the tub placed in front of the fireplace and had a bath. Amanda was not present, of course, but later as she and Theo met in the hall, he reported that the stranger refused to be helped with the bathing and once or twice made an obscure and bitter remark about some woman named Gretta.

"I only bring up the female's name, miss," Theo said with a shamefaced look, "in the hopes that it'd help ye find the bloke's kin. Do ye reckon she's 'is sister?"

"I have already discussed the woman known as Gretta with the gentleman," Amanda replied calmly, but with secret amusement. "Indeed, Theo, she is *not* his sister, nor anyone even remotely related to him."

Theo accepted this explanation with a sober nod

and a faint blush. "Well, least ways he's clean now and tucked into bed again. He wouldn't let me touch 'im, so he shaved hisself whilst sittin' in the tub."

This revelation brought such a vivid picture to Amanda's mind—John's chest dotted with lather, his strong brown knees jutting out of the water like volcanic islands in a frothy sea, his lean fingers deftly carving away the stubble of a black pirate's beard—that she had to shake her head to clear it.

"What about his clothes, Theo?" she prompted, anxious to be assured that she wouldn't have to spend another night in a room with a naked man. Last night he was unconscious and sick; tonight he was conscious and gaining strength by the minute.

"Mrs. Beane found 'im a shirt to sleep in, seein' as how he wanted to keep 'is fancy togs neat fer tomorrow." Theo bent a wary gaze on Amanda. "We're not takin' 'im with us, are we, miss?"

"I can't leave him with Mrs. Beane, Theo," said Amanda with a sigh. "The doctor said he could have bouts of confusion before his memory returns, so he definitely needs to be watched over carefully until he can be reunited with friends or family."

"He might never regain his memory, miss," Theo argued. "I don't reckon ye mean to take 'im clear back to Darlington Hall!"

"Of course not. But during this initial stage of his recovery from the accident, I'm certainly not going to abandon him. Perhaps by the time we get to Chichester, he'll be well enough to leave with the authorities. I won't take him to Thorney Island with us."

"It'd be best fer everyone if'n we skipped Thorney Island altogether, if'n ye ask me," Theo grumbled.

"But no one asked you, Theo," Amanda said curtly, edging toward the door to her room.

"Truth to tell, I think ye're makin' a mistake, miss, bringing that little merry-begotten of yer pa's back to Darlington Hall," Theo stated with the boldness of a longtime, trusted servant. "It's causin' nothin' but problems. Ye ought not t' be sleepin' in the same room with that man, neither. But none of this'd happened if'n ye hadn't lied to Mrs. Beane in the first place, ner left yer home without a chaperon. The master and the missus taught ye better'n that, Miss Darlington—"

"That's enough, Theo," Amanda said sternly, her usual soft voice slightly raised. Theo looked at her in surprise and chagrin, but Amanda had patiently allowed him to fuss over her and nag at her during the trip because she knew he held her in genuine affection and was truly concerned for her welfare. But she couldn't allow him to bring up her parents as an example or unfavorably compare her behavior with theirs, particularly since he knew how despicably her father had behaved.

"I don't like being short with you, Theo," said Amanda in a softened tone, "but you sometimes forget that I'm not a little girl any longer. I know perfectly well what I'm doing, and even if I didn't, it's not your place to lecture me."

"Yes, miss," said Theo, mortified.

"Now, go and have your supper and go to bed," she ordered. "We all need our rest for the trip tomorrow."

Theo bowed stiffly and departed, leaving Amanda feeling like a brute. She hated wounding his pride and hurting his feelings, but the last thing she wanted to hear was how well her parents had taught her. Their lessons were sheer hypocrisy, and Amanda knew that even if she made mistakes along the way, from then on she would base her decisions on her *own* determination of right and wrong.

Because of her contretemps with Theo, when Amanda reentered the room she shared with "John" she was in a rather tetchy mood. And it did not help matters to find her supposed husband expertly entertaining the chambermaid, who was sitting on the side of the bed and laughing till it looked like her seams would split and her womanly charms would jiggle out of her low-cut bodice.

After his bath and shave, and despite the nick on his chin from an out-of-practice handling of the razor, John looked wonderful. His hair shone ebony black above his fresh bandage, the thick waves tamed into a semblance of neatness but still looking tousled and touchable.

His skin glowed from the bath, and his eyes gleamed with renewed vitality after having polished off a hearty dinner approved by the doctor.

He was wearing the nightshirt Mrs. Beane must have pulled out of a bottom drawer of her dead husband's old wardrobe chest, but even the plain dun-colored garment did not detract from the vital beauty of the man wearing it.

As the chambermaid's laughter subsided at last into giggles, she turned and noticed Amanda standing just inside the door. Leaping to her feet, she made a hasty curtsy and sidled away from the bed. "Oh, milady, it's *you!*" she said nervously, as if Amanda had caught them playing slap and tickle under the covers. John simply sat there, looking relaxed and happy and not a bit like a man who'd recently suffered an accident and lost his memory.

"Well, of course it's me," Amanda said with forced lightness, wondering how she'd feel about stumbling onto such a scene—however innocent it might truly be—if she were actually married to this handsome stranger. Even now, with no claim whatsoever to his love or loyalty, she felt an irritating twinge of jealousy. "What has my husband said to amuse you so well?" She shifted her speculative gaze to John and raised a brow. He gave an infinitesimal shrug and smiled even broader.

"His lordship was just tellin' me a comical story, milady," said the chambermaid, still hiding smiles and giggles behind her hand. "He's ever so full of jest, he is."

"That's my husband," Amanda said dryly, "always the life and soul of every party." She moved into the room, leaving the door open behind her as a hint to the chambermaid. The hint did not fall short of its mark, and after tittering through two more curtsies, the chambermaid left them alone.

"If you can remember comical stories to tell the servants, does that mean you've got your memory back?" Amanda asked John, taking her usual position at the end of the bed.

"Why do you always stand at such a distance when you talk to me?" John countered her question with another. "Sally's not afraid of me."

Amanda raised her brows at the familiar use of the chambermaid's name. "I'm not afraid of you, either," she lied, "but I don't need to be sitting in your lap in order to hold a conversation with you, do I?"

John appeared to be considering this arrangement. "You don't *have* to, but it *would* be rather cozy."

"Things are quite cozy enough as it is," Amanda retorted. "Now, do answer my question, John. Are you beginning to remember things?"

John made a slight grimace and shook his head. "No, not *important* things. I remembered a few bawdy jokes I must have heard in a men's club, but I don't have the vaguest recollection of who might have repeated them to me. Odd, isn't it?"

"*Very* odd," Amanda agreed, tapping her toe on the carpet.

"You do believe I can't remember, don't you?" John asked her with a sharp look.

"I can't think of any reason why you'd lie about it," Amanda answered honestly. "But your memory loss seems so . . . *selective*."

"Yes, it does. Which makes me wonder if there's something I really don't *want* to remember," Jack admitted with a thoughtful frown.

Amanda looked down and absently gave the front of her skirt an arranging stroke. "I've wondered—" She stopped, not sure whether she should proceed with a theory she'd been mulling over.

"What, Miss Darlington?" John prompted her.

"I've been wondering if perhaps you're in some kind of trouble ... or danger." She looked up to gauge the stranger's reaction to her suggestion. He looked serious and interested, but he didn't look frightened.

"That's an intriguing idea," he said, leaning back against his pillows and laying his hands flat on his chest. While seeming to meditate on the ceiling, he continued, "Because I was wandering alone in what was essentially a wilderness, you're speculating that someone might have ... er ... *dumped* me there, eh?"

"The thought had crossed my mind," she admitted. "Why else would you be there?"

"The possibilities are endless," said John. He stretched his arms above his head in a leisurely fashion, then crossed them behind his neck. Looking oh so comfortable, he smiled and engaged her eyes. Whenever the dratted man looked at her, Amanda found it impossible to look away. "The possibilities of who I am are endless, as well," he added provocatively. "Doesn't that make you nervous, Miss Darlington?"

Everything about him made her nervous, but Amanda wasn't about to admit that fact. "Your clothes, your manner of speaking ... your general *air* indicate that you are high-born, John, and probably peerage. Perhaps I wasn't lying to Mrs. Beane when I told her you are an earl."

John got a look about him like a preening peacock. "My air, you say? An *earl*, you say?"

"But that doesn't mean you're a *good* man," Amanda reminded him, not too eager to add to the fellow's cockiness. "Any fear I might have of you, John, would have nothing to do with your rank in life but would have everything to do with whether or not I could trust you to behave honorably."

"I've wondered about that. . . ."

"About what?"

"About whether or not I'm honorable . . . whether or not I'm a good man," said John in a considering tone. "What kind of man do *you* think I am, Miss Darlington?"

I think you're much addicted to flirting, a knave, a rascal, maybe even a wastrel . . . and utterly charming, Amanda said to herself. To John she simply said, "I don't know."

"Which is rather dangerous for you, is it not?"

Jack watched as Miss Darlington gave his teasing remark more serious thought than he'd expected . . . indeed, much more than it deserved.

"You would never hurt me," she said at last, her sincerity obvious. *Anyway, not purposely,* she added to herself.

"How do you know that?" he quickly countered.

"I just do."

Jack was floored. He didn't know how to respond. Indeed, he was so surprisingly touched and embarrassed by her naive trust in him, he didn't even know where to look. He covered his confused emotion with a cavalier laugh, saying, "Well then, you know more about me than I know about myself! Suffice it to say, I remain a mystery to us both. Now let's talk about *you*, Miss Darlington."

"There's no need to talk about me. My memory is intact, and my present history is very boring," said Miss Darlington in a dampening tone, turning to pick up a long piece of kindling and poke at the fire. "There's nothing at all mysterious about *me*."

"I beg to differ. I had concluded that you wore black because you were trying to camouflage your beauty, but it's true what the doctor said, isn't you? You *are* in mourning."

All Jack could see of her face was the hint of a blooming cheek, but the cheek paled and the edge of her mouth suddenly drooped. He was immediately angry at allowing his curiosity to cause the lady pain. "If you'd rather not talk about it—"

She turned and managed a weak smile. "Don't be ridiculous. I don't mind talking about it. My parents died six months ago."

"My condolences."

She turned back to the fire and resumed her idle occupation, never answering. Tactfully, he dropped the subject. But since his intense curiosity about Miss Darlington wasn't even slightly appeased, he couldn't help asking more questions on other matters.

"Why are you traveling alone?"

"Because as an independent woman of substantial means, I am able to do so and choose to do so. Do I need another reason?"

"No, I suppose not. But it's dangerous."

"It is a risk I'm willing to take."

"Indeed, you are a willful woman, Miss Darlington."

"Not until recently," she murmured faintly, the words barely audible.

Jack found that comment revealing and intriguing. What had happened lately to change Miss Darlington into a willful female who jaunted about the countryside without an escort?

"Whom are you rescuing, Miss Darlington?"

She forced a brittle laugh. "No one. Where did you get such an idea?"

"From you. You said you needed to leave soon to rescue someone, but you didn't finish the sentence."

"And I won't, because it's none of your business."

"You won't even tell me where you're going? How disobliging of you!" He lowered his voice. "You say you are not mysterious, Miss Darlington, but such secrecy smacks of mystery."

She turned, the firelight catching rosy highlights in her hair, her skin. "Well, John," she said dulcetly, "it seems we are each a mystery to the other. But since we are presently together only because of the oddest and most inopportune of circumstances, and are not destined to spend our lives together, I don't think it matters much. Now if you don't mind, I'm going to bed."

Jack wasn't the least bit sleepy, but he decided that he'd questioned and harassed Miss Darlington enough for one night and obediently blew out the candle at his bedside, turning his face toward the wall so that his reluctant roommate would have a little privacy.

By firelight, she unpinned and brushed out her hair. He couldn't see her doing it, of course, but he could hear every silky stroke of the brush and had no trouble remembering how lovely she'd looked that morning as she'd performed the same task.

He lay very still, getting drowsy. He was convinced that he normally slept alone . . . except for the occasional night with a ladybird, of course. And he was still quite positive he wasn't married, which made it all the more disconcerting that he found the sounds and scents of another human being in the room with him so comforting . . . so welcome. So restful.

Half-dozing, he rolled on his back, expecting to see Miss Darlington's dormant form huddled under a blanket on the cot. His eyes blinked open; his heart started hammering in his chest. No doubt thinking he was asleep, Miss Darlington had slipped behind the changing screen to have a sponge bath. She'd taken a candle and set it on the table behind her. The result was that she'd rendered the thin folding screen practically transparent. Her shadow—every slender, womanly curve—was silhouetted against the candle's glow.

She moved slowly, quietly, trying to make as little noise as possible, but Jack was already awake . . . wide awake and absolutely mesmerized. Her movements were graceful and sensuous as she dipped her cloth in the basin and smoothed it over her arms and chest. Once she turned and the profile of a breast was clearly discernible . . . right down to the hard nub of the nipple.

Jack swallowed hard. She'd said she trusted him. To deserve that trust, the honorable thing to do would be to turn over and go back to sleep. With a supreme struggle, he finally forced himself to look away, then to turn and face the wall again. Sleep, however, was out of the question.

He sighed. Well, he guessed he knew his answer to the rhetorical question he'd posed earlier . . . the one concerning whether or not he was a good man, a man given to honorable impulses. Apparently he was. *Damn it.*

Chapter 7

Amanda awoke to the sound of a rooster crowing. She sat up in her narrow cot, her eyes heavy from a restless night, and looked around. The room was filled with the hazy gray predawn light, and John was fast asleep. It was the perfect time to get up and dress before she was hampered by the company of her impertinent roommate. She wouldn't even take the time to stoke up the fire for a little warmth; it was far more important to have a bit of privacy while attending to her personal needs.

Swiftly slipping her arms into her dressing gown, she stood up and hurried behind the screen. She'd waited last night till John's deep and steady breathing indicated he had fallen asleep, then quietly had a sponge bath and laid out a fresh black traveling gown for the trip this morning. She was grateful the rogue was a sound sleeper and was hoping he'd sleep just as soundly this morning while she dressed and arranged her hair.

As Amanda went about the tedious chore of doing up all her buttons, she pondered the events that had made her night so restless. Just having to share a bedchamber with a man was enough to disturb a maiden lady's rest, but John had talked in his sleep again. She'd gone to his bedside more than once to lightly lay a hand on his forehead and test his temperature. She had been greatly relieved that there was no fever, but his disjointed and agitated murmurs disturbed her.

The man was obviously troubled about something . . . something that plagued him in his sleep and disappeared from his memory during waking hours. She couldn't help wondering what worried him so.

Buttoned into her severe gown and with her wavy hair forced into the usual tight coil at the nape of her neck, Amanda felt back in control. But as she came out from behind the screen, her eyes were drawn immediately to the bed and the man in it. She released a relieved sigh when she observed that he still slept; she'd have time to locate Theo and send him in to help John dress.

Amanda was beyond worrying what Mrs. Beane would think about giving over her nursing duties to a mere coachman. Since the stranger had regained his consciousness and begun to tease and question her so persistently, Amanda felt less and less able to cope with him. Besides, they were leaving that morning, and it no longer mattered what Mrs. Beane thought of her aristocratic guests.

Amanda went to the door but lingered there for a moment before leaving. John looked so appealing while he slept. His hair was tantalizingly rumpled, his thick black lashes shadowed his chiseled cheeks, and his mouth was nicely molded and firm, not gaping open like her father's used to do when he snored.

Yes, it was very nice that John didn't snore. Now, if only he didn't talk in his sleep! But, thank goodness, last night was the last time she'd have to worry about John's sleeping habits.

Theo was easily found and only too eager to make up for his disrespectful behavior of the previous evening by hastily agreeing to anything Amanda asked him to do. While Amanda strolled and lingered in the grassy field behind the inn, Theo attended to John. After nearly an hour of this purposeful loitering, Amanda grew hungry for her breakfast and returned to the room.

When she discreetly knocked on the door, John's deep voice called out "Come!" and she hesitantly entered, not entirely sure why she suddenly felt so shy. But as soon as she clapped eyes on John, she knew her nervous uncertainty was justified.

Previously she had only seen the stranger lying down or sitting up. Seeing him now, standing by the fire in a nonchalant pose with one elbow carelessly propped on the mantel, she was more than a little intimidated.

John was taller than she imagined, and looked much bigger and more masculine in an upright position. And with his burgundy jacket and light gray trousers cleaned and pressed, his boots polished, his hair brushed to glossy perfection, and his snowy neckcloth arranged in an elegant style fit for Almacks, he was quite impressive. Amanda felt her jaw loosen and her knees go weak.

"Good morning, Miss Darlington," said John, a ghost of a smile tugging at his lips.

As Amanda was sure John's smile reflected his amusement at her dumfounded expression, she quickly gathered her composure and answered with prim civility, "Good morning to you, sir. You look as though you are feeling more yourself today. Is it too much to hope that you actually *are* more yourself . . . that you have regained your memory and can tell me your true identity?"

"Ah, I wish I could tell you who I am, Miss Darlington," he said with a dubious show of regret. "But, alas, I know no more today than I did yesterday. I'm afraid you're going to have to put up with me a little longer."

"But only so far as Chichester," she said decisively, taking satisfaction in replacing his confident look with one of displeased surprise. "If you are strong enough to stand and walk, and travel in a rattling carriage for fifty miles or more, you are well enough to be given over to the authorities. They will have means to identify you and get you safely back home. I haven't the slightest doubt that once you show your face in London, you'll be instantly recognized. If I had the time, I'd take you there myself, but—"

"I won't be sent to London!"

John's insouciant attitude entirely disappeared. He pushed away from the mantel and paced the floor, a grim, distracted expression on his face and both hands curled into fists. She noticed he had a slight limp.

"Why not? If you frequent the usual haunts of the *ton*, if you belong to Whites or use Weston as a tailor—which seems quite likely to me—London is the most logical place to find acquaintances."

"I don't know why I have an aversion to the city, but I do," John said gruffly, still pacing. "And, furthermore, I have no desire to embarrass myself by being displayed like a shop-window dummy for all and sundry to gape at till someone recognizes my face."

"I'm sure the constabulary has more discreet means of finding out one's identity."

He stopped pacing and turned on her, glowering. "If you mean those likenesses they nail to trees and distribute amongst the rabble, I don't fancy that method, either. I would rather remember who I am and where I belong on my own, thank you very much."

"You cannot do it on your own, John," Amanda reminded him. "But you won't go to the authorities, you won't stay with Mrs. Beane, and you won't go to London. That leaves only one alternative . . . that you remain with me, which I don't mind telling you has thus far proven to be dashed inconvenient!"

"If you're itching so badly to be rid of me, Miss Darlington," John said with asperity, "I could rack up in a room somewhere ... but not *here*! I daresay in time I would remember something."

Amanda felt herself relenting. Her anger was really only a defense against her attraction to this man, and she had no desire to place him in danger just to make herself more comfortable.

"Dr. Bledsoe said you were liable to have bouts of confusion," she said, reluctant to voice her own concerns for John's safety but perfectly willing to repeat the doctor's. " 'Tis out of the question for you to stay in rented lodgings alone. Besides, I *am* partly responsible for the fix you're in, so—"

"So why are we having this conversation?" John asked, brightening as it became obvious that he was winning his point. "Though you won't confide the particulars to me, I know you are anxious to get somewhere quickly. We're wasting time arguing, so why don't we climb aboard the carriage and be off? If we still feel inclined to argue, we can do it just as well en route."

Amanda could not argue this point, so with stiff dignity she directed Theo, Harley, and Joe in the loading up of her portmanteaux. Then she played the dutiful wife by escorting her injured husband—who certainly needed no escort, as he was as strong as a horse and as steady as a teetotaler!—down the stairs and to the front door. There she waited while John paid Mrs. Beane quite handsomely out of his own purse.

When they were finally aboard the carriage and on their way, Amanda turned her face to the window and pointedly ignored her traveling companion. Thankfully, John took the hint that she was feeling too prickly for conversation and did not utter a single word.

If nothing good could be said for the circumstances of her life in the last two days, Amanda supposed she should at least be happy that the weather was conducive to a journey that morning. It was a beautiful day. The sun was strong, and only a very gentle breeze stirred the gold and russet leaves of the trees that lined the country road they traveled on.

They were passing over the South Downs, a section of England known for its proliferation of prehistoric settlements, quaint medieval villages, and ever-changing natural scenery as the land undulated toward the sea. As they left the village of Horsham, which was situated in a deep woodland, the aspect from Amanda's window opened up to bracken-covered heathland filled with deer and other wild field animals.

They were headed southwest toward Arundel, which Amanda hoped they would make by noon, then on to Chichester for dinner and lodgings for the night.

But in the meantime, she was encapsulated in a very small space with a very large man. Amanda was sure she'd not be able to ignore him all day, especially if he did not choose to be ignored. Her neck would get a painful crick in it if she continually faced the window, but conversation was dangerous. John could tell her nothing about himself . . . and he was too dashed curious about *her*!

Amanda was beginning to think that another lie would be necessary to appease the fellow. For example, if she told him that she was going to Thorney Island to pick up . . . say . . . her *nephew* for a short visit, his curiosity would probably be satisfied.

Yes, Amanda admitted to herself, it would be better to tell another lie than to have him continually after her to 'fess up about her "secret rescue mission."

She turned toward the stranger, fully expecting him to be staring at her and one of his wicked brows lifted imperiously. But he was asleep ... his head lulling against the soft squabs of Amanda's comfortable carriage.

So, thought Amanda, despite the fellow's inherent physical strength and stubbornness, he could not completely escape the fatigue occasioned by a nasty bump on the head and several hours of unconsciousness, fever, delirium, and forced bed rest. Like all mortal men, he needed time to recuperate.

Amanda smiled to herself, very well pleased to discover that however Adonis-like the stranger appeared, he was only mortal after all.

Mrs. Beane had just finished her noon meal and a strong cup of tea. Now she was settled in her kitchen, quite alone, with her feet propped up on an opposite chair. Though she was a bit disappointed that the earl and his small entourage had not stayed longer and spent more money, she was well pleased with the payment he'd made for little more than a day's worth of grudging hospitality.

She hated being an innkeeper; it did not suit her solitary disposition at all. But when her husband was so disobliging as to turn up his toes, she'd had no choice but to carry on with the business or go hungry. That morning all but one guest had left the premises, and a nearly empty house suited her excellently. Besides, it would fill up again soon enough ... though not with the likes of Lord Thornfield or some other rich nob. They rarely saw his sort at such a modest establishment as the Three Nuns. She closed her eyes and rested her head against the back of the chair.

"Mrs. Beane? Sorry to disturb ye, mum, but there's a gentl'man out front wishin' to speak to ye."

Mrs. Beane opened her eyes and glared at the timid chambermaid, hovering just inside the door. "If he wants a room, Sally, go ahead and take 'im upstairs. 'Tis too early in the day fer me t' want to gabble with the customers."

"Oh, he don't want a room, mum," said Sally, wide-eyed. "He wants particular to speak to you."

Mrs. Beane scowled and sat up, lifting her feet from their comfortable prop and dropping them to the floor. "What about?" she demanded shortly.

"I don't know, mum." Sally nervously plucked at her apron front, then added earnestly, "But he don't look like the type o' man what's accustomed t' bein' refused."

"What rubbish you speak, girl!" Mrs. Beane's curiosity was piqued, but she hid her interest behind a sour face as she stood up and stalked to the door. "People get refused all the time. I'm sure this bloke's no different than the rest."

But when Mrs. Beane entered the parlor where the stranger awaited her, she was forced to admit that Sally was right. This man *was* different. In fact, she couldn't imagine anyone ever saying no to such a commanding-looking gentleman.

Mrs. Beane kept the inn clean and in good repair, but the stranger's imposing height, his fine patrician features, his elegant clothes, and his haughty demeanor made the small room look dingy and shabby by comparison. Though she was admittedly impressed by rank and swayed by money, Mrs. Beane was almost never truly intimidated. However, she'd never before clapped eyes on someone who so perfectly personified English highborn breeding as this man did. Convinced she was face-to-face with no less than a duke, Mrs. Beane was rendered speechless. She simply stood and gawked.

The gentleman raised a tawny, gracefully arched brow. "Are you the proprietress of this establishment?"

His voice was deep, assured, perfectly modulated. Mrs. Beane cleared her throat. "Aye." Her own voice sounded coarse and unpleasant to her ears after hearing his. "Yes, sir, I am. What ... what can I do for ye?"

The stranger crossed his arms over a broad chest outfitted in a superfine jacket of deep Devonshire brown, worn over a waistcoat of palest butter yellow. Buff trousers and tall black boots encased the gentleman's extremely long legs, and for the first time in her life, Mrs. Beane found herself staring lustfully at a man's limbs.

Her reeling wits were righted, however, when the gentleman spoke again, his cool authority and aristocratic accent ready reminders of the differences between them. "I need some information, madam."

She hadn't the slightest idea of refusing him. "Indeed, sir, what sort of information?"

"I'm looking for someone who may have come this way recently. A man of two-and-thirty, exactly two inches shorter than myself, well dressed, and very dark. He has a scar on his right cheek."

Mrs. Beane immediately recognized her recent guest, the Earl of Thornfield, in this description. "You must be talking about Lord Thornfield," said Mrs. Beane, happy to be of service to such an impressive man ... and, by the looks of him, he could afford to reward her generously for her trouble.

The man's pale but vivid blue eyes sharpened with interest, but instead of smiling as if pleased, he frowned. "You have seen a man bearing such a description, but he calls himself Lord *Thornfield*?"

"Aye, sir," she affirmed, then felt a prick of uneasiness. If they weren't talking about the same man, the gentry cove would likely not deign to reward her. "Isn't he the gent ye're looking for, then?"

"How recently was he here?"

"He only just left this morning, about eight. The doctor cautioned 'im not to travel too soon after the accident, but he—"

"An accident, you say? The gentleman was injured?"

"He had a bump on 'is noggin. His wife said he fell and hit his head on a rock when he—"

"His *wife*?"

"Aye, sir. Lady Thornfield was the one who brought him here night before last. He was unconscious and looked as though someone had tried to put 'im to bed with a shovel, so to speak."

"Was he well when he left this morning?"

"Well enough. He was walkin' and talkin', and he ate a hearty breakfast."

She could almost imagine she saw the grand gentleman heave a relieved sigh beneath his elegant waistcoat. "Did they say where they were going?"

"No, but they were in a great hurry."

"Do you know what direction they were headed?"

"West, I think."

"Can you describe the carriage?"

"Have you never seen it, then?"

"Of course I have. But I want to hear *your* description."

"It's painted a pale gray, touched here and there with white. Very modest-looking for the coach of an earl. And there's no crest. I thought it odd, but Lady Thornfield said they was in mourning. Dressed all in black, she was."

"Hmmm," was all the man said, his high brow furrowed.

"Is it Lord Thornfield you're lookin' for, then?"

"I . . . think so."

Mrs. Beane thought that was a queer comment but

respectfully forbore from saying so. He stood as if in deep thought for a moment, then roused himself and plucked a few guineas from his pocket and poured them into her ready hand. "Thank you for your information, madam."

"You're *very* welcome, sir," said Mrs. Beane, hardly believing her good luck in being useful to two such rich nobs in little over four-and-twenty hours.

When the man turned to go, Mrs. Beane thought of another bit of information that might be of interest to him and, therefore, profitable to her. "He's lost his memory."

The irritable look disappeared to be replaced by pale disbelief. "Jack has lost his memory?" he said faintly.

"*Jack*, sir?" said Mrs. Beane, puzzled by this odd insertion of someone else's name. "We were speaking of Demetri, Lord Thornfield—"

"Yes, Lord Thornfield. You say he's lost his memory?"

"Aye. As the doctor said himself, he was lucky he was traveling with his wife or the poor fellow would be totally at the mercy of strangers, not knowing where or to whom he belonged."

"Yes," he said, his voice more thoughtful than ever.

"You're a friend of his?" asked Mrs. Beane.

The gentleman stirred, seeming to shake off the grim reverie he'd fallen into. He stood tall and gave his chin a purposeful thrust. "Yes, I'm a friend of his," said the gentleman, "and I'm going to catch up with him and his . . . er . . . lovely wife if it's the last thing I do!"

The stranger then turned on his refined heels and marched away, somehow managing to look dignified despite the giant strides he took to the crested carriage that awaited him. He had a brief, quiet, but extremely intense conversation with his coachman, then stepped inside the beautifully appointed vehicle and was off in three shakes of a lamb's tail.

Mrs. Beane watched him go, admiring the glossy black paint of the coach, trimmed tastefully with silver, and the four beautiful black high-steppers that propelled it at such an astonishing speed.

As the dust plumed behind them, Mrs. Beane shook her head, wondering what the hurry was and why the gentleman was determined to catch up with his friend "if it was the last thing he ever did." Certainly with all *his* money, the stranger could do whatever he pleased.

Then she remembered that she'd hoped for a little more restitution from the gent for that last juicy bit of information, and he'd disappointed her. She vented her wrath by shaking her fist at the carriage, which was fast becoming merely a faraway speck on the road to Arundel.

Long before Jack and Miss Darlington arrived in Arundel, as they approached the small village of Patching, an especially deep rut in the road bounced them in their seats. Theo thought he heard an ominous splintering sound and pulled the carriage over to investigate. Upon inspection he found a cracked felloe in the front right wheel.

This condition required immediate attention, so Theo carefully drove the carriage into the village and looked about for the wheelwright's place of business. He found the small building and stable yard quite soon and led the team into an adjacent orchard where the horses could graze, then instructed Harley and Joe to water the cattle, and went in search of the wheelwright.

Thoroughly awake now and refreshed by his long nap, Jack opened the door and squinted into the noon sunshine that bathed the autumn-frocked countryside. "God, it's a beautiful day," he ventured, sliding a speculative look toward Miss Darlington.

"I hadn't noticed," she snapped, obviously very frustrated by the delay and determinedly avoiding Jack's eyes by looking out the window on her side of the carriage.

"Why don't you get out and stretch your legs?" he advised.

"We won't be here that long."

"Surely, Miss Darlington, you overestimate the efficiency of country wheelwrights," Jack said with good-humored reason. "I daresay we'll even have time to get a bit of lunch while we wait."

"I mean to have lunch in Arundel," Miss Darlington said stubbornly.

Jack rubbed his chin and eyed Miss Darlington consideringly. "I know how desperately you want to get to your destination, Miss Darlington, but sitting uncomfortably in a stuffy carriage when you could be outside in one of the last truly beautiful days of the season will not get you there any faster. Nor will your self-induced discomfort speed along the process of repairing the carriage wheel. You can't control every event of your life, Miss Darlington, so you might as well enjoy each moment you can and grasp each lovely opportunity that comes your way . . . such as this glorious, sunny day."

He watched the effect of his little sermon on Miss Darlington. Her chin went up a notch and she flitted an embarrassed glance toward Joe and Harley—who were pretending not to listen—but she said nothing.

"Such intensity," he remarked teasingly. "Such devotion! Indeed, you must be in such a great hurry to resume your journey because you have an assignation with a lover!"

Miss Darlington's head jerked round, and she glared at Jack. "If you must know, sir, I'm going to a remote spot on the coast called Thorney Island to pick up my nephew. My ... er ... sister and her husband are going on holiday, and like a good and useful spinster aunt, I've agreed to take the child back to my home in Surrey till his parents return." Her eyes gleamed a challenge. "Now are you satisfied?"

Jack raised a brow, not the least satisfied because he knew she was lying. Who would trust giving over the care of their child to an eccentric aunt who jaunted about the countryside wholly without escort? "I only wonder why you've been so reluctant to explain yourself before now," he remarked.

She turned away and said petulantly, "I never supposed it was any of your business, sir."

"But we're friends now, are we not, Miss Darlington? I think we got to know each other rather well at the Three Nuns."

Miss Darlington's face took on a delicate pink hue, as if she were remembering just how well she *had* got to know him. That she'd seen him naked pleased Jack rather than embarrassed him. The forced intimacy brought an edge of excitement to their relationship that he enjoyed, even though he knew he could never act on his attraction to the lady ... simply because she *was* a lady.

Jack wished he knew the true reason for her visit to Thorney Island—a quaint sounding place, that— but he knew he'd never find out by directly asking. He had to be subtle. He had to bide his time and watch for an opportunity to ferret out the information, taking Miss Darlington unawares. But Jack had all the time in the world. Any appointments he might have made for the near future were blessedly forgotten.

Jack got out of the carriage, took a deep breath of the unpolluted country air, and stretched his arms above his head.

A slight sway of the carriage alerted Jack to the

fact that Miss Darlington was preparing to descend as well, despite her declarations to the contrary. He stood at the door, ready to assist her in stepping down. However, after a narrow look his way, she chose to alight from the opposite side. Jack hurried to the other side of the coach to offer his hand, but she was too fast for him. By the time he got there, she was out and already striding into the shady interior of the grove.

Undaunted, rather enjoying the chase, so to speak, Jack followed. "Why are you so prickly today, Miss Darlington?" he asked her. "You act as though I've got the typhus."

Miss Darlington turned and looked Jack over scathingly. Confused, he glanced down at his clothing, looking for a spot or a wrinkle. "Is there something amiss with the way I look?" he inquired.

Miss Darlington shook her head. "Oh no, John," she answered wryly. "You look fine as a fivepence. You're a very dashing fellow, indeed."

"Is there something wrong with putting one's best polished foot forward, Miss Darlington?" asked Jack, a laugh in his voice.

Ignoring the question, she continued warmly, "Furthermore, you're a dreadful flirt and have no qualms about vexing a poor spinster woman like myself, who, I might remind you, has only tried to help you ever since—"

"Ever since the moment you ran me down with your coach?"

Miss Darlington was about to make an angry reply but was diverted by something or someone behind Jack. He turned and watched Theo approaching with the usual scowl he wore whenever Jack was anywhere near Miss Darlington.

"What's the matter, Theo?" said Miss Darlington.

"I can't find the wheelwright, miss," he answered,

lifting his hands in an exasperated gesture. "I can't find no one nowhere. The town seems deserted."

Intrigued, Jack walked out of the grove to stand at the edge of the road and look up and down the short row of principal buildings that made up the small village. Theo and Miss Darlington followed and stood beside him. Together they listened ... and heard nothing.

"Heavens," said Miss Darlington in a whisper, which seemed appropriate for the ghostlike atmosphere of the place. "Where could they all have gone?"

"There's evidence of recent occupation," Jack observed aloud, "so they can't have gone far."

"But what could make them all disappear at once?"

"A funeral or a wedding," Theo offered.

"Is there a difference between the two?" Jack muttered.

"In a small town where folks know all their neighbors," Theo continued, tactfully overlooking Jack's cynical aside, "when there's a marriage or a wake, everyone turns out in their best togs for the festivities."

"There's a church just down the road a bit," said Jack, spying a brown stone building with a steeple, surrounded by a weathered picket fence and a graveyard. "Maybe we should investigate."

Miss Darlington agreed with a nod, then turned to Theo and said, "Wait with Harley and Joe at the coach, please. Hopefully we'll locate a wheelwright soon and bring him to the grove."

Theo obeyed reluctantly, with his usual suspicious glance toward Jack. Then Amanda and Jack walked down the road till they stood opposite the arched front doors of the ancient church. Suddenly the doors burst open and throngs of people spilled out. As if carried forward by the sheer enthusiasm of the group, in the middle of this mass of happy humanity were a bride and groom.

"Well, it's not a funeral," Jack said glumly.

He'd had that dream again last night, the dream with the anonymous bride and his own neck caught tight in the nuptial noose. Now his nightmares seemed to be haunting his waking hours, too.

But at least in this case he was *not* the groom. For that wondrous fact alone he was grateful. Very grateful, indeed.

Chapter 8

It appeared that the whole town, indeed, had turned out for the wedding of a most popular couple. Amanda was astounded and curiously moved by the sight of so many merry people streaming through the chapel doors to congregate on the freshly scythed lawn and in the quaint and pretty graveyard.

These were country folk in their best finery: little boys in homemade short pants running pell-mell through the tombstones; beribboned little girls with ruffled pantalettes showing under their skirts; blooming, envious young women in sprigged muslins and bonnets festooned with crimson autumn roses; dowagers in faded silk and fusty old hats twenty years out of style; young bucks with red necks uncomfortably chafed by starched collars; and grand old squires, shopkeepers, and farmers with florid faces and middle-aged bellies straining against wildly patterned waistcoats.

And somewhere in that colorful crowd was the wheelwright and their only hope of resuming their journey in the foreseeable future.

"How shall we *ever* find him in such a throng?" said Amanda, her voice reflecting her discourage-

ment. She couldn't believe all the encumbrances that
kept cropping up on her way to Thorney Island. At
the rate she was going, her sibling would be a grand-
parent before she arrived!

"We shall simply ask someone to point him out to
us," John said matter-of-factly. "We've already
drawn a great deal of attention."

John was right. They were the object of many curious eyes. Suddenly feeling shy, Amanda impetuously
grabbed hold of John's arm just before he crossed the
street. He peered under the brim of her unadorned
black bonnet and smiled at her. She braced herself
for some sort of teasing remark, but he surprised
her by saying only, "Don't worry, Miss Darlington,
I daresay these people are just as friendly as they
look." Then he took her arm and tucked it against
his side in the manner of a promenading couple.

His confident, kind manner and words reassured
Amanda, and she did not pull free even though she
noticed Theo frowning disapprovingly as they
walked away.

There were hushed whispers and muted exclamations as they approached the crowd. Soon a natural
division occurred as people stood to the side and
allowed Amanda and John to pass through. A path-
way was formed leading directly to the newlyweds
and their immediate family. Amanda did not enjoy
such a conspicuous arrival, but she supposed they
did present a rather queer picture.

Not only were they strangers, but they were obviously of a different class and unlikely to be invited
guests. She was draped from head to toe in black
mourning attire. John looked just as odd, as he was
hatless and sported a large bandage round his head.
Indeed, they looked very much out of place.

Dressed in white muslin, with a halo of ivy in her
hair, the pretty bride looked up from the bouquet of
field flowers she'd buried her nose in and stared at

John and Amanda. Her groom was shaking hands
and having a hearty laugh with an older gentleman
who, judging by the striking physical resemblance
between them, must have been his father: they were
both tall and thin with sunburned faces, big noses,
and large Adam's apples.

The bride nudged her groom, and suddenly everyone's attention was on Amanda and John.

John produced a charming smile and addressed
himself to the groom. "How do you do, sir?"

"How do you do?" the groom returned politely
but with a puzzled expression.

"I see congratulations are in order," John
continued.

"That's right, sir," broke in the rough, deep-
timbered voice of a swarthy, black-bearded, muscular
man standing to the bride's right. " 'Tis a happy occasion, and we're all as merry as the birds in May.
But what, sir, kin we do fer you and yer missus?"

John did not correct the gentleman's mistake in
assuming Amanda was his wife. She supposed it
wasn't important in the present circumstances, and
she did not really mind it, anyway. She was beginning to appreciate the benefits of a male escort on a
long trip. And it was much better to go along with
the honest blunder than to try to make awkward
explanations.

"We're on our way to Arundel, but our front left
wheel has a cracked felloe. We dare not drive it further in such a condition, so we're naturally looking
for the wheelwright. We are greatly dismayed to
have disrupted your happy occasion, but could you
point out the good fellow? We shall be prodigiously
glad to make his acquaintance."

By the way the man beamed at John, Amanda was
sure they'd be face-to-face with the wheelwright in
no time at all. She was correct.

"You're lookin' at the good fellow right now, sir,"

said the man, giving his loosely tied cravat a straightening tug. "I'm the wheelwright of this 'ere town of Patching and proud of it."

"Delightful," said John, his smile widening with satisfaction. "Can we drag you away from the festivities for a bit, then? It should only take a little while to repair the wheel, then we'll be off and out of your way."

" 'Fraid that's impossible, sir," said the wheelwright, his smile collapsing into a grave frown.

John suppressed his justifiable surprise and simply asked, "Why so, sir?"

In a slightly truculent voice, as if he were anticipating an argument, the wheelwright said, "Because I'm the bride's father and the provider of the feast we're about to partake of. Ye don't imagine I'm about to miss out on me own daughter's weddin' party, do ye?"

While Amanda was aggrieved and mystified by her continued bad luck, John chewed his lip consideringly. "You have a point, sir," he conceded, then continued with utmost politeness, "How long do you think it will be before you can leave the festivities and attend to our wheel?"

The wheelwright was so surprised and pleased by such a reasonable and courteous attitude from an obvious aristocrat, his smile returned full-force. "Give me an hour or two, sir. Then I'll be much obliged to mend your wheel . . . and for free, too!"

"Giving away your services won't be necessary," John assured him. "But while we wait, can you recommend where my wife and I and our servants might procure refreshment?"

"There's nothin' open in the village, sir," the wheelwright answered apologetically.

"I was afraid of that," said John. "But never mind. We shall simply await you in the yonder grove. Just let us know when—"

"Nonsense, sir," said the burly fellow with an expansive and congenial smile. "Seein' as how you're bein' so patient and understandin' of a man's natural wish t' eat with 'is new-married daughter, I'd like t' repay the favor. Join us for the wedding feast! Your servants are welcome, too."

John glanced down at Amanda, gauging her reaction to the suggestion. But Amanda hardly knew how to react. She was definitely hungry, and she had no compunction about rubbing elbows with the yeomanry and tradesmen of Patching, but she couldn't help but think her and John's presence would put a damper on things.

She got up on tiptoe and voiced her reservations in a whisper directed at John's ear. "Wouldn't we be intruding?"

But the wheelwright had bent near to catch the soft-spoken words and firmly disputed such an idea. "There's plenty of food and spirits, madam, and plenty of jolly company, as well. We're a friendly lot and are more than willing, on this happy occasion, to share our simple fare."

The invitation was issued with much kindness and in a charming, courtly manner Amanda found irresistible. Just as she opened her mouth to accept, however, she remembered that she probably ought to defer to her "husband's" wishes. She glanced up at John and saw that he wanted to stay, too. Without exchanging a word, they each understood the feelings of the other and turned to face the wheelwright.

"We'd be delighted to join your party," John said.

"And we'd be honored t' have ye," said the wheelwright, extending his large, calloused hand for a robust shake. "I'm Richard Clarke."

"I'm John Darlington, Lord Thornfield," replied John, without a bit of confusion or blink of an eye. He made an elegant gesture in Amanda's direction. "And, as you know already, this is my lovely wife, Lady Thornfield."

A few eyes goggled at the mention of lord and lady, but Richard Clarke, with gracious composure and pardonable pride, introduced the rest of his large family, the groom's family, and even a few people standing in the general vicinity. Amanda's head was swimming with names, but she nodded and smiled and tried to remember them all.

Presently Richard decided that it was time to start the festivities and, with his plump wife on his arm, began to lead the way to wherever it was the wedding reception was to take place. Amanda and John were immediately swallowed up and pressed along with the crowd across the grassy lawn.

Amanda was too far back to see, but as they progressed toward the street, she could hear a carriage tearing down the road at breakneck speed. It passed just before the wedding party reached the road and kept them waiting at the edge till the cloud of dust settled. Amanda sighed and envied the driver of the fast-moving equipage, wishing her own carriage were just as sound and headed just as quickly in the direction of Thorney Island.

They crossed the narrow street amid excited chatter and faces wreathed with smiles in anticipation of the upcoming fun. The festive mood was infectious, and Amanda began to reason away her worries about Thorney Island. After all, what could she do at present to change the situation? They were stuck in Patching till the wheel was mended, and it would not be mended till the wheelwright had celebrated the marriage of his daughter. So, as John had advised her to do, she might as well enjoy the moment.

The very idea of forgetting her troubles for a while was intoxicating to Amanda. The thought of such freedom put a spring in her step, and she was fairly skipping alongside John by the time they reached their destination. Stealing a peek at her pretend spouse, she noticed that John looked as cheerful as she did. Amanda felt a fluttering sensation in the vicinity of her heart. She was proud and excited to be thought of as this man's wife. For an hour or two she would allow herself to enjoy the masquerade.

The wedding party was to be held in a huge barn that had been swept and scrubbed till the wood walls and floors looked new. Sweet, fresh hay had been scattered on the floor along with a little sawdust in preparation for dancing. The rafters were hung with flowers and vines, and every corner of the barn was artfully arranged with pumpkins and sprays of long-stemmed sunflowers and pussy willow. Bales of hay were arranged in groups here and there to be used for seats.

At the far end of the barn were rough-hewn tables and a hodgepodge of unmatched chairs borrowed, no doubt, from every house in Patching. Ham, chicken, pheasant, rabbit, and mutton, all roasted to a crisp, succulent brown; bowls full of every variety of vegetable from the garden; breads and biscuits; and cheese, pastries, and cakes covered the tables from end to end.

There was a general scramble as everyone found a place to sit, with Richard saving seats for Amanda and John at the table of the bride and groom. But Amanda suddenly remembered Theo and Harley and Joe, and asked John if he would go back to the grove and fetch them.

"Certainly, my *darling*," John replied like a dutiful husband but with a mischievous twinkle in his eyes. He had made good his playful threat to use the intimate endearment she'd scolded him for using the day before. But what could she do? thought Amanda. It was perfectly natural for married couples to use endearments.

As John walked away, Amanda admired his straight, tall figure and decided that she'd allow him to call her "my darling" as much as he pleased in the next short hour or two. It was rather pleasant.

And since they were only pretending, what harm could it do?

John returned with Theo and the others, and directly after a quick prayer fervently offered in the booming baritone of Richard Clarke, everyone commenced eating with a relish.

"Here, my darling," said John, filling a large tumbler half-full with a dark red beverage. "Try this. Richard tells me it's his own special recipe."

"What is it?" asked Amanda, eyeing the drink with suspicion.

"It's a sweet elderberry wine," he answered, taking a long sip from his own tumbler.

Amanda frowned at him. "Do you think you should be drinking spirits so soon after your concussion?"

"Nonsense," scoffed John with a laugh. "This can hardly be classed in the category of spirits. Why, even the little children are drinking a slightly watered-down version of it. Even *you* might feel perfectly safe in indulging yourself a little."

Amanda debated and, as she had never drank wine in her life, was about to pass up the experience when John leaned very close and whispered in her ear, "Indulging yourself is something you never do. Aren't I right, Miss Darlington?"

He was perfectly right, but Amanda had no intention of telling him so. "I indulge myself regularly, sir," she informed him frostily.

"What with?" he taunted her. "An extra shaving of sugar in your tea? Or perhaps you let your chamomile blend steep a little longer now and then? A strong cup of tea is very dangerous indeed, Miss Darlington! The extra stimulant might keep you up past nine!"

Amanda was quite flustered. Her parents had never allowed fermented drinks in the house, and she had accepted the practice as a safe, sensible one, even though she knew many people drank wine and other similar beverages moderately and without becoming drunken regulars at the local pub.

She wasn't sure about John, though. He'd been drunk as a sailor the night he'd wandered into the path of her horses, and she was a little wary of how he'd handle Richard Clarke's elderberry wine.

"You are a poor one to try to advise me that a little indulgence is desirable. Obviously *you* indulge too much or you'd still have your memory," she informed him with a disdainful sniff.

"Well, my darling," said John, not the least offended by Amanda's snippity speech, "I had much rather take the risk of indulging a little too much now and then than to *never* enjoy myself. How spare and dull and dry one's life would be without a little risk, eh?"

Amanda knew exactly how spare and dull and dry one's life could be without a little risk because *her* life was a perfect example. It was a gloomy reflection.

"Wandering into the path of galloping horses is an extreme case," John continued in a contemplative tone. "Although I don't remember, of course, I feel fairly sure that I've *never* been that drunk or that thoughtless before." His brows furrowed. "There was something unique about the circumstances of that night."

"I think so, too," Amanda agreed, but when she would have engaged in continued speculation, John dismissed the subject with a shrug of his broad shoulders.

"Never fear, Miss Darlington," he assured her with a rakish grin and in a confiding voice no one else could hear. "I have no intentions of becoming inebriated with elderberry wine. Since I'm determined to be so *dreadfully* good, why don't you consent to be just a *little* bit bad. Taste it, Miss Darlington. If you fall into a drunken stupor, I promise not to compromise you."

"You are really too ridiculous, John," Amanda chided him in an attempt to appear amused and unconcerned by his remarks. "I won't be goaded by you into drinking this wine, but when Mr. Clarke decides to toast his daughter, I shall certainly join in most willingly."

As if he were in cahoots with John, Richard Clarke decided at that moment to raise his glass to the happiness, health, prosperity, and fruitfulness of the recent union between his daughter and her swain. But not all at once. Each was a different toast. And by the time he was through, his daughter's face was nearly as rosy as the wine itself. The toast for "fruitfulness" produced the most colorful blush of all.

As for Amanda, she was sure her cheeks were as pink as the bride's. But not from embarrassment . . . from the wine. Far surpassing the stimulating properties of tea, wine seemed to be able to warm one from the roots of one's hair to the tips of one's toes. Amanda could now appreciate why people drank spirits on cold nights. Indeed, after the fourth toast and in a giddy state of mind, she could understand its appeal even on the warmest day in June.

Trying to prove she was no milquetoast, she had taken two or three hearty gulps with each toast, nearly choking on the first one but stoically showing a brave front even though her eyes watered and her throat burned. But after the second toast she had become quite used to the potent properties of the wine and could down it with ease. After the third and fourth toast, she was quite relaxed.

Jack wondered if he'd gone too far by teasing Miss Darlington about the wine. He supposed she occasionally drank a weak ratafia at social functions or took a delicate sip or two of sherry or claret after dinner. But by the way she'd gulped down Richard

Clarke's elderberry wine, it was obvious she never drank and was drinking now only on a dare. *His* dare. And by the glowing, giggly look of her, she was well on her way to becoming thoroughly foxed.

While Miss Darlington chatted animatedly with a deaf, elderly woman to her left, Jack took away what was left of her wine. If she drank the rest of it and compromised her dignity in front of all these people, she might regret it till her dying day. Jack was not prepared to allow her to take that sort of risk, no matter how cavalier he was about his own risk-taking.

Presently she turned and seemed to be looking about for her tumbler, but Jack diverted her attention to the fiddle player who had propped himself in a corner on a bale of hay and was doing some preliminary plucking, scratching, and tuning.

Jack leaned close to Miss Darlington and whispered, "Since—as I just bragged to the nervous groom—we've been married for several years, I should already know this about you, my darling. But refresh my memory, won't you? Do you like to dance?"

By now the fiddle player had struck up a lively jig, and half the townspeople were hopping and prancing in the middle of the room. The spectators turned their chairs to get a better view. Amanda avidly watched the performances—which were done with enthusiasm if not with skill or grace—her eyes dancing, her lips smiling, and her toes tapping.

Without taking her gaze away from the dancers, Miss Darlington said, "I love watching others dance. I always thought I would enjoy dancing, too, but I don't remember feeling much enjoyment during the few times I danced in London when I had my coming out."

"But in London you were dancing with strangers, were you not?"

"Yes. I never got very well acquainted with anyone, you know. Especially men. I was too shy."

"But you know me *extremely* well, Miss Darlington," Jack suggested, hoping to catch her eye and drive home that point with a teasing leer.

"You're quite wrong, John," Miss Darlington said, still keeping her delighted gaze fastened on the dancers. "I may have nursed you through a fever, but I know absolutely nothing about you." She turned then, a tiny furrow appearing in her otherwise smooth brow. "But I think I like that most about you."

Jack was genuinely puzzled. "*What* do you like most about me?"

"Your anonymity," she said with a faint, almost coy, smile.

He raised his brows. "Why is that?"

She leaned her head to the side and seemed to ponder. "I suppose because it allows me to be less reserved."

Jack's brows rose even higher. "In the last two days, I don't know how you could have been *more* reserved, Miss Darlington!"

"Oh, but I'm usually *much* more reserved," she assured him.

"Indeed!"

"But that's beginning to change. A recent event in my life has led me to believe that it is more important to act on *feelings* than to allow our actions to be totally regulated by certain rules that have been drilled into us since birth."

Jack smiled ruefully but was thoroughly enjoying Miss Darlington's sudden inclination to confide in him. "It is not *always* wise to act on feelings, Miss Darlington. Impulsiveness can often have disastrous consequences. But you are quite right to try to be a little less ... er ... rigid."

"I quite agree with you!"

"If you're agreeing with *me*, Miss Darlington, I can

only suppose that the wine is affecting your thinking," Jack suggested, only half teasing.

"No, it's not the wine," Miss Darlington insisted seriously. She turned her gleaming eyes to his. "Aren't these people lovely, John? I've never been around people so free and easy and affectionate. Have you noticed how Mr. Clarke pinches and pats his wife? My parents never acted so."

"Well, I—"

"Even the newlyweds are cozy, when I should have supposed they'd have needed time to get used to each other."

"I thought *all* newlyweds were cozy! Insufferably so," he added with a shudder of distaste.

Miss Darlington heaved a happy sigh and turned her gaze back to the dancers. "I know I should be well on my way to Thorney Island by now, but it's not my fault the carriage wheel broke. In fact, I believe I'm actually *glad* the wheel broke or I should never have known such bliss."

Jack was growing rather alarmed at the heights to which the elderberry wine had lifted Miss Darlington's spirits, which were usually so sober and serious. A little relaxation and pleasure derived from liquor were desirable, but such a euphoric mood as Miss Darlington was experiencing could only end in a corresponding depth of depression once the effects of the drink wore off. Furthermore, she seemed to have completely forgotten about her urgent business on Thorney Island.

Miss Darlington suddenly turned and grasped Jack's hands. "Do you think it would be thought *dreadfully* improper of me if I danced?"

Jack was shocked. He'd never thought for a moment that he'd actually be able to talk Miss Darlington into dancing. After all, she was still in mourning clothes. Many women went into half-mourning after six months, but Miss Darlington was covered in black from the crown of her hat to the sole of her neat little nankeen boots.

"You might raise a few critical brows amongst the stiff-rumped of the bunch," Jack admitted, "but I don't think the majority of the townsfolk of Patching would care a fig if you danced, Miss Darlington. But are you quite sure?"

"I'm very sure," she said with a decided nod, then looked eagerly about the room. "Whom do you think I should ask?"

"My dear girl," Jack expostulated, "of course you'll dance with *me!*"

"But your head, and your knee—"

He stood up and peremptorily pulled Miss Darlington to her feet. The very idea of her seeking out some young buck to jig her about the room—now he knew she wasn't thinking straight. Besides, if anyone was going to dance with his wife, it was going to be him!

The fiddler launched into a quick-paced country dance, and Jack swung his partner onto the floor. Their appearance caused a stir among the townspeople, but once the surprise wore off most of the stares directed their way were admiring ones. And there was much to admire, Jack thought with pride. They danced well together.

Miss Darlington was light on her feet and very graceful. It was a pleasure swinging her down the line of dancers and watching her face glow from the exercise and sheer enjoyment of the activity. During one especially brisk turn, her bonnet ribbons loosened and her bonnet flew off and onto the floor. A child ran forward to pick it up and keep it for the "gran' lady" till the dance was done. Miss Darlington merely laughed, throwing back her head till her abundant hair loosened and the escaping golden waves bobbed around her face.

Jack was entranced. He'd thought from the moment he'd first clapped eyes on Miss Darlington that she was capable of such vital beauty and energy, but he never thought he'd be around long enough to watch her blossom so dramatically. She was always so proper, so serious, so conscientious, so reserved, so *sad* and so worried about something. . . .

He found it hard to accept that this incredible transformation was brought about merely by Richard Clarke's special recipe for elderberry wine. If the wine were so potent in relaxing a person's inhibitions, the wheelwright would be well advised to bottle it in small vials and market it as an aphrodisiac!

After two country dances and an Irish jig, Miss Darlington was finally persuaded to sit down. Jack's knee ached like the blazes, he was slightly dizzy, and his head hurt from the constant rotations and bouncing required, but he wasn't about to admit as much to Miss Darlington.

"Lord Thornfield. My lord?"

Jack finally realized that Richard Clarke was trying to catch his attention. He'd been dancing, too, and sweat trickled down his broad forehead like rain off a roof. The fellow dabbed at the deluge with a handkerchief and breathed heavily.

"Mr. Clarke," Jack said with a commiserative smile. "You're about done up, old fellow. Me, too, I'm afraid."

"Aye, the ladies could dance all night, couldn't they? But I'm ready to leave for a while and see to the fixin' of your wheel. Are you ready?"

"Yes, of course. How long do you think it will take?"

"No more than half an hour."

"You know where the coach is, so I'll leave you to it. Lady Thornfield and I are going to take a restorative walk ... slow and easy ... by that pleasant brook I caught sight of earlier that runs behind the chapel."

"An excellent idea," said Mr. Clarke, nodding his approval and pleasure. "We've a pleasant little town. Do enjoy it while ye're here."

Jack was not so intent on enjoying the beauty of the region as he was on calming down Miss Darlington. The dancing had only exhilarated her further, and he wanted to get her away to a quiet spot where she could regain her composure. Not that he didn't like her all rosy and animated, but he expected a change in mood any moment. Better she was away from public view when that radical change occurred.

Miss Darlington kissed the little boy that had rescued her hat from the floor when it flew off her head, then bade farewell to Mrs. Clarke, the bride and groom, and sundry other people with whom she'd become instantly friendly. She was still waving goodbye as John took her arm and escorted her through the wide doors, which were already open to the mild October day, and across the road to the graveyard.

"Where are we going?" Miss Darlington inquired, looking curiously about her. "The carriage is the other way."

"I thought it would be pleasant to stroll by the stream while Mr. Clarke fixes the wheel. Do you object?"

"Not at all," Miss Darlington replied unhesitatingly, slipping her arm in his. "As you said earlier, there's no point in sitting in a stuffy carriage when we could be outside on such a glorious day."

Jack looked down at her smiling face, her cheeks flushed from dancing, her eyes bright and clear. Her hair was unbound, and the sun made it shine like gold. He had an almost overwhelming urge to sift his fingers through the loose tresses but controlled himself with an effort.

"You don't seem as anxious as you were to get to Thorney Island," he said.

That tiny furrow reappeared between her brows.

"It's still just as important that I get there in a timely manner—" Her eyes shifted to his face for an instant; then she stared straight ahead. "—because my brother and his wife have a schedule to keep. But we have to wait for the wheel to be fixed anyway, so we might as well enjoy a walk. How long do we have?"

Jack noted that she had said earlier that her sister lived on Thorney Island, not her brother. "About half an hour."

"Good," she said with a satisfied sigh.

Jack was entranced ... and confused. He had been attributing Miss Darlington's uncharacteristic behavior to the wine, but she no longer appeared giddy or overexcited. She had not become depressed, either. She certainly seemed much more relaxed than usual, but she also seemed completely in control of herself. She seemed ... content.

Yes, that word summed it up best of all. For the first time since he'd met her, Miss Darlington seemed quite content. Instead of analyzing the situation, Jack decided to take his own advice and simply enjoy the moment. He knew better than to expect such a halcyon mood to last.

They walked across the graveyard, weaving through the tombstones, down a sloping footpath to the edge of a creek that was lined with ancient sallows. They looked up and down the gently cascading flow of water as it bumped and bubbled over a bed of rocks and rushes, then instinctively turned toward each other.

The gurgle of the brook was soothing, the sun was warm, the breeze was mild but with just enough lift to scatter Miss Darlington's hair about her face in a very charming manner. Jack had just reached up to push a tress out of her eyes when she slipped on a slick tuft of grass. He kept her from falling by grabbing hold of her waist with both hands.

"Steady," he cautioned, staring down into her startled blue eyes, his gaze straying uncontrollably to her lips, which were parted and frozen in an unspoken exclamation of surprise.

"Yes . . . steady," she repeated breathlessly, bracing the palms of her hands against his chest.

Jack's heart hammered against his ribs, he couldn't catch his breath, and he couldn't tear his gaze away from Miss Darlington's inviting mouth . . . looking all pink and dewy and tender.

His hands tightened on her waist. "Miss Darlington, do you know how beautiful you are?" he whispered.

She gave a soft gasp, and her lashes fluttered down over her eyes. He watched her blush, the color tinting her cheekbones an alluring pale rose.

"Am . . . I . . . beautiful?" she said haltingly.

He slid his hand under her satin-soft chin and tilted her face, urging her to look at him. Shyly, she met his gaze. He smiled. "Oh, yes," he assured her. "You're very beautiful. And standing so close to you like this is playing havoc with my self-control and making me wish I weren't a gentleman. You are the sweetest, the most delectable temptation to come my way"—he grinned—"in recent memory."

She smiled slightly at his witticism and looked down again. He studied the graceful sweep of her lashes against her porcelain skin, the curve of her lips, the delicate cleft in her chin. Her hands had remained on his chest, and now her fingers were splayed and were lightly—unconsciously?—caressing him. He could tell she was a sensuous woman underneath her prim exterior.

"Miss Darlington, have you ever been kissed?" he found himself inquiring in a husky tone.

Her eyes lifted to stare into his. "Yes," she replied in a tremulous whisper. "But . . . not by you."

Chapter 9

Jack could swear he'd just heard an invitation from Miss Darlington to kiss her! It seemed too good to be true, and definitely out of character coming from such a proper female. After all, it was the sort of indirect invitation seasoned flirts delivered with a coy smile and fluttering lashes. Miss Darlington had said it with the simple straightforwardness he'd come to expect of her, but was it really Miss Darlington talking, or was it the elderberry wine?

Despite the possibility that Miss Darlington's judgment was a trifle fuzzy, Jack was sorely tempted. The fact was, he'd been planning to steal a kiss from her sometime before they parted ways, and now was his chance. Hell, he'd kick himself later if he didn't take advantage of such a golden opportunity! And it was a delightful bonus to find out she was as interested in sharing a kiss as he was.

Maybe he'd been wrong to assume she was the cloistered little nunlike creature she appeared to be. Or was that just wishful thinking on his part? He wanted to kiss her, therefore he wanted to believe she was far more experienced than he'd previously supposed. It all came back to the wine. Was she inebriated or wasn't she?

Jack really didn't want to take unfair advantage, so he looked at Miss Darlington keenly and said, "Tell me truthfully, are you foxed, m'dear?"

"Not at all, John," she said with quiet assurance. Then her hands on his waistcoat began to stray, to begin a shy, tentative exploration of his chest. Her eyes followed the movement of her hands. Her rapt concentration was damned arousing.

Jack swallowed hard. "I could be married," he warned her. His own hands were moving ... had perhaps been moving all along ... up and down her smooth, slender back.

She lifted her gaze to his and smiled. Her expression was a little dazed, and her whole face was aglow. She was enchanting. "You said you weren't married, and I believe you. You'd never forget something that important." Her hands continued to move, warming his skin underneath the layers of clothing. Heat collected in his loins. Her lips were mere inches away.

"More importantly," he added huskily, "I've no intention of *getting* married."

"I gathered as much from some of your comments," she replied with a distracted nod. Her gaze shifted back to the movement of her hands, which now roamed over his shoulders.

"I don't even know your Christian name," he continued to reason somewhat desperately. "You instructed me to call you Miss Darlington ... remember?"

Her voice softened and lowered to an intimate murmur as she said, "My name is Amanda."

"Amanda, look at me," he ordered.

She looked at him.

He grasped her lovely, roving hands and held them against his chest so he wouldn't be distracted. He sighed heavily. "As desperately as I want to, I don't think it would be a good idea to kiss you."

Much to Jack's chagrin, she immediately lowered her gaze, nodded, then quietly said, "I'll go back to the coach." She began to move away.

"Like hell you will!" Jack grated, grabbing her by the shoulders and pulling her back against his chest and into his arms. He had not expected such a quick and complete capitulation! He wanted to kiss her and he was going to kiss her ... his conscience be damned!

"Amanda...." he crooned. Then he cupped her head in his right hand, slid his left arm about her waist, and kissed her.

Amanda felt as though she'd waited forever—all her life, in fact—for such a kiss. His lips were firm and soft and lavishly warm. A sweet ache blossomed in her chest and wandered uncontrollably through her body. Her head tilted, her body arched as she melted into him. His lips molded her mouth to his, and she followed his lead as he led her deeper and deeper into a sensual paradise.

Amanda had been kissed before. Once by Benjamin Walker, a local squire's son when they were both thirteen, and twice by the rector at the parish in Edenbridge during a brief courtship two years ago. Benjamin's kiss was wet and sticky and never repeated because Amanda was never so obtuse as to go into a deserted barn with him again. Rector Mitford's kiss was dry and cold and singularly uninspiring. Determined to give him another chance, Amanda allowed the good rector to kiss her again, but the result was the same.

Perhaps even then she understood how barren her parents' marriage was and had resolved, unconsciously, never to fall into a similar trap. She gently declined further visits from the rector.

John's kiss was different from either of these. Very different, indeed. Every nerve and fiber of her body was tingling. Her blood thrummed through her veins. She felt faint and curiously energized at the same time.

Then he deepened the kiss, parting her lips with his tongue and delving inside the sleek borders of her mouth. A drenching pleasure washed through her, and she moaned and pressed herself hard against him. He responded with a gasp, and she felt his hands roam over her back, her arms, her neck, and then her breasts. . . . Her skin was on fire.

She had no sense of right or wrong, no sense of time or place. She felt a wild urge to strip herself of every black scrap of clothing she wore, right down to her undergarments, to stand bare and brazen in this man's arms. She remembered the look of him, the feel of him, when he lay naked on the bed at the inn. And she yearned to see him, to feel him again.

Braced against his waistcoat, her hands began a tentative exploration. Oh, how well she remembered the hard planes of his chest, the taut hollow of his belly, the angle of his narrow hips, the muscled curve of his thighs, the jut of his magnificent manhood. . . .

Her knees weakened. Her weight shifted into the circle of John's arms as she leaned forward, and he began to urgently lower her toward the soft, downy grass. . . .

"Ahem. Er . . . *miss*?"

Amanda lurched backward, nearly falling flat on her rump. She stumbled and gained her balance, then whirled around to face . . . Theo. He stood ramrod straight, his eyes averted, his mouth pulled into a stern pucker of disapproval.

"The wheel is repaired, miss."

Amanda was horrified. She felt exposed, as though Theo—if he dared to look at her—could actually see her breasts throbbing with heat against the chafing, stifling fabric of her traveling gown. As though he knew how slick and wet she felt at her core. But of course he couldn't see those intimate parts of her, couldn't know how wanton and aroused she felt.

He could, however, see the disarray of her loosened hair, her kiss-swollen lips, and the mortified blush that stained her cheeks. And she *was* mortified. Nothing could have brought her senses back to reason faster than a trusted old servant's disappointed and disapproving demeanor. Amanda couldn't imagine what she'd been thinking. For the past hour, she'd frankly forgotten who she was. Was amnesia contagious? she wondered with grim humor.

"Th-thank you, Theo," she said, finally able to form the words through lips that were stiff and numb from shock ... lips that moments before had been as pliable as warm honey. "I'll be along in a moment."

Theo had been dismissed, but he did not budge. Part of Amanda was desperate to run away to the coach and pretend that nothing had happened between her and John, but she knew that would not settle anything. She knew she must stay and set things straight with John, but she refused to do so while her servant looked on.

"Theo, go back to the carriage," she said in an even, firm voice.

Finally he looked at her, his expression half-embarrassed, half-reproachful. "Will ye be comin' in a minute, then?" he inquired roughly.

"I assure you, Theo," Amanda said earnestly, "I will follow you instantly. I just need a short word with John."

Theo threw a hateful look John's way, then turned sharply on his heel, climbed the rise of ground to the graveyard, and disappeared.

Amanda turned reluctantly and faced John. He was standing nonchalantly, his weight thrown on one hip, his arms crossed low on his chest, his expression a cool mix of amusement and chagrin. "How ill-timed," he said.

"How ill-judged," Amanda retorted, flustered. "There should have been nothing for Theo to see."

"If he'd shown up five minutes later, there'd have been even more to see, I daresay."

Amanda squeezed her eyes shut and held up a restraining hand. "No, please don't say that."

John's expressive brows lifted. "So that's how the wind blows, eh? So, it *was* the wine making you behave so uninhibitedly?"

Amanda was about to argue that the effects of the wine had worn off long ago, then realized that her indulgence in the alcoholic beverage was a wonderful and convenient excuse for her actions during the last few minutes. She couldn't explain her behavior—even to herself—so she allowed the blame to fall on Richard Clarke's elderberry wine.

"You should have known it was the wine and behaved like a gentleman," she said accusingly, all the while simmering in her own sense of guilt.

"You invited *me* to kiss *you*, not the other way around," he reminded her.

"I don't remember inviting you to do anything!" she insisted stubbornly, though she knew better.

John grinned. "If that wasn't an invitation, then I'm a monkey's uncle."

"You should have controlled yourself," she sniffed.

"I daresay you're quite right. I should have controlled myself," was his generous reply.

"And ... and if I *did* invite you to kiss me, you can be sure I'll never do so again!" she further informed him.

"Very wise of you, Amanda," he said dryly. "Now I suppose you understand what I meant when I said it is sometimes disastrous to impulsively act upon one's feelings, eh?"

"Don't remind me of things I said while under

the influence of a fermented beverage," she replied angrily. "And don't call me Amanda!"

"All right, *darling*," he said with a debonair grin.

"Oh, you insufferable man!" Amanda exclaimed, grasping her skirts in her fists and turning to stride quickly up the hill. "It would serve you right if I left you here to fend for yourself," she flung at him over her shoulder, then stomped away in great indignation.

Jack watched Amanda's black skirt swish behind her as she disappeared over the rise of the hill, her slim hips swaying tantalizingly. The minute she was gone, his suave smile fell away. Far from feeling roguish and urbane, he was shaken to the very center of his being. Even though he couldn't remember his name, who his family was, what he was doing last week or last year, he knew he'd remember if he'd ever been so stirred by a kiss. And he was very sure he never had. . . .

Jack was intrigued and entranced by Amanda Darlington. She was a mystery—prim and prickly one moment, wanton and full of innocent wiles the next. She was strong and willful, yet touchingly vulnerable at the same time. He wanted to take her to bed . . . and he wanted to protect her. He wanted to be her lover . . . and her friend. These impulses seemed distressingly at odds with one another. He was confused.

One thing he did understand about the situation was that things would be much clearer, his mind much less a muddle, if he knew the real reason why Miss Darlington was traveling alone and why she was in such a tizzy to get to some remote island with the unprepossessing name of Thorney.

Quite obviously she'd much rather not have him and his amnesia around to worry about in the interim, but fate had flung them together. And if he could allow himself to give in to a little vanity, he was convinced that she was just as attracted to him as he was to her. She'd said so, hadn't she? And why else would she allow him to kiss her?

But then Jack's brows furrowed in a frown. She had also confided that she liked him for his "anonymity." It would be lowering to be liked simply because one was temporarily a nonperson ... but he couldn't help but think there was something more to the attraction than *that*.

Taking a deep breath, Jack uncrossed his arms and trudged up the hill. It had taken all his self-command to cool the ardor he felt for Miss Darlington, and he knew it only required one glance, one touch to send his senses reeling again. If Theo hadn't interrupted them, he'd have made love to her right there in the grass, regardless of who might have chanced upon them. He'd been that lost to passion.

Walking through the graveyard, crossing the street, greeting wedding guests who were starting to mill and stagger about town, and braving Theo's scorching look of warning, however, stripped him of the last bit of carnal lust he still harbored as he entered the grove and approached the carriage parked snugly under the trees.

The horses were already harnessed, Joe was sitting in his usual station beside Theo, and Harley was perched on the rumble.

"Where's Mr. Clarke?" Jack inquired.

"T' mistress 'as already paid 'im," Theo replied stiffly, pulling back slightly on the reigns and making the lead horse rear his head and snort restlessly.

Jack took the hint. He threw Theo a bland look of innocence and climbed aboard. As he expected, Miss Darlington was conscientiously staring out the opposite window. Her hair was pulled into its usual tight coil at the nape of her lovely neck, with no wisps or waves daring to escape.

"Too bad Clarke didn't stick around to say good-bye," said Jack, testing the waters with the conversational comment. "I thought him a very pleasant man."

Miss Darlington turned and glared at him. "I told him I would relay his best wishes to you, etcetera . . . so consider it done."

Brrrr. The waters were decidedly cold. Jack was quite sure Mr. Clarke's best wishes would not have given him such a chill had they been relayed by the gentleman himself.

He sighed, resigned to a view of Miss Darlington's chipped-in-ice profile till they reached Chichester. Then she'd thaw just long enough to hand him over to the authorities. Or try to. He had no intention of being detained by some local constable or dragged off to London like a prisoner. And he likewise had no intention of abandoning Miss Darlington until he was quite sure she was going to be safe for the duration of her mysterious journey. As long as his memory eluded him, he didn't think she'd abandon him, either . . . not even to the constabulary.

Theo handily maneuvered the carriage onto the road, and since many people strolled about—most of them probably full of elderberry wine—he was basically walking the horses till they were clear of the village. People waved and shouted good-bye as the carriage drove slowly past.

Miss Darlington bestirred herself to smile and wave through the window, and Jack did, too. He'd had as good a time at the wedding feast and dance as Miss Darlington had. He liked and admired the simple, honest goodwill of the people of Patching very much.

They were driving past the church, and Jack observed that the bride and groom, for some reason, had wandered back to the sacred building in which they'd taken their vows. They were standing side by side in front of the arched door, their heads bent together as they no doubt murmured sentimental claptrap to each other. It was a touching tableau and would have warmed the heart of anyone not so averse to the matrimonial state as Jack was.

He was about to look away and sit back in his seat when something amazing happened. Right before his startled eyes, the bride's appearance changed! She was transformed by his imagination, or some other mismanagement of his recently knocked-about brain, from blond, plump, and rosy to pale, elegant, and auburn-haired! Jack was beginning to suspect the elderberry wine of having traces of opium, or else why would he be having such a strange hallucination?

He rubbed his eyes and stared again, but the auburn-haired female was still there. He didn't recognize the woman, couldn't put a name to her, but he had the distinct impression that he knew her exceedingly well. Then—horror of horrors—the gawky country boy next to her suddenly changed faces, too. And the face he changed into was his very own!

The imagined transformation became dismantled and clouded as they drove farther and farther away from the church. Jack's last sight of the couple was a rather blurred view of their former selves.

Jack jerked his gaze away from the couple and slumped in his seat. He closed his eyes. He was breathing hard and sweating as though he'd been running alongside the carriage instead of riding quite comfortably inside.

The nightmares he'd been having since the accident took on the hideous form of reality. It was true, then. He was married . . . or destined to be. But to whom?

The name came to him like a distant echo. *Charlotte. Charlotte Batsford.*

Another echo, much louder and clearer, revealed his own name. *Jackson Montgomery, Viscount Durham.*

Then the echoes turned to shouts and trumpets

and a fanfare fit to welcome royalty ... but all the fuss and folderol was simply the return of his errant memory. It came back in a huge rush. He went from remembering nothing to remembering everything in the time it took to blink. And accompanying his memory came a monstrous weight that crushed his very spirit.

Gone was the delightful sensation of freedom he'd enjoyed over the past two days. He'd never be free again. He was betrothed to wed Charlotte Batsford, and if he'd not been nearly run down by Miss Darlington's carriage, he'd be married and on his honeymoon this very instant. What a dismal thought, indeed.

Jack was roused from his melancholia by a gentle nudge of his arm. He looked up from a dazed contemplation of his hands—clenched into fists and resting on his knees—and discovered Miss Darlington peering with a grave and anxious expression into his face.

"Are you all right, John?" she inquired, her anger apparently forgotten for the moment by her concern for him. "You look distressed. I've spoken to you several times, but you've seemed in a trance. Don't you feel well? Has anything happened? Have you remembered something?"

John looked at Miss Darlington, at her wide, innocent blue eyes, and quite blatantly told the biggest lie of his life. "I'm quite all right, Miss Darlington." He smiled gamely and dabbed at his damp forehead with his handkerchief. "I just felt a bit topsy-turvy in my stomach for a moment, that's all. Unfortunately it had nothing to do with my memory. I still remember nothing ... absolutely nothing at all. Terribly sorry. Looks like you're stuck with me for a while longer."

Chichester was a fairly populous town with several inns to choose from, leaving Julian no recourse but to spend the afternoon making inquiries at each establishment. He'd driven like the very devil himself to try to overtake the carriage described by Mrs. Beane as the vehicle his brother had departed in that morning, but to no avail. Jack's party was either driving just as fast as he was, or they'd taken another route and were headed somewhere other than Chichester.

After receiving no encouraging information from the innkeepers, Julian rented a private parlor in the Charleston Arms, a hostelry located on the main thoroughfare of town. The chief attraction of the first-floor parlor was a window that looked down on the activity of the street below. Julian could refresh himself with a large quantity of strong tea while he kept watch at the window for anyone resembling a well-dressed gypsy with a bandage round his head, accompanied by a woman in black.

Julian had likewise made arrangements for the comforts of his servants and horses, the first being served refreshment in the kitchen and the second being brushed down, watered, and fed oats in the stable. He'd given orders to "spring 'um!" as they'd left Horsham, eager to put an end to the thousand questions racing through his mind concerning the health and welfare of his ramshackle brother. As a result, the horses had arrived in a steaming lather, and his servants felt "fair pulled t' pieces," as Caleb the coachman confided to his master. They'd all been pretty well tossed about in the course of traveling the rutted and rocky country roads.

Now Julian sat with his booted feet propped on a fringed ottoman, his legs crossed at the ankles, his fourth cup of tea cooling as he held it aloft and gazed intently out the window into the stream of people walking, riding, or driving up and down the street.

Eventually he set the cup and saucer on the pie-crust table by the chair, stood up, and walked to the window. With his hands clasped behind him and his legs slightly spread, he stared broodingly down at the walkway, only vaguely aware now and then of a female gaping up at him or openly flirting.

The last thing Julian cared about at the moment was whether or not he cut a dashing figure. He was trying to sort out the information he'd received so far concerning Jack's disappearance and make some sense out of it. He had little to go on. He knew Jack had been injured after he left The Spotted Dog, but how he acquired the injury was pure speculation. Mrs. Beane said he'd fallen and hit his head on a rock, but he could just as easily have been throttled by someone.

As well, the woman had said he'd lost his memory. If this was true, it was most disconcerting. If Jack had no idea who he was, what defense did he have against people who might wish to use his memory lapse as a means to control him? It all sounded much too melodramatic, of course, but even in civilized England nefarious deeds were done. Julian only hoped that this was not the case with Jack. But why else would he be headed in the opposite direction than where he *should* be headed?

If Jack knew who he was, he'd know people would be worried about him, he'd know he was engaged to be married and had virtually left standing at the altar an innocent woman who did not deserve such shabby treatment.

And who was this mysterious female Jack was traveling with? Why was she dressed all in black? And why were they introducing themselves as Lord and Lady Thornfield? Julian did not believe that his honorable brother was capable of deliberately jilting his betrothed at the last minute and running off with a femme fatale . . . and, to of all places, Chichester!

No, none of it made any sense. But then, since all this mystery and confusion was connected to Jack,

Julian ought not to be so *very* surprised. He allowed himself a rueful grin and an infinitesimal shake of his head. Jack was still alive, and that was all that mattered. And since he still breathed the same sweet English air as Julian did, there was every reason to expect that all would be well in the end.

Julian's smile fell away and his patrician lips compressed into a grim, determined line. He would make bloody sure that all would be well in the end ... or his name was not Julian Fitzwilliam Montgomery the Third, Eighth Marquess of Serling.

"According to Theo, the best inn in Chichester is the Charleston Arms. You look as though you are accustomed to demanding the finest accommodations when you travel, so I don't understand your disinclination to stop there!" Amanda stared at John with a look of puzzled irritation.

"I just think we should be a little more discreet, Miss Darlington," John replied.

"Discreet? I should think you'd want to be recognized. How else are you going to get your memory and your life back?" John shrugged noncommittally, and Amanda heaved an exasperated sigh. "Sometimes I think you don't *want* your life back, John!"

"Maybe I don't," he mumbled, turning to look broodingly through the window at the outlying farms and growing congestion of buildings on their approach to Chichester.

Amanda couldn't pretend not to know what John meant. There was some question about the amiability of the life he'd led prior to stepping into the path of her coach-and-four. Although he was well dressed and educated ... obviously upper-crust ... that certainly didn't guarantee that he'd been happy before.

And even if he *had* been leading a happy life, Amanda had begun to understand how he might feel some reluctance to regain his memory. There was a certain charm to not knowing who you were. In a burst of candor, she'd told John she was attracted to him partially because of his anonymity. Perhaps she was also *envious* of his anonymity.

Yes, it would be lovely not to remember the heartaches, the mistakes, and the disillusionments of the past. And it would be quite exhilarating to feel that you could choose your path in life without the encumbrances of prejudices and reservations instilled in your youth.

Of course Amanda was thinking of her parents and the life she'd led up till then because she'd slavishly followed their example. And in the final reckoning, their example proved to be false and their way of life nothing like what she wanted.

Today at Patching, dancing and socializing with people who worked hard and played hard, Amanda was beguiled by elderberry wine and a fierce desperation to throw off all the restraints she'd been shackled with for the whole of her three-and-twenty years. And the result had been that she'd thrown herself into John's arms and demanded a kiss.

Even now, hours after their encounter by the stream, Amanda was warmed and stirred by the memory of their kisses and of John's hands on her body. She glanced at him and was relieved to see him still gazing steadfastly out the window. She didn't want him to see her face kindle with heat at the mere thought of their intimacies.

In the course of their afternoon's journey, John had apologized three separate times for kissing her. And while she had privately forgiven him, she had been too stubborn and too afraid to acknowledge that forgiveness out loud. She feared that if she relented and honestly took her considerable share of the blame for what had happened between them, something might happen again. Sitting in such a small enclosure for such a length of time had sorely taxed her powers of resistance already. Every moment she'd wanted to reach out and touch him.

John had warned her that acting on one's impulses could be disastrous, but while he held her and kissed her Amanda had felt nothing but sheer bliss. She wasn't sure anymore what was right or wrong. She used to think moral decisions were as clear as black and white, but now she knew there were dangerous, delightful shades of gray.

One thing she did know for sure was that she intended to leave John with the constables in Chichester. She couldn't allow him to continue on with her to Thorney Island and discover her family secret. And with her conscience in a muddle, the sooner John was out of her life and back in his, the better it would be for everyone concerned. No matter what she felt for him, after tonight John would be out of her life forever.

Amanda had never felt so depressed.

"So you still want to go to the Charleston Arms, eh?" inquired John, turning from the window. He looked oddly wistful, and Amanda's heart twisted in her chest. It was almost as though he knew she was going to desert him in Chichester and was just as reluctant to part company as she was.

Then she firmly told herself that she was behaving like a mooncalf and indulging in wishful thinking. John was a lady's man and was used to women swooning in his arms. Their intimacies that afternoon had meant nothing to him. If they'd made love, she'd have been just another notch in his figurative bedpost.

But making love with John would have meant something to Amanda, something very special indeed. And it would have given her something to remember throughout her lonely spinster's life.

Amanda shook her head, trying to dislodge the delicious images of her and John lying naked on a bed of sweet grass, their arms wrapped around each other. . . .

"Miss Darlington?"

The subject of her fantasy had been close enough to touch all day, and now he was even closer. He leaned forward with a questioning look on his arrestingly handsome face. The golden-brown eyes were eloquent with feeling; the mouth was drawn into a serious line. In that moment, Amanda decided that she needed just a little more time with him, just a few more memories to be carefully treasured over the years.

"Are you all right?" John inquired gently.

"No, I am not," she admitted with a weak and rueful smile.

His brows lowered in a concerned frown. "What can I do to assist you, madam?"

"You can open the trapdoor in the ceiling and tell Theo that we are *not* to stop at the Charleston Arms."

"Indeed? And where are we going to stop?" he wanted to know.

She shyly averted her eyes. "Somewhere more . . . *discreet*."

Chapter 10

The Angel Inn was several blocks from the center of town and out of the way of the general flow of traffic. It was a clean, modest establishment with a gracious landlord and, best of all, enough vacant rooms that Amanda and John were not compelled to share a bedchamber again.

Without consulting her, John introduced them as husband and wife. Amanda was a bit miffed at John's high-handedness at first but then realized that one more night pretending to be his wife was exactly what she wanted, anyway. That was why she'd decided to go along with his wish to stay in a more discreet location than the very prominent Charleston Arms. He seemed to want a few more hours of anonymity without the chance of running into someone he knew in town, and she wanted a few more hours of his company.

Remembering how exciting it felt to be with a man like John would console and amuse her during many lonely nights in the future. She forced away thoughts of all the people who were probably worried about John and told herself that it was all right to be selfish just this once. *They*—whoever they were—could have him back tomorrow. Tonight, she wanted him all to herself.

Not in her bed, of course; she was not that lost to reason and common sense. However, she knew she was courting temptation by spending another night with him under the same roof. But it seemed that she and temptation had lately become bosom beaux.

As the landlord, Mr. Tebbs, preceded them up the stairs to their chambers, he kept up a friendly, steady chatter. Amanda was thankful for this because ever since she'd told John that she preferred not to stay at the Charleston Arms, an awkward silence had built up between them. She'd taken him by surprise.

Once or twice she'd caught him giving her speculative, measuring glances. He was obviously wondering what she intended. But his expression was puzzled and wary rather than lecherous. However, if he *had* leered at her, who could blame him for doing so after what happened that afternoon behind the church? She hadn't exactly been a shrinking violet.

"Here we are, milord, milady. Two rooms exactly next to the other and with a door betwixt fer yer convenience." Mr. Tebbs, a short, rotund man with a hospitable smile, bobbed his bald head genially. He opened both doors and stood aside for Amanda's and John's inspection. "I hope they'll do?"

Amanda felt herself blushing at the "convenient" arrangement. The kindly landlord must have noticed her heightened color, and before John could reply to his first question, he asked a second question. "Are ye newlyweds, then?"

"Yes, er . . . we are," John replied. "About as new as they come," he added dryly.

"Too bad ye had a bereavement so soon after yer nuptials," Mr. Tebbs murmured sympathetically, making a somber face as he seemed to suddenly notice Amanda's black dress. His smile came back full force as he went on, "But ye're young and ye've got yer whole lives t'gether. There's ups and downs, but ye've got each other to help get through the downs, eh?"

Amanda glanced at John to see how he was taking the landlord's familiar manners and his folksy philosophizing. She was relieved to observe that he wasn't acting a bit high-in-the-instep, like so many men in his station of life might do, but was readily returning the landlord's smile.

"Thank you, sir, the rooms will do perfectly," he said with a friendly but authoritative nod of dismissal. "Remember, we want the private parlor for dinner at eight."

"Right ye are, milord," said Mr. Tebbs, bowing himself down the hall, his smile still intact. "Dinner at eight with all the trimmings, just like yer lordship said."

When the landlord disappeared round a corner in the narrow hallway, John turned to Amanda. "He's a great improvement over Mrs. Beane, isn't he?"

"Indeed he is," Amanda agreed, finding it impossible to meet John's eyes now that they were alone.

John lifted her chin with his forefinger and made her look at him. "You do plan to take dinner with me, don't you?" He was standing much too close, and Amanda felt desire rise inside her, steamy and vaporous.

Against her better judgment, she replied, "Yes. I have to eat, don't I?"

A smile tugged briefly at the corners of his mouth. "But I wouldn't put it past you to eat in your room, refusing my company altogether ... after what happened today."

"I was as much at fault for what happened today as you were."

At her halting admission, John's eyes took on a tender expression that caused her heart to beat erratically. "You're very generous," he murmured, sliding his knuckles down the side of her face, then cupping her chin lightly. "But a true gentleman would have considered the influence of the elderberry wine and not taken advantage of you as I did."

Amanda struggled internally, then bravely informed him, "That's very generous of *you*, but I must also confess that the elderberry wine had nothing whatsoever to do with my forward behavior."

For a long moment John seemed to consider this last impetuous burst of honesty. It was a moment charged with a tension that hinted at possibilities . . . possibilities they both considered but which neither of them dared speak of. His warm fingers, still curled over the curve of her jaw as he cupped her chin, tightened. He lowered his head, then halted halfway down, seeming to think better of it before he actually kissed her. His hand dropped to his side, and he stepped back a pace.

Amanda was glad he commanded a measure of self-control she so obviously lacked. Her lips pulsed with longing, but reason told her it was better this way. She knew only too well that it would be difficult—nay, impossible—to stop with a kiss.

"There's time to rest before dinner," he told her, his manner altered to a cautious politeness. "It's been a long day."

She nodded meekly and backed into the room. "Will you be resting, too?"

"Yes. But first I need to speak to Theo."

"To Theo? Why?"

"I need him, or one of your other servants, to run an errand for me. I borrowed Mrs. Beane's dead husband's dull razor to shave myself yesterday . . . with disastrous results." He rubbed his raspy jaw and smiled ruefully. "I want a new blade. Since I am dining with a lady tonight, I am determined to look the gentleman." *And act the gentleman, too*, was the message his dark eyes conveyed.

Amanda was flattered and thankful that John respected her, but a part of her wished they could forget for a few hours who she was and allow respect to give way to desire. She firmly pushed aside the improper thoughts and smiled gratefully at John.

"Shall we meet here in the hall at eight?" he suggested.

"Yes. At eight," she agreed, then slowly shut the door, peering round the edge of it at John till the very last moment.

With the door finally closed, she leaned against it with her eyes shut, trying to compose herself. Who was she trying to fool? There was no use languishing by the door; she'd not be able to compose herself till John was out of her life forever. But she had one more night to enjoy her discomposure, and she walked eagerly to the bellpull by the bed and gave it a yank, summoning the chambermaid. She was going to have a bath.

Jack sought out Theo and found him in the taproom, a long, narrow chamber with a stone floor and a large stone fireplace with a fire burning brightly on the grate. Several wooden tables with benches were placed in straight rows on one side of the room, and on the other side of the room was a wooden counter, behind which were some shelves holding bottles and mugs. At the end of the counter was a barrel with a spigot.

Theo sat near the barrel on a stool at the bar, watching the barkeep fill a mug with a golden-brown liquid topped with froth. Judging by his mellow demeanor, he'd already downed a few mugs. All the better to ferret information out of him, thought Jack. There were other people and a fair amount of noise in the room, but Theo seemed to sense Jack's approach and turned to watch him as he walked to the bar and sat down in the vacant stool next to him.

"Hello, Theo," said Jack, crossing his arms and leaning on the bar.

Theo stared straight ahead and took a long sip from his mug before answering with grudging respect, "Good evenin' to you, sir."

"You don't like me very much, do you, Theo?"

Theo smiled grimly. "If I answered truthfully, sir, it'd be considered disrespectful on my part . . . *sir*."

"You don't owe me any respect. You don't know me from Adam."

"It's plain t' see, sir, ye're a *swell*. It's my bound'n duty to kowtow t' me betters. Part of the job, y' see."

"Your job is to drive Miss Darlington about England as well as to protect her when need be."

Theo turned and eyed Jack balefully. "That's what I've been tryin' t' do, but ye've made my job considerable harder."

"I assure you, Theo, I have no desire to harm your mistress."

"That's not what I see'd when I caught you two by the stream today," Theo said accusingly.

"That was a mistake," Jack replied briefly, then hurried on to the matter he had come to discuss. "But it does prove what can happen when a woman travels alone . . . even with devoted servants for protection. I wonder that her brother allows it."

"She ain't got a brother. Where'd you get such an idea? She ain't got no one but her old-maid aunts since her mother and father died six months ago."

So here was the definitive proof he'd needed to support his conviction that she'd been lying about picking up her brother's—or was it her sister's?—child to tend while he or she went on holiday with his or her spouse. Now, what was the truth?

"All the more reason to be alarmed at her undertaking this trip to Thorney Island alone," he ventured further. He lowered his voice and spoke confidingly. "The nature of Miss Darlington's business there is distressing, is it not?"

Theo peered suspiciously over the rim of his raised mug. He took another long sip, then said, "Miss Darlington's business on Thorney Island is none of *yer* business, sir."

Jack rested his jaw on one fist and shrugged nonchalantly. "Ah, but she's already told me all about it. Don't you think it a shocking situation?" Jack considered "shocking" a fairly safe adjective to use. Almost anything of a serious nature could be called shocking.

Theo stared at Jack for a long, considering moment. Jack maintained his sober expression and endeavored to look as sincere as possible. He apparently convinced Theo that he enjoyed Miss Darlington's confidence, because the coachman shook his head disgustedly and said, "Bah! I can't believe she'd go and tell ye such a thing. It's shocking, all right. And it's my opinion that the lit'l bastard had ought t' be left where it is. It's a shame t' the family. The late master and missus wouldn't allow the child t' be brought t' Darlington Hall when they was alive, and I say it ought not t' come now after they're dead and gone. Leave well enough alone, is what I say!"

This little diatribe evidently made Theo thirsty, as he buried his face in his brew and finished it off. Jack was apparently not expected to reply. He was glad of the reprieve because he frankly did not know what to say! He was in shock!

Part of what Miss Darlington had told him about her reason for going to Thorney Island was true; she was indeed picking up a child. But the child was not her nonexistent brother's offspring ... it was *hers*! Miss Darlington was the mother of an illegitimate child!

"Barkeep," said Jack, his voice a thready rasp. "I'll

have a tumbler of Scotch. And be quick about it, if you please."

Amanda checked her appearance in the mirror above the tallboy. Her complexion glowed from her recent bath, and she felt fresh and warm and rosy. A sense of excitement, of anticipation, also contributed to her blushing cheeks. After all, she was going to dine and spend the evening with a very amusing, charming, and attractive man. And she was determined, for once, to enjoy herself without suffering pangs of ridiculous guilt.

She'd even gone so far as to alter her mourning apparel to something a little less severe. She had brought only black gowns with her, so there was no changing that, but she had also brought along a silk shawl Aunt Prissy had given her for Christmas last year. It was black, but it was thickly embroidered with exotic flowers in soft pastel colors and edged with a long knotted fringe.

Since her parents had died, she'd never worn it in public, thinking it unseemly and far too pretty to be seen in while she remained in a state of mourning. But tonight she was going to make an exception to that inflexible rule. Tonight she wanted to look her best.

The dress she'd chosen for the evening was a lightweight flowing silk with a high collar trimmed with a velvet band. There were a dozen shiny round black buttons down the bodice to the empire waist, and puffed sleeves with a deep flounce of black lace falling to below her elbows. With the shawl draped over her shoulders and flowing over the natural bend of her arms, the effect was quite elegant.

Her hair, too, was different. Instead of pulling it back into a tight knot at the base of her skull, she wound it into a loose coil and pinned it up much higher than usual. The result was extremely flattering, the natural waves of her hair framing her oval face with a fuller, softer look.

Tentatively pleased by her less severe appearance but a little afraid of the underlying reasons why she was taking such pains to look nice, she stepped away from the mirror and moved to the window that looked out over the limestone walls that enclosed the stable yard at the back of the inn.

To the sides of the cobbled yard, she could see other buildings and part of a stretch of the road that led into the more populous area of Chichester. People were still trudging up and down the walkway, their wraps pulled snugly about them as the chill and fog of an autumn evening crept over the town.

It was the last eerily gray moments of dusk, and as Amanda watched, it started raining. The aspect grew instantly quite dark and dreary, and she could hear the distant rumble of thunder and see flickers of lightning. It appeared that the storm was building in intensity and moving in their direction. She hoped Theo had returned from his errands in town and would not get caught in a sudden deluge.

Amanda turned away from the window, walked to the bed, and sat down. She was nervous. She glanced at the small clock perched atop the narrow mantel above the fireplace. It was half past seven. Thirty more minutes before dinner. She played nervously with the top button of her gown, rolling the smooth porcelain between her thumb and forefinger.

She frowned, thinking about how disconcerted she'd felt when John announced that he was sending Theo into town for a new razor blade. She had hoped that Theo had not already left the premises to undertake her own commission to run an errand, therefore giving John reason to suspect something was afoot.

Something *was* afoot, of course. When they'd arrived at the Angel, Amanda had given Theo a note to take to the local constable's office as soon as he'd whet his whistle in the taproom and rested up a bit. The note indicated that John needed assistance in locating relatives in order to establish his identity. But she instructed the police to come in the morning to fetch him and not before, as he needed a restorative night's sleep before facing the gruelling aspect of a long trip to London on the morrow.

Amanda felt like a traitor. She knew John didn't want his amnesia dealt with in the usual ham-handed fashion by the local police, and for some reason, he had an aversion to going to London. But what else could she do? As his memory had not returned yet, it seemed a stubborn case and one which probably required as its cure the jolt of seeing someone he knew intimately. She could not assist him in this matter as she had important matters of her own to attend to. Matters he could know nothing about. She had no choice but to notify the authorities and relinquish John and his problems to them.

Suddenly the room darkened, and rain blasted against the casement window. The flames in the fireplace shuddered and danced from a burst of air coming down the flue. A flash of lightning and an immediate crash of thunder fairly shook the decorative copper plates off the mantel. Amanda pulled her shawl close about her and moved to the window.

The wind was playing havoc with everything and everyone in its path. People were huddled in their coats and rushing for shelter. There was a tempest brewing, and Amanda stood and watched it with a curiously delighted smile on her lips. She enjoyed a good storm. She always had. But tonight she felt more than usually stirred by the kickup Mother Nature was waging.

In a burst of enlightenment, she understood the connection between herself and this particular storm. Tonight, and indeed ever since she'd met John, her own heart and soul were a tempest . . . a tempest of feelings and yearnings she could hardly contain. With each clap of thunder and each preternatural glow of electricity that momentarily brightened the room, her restlessness increased. She started pacing.

Her usual enjoyment of a storm was intensified tenfold. This time she was stirred to a point of feverish excitement that was growing moment by moment quite strangely . . . *uncomfortable*. It seemed there needed to be a climax . . . a blinding blaze of lightning, a deafening roar of thunder, then a soothing quiet with only the mesmeric drip, drip, drip of rain off the roof.

Amanda ached for an easing of this tension, a soothing aftermath to the storm. But she knew it wouldn't come, it couldn't come till she'd weathered the tempest . . . her own personal tempest, her own storm of emotions.

Amanda suddenly stopped pacing. She heard the cry of a child. She wasn't sure where the sound was coming from. There was only one room next to hers, and that was John's, so she guessed the crying child was in a room across the hall. She listened, expecting to hear the voice of an adult soothing the child, quieting its quite natural fears of the loud thunderstorm.

But the child continued to cry, sounding more and more desperate and frightened as the rain beat against the windows, loose shutters slammed against the walls, and tree limbs creaked ominously in the wind.

The idea of the child braving the terrors of the storm alone filled Amanda with sympathy . . . and indignation. "This will not do," she said to herself, moving to the door and flinging it open. "Whoever is supposed to be taking care of that child should be horsewhipped!"

It did not take her long to ascertain that the child was indeed in the room directly across the hall from hers. She knocked on the door, but no one answered.

She turned the knob and discovered the door unlocked, then eased it open and peered into the dark.

"Is someone here?" she inquired on the slim
chance that an adult was sleeping in the room or was
otherwise occupied to the point that they could not
attend to their own child. But no one replied, and
the child continued to weep.

"I'm here to help you," Amanda called softly,
squinting to see and wishing she'd had the foresight
to bring a brace of candles with her. Another flash
of lightning, another cry of fear in accompaniment to
the boom of thunder, enabled Amanda to locate the
child. There, huddled in the corner farthest from the
window, was a little girl about three or four years
old, in her nightdress, her face wet and swollen from
crying and her pale hair tangled and hanging in
her face.

"Don't move, sweetheart," Amanda told her. "I'll
be right back." Then she hurried across the hall,
grabbed the brace of candles on her bedside table,
and returned to the little girl's room. She set the candles down on a nearby chest and held out her arms
to the child.

"Come here, my dear," she said in a gentle, cajol-
ing voice. "I know you're afraid of the storm, and
I'll stay with you till it's over."

"I want my mama," the little girl sobbed weakly.
"Where's my mama?"

Amanda's heart ached at the plaintive question.
"Darling, I don't know. I'll fetch her for you in a
moment, but wouldn't you like me to hold you and
dry away those tears first?"

Another burst of thunder and lightning made the
little girl tremble violently. Amanda could stand it
no longer, and she moved across the room, scooped
up the little girl, and clasped her against her chest.
The child's arms immediately wrapped around
Amanda's neck, and she clung to her, happy for now

to take a kind stranger as substitute for her absent mother.

Amanda walked to the bed and sat down on the side edge, holding the little girl in her lap. Her small legs and feet were bare and cold as they stuck out at the bottom of her nightdress, and Amanda took a quilt from the foot of the bed and tucked it around the child. She was trembling from both fear and cold, the poor thing, and Amanda's feelings went back and forth between anger toward the child's delinquent parents and an overwhelming surge of protectiveness toward the child.

How could someone leave such a small child alone during such a terrible storm? How could they leave her alone at *all*, especially at a public inn that could harbor all sorts of human riffraff ... and with the door unlocked?

Amanda focused on comforting the child instead of her anger. She'd have it out with the parents later. She crooned reassuring words to the little girl, rocked her back and forth, smoothed her disheveled hair out of her eyes, and dabbed at her wet cheeks with a clean handkerchief. After a few short minutes, the child's crying subsided to an occasional hiccup and a shuddering sigh. Soon she was fast asleep.

Amanda held the child close, her small head tucked under Amanda's chin, her thin arms still wrapped around Amanda's neck even in sleep. The storm still raged, but the worst was over. The thunder and lightning were further apart and more distant as the tempest moved inland to disturb the pastoral peace of the farmers in their snug cottages on the weald.

Amanda drew a measure of peace from the warmth of the little body she held against her breast. She was glad she'd been able to still the child's fears to the point that she'd actually dozed off in her arms.

Amanda decided that she liked giving comfort,

cuddling and showing affection to another human being. And she realized how seldom she was able to do something so elemental, so basic to human happiness in her own circle of influence. She'd only her aunts to hug and fuss over, and they were almost as reserved about demonstrations of affection as she was.

She wanted more. She craved the love of a child ... and a man. A husband, ideally. She wished she were comfortable enough with the opposite sex to get past courtship and on to commitment, but she'd never been able to thus far. She'd botched her chances of making a match during her season in London by being too shy, by making the men think she was frigid. And at Edenbridge there was no one eligible in the neighborhood ... except Rector Mitford. But with his cold lips he'd never be able to give her the love and affection she craved.

Maybe the child on Thorney Island was the answer to Amanda's prayers. And maybe she was the answer to the child's prayers, too. Amanda could make sure her sibling, whether a boy or a girl, was given the affection she'd missed as a child. It disturbed her greatly to imagine that her brother or sister had already been denied the love he or she deserved. Amanda wanted desperately to make amends for her parents' callousness.

In the fervor of her feelings, Amanda blinked back the tears that threatened to spill over onto her cheeks. She squeezed the child tighter against her chest, wishing, longing, yearning for something of her own to hang on to.

Jack walked up the stairs from the parlor. He had spent the last few minutes making sure that everything was arranged just as he'd ordered. It was exactly two minutes before eight, and he was looking forward to his dinner with Miss Darlington with mixed feelings.

After a single drink with Theo that afternoon, during which he'd learned that Miss Darlington was on her way to Thorney Island to collect her illegitimate child—a child her parents apparently refused to allow her to keep after it was born—Jack had returned to his room and spent the remainder of the day pondering the surprising twists and turns of life. He'd never have believed in a million years that the prim Miss Darlington was anything other than a virgin.

He found himself inordinately curious about the details of her affair with the child's father. Who was he? How old was she when the affair occurred? Why didn't he marry her? Did he hurt her? Did he love her? More importantly . . . did she love him?

Jack was surprised by his intense interest in the answers to these questions. He barely knew Miss Darlington, but he couldn't bear the thought of some man callously using her, then deserting her. But maybe she'd been a willing party in the affair and had not expected anything more than a passionate interlude in what Jack had begun to imagine was quite a prosaic and stifling life.

One thing he knew for sure: he didn't respect her any less for what she'd done. It only proved she was human. And nothing could make him think very ill of a woman who had nursed him through a life-threatening fever and put up with his nonsense for the past two days. The very fact that she was now determined to fetch her child and take it back to Edenbridge, disregarding the social consequences—the snubbing, the gossip—proved she was a brave and remarkable woman.

No, Jack didn't think any less of Miss Amanda Darlington. In fact, he was more determined than ever to help her get to Thorney Island to reunite with her child. He understood now why she was traveling alone, the little nodcock. She was trying to be discreet! But traveling alone only made her stand out like a sore thumb, which proved she was quite naive about such things despite her rather scandalous history.

She needed someone to watch over her, Jack decided again. And by being that someone he was only returning the kindness she'd shown him by saving his life. He refused to believe there was another motive for wanting to help her.

At the landing at the top of the first floor, Jack turned toward his and Amanda's adjoining chambers. But as he approached, he noticed that Amanda's door was standing open and so was the door opposite to her room. Amanda, however, was nowhere to be seen. This did not bode well and Jack walked quickly to investigate, his heart hammering in his chest, fear rising in his throat like a geyser.

A clap of thunder from the receding storm sounded just as he reached the opened doors. He glanced quickly inside Amanda's room, saw nothing, then crossed the hall and saw Amanda sitting on the edge of a bed holding a child.

Amanda's face was turned away, her cheek resting against the child's head. She was unaware of Jack's presence. He stood and watched as she rocked the child and crooned soothing words while curious emotions roiled in his chest. He thought of the child she'd been forced to give up, and his heart ached for her.

Obviously the prim Miss Amanda Darlington was capable of the deepest and most tender feelings, the kind of feelings only mothers understood. And for a brief, alarmed instant he imagined Amanda mothering his own child . . . *their* child.

Thrusting aside the unwelcome, dangerous, and uncharacteristically sentimental thought, Jack stepped into the room and cleared his throat. "Miss Darlington?"

When Amanda turned quickly to look at him, he was startled to see the tracks of tears on her cheeks. He took an instinctive step forward as if to comfort her, checked himself, then stood with his hands clenched in impotent fists. He couldn't bear to see her hurting.

The questions came out in a rush. "What's the matter, Miss Darlington? Has someone hurt you?"

Looking embarrassed, Amanda quickly removed one arm from around the child and wiped away her tears with the back of her hand. Smiling gamely, she said, "No, nothing's the matter with me. I'm just a little angry, that's all."

"Angry at whom, and for what?" Jack's voice rose in volume and his fists clenched a little tighter.

Amanda pressed a finger against her lips, her brows dipping in a frown. "Hush," she said, her own voice barely above a whisper. "You'll wake her up, and I just barely got her to sleep."

Jack glanced about the room. "Where are her parents?"

Amanda's jaw tightened. "That's what I'd like to know. I was dressing for dinner when I heard this child's cries above the racket of the storm. I knocked on the door, and when no one answered I entered and found this tiny girl crouched in the corner, terrified! The room was entirely in the dark. I can't imagine what her parents were thinking of by leaving her alone like this! Where do you suppose they are?"

"I don't know, but I'll find out," said Jack, moving to the door. "I'll start by inquiring below."

"Thank you, John," said Amanda, smiling gratefully.

Jack acknowledged her gratitude with a rather grim smile in return. He was anxious for the child's welfare and angry at the parents as well. But he was most anxious about getting things settled so that his dinner with Amanda could go ahead as planned. She needed a little relaxation and amusement, and he was determined to see that she get them both.

Chapter 11

The child's parents were found taking refreshment in the taproom, lingering over a mug of brew and chatting amiably with some fellow travelers. They were a respectable, middle-class couple on holiday, headed for a seaside sojourn at a little resort near Brighton called Goring-by-Sea.

They were quite mortified and distressed to discover that their little Charity had awakened during the storm and disturbed Amanda, but they had left her fast asleep and had only been gone from the room some forty-five minutes ... or so they said. As Charity had been quite exhausted when they arrived at the inn, they'd had no notion she'd awaken before morning.

They apologized profusely and looked chagrined, but Amanda suspected that they were more embarrassed by the incident than concerned about Charity's ordeal during the storm.

Sitting in a wing chair by the fire in the cozy parlor with John, Amanda clutched a barely touched tumbler of apple cider and was totally absorbed by worrisome thoughts of Charity and scathing thoughts of the little girl's parents. She knew her natural empathy for Charity was made even stronger because of her anxiety about the child on Thorney Island and her own memories of a barren childhood, but she could not reason away the tension and melancholy that was the result of these intermingled concerns.

"Miss Darlington?"

Amanda was roused from her brooding reflections by John's voice. She looked up and saw that he was leaning against the mantel, his long legs crossed at the ankles in a relaxed pose.

"Yes?" she said, feeling slightly dazed.

He peered at her intently, then raised a brow. "Where *are* you, Miss Darlington?"

Her brows knitted. "What do you mean? I'm in a parlor at the Angel Inn . . . with you."

"No, you are not in the parlor with me. In fact, you are miles away . . . in thought, if not in person."

"I beg your pardon," she replied a little stiffly. "I cannot forget that child's predicament so easily as you do."

He pushed off from the mantel and stood in front of her. With his arms crossed over his chest, he scowled down at her, much in the manner of a sultan eyeing with displeasure a naughty concubine.

Despite her worries, a quiver of feminine awareness rippled through Amanda like a pleasant shock. It was impossible to stay immersed in one's thoughts with such a distraction as John in the room . . . and standing so close. He was so close, in fact, she could smell the clean scent of him: the subtle spice of a gentleman's soap, the freshly laundered and starched cravat that glowed snowy white at his strong throat.

She knew he'd had a bath because she'd heard the servants carting up the tub and the buckets of hot water that afternoon, but just looking at him now there was no doubt that John had spent considerable time grooming for tonight.

A new razor, and a steadier hand than he'd had two days ago, had allowed for a close shave without a single nick. His jaw was bare and smooth and begged to be caressed.

His hair was squeaky clean, the lustrous black curls a careless, disarming tumble that begged to be sifted through by eager feminine fingers.

His piratelike bandage was gone, too, replaced by a small square of gauze secured at the edges by some sort of clever adhesive.

Everything he wore from jacket to waistcoat to trousers to tall boots was freshly brushed, pressed, or polished. Amanda's breath quickened at the idea that he'd been as anxious to look to advantage tonight as she had. *Why?* she wondered, a shiver coursing down her spine. Did he have seduction in mind? And if he did, would she have the strength to refuse him?

"Why do you consider the child in a 'predicament,' Miss Darlington?"

Amanda blinked, her mind working overtime to dispel thoughts of seduction and return to the original topic. "Oh, you mean Charity?"

"We *were* talking of the child," he reminded her with a touch of amusement in his tone. "You accused me of caring less than you for her 'predicament.' I do not consider the child to be in a predicament. As a whole, she is well cared for. Her parents simply misjudged in this case."

"They should have known she'd awaken and be frightened during the storm."

"Not everyone is so perceptive and conscientious as you are, Miss Darlington," John suggested, uncrossing his arms and stepping back to his former position by the mantel. He stared at her with a strange expression. The firelight flickered over his face and picked out the warm golden flecks in his eyes. "You'll make a wonderful mother," he said softly.

Amanda shifted uncomfortably in her seat. "Why

do you say that? You must know that I am destined to be a spinster." She raised her chin with a show of dignified unconcern. "And I do not mind it, you know. I ... I will have my nieces and nephews to keep me well enough alarmed and entertained through their growing-up escapades. It is much more comfortable to have nephews and nieces, you know, than children of your own."

"I believe you said it was your *sister's* child you're picking up at Thorney Island?"

Amanda couldn't remember whether she'd said brother or sister, but either would do, so she answered, "Yes ... er ... my sister."

John chewed his inside lip and nodded consideringly. "Yes. Well, if I had the natural instinct you do for children, Miss Darlington, I certainly wouldn't wait for my sibling to supply me with infants to attach my interests and affections." He suddenly got a faraway look in his eyes and a rueful half-smile on his lips. "If I were to wait for *my* brother to wed—"

"*Your* brother?" Amanda sat forward in her seat and set the tumbler of cider on a nearby table. "Then you've remembered something, John?" Perhaps she wouldn't have to turn him over to the authorities after all!

A mixture of alarm and confusion dawned then disappeared on John's handsome face. He chuckled self-consciously. "*If* I had a brother, Miss Darlington. I was only speaking hypothetically, you see," he explained. "I'm sorry if I got your hopes up." He smiled apologetically. "I know you're dashed anxious to be rid of me, but I still remember nothing."

Amanda frowned. "It sounded so much like you were remembering ... as if you'd a very specific brother formed in your mind's eye. You spoke with such a familiar tone, you know."

"I only wish I could remember a brother, or any

relative for that matter. Now, if you're done with your cider, Miss Darlington, I'll ring for dinner."

Jack hoped the sudden change of subject would deter Amanda from further speculation on his "tone." Damn, but he'd almost emptied the budget that time! He was going to have to be more careful. If Amanda suspected that he'd got his memory back, he'd no longer have any excuse to stay with her. And stay with her he must!

The little frown seemed stubbornly fixed on Amanda's face, however, as she stood up and moved to the table. As Jack took her hand and helped her to her seat, scooted her chair in, and walked around to his own seat on the opposite side of the small square table, her air of preoccupation remained. If she was having suspicions, she might try to catch him in another error. But why would she suspect him of faking amnesia? Even Jack was amazed at himself for the ruse he was practicing just to stay close to a woman he barely knew.

Julian would think he was crazy. And maybe he was. . . . Jack's older brother was never far from his thoughts, which could possibly account for nearly mentioning him just now. Jack knew Julian, and he knew he was out looking for him at that very instant. Julian was beastly clever, too, and Jack was well aware that time was limited before his brother tracked him down. All the more reason to avoid the hub of Chichester and any place very public.

Mr. Tebbs and two female servants entered the room and began placing numerous covered dishes on the pristine white tablecloth, and Jack and Amanda sat, silent and polite. Jack could only guess at Amanda's thoughts, but his thoughts had progressed from his brother to Charlotte Batsford, his fiancée.

Actually, he'd been thinking a great deal of Charlotte all afternoon. He was sure she'd been distraught to discover that her groom had disappeared on the very night before their wedding! She was an affectionate girl, and he truly believed she cared for him ... not very passionately, of course, but enough to be sorry if he'd fallen into a deadly scrape of some kind. He'd certainly feel the same sort of compassion and concern for her.

Lady Batsford, of course, would be in the boughs, stewing and wailing and fretting and swooning, with a vinaigrette under her nose and a handkerchief soaked in lavender water to bathe her brow. The brunt of the embarrassment attached to the aborted wedding would be felt by Charlotte's shallow and ambitious mother, rather than Charlotte herself.

Of course, Jack had every intention of returning to London as soon as he'd made sure Amanda was safely back in Edenbridge. Then he would make amends with Charlotte, explain his absence due to amnesia, stoically endure the wedding, and make everyone happy. . . .

Everyone, that is, except himself. If there was one thing Jack had learned by butting heads with a rock, it was that he was not ready to get married. If he weren't already bound by honor to marry Charlotte, Jack would happily wait till he was in his dotage to tie the nuptial knot and have children. And even if he didn't come through with a spare heir in the event that Julian didn't marry, it was really his older brother's duty to perpetuate the Montgomery line, not his.

When Mr. Tebbs and his helpers had bowed themselves out of the room, Jack shook off his heavy thoughts and lifted his goblet of wine as if he were about to propose a toast. "Miss Darlington?"

"Yes?" said the lady, looking up from the process of arranging her napkin over her skirts.

"I have a proposition." He smiled roguishly. "Are you interested?"

Amanda's eyes widened. "I suppose that depends on what you ... er ... *propose*, John."

He lowered his glass and leaned forward. "I propose that you and I have a delightful dinner."

"That is a reasonable hope—" she began, gesturing toward all the covered dishes.

"I don't mean let's simply enjoy our food, Miss Darlington," Jack scoffed with a grin. "I mean, let's forget all our troubles for tonight and concentrate on simply enjoying ourselves. You seem quite burdened down with serious thoughts, m'dear, and that just won't do!"

Amanda blushed and fidgeted with her cutlery, fussily lining up the forks with the spoons and knives. "I will admit I have been thinking of Charity since the storm, but don't imagine, sir, that I'm overly beset with worries. I have nothing to worry about!"

Brave girl, thought Jack. *Nothing to worry about, indeed! Nothing but an illegitimate child to collect and a hostile society to face down once you return to Edenbridge.*

But he kept his thoughts to himself and said, instead, "That's what I mean, Miss Darlington. You're very tense and depressed about Charity, and since I will probably regain my memory any day ... any moment ... I propose we enjoy tonight as if it were our last night together. I know I've been a royal pain in the ... er ... neck since we nearly collided on the road three nights ago, but I'm eternally grateful to you for nursing me back to health and have actually quite enjoyed your company in the interim. I hope you have sometimes found *me* amusing, Miss Darlington?" he finished, lifting his brows hopefully.

"Yes, you are sometimes *quite* amusing, John," she admitted with a faint smile. He thought he noticed a slight easing of her shoulders as she smiled, a less rigid way of sitting. That was good.

Encouraged, he grinned and raised his glass again.

"Then I propose that for tonight you and I forget about any troubles we might have ... past, present, or future. I propose we forget that there's another world outside this pleasant room"—he made a sweeping gesture—"or that there's another day coming to vex us in a few hours. Let's forget what everyone expects of us, or who everyone thinks we should be. Let's quite simply forget for a few precious hours, Miss Darlington ... *who we are.*"

Amanda smiled, shook her head ruefully, and lifted her own nonalcoholic drink ... milk. "All of which is quite easy for you to do, John. You *don't* know who you are. Or have you forgotten you have amnesia?"

Jack put his finger to his chin in a playful pose, saying, "I have amnesia? Dashed if it didn't slip my mind!"

They both laughed and touched glasses, the cheerful chink of crystal sounding through the room. Amanda took a sip of milk, and Jack watched her appreciatively. She looked lovely tonight. That colorful shawl added warmth and a glow to Amanda's delicate complexion. And her hair ... she'd arranged it differently. It was softer, more feminine and flattering.

And perhaps most telling of all, the top two buttons of her gown were undone. Amanda Darlington's prodigious use of buttons to secure her garments had become a symbol of chastity to Jack ... and possibly a figurative safeguard against temptation for her as well. After all, she *had* given in to temptation once and was perhaps frightened to do so again. So what exactly did the two undone buttons mean? Maybe it was best he didn't know.

"What do you say, Miss Darlington? Will you agree to forget who you are for a few hours?"

Amanda felt as though she'd been knocked on the noggin with a wand wielded by a well-meaning but misguided fairy godmother. Of course she wanted to forget who she was for a few hours. She'd been wishing as much all day. But was it wise?

"Don't think about it. Just make your decision and dive right in, m'dear," John advised.

"But you once advised me not to be too impulsive, sir," she reminded him.

"So I did," he began with mock seriousness, but then the expression in his eyes became sincerely sober. "But what if I promise to be the gentleman, no matter how giddy and impulsive you become? If you're worried that I'll compromise you, m'dear, I'll pledge my honor that that won't happen."

Amanda had very mixed feelings about John pledging his honor. Part of the charm of forgetting who she was was the excitement and danger naturally attached to such a daring idea.

"Very well," Amanda suddenly agreed with a happy smile. "For tonight I'm not myself."

"Bravo!" John lauded her with a friendly wink as he uncovered the first of the dishes. "Now, how shall you begin this experiment, Miss Darlington? I say . . . do you like peas?"

"No, I don't," Amanda declared roundly. "I've *never* liked peas, but I've always eaten them because Mr. Grenville, our apothecary, says they're very good for me. Miss Amanda Jane Darlington is always very attentive to her doctor's instructions, but since I've quite forgotten I *am* Miss Amanda Jane Darlington, or what that lady usually does when faced with a bowl of those green mushy things, I refuse to eat a single pea!"

"Very wise. Very wise, indeed," said John. He leaned forward, his face alight with mischief. "This is a very promising beginning. I like peas, you know, but I don't like them half as well as I like custard with caramel sauce. And I've asked Mr. Tebbs to prepare a large dish of the stuff." He gave her a significant look.

Amanda caught on and very obligingly helped John along to his desired end. "But aren't you sometimes a little too full at the end of a meal to enjoy your custard with caramel sauce?"

"Yes, sometimes I am," John admitted with an exaggerated sigh.

"Then perhaps you should have it as your first course!" Amanda said with the air of one having just conceived a brilliant idea.

"You're not suggesting that I eat my dessert *first*, are you?" said John in a horrified voice.

Amanda shrugged. "I wouldn't usually make such a shocking suggestion, but since I'm not myself tonight, I highly recommend that you eat your fill of custard before you even consider taking the merest nibble of a pea."

John immediately summoned the landlord by ringing a bell placed handily at his elbow and informed him when he appeared that dinner was to be served in reverse. Mr. Tebbs was initially surprised and perplexed, but John assured him that they'd just taken a notion to do things backward for once, and would he be a Trojan and put up with their nonsense for the evening?

Mr. Tebbs was an amiable man and not unfamiliar with the sometimes strange fetishes of the aristocracy. Lord and Lady Thornfield, though friendly and not too toplofty, were obviously of the aristocracy and, therefore, entitled to fetishes. He shrugged and agreed to the strange request without further ado.

As Amanda and John luxuriated in the creamy sweetness of custard with caramel sauce, Amanda leaned across the table and said, "You know you're probably going to have a devilish case of indigestion on the morrow."

John rolled the custard around on his tongue, his

eyes closed in dreamy pleasure, before answering. "You forget, m'dear. We agreed that we would behave as though there *is* no tomorrow. If tomorrow doesn't exist, I have nothing to fear from a sour stomach."

"You're so right," she said with a decided nod.

John grinned and Amanda giggled, truly amazed to find herself involved in such a silly game. But for all its silliness, the game was just what she needed at the moment. She wanted to forget about tomorrow, not just for the sake of her stomach but because tomorrow the authorities would arrive and take John down to the office to question him, then employ bureaucratic interference in helping him regain his identity. He'd be furious, of course, but it was for his own good. And *her* own good, too.

Amanda thrust away these intrusive thoughts. By thinking so seriously, she was disobeying the rules of the game. She smiled at John as they next tackled the roast leg of lamb.

"What are you thinking now, m'dear?" John asked her, carving away.

Amanda pinched a crispy piece of meat off the plate and put it in her mouth. "I was wondering, John," she said, as she licked her fingers in a most unladylike manner, "do you know how to waltz?"

John concentrated, then announced, "I don't know, but I daresay if we had a go at it, I'd remember enough to get by."

This was good enough for Amanda, who had never waltzed before in her life and was thinking that dancing with John would be a perfect after-dinner activity ... and a blissful experience to store away with her other memories.

They continued the meal with an air of festive abandon, savoring the food and the conversation. It was a strange, lopsided conversation, however, since John's amnesia limited a great many topics and sources that he ordinarily could have drawn upon for something to say. As a result, Amanda was drawn out to talk about herself. She found herself telling him all about her aunts and their endearing eccentricities and fervid charity work, her large farm at Edenbridge, her love of reading and painting, and even her disastrous season in London.

She was relating a story about a clumsy partner at Almacks who stepped on her demi-train and apologized at least eighteen times before she implored him to stop, and then swung her during a country dance smack into a potted palm.

John laughed till mirthful tears leaked from his eyes. Amanda laughed, too. "At the time, I didn't think the incident so amusing," she confessed, gasping and holding her side. "But in retrospect I suppose it does seem rather ridiculous!"

"Time and distance give us perspective," said John, smiling and wiping his damp cheeks with the back of his hand. "And you do have a knack for telling stories, Miss Darlington. I find it hard to believe that you weren't an instant success in London."

"I told you I was reserved and shy," she reminded him.

He waggled a brow. "But you're not shy with me."

She poked out her chin in a charming pose of rebellion and said, "And I've resolved never to be shy again!"

"I gather your parents were reserved?"

Jack had noticed that when Amanda told about herself, her home, and her family, she omitted any comments about her parents. Resentment toward them for denying her the right to keep her illegitimate child could account for this, of course, but he found himself curious to know more about Amanda's upbringing. He wished, too, that she'd confide in him about the real reason for going to Thorney Island. It would make it a lot easier to include himself in the final journey and reunion if Amanda trusted him.

"My parents would never eat dessert first," said Amanda, absently poking at the cold potatoes on her plate, "even if their lives depended on it." She looked up at Jack with a wan smile. "And they always ate their peas ... every single one." She sighed. "That about sums them up."

"In other words, they were no fun and have no business being discussed on such a jolly occasion," Jack said, sorry he'd allowed his curiosity to put a damper on Amanda's happy mood and eager to get things back to a proper footing. He stood up and bowed gallantly. "Did I hear you mention something about waltzing, Miss Darlington?"

To Jack's delight, Amanda's face immediately lit up. "Yes," she said eagerly, clasping her hands together like an excited child. "But there's no music, John. Do you think it would be utterly ridiculous of us to dance without music?"

"I have a vague recollection of the ability to carry a tune, Miss Darlington," he informed her gravely as he extended his hand for hers. "I'll hum."

Amanda laughed, took Jack's proffered hand, and stood up.

"Maybe you should take off your shawl," he suggested. "It is quite lovely, but waltzing is an energetic activity and might make you feel rather warm."

Amanda readily complied with this suggestion, folding the shawl over the back of her chair. Jack considered telling her to undo a couple more of the buttons that marched up her throat, but decided he'd be pressing his luck.

The parlor was small, so Jack pushed the dining table and other pieces of light furniture against the walls to make room for dancing. The resulting racket drew the attention of Mr. Tebbs, who entered the room, blinked once or twice in surprise, shrugged, then obligingly cleared the table of the dirty dishes before bowing himself out with a smile and the assurance that he'd "leave you two newlyweds alone."

Jack pretended not to notice Amanda's resulting blush but moved to the center of the room, held out his arms in a wide arc, and said with a commanding air and a huge smile, "Come here, Lady Thornfield, and dance with your husband."

She hesitated for a second, like a timid child standing at the entrance doors to Astley's Royal Circus but afraid to go in. He watched her come, her hands pressed against her diaphragm as if she were willing herself to breathe, her eyes alight, her cheeks flushed, and her lips smiling. Even the black dress showed her to advantage tonight, countering her pale porcelain beauty and accentuating the smallness of her waist and the firm shape of her breasts.

He gritted his teeth even as he smiled, telling himself he must remember not to embrace her and kiss her when she got near enough but simply assume the usual position for waltzing—one hand at her waist and the other lightly holding her hand aloft—and behave as he promised he would . . . like a gentleman.

As she walked into John's outstretched arms, Amanda felt as though she were entering the pearly gates of heaven. He chastely curved his long fingers around her waist, took her other hand in his, and extended it in the usual position for the waltz, but if he'd been bolder, if he'd taken liberties, she'd have been helplessly in his power. Thank goodness he had pledged his honor.

"Just follow my lead, Miss Darlington," said John in what Amanda thought was a strangely husky voice. Then he began to hum, and they began to move.

He had a wonderful, deep melodic voice. Its resonance thrummed in Amanda's blood, stirring it up.

She glanced shyly up and saw the strong curve of his jaw. If she stood on tiptoe, she could kiss him there, if she dared. . . .

"Who composed this tune, I wonder?" she asked, seeking safety in conversation. His light hand at her waist seemed to burn right through her garments to set her skin on fire.

"I don't know," he replied. "I'm sure it's something I've danced to."

"I'm sure it is," she agreed, feeling jealous of all the other women he'd held in his arms like this ... and in other ways, too.

"I suppose your parents didn't allow you to waltz?" said John.

"The *Lady's Magazine* had an article in it cautioning all young women to beware the dangers of waltzing. It was their scholarly opinion that human nature is so depraved that even men of great purity cannot be trusted in such close proximity to the female sex. My mother agreed with their opinion."

John leaned back to look down at her. "Your mother was wrong. Here we are, dancing quite closely together, and I'm behaving very properly. Wouldn't you say so, Miss Darlington?"

Amanda had no trouble recognizing that John's smile was strained. Was he as attracted to her as she was to him? Did he want to kiss her as much as she wanted him to?

"Yes," she assured him in a rather strangled voice. "You are behaving *very* properly." Then she snuggled her head against his chest, and his arms tightened around her.

Amanda could feel and hear John's heart; it was beating as hard and fast as hers. They glided slowly, sinuously about the room. John's hum became more and more faint till it finally ceased altogether. Then by degrees the dancing stopped, too, so that they were simply standing in the center of the room, holding each other, swaying ever so slightly to some imagined tune.

The only sound in the room was the soft patter of rain against the window glass and the snap and crackle of the fire. Dazed, warmed, aroused, exhilarated, Amanda looked up and John looked down. Their lips were inches apart.

In that moment, Amanda made a decision. She wanted to take the game as far as it could possibly go. She wanted to believe with all her heart that tomorrow wouldn't come, or if it did, that it wouldn't matter anyway. She'd have memories, lovely memories of tonight to keep her warm through the rest of her life.

She wanted John to make love to her.

Chapter 12

"I said I'd never invite you to kiss me again, but . . ."

Amanda's sweet breath fanned over Jack's mouth, making his lips tingle and pulse with anticipation. "I want to kiss you, Amanda, more than you'll ever know," he rasped. "But I pledged my honor."

"I release you of that pledge."

He groaned. "You don't know what you're saying."

"What makes you think that? I haven't been drinking wine or anything stronger than apple cider and milk." She smiled and her lips trembled. "At least I can vouch for *my* clear-headedness."

"Well, I can't vouch for mine," Jack said roughly. "You're driving me crazy. I can't think straight! I promised not to compromise you, and you're tempting me beyond endurance, Amanda. I can't—" He broke off. He was about to say he couldn't remember ever wanting a woman as much as he wanted her, but it would be a mistake to allude to memories. He didn't want to excite her suspicions.

"You can't what?"

"If I kiss you, I can't promise that I'll be able to stop."

"I don't want you to stop." Her voice was a mere whisper. "I want you to make love to me."

Jack's knees were weak with desire. He wanted to lower her to the floor then and there and take her. He shook his head, straightened his spine . . . and his resolve. "You don't even know me. You don't know anything about me."

Amanda's hands on his back began to move in a luxurious caress. "I know everything I need to know about you. You're tender and kind and funny. I love the way you touch me, and I love touching you."

Her magic hands wended their way up to the nape of his neck, her fingers threading into the thick hair that spilled over his collar. He fought the urge to close his eyes and concentrate on the lush sensations she was stirring in him. "John, you said this could be the last night we spend together. I want to remember it always."

Jack clenched his jaw. "Amanda, you say you're destined to be a spinster. I don't believe that. Someday you'll fall in love. Someday you'll marry, and you'll wish this night had never happened."

"I don't believe that. I'll never regret the kind of bliss I felt in your arms today behind the church, and how alive I feel tonight in your arms."

"But you *will*."

She placed a finger on his lips, silencing him. "I'll never regret it, no matter what happens. Make love to me, John."

Jack was torn between consuming desire and his screaming conscience. His body ached and throbbed with wanting her. He reasoned that she was a grown woman in full possession of her senses and completely in command of her actions. She seemed to know what she wanted, and she apparently wanted *him*. He had done nothing to persuade her or seduce her or trick her into submission. And she wasn't a virgin, so it wouldn't be like despoiling an innocent. . . .

Jack was a little ashamed of that last rationalization. He didn't know how her child had been conceived. She might not have been as willing then as she was now.

Jack's conscience made a last-ditch effort to be heard. It was reasonable to assume that she was willing and experienced, but Amanda still seemed so . . . well . . . vulnerable. And he wasn't being honest with her. He'd got his memory back hours ago, and he'd kept that fact to himself. He was keeping it to himself so that he could travel with her and protect her, but was that a good enough reason to lie and deceive . . . particularly in light of the fact that they might be indulging in the most intimate of activities?

"Kiss me, John."

Jack was in a turmoil of thoughts and feelings. But he wanted to stop thinking and worrying and reasoning and just give in to sweet seduction. He wanted to kiss Amanda Jane Darlington more than he wanted his next breath. He wanted her with every particle of his being. He admired her, respected her, and cared about her, so why . . . he reasoned desperately . . . *why* shouldn't he kiss her?

It seemed to take a millennium to convince him, but when John finally lowered his head and touched his lips to hers, Amanda flushed hot with pleasure from head to toe.

As before, the kiss began with tender restraint, but the passion that exploded between them could not be held in check. John's arms tightened, and he pulled Amanda hard against him, his palm pressed against the small of her back and his tongue coming fully into her mouth. The whole length of him was against her, and through the many layers of clothes—hers and his—Amanda could feel his arousal outlined against her stomach.

On a gasp of dizzying pleasure, her mouth opened to his and her arms wrapped eagerly around his neck. His chest and shoulders felt firm and smooth under her hands, his legs long and hard with muscle as they pressed against her own. She imagined his weight on her, around her, *inside her*, and she became weak with longing.

He kissed her throat, her neck, then found her mouth again . . . and again. Suddenly he pulled away and held her at arm's length. His look was intense and fiery.

"I have to tell you something, Amanda, and I want you to listen very carefully."

"Yes, John?" she quavered, sapped of strength and hardly able to stand on her own.

"I mean every word I'm about to say."

"Yes, John. I'm . . . I'm listening."

"If we make love tonight, I'll not be able to promise you anything in return. Do you understand, Amanda?"

She nodded.

He shook her a little and said, "Are you sure?" His voice was steeped with anguish. "Because despite our little game tonight, I *do* have a life out there beyond this room. A life that I may have to face tomorrow, or if not tomorrow, very soon. Sooner than I'd like," he added gruffly. "Then I'll be gone and all you'll have left—"

"Are my memories," she said with a smile, a smile so tender and wise and sure, Jack was ready to throw up his hands in defeat. But what sweet defeat . . .

"I'm going upstairs now," he continued, running a shaking hand through his hair. "I'm going to my room. I'm giving you the chance to clear your head and change your mind, Amanda. Take all the time you need. But if . . . if you still want me, I'll be waiting. And if you decide not to come to my room, when I see you tomorrow I won't speak a word of what passed between us tonight. Agreed?"

Amanda nodded again and caught hold of a nearby chair to steady herself as John finally, reluctantly let go of her. With one last yearning and turbulent look, he left the room.

Jack was lying on the bed dressed only in his shirt and breeches. An hour had passed, and he was both relieved and disappointed that his delaying tactic had worked and made Amanda think better of sleeping with him.

She was still up. He could tell by the light that peeped from under the door that connected their chambers. What was she doing? he wondered. What was she thinking? Wearing? He imagined her in her nightdress, her hair loose and flowing.

Then, suddenly, he no longer needed to imagine. The door opened, and Amanda stepped into his room.

It was the first time he'd seen her in something other than black. He propped up on his elbows and stared. He couldn't help himself; he was utterly enraptured. She was an angel.

The loose neck of her white gown hung to the side, nearly baring one round, silky-looking shoulder. Her hair was longer than he remembered, the pale blond waves reaching to below her waist. Her eyes were huge and luminous and liquid blue in the candlelight. In their depths he saw desire warring with a natural and appealing shyness.

He sat up and swung his legs over the side of the bed. "You came," he said, unable to keep the wonder and the husky edge of arousal out of his voice.

"There was never any question in *my* mind," she informed him with an alluring smile that seemed at variance with her celestial appearance.

"As long as you're sure, Amanda," he said, still

demanding a guarantee from her that she knew exactly what she was doing.

"I've never been more sure of anything in my life," she told him, lifting her chin in that adorable way she had. She took another step into the room and closed the door behind her.

Spellbound by her lovely face and the eloquent expression in her eyes when she'd first entered the room, Jack's gaze had not strayed below her shoulders. But it did now. Her nightdress was made of a thin lawn material that was rendered practically transparent by the candlelight. The outline of her firm, uncorsetted breasts and the tight knot of her rosy nipples sent a shock of almost painful awareness through his bloodstream.

"You know I've never done this before," she said, taking a step closer, her hands clasped at waist level. "I've never come to a man like this and asked him to . . . to love me."

Jack searched her face. He saw the tension in her delicate features, the uncertainty in her eyes. He believed she was telling the truth, which made him wonder all the more about the relationship she'd had with the father of her child. He had a wrenching feeling inside that it hadn't been a happy liaison, and then a most unreasonable urge to throttle the man who had made love to her first . . . *before* Jack.

Jack cast aside such ridiculous, possessive ideas and swore that even though he had only one night with her, he'd make it a night she'd remember forever.

"Come here, Amanda," he murmured. She came and snuggled against his chest, tucking her head under his chin. He wrapped her in his warmth and simply held her, tenderness for the moment overriding passion.

But not for long. She felt too good in his arms. Her firm, rounded figure hinted at tantalizing curves to be explored. He wanted to pleasure her, love her, release her from every care and restraint that had been thrust upon her in the three-and-twenty years she'd spent on earth.

He put his hands on her waist, set her back from him a few inches, then held her gaze. Without breaking eye contact, he skimmed his hands up her sides to cradle her breasts through her flimsy nightdress. He rolled the tender tips of her breasts between his fingers and watched her eyes widen then droop with pleasure. He saw gooseflesh erupt on her arms, and her shoulders gave a tiny shiver.

"John," she whispered hoarsely, and Jack frowned. He wouldn't even hear his own name on her lips! In the throes of passion, she'd cry out the name she'd given him ... not *his* name!

"John? What's the matter?"

Jack schooled his face to hide his disappointment, then told himself he'd let Amanda call him any name in the book just for the thrill of loving her. With this thought in mind, his smile came back naturally.

"Nothing, love," he assured her, cupping her shoulders and pulling her to him. "Come here. I just can't get enough of you."

He bent his head and kissed her, claiming her mouth with full and heated intent. His tongue dipped and delved, teased and tantalized. He ravished her mouth, tugging, nipping, licking. When he finally pulled back, his breath was a rasp. Amanda had no breath, no sense of reality beyond the moment. There was no tomorrow, no other place on earth but the Angel Inn, no one who mattered but ... John. *John.*

He nuzzled her neck, kissed the lobe of her ear, and tongued the hollow gently, fleetingly. Then he reached behind her, caught her buttocks in his hands, and pulled her against his aching loins to rub his erection against her.

A furnace of desire fired through Amanda's belly. John's touch was like nothing she'd ever known or even imagined. It was unearthly, almost indecent to feel so drenched with pleasure. Her bones were melting. Her heart was beating out of her chest. And he was far from through, the night far from over. . . .

"Darling, I want you out of this," he said, rubbing Amanda's shoulders, his eyes dark with impatient desire as he searched the gown for buttons to undo or ribbons to untie.

Amanda blanched at the idea of standing completely naked in front of John. She'd never been seen by anyone without some sort of clothing on. She even modestly averted her own eyes from the mirror when she rose from her bath.

"Maybe I should leave it on," she suggested timidly.

He raised that incorrigible brow of his, and a wicked gleam shone in his golden-brown eyes, but he only said, "All right. Leave it on if you want to. Maybe later you'll want to take it off. But, if it's all the same to you, darling, I'm going to take off every stitch of *my* clothes. Beastly restraining things! It's all right, isn't it? After all, you've already seen *me* as bare as a newborn babe."

Amanda could only swallow and nod, then watch with guilty pleasure and wide-eyed fascination as John proceeded to disrobe. She had never imagined anything could be so erotic as watching a man take off his clothes. With not a scrap of modesty about him, John undid the buttons on his shirt with skillful efficiency. His strong brown dexterous fingers were almost as captivating to watch as the ever-growing expanse of broad chest appearing between the white hemmed edges of his shirt.

He tugged the tail of the shirt out of his trousers, slipped his arms free and tossed the shirt on a nearby chair. Then, with a sly grin, he went to work on the front placket of his trousers. She watched the ripple of lean muscles in his chest, his arms, his back, as he loosed one button after the other. Her eyes followed his hands again as he pulled the trousers down, then peeled them off in no time at all.

Certainly it was all done too quickly for Amanda to prepare herself for what she saw. She'd seen him naked before, but she hadn't expected the state of his arousal to have changed his anatomy to such magnificent proportions.

"Good lord, I've scared you, haven't I? Sorry, darling."

Amanda tore her gaze away from his manhood and looked dazedly into his eyes. His expression was chagrined, apologetic . . . proud?

"You're no more sorry than I am, John," Amanda accused him breathlessly and with a wry smile that twitched a little nervously at the corners.

Her saucy retort delighted him, and he picked her up and carried her to the bed. She laughed with alarm and joy as he plopped her into the middle of the feather bed and lay down beside her.

"Now, m'dear, I've got you just where I want you," he warned her with a teasing leer. "Surrender yourself to me, Miss Darlington, or . . . or . . ."

"Or what?" she demanded with a grin.

He sobered and smiled, then tenderly traced her cheek with his finger. "Or I'll quite simply expire on the spot. I want you, Amanda, more than you'll ever know."

"Then take me, John," she said with quiet ferocity. "Take me now."

Without further ado, he pressed her into the bedclothes, covering her face with kisses, thrilling her body with warm, skillful caresses. He shifted the wide opening of her nightdress till her breasts were exposed, then he caught each nipple in turn in the hot moistness of his mouth. He nibbled each pebble-hard tip, raking it with his teeth, sucking, swirling his tongue around the dusky, sensitive skin till icy-hot pleasure vibrated in every nerve of Amanda's body.

Then he eased up Amanda's nightdress to the edge of her bottom. Their legs were tangled, and John's erection was pressed against her stomach. The only thing between the slick, heated core of Amanda's womanhood and ultimate pleasure was the dratted nightdress she'd refused to take off ... wadded up in an uncomfortable ball!

"John," she said breathlessly, pushing at his shoulders. "I've changed my mind."

Amanda felt John go stiff in her arms. He braced his hands on either side of her head and looked down at her with disbelief in his eyes. "You've ... you've changed your mind ... *now*?" he rasped. "My God, Amanda. You're going to be the death of me."

As he rolled to the side and expelled a long-suffering sigh, Amanda realized that he'd misunderstood her. She grabbed his shoulders and choked out in a voice that was half-panicked, half-amused, "No, John. I don't mean I've changed my mind about making love!"

He stopped, confusion clearly written on his face. "Then what, love?"

She felt her face flame with color. "My ... my nightgown. I ... I want it ... *off*."

It was extremely gratifying watching John's expression change from pained resignation to one of joyful relief and building excitement. He broke out in a delighted smile that quickly turned sly and sensual. "Well, my dear, that can be done in a trice."

But he didn't do it in a trice. He kissed the gown off her inch by delicious, shivery inch. By the time she lay naked beneath him, she had lost all sense of anything beyond the circle of John's arms. She was in a stupor of consuming pleasure, but with a sharp edge of need and anticipation that could only be assuaged by their ultimate joining.

Amanda knew there was no turning back now, no changing her mind about anything. She was powerless to deny her need. She would take what he offered and keep it close to her heart for the rest of her life. She would cherish this night forever.

Jack tried to go slow. He tried to be gentle. He wanted to be sure he'd urged Amanda to the limits of sensual pleasure before entering her. But as she lay beneath him, so tempting, so beautiful, he knew he couldn't wait another second. He needed to possess her, to make her his . . . even if it was only for one night out of a lifetime.

He lifted and entered the hot, weeping center of her slowly, sinuously, pacing himself so that the first jolt of pleasure wouldn't send him reeling over the edge. But as his hard, aching flesh invaded her moist heat, his eyes opened in surprise, and he searched Amanda's flushed face. There was a natural resistance . . . a barrier. She was a virgin!

In that moment of revelation, every conclusion Jack had come to about Miss Amanda Jane Darlington bit the dust! He stilled in her arms, alarm, guilt, desire, and desperation racking his mind and body. He'd been wrong about her having an illegitimate child. He'd been dead wrong about that . . . and about how many other things?

This woman with whom he was sharing the most intimate, the most beautiful of human communications, was still a mystery.

She opened her eyes, staring at him through dusky lashes. Her need, her desire was startling. His own need still commanded his body. His desire for her surged through his bloodstream like a raging tempest.

"John . . . now," she whispered. "Please."

Who could resist such a plea? Not Jack. Her tight,

sweet womanliness was wrapped around him, and
it was as though he no longer controlled his destiny
for the next few minutes or hours. He would consider the consequences later. Much later.

"Darling," he whispered, stroking her face, her
hair. "It's going to hurt a little at first."

She nodded solemnly. "I know."

"I'll try to be gentle," he promised, then bent his
head to claim her mouth in a kiss, and with one
quick thrust took her virginity. She tensed and made
a small moaning sound, but he caressed her and
kissed her till he felt her body relax beneath him
again.

"Are you all right, Amanda?"

Amanda bit her lip and nodded. "Yes. The pain is
gone." And it was. It had only been fleeting, anyway,
and was little enough to pay for the bliss of being in
John's arms. But when she'd thought she'd reached
the heights of pleasure and could go no higher, John
began to move. A new urgency blossomed within
her.

The feel of him inside her was like nothing she'd
ever dreamed possible. The tender flesh of her woman's core was pulsing with sensation. But she felt
more than euphoric physical enjoyment. . . . He was
filling her. Filling the emptiness of her life with a
tender passion she'd never forget. She felt joy ex-
panding her chest like sweet, fresh air on a spring
morning. She was exhilarated, enraptured. She was
in love. . . .

Dear God, she *loved* him!

Amanda wrapped John in her legs, holding on for
dear life as she began to soar on their shared desires.
John plunged deeper, setting a rhythm Amanda
matched with an abandoned enthusiasm.

Then, suddenly, she felt a curious floating sensation,
followed by a blinding flash. Amanda clutched John to
her breasts and cried out his name as ripple after ripple

of dizzying pleasure claimed her. John arched and found his own release, calling her name, too.

With both hearts beating as if they were one, he held her till their breathing slowed, till their scattered, shattered senses were recalled to the here and now. Then John lifted his head, kissing her neck and face as he gently withdrew and slid to the bed beside her. He pulled her against his chest and wrapped his arm around her shoulder.

Amanda caught his hand and brought it to her lips, brushing a kiss across the warm skin. She kept her eyes shut, afraid to open them, willing time to freeze at this one moment of complete repletion and happiness. But already the seconds were ticking away, bringing tomorrow and hard, cold reality.

Tomorrow. Tomorrow she would wonder if this all had been a dream. Tomorrow John might remember his name ... and forget hers. Tomorrow they would come and take him away.

She moved in his embrace, thinking it best to initiate the separation early. She'd go to her own bed, forfeit the pleasure of feeling his hard, warm body against hers as he slept ... and lie awake, thinking about him, loving him. But John foiled her plans with a few words.

"Don't go, Amanda. Stay, sweetheart."

Amanda opened her eyes as John shifted, turning her to face him. His eyes were deepest brown, the expression warm and loving. "The night's not over yet," he told her with a lazy, boyish grin. "Give me just a few minutes, and I'll make love to you again."

How could Amanda resist? Tomorrow belonged to reality, but this one bright, beautiful night was theirs.

Jack made love to her again.

And again.

In the morning, Jack awoke to a room filled with light, an empty bed, and a guilty conscience. Last night had been an earthly slice of heaven at the Angel Inn, and Jack would never forget it. But had he been right to take the ecstasy Amanda offered him so willingly?

He had thought she was experienced, but she was a virgin. Never mind that he hadn't found that out till he'd already compromised her beyond repair; the fact that she'd been an innocent maid before their lovemaking made all the difference in the world. At least after the first time they'd made love, he'd taken precautions against pregnancy. He knew he should have thought of that sooner. But odds were, one unprotected sexual act would not result in a pregnancy.

What was her state of mind this morning? he wondered. Did she regret their lovemaking? He'd told her beforehand that he could offer her nothing in return, and she'd seemed to readily accept that fact, but Jack's sense of honor was nagging at him like a fishwife. However, since he was already engaged to one woman—Charlotte—he wasn't free to do the honorable thing by the other women—Amanda— even if he wanted to.

Did he want to? Jack wasn't sure what he wanted. He knew he had some rather extraordinary feelings for Amanda, but since he had only made her acquaintance three days ago, it would be idiotic to imagine himself in love with her.

Wouldn't it?

Jack sat up, grimly amused by the tangled bedclothes. They hadn't slept much. He'd been astounded by his stamina last night and the instant recurrence of arousal each time after they'd made love. And Amanda had returned his ardor with equal feeling. They'd both felt an urgency to make good use of the limited time they had together. It was as if they were on a one-night honeymoon.

Jack sobered still more, wondering if he'd feel the same intensity of passion for Charlotte Batsford when

he made her his bride and began his real honeymoon. He sighed, doubting it very much. He'd never
felt so much passion for anyone as he had for
Amanda last night, and he'd had more than his fair
share of experience with voluptuous, skillful
ladybirds.

But he knew it wasn't Amanda's skill that made
her so irresistible. Her passionate responses were innocent and instinctual, not learned. She was open
and unguarded and eager. She made his heart soar
with emotion when he made love to her. She made
him feel as though the sexual act they shared was
more than physical . . . that it was spiritual, too.

Jack shook his head ruefully, swung his legs over
the side of the bed, and stood up. He needed to
splash some cold water on his face before he'd talked
himself into believing he was in love with Amanda
Jane Darlington. That wouldn't do. It wouldn't do
because he couldn't do anything about it even if he
were in love with her.

Jack washed up, shaved, got dressed, then knocked
on the door between their rooms. When Amanda
didn't answer, he pulled his watch from a waistcoat
pocket and checked the time. It was barely seven, so
he was surprised that she'd left her room so early to
take breakfast. And why hadn't she awakened him?

Jack frowned, unwelcome suspicions grabbing at
him from all sides. She wouldn't go on to Thorney
Island without him, would she? She wouldn't simply
leave him behind . . . would she? But how could he
possibly anticipate what Amanda would do? He'd
made love to her, but he still didn't know her.

With his jaw set grimly, Jack opened the door and
went into her chamber. Just as he feared, not a single
personal article belonging to Amanda was left in the
room. The wardrobe was empty, the dresser top was
bare of brushes and hairpins. Amanda was gone.

Seething with anger, Jack strode to the door and

yanked it open. He took the narrow stairs two at a time, but when he gained the entrance hall, he wasn't sure what to do, where to go. He heard Mr. Tebbs talking to someone in the parlor he and Amanda had used the night before, and he barged through the half-open door with a vengeance.

He was stopped in his tracks, feeling foolish and embarrassed, when he found Amanda sitting at the table, quietly attending to her breakfast. Both she and Mr. Tebbs, who was serving her from a platter of ham, turned and looked at Jack with surprise on their faces at his abrupt entrance. He'd no doubt the fierce expression on his face was rather startling, too.

"My lord!" said Mr. Tebbs, recovering first and pasting a pleasant, obsequious look on his face. "Er . . . didn't you sleep well last night, my lord?"

Jack collected his composure and subdued his unwarranted anger. Amanda hadn't left him at all. It made him feel decidedly sheepish now to realize how upset he'd become at the very idea of her leaving him behind. And he wasn't sure exactly *why*. . . .

There were a number of reasons, of course, why he wanted to continue on with her to Thorney Island, but he had a gut feeling his pained and desperate emotions at the very idea of her unannounced departure right after they'd spent the night making passionate love had their source in a more personal explanation. But he'd no time to analyze his half-crazed reaction and summoned all his sangfroid to try for a more dignified entrance.

Jack gave his shirt cuffs a tug, lifted his chin, and endeavored to look nonchalant. Whenever he wanted to look very debonair and toplofty, he recalled Julian's imperious manner and copied that. The result was never as daunting as his brother's patrician mien, but it had helped him through some tight spots before.

"I slept exceedingly well, thank you," Jack in-

formed Mr. Tebbs with a brilliant show of aristocratic teeth.

Mr. Tebbs was reassured, chalking up his lordship's initial look of extreme displeasure as morning
ruminations on a pesky estate matter or some other
quandary exclusive to the landed gentry. He pulled
out Jack's chair and bustled about, filling his plate
with all sorts of savory-smelling breakfast courses.
Mr. Tebbs was finally satisfied that his lordship
would not swoon from hunger, and he bowed himself out, finally leaving Jack alone with Amanda.

That lady was self-consciously cracking a boiled
egg with her spoon when she apparently felt Jack's
eyes upon her and looked up, a becoming glow on
her cheeks and in her eyes.

"You look beautiful this morning, Amanda."

She blushed. "Thank you."

Jack stared at her for another lingering moment,
tamping down a strong urge to leap to his feet, whisk
the food and plateware off the table, and initiate Miss
Darlington to the delights of morning sex. Instead,
he snapped open his napkin and said, "You left the
bed too soon, m'dear."

She blushed even deeper. "We've a busy day
ahead, John," was her only reply, said in her usual
prim way.

"Yes. On to Thorney Island." He chuckled. "Do
you know that when I got up and found you missing
and your belongings all packed up and gone from
your room, I thought you'd deserted me! I should
have known you'd never do anything so shabby."

She gave him a quick, startled look and dropped
her egg on the floor.

"Never mind," said Jack, dismissing the accident
but wondering why Amanda seemed so nervous. He
could only suppose she was feeling some natural
awkwardness after last night. And some regret,

maybe? "Mr. Sweeney gave me four eggs. I'll never eat so many. You can have one of mine."

"But it's such a mess," she said in a distraught tone, staring down at the soft yolk making a yellow puddle on the carpet.

"But it's nothing to get all worked up about, m'dear," John reasoned soothingly. "Mr. Sweeney has dealt with worse messes, I'm sure." He rang the bell to summon someone to clean up the egg.

When she continued to stare at the floor, John got up and knelt down beside her chair with napkin in hand. "I'll dab it up; then the maids won't have much to do to finish the job. Don't fret, Amanda," he said cheerfully.

Jack cleaned up the egg as best he could. Then, while he was still on his knees, he looked up at Amanda and was surprised to see tears in her eyes. Jack felt a strong contraction in his chest. He lifted his hand, stroked her cheek, then cupped her chin. "What's the matter, Amanda?" he asked gently. "You're not crying over this silly egg, are you?"

"No," she said, the tears streaming over her bottom lashes and coursing down her cheeks. "I'm feeling wretched, John, because I *am* deserting you!"

Jack stiffened and frowned. "What do you mean?"

Suddenly the door opened, and two uniformed constables entered the room.

Amanda's eyes widened, and she covered her mouth with her hand. "Oh ... no. Not yet," she mumbled through her fingers. "He hasn't even eaten his breakfast!"

Chapter 13

Amanda couldn't bear the accusing way John was glaring at her. "I had no choice, John," she said with a beseeching look. "This is the best way to find out who you are."

"At any rate, it's probably the fastest way," John said grimly, as he stood up and threw his napkin on the table. "And since you're itching to be rid of me, I ought not to be so *very* surprised to see these gentlemen here this morning."

Amanda stood up, too. She felt weak and trembling inside, not just because John was angry and hurt because he considered her involvement of the police a betrayal, but because she didn't want him to go! Last night had been heavenly, and she could hardly bear the thought that she'd probably never see him again.

Amanda wrenched her gaze from John and addressed the older of the two constables, a man with a shock of black hair, a bulbous nose, and a walruslike mustache. "I did not suppose you'd come so very early. He's not even had his breakfast yet!"

"I was just told to come this mornin', miss," said the constable, exuding stalwart authority. "And it

206

seems the sooner this business is commenced, the better it'll be for all concerned."

Behind the constables, Amanda noticed Mr. Tebbs's anxious face looking in at the door and a couple of mobcapped maids.

"You aren't arresting me, are you?" John demanded to know.

"Not exactly, sir," the constable said after a considering pause.

John's brows lifted. "Then by what authority and to what purpose do you intend to take me into custody? I certainly haven't broken any laws."

The constable pointed to Amanda with his nightstick, making her feel even guiltier. "This here lady says that due to an accident, you've plum forgot who you are, sir. We can help you establish your identity."

"How Good Samaritan of you, to be sure," John said caustically. "But what if I don't need or want your help?" He stood straighter. "What if I refuse to willingly go with you?"

The younger constable, a thin youth with a spotted face, shifted from foot to foot and glanced nervously at his superior.

"Well," began the senior constable, "first I'd figure that there's something havey-cavey goin' on if you don't want to know who you are. I might conclude that you're playin' fast and loose with the law. Maybe you're a wanted man . . . a smuggler or a thief gone incognito."

John smiled contemptuously. "You have an active imagination. I can assure you I'm neither of those things."

The constable shrugged. "If you've got nothin' to hide, sir, by my reckoning there's no logical reason why you wouldn't want to know who you are."

"But I dislike your methods. Is there no other way to resolve this dilemma?"

"As the lady is no longer willing to take responsibility for you, sir, and if you refuse our assistance, there's only one alternative."

"And pray what is that?"

"The hospital asylum, sir, for the mentally deranged."

John laughed. "I'm not mad. I've simply lost my memory!"

Amanda began to wring her hands. She had not expected John to be so uncooperative, nor the police to be so stern and businesslike. And the very idea of John going to Bedlam or such was unthinkable! She'd take him to Thorney Island with her, and even Darlington Hall, before she'd let that happen.

"Come along quietly, sir, and we won't have to restrain you."

Amanda's eyes widened with horror as she noticed for the first time that the younger constable was holding a length of rope.

"Gentlemen!" she exclaimed. "Surely it won't be necessary to tie him up!" She turned to John. "Oh, do please go with them quietly, John! They mean you no harm and only wish to help you!"

John gave her a gently rebuking glance, then spoke again to the constable. "It should be perfectly obvious that I'm neither a criminal nor a madman. I've got plenty of blunt and have no more need of this lady's assistance than I have of yours."

He took out his purse and cradled it in one palm. The two constables exchanged glances.

"I can rack up in an inn and wait till my memory returns, if need be. So why don't you tell me, sirs, just what it will take to get you off my *arse*." John plopped the purse into his other palm with a jingle of coins and waited.

Amanda thought it looked very much as though John were attempting to bribe the two officers of the law. The keen expression in the senior constable's eyes was either avarice or righteous indignation. It turned out to be the latter.

"If you think you can bribe me, sir," he growled, "you're dead wrong. And if you don't want to be arrested for doin' just that, I think you'd better put away that plump purse of yours."

John hesitated, glowering belligerently, but finally put the purse away in his coat pocket. Amanda could actually see the tension ease out of the senior constable's broad shoulders a little. He didn't want trouble, either.

"In answer to your question, the only way to get us off your *arse*, sir, would be for you to tell us who you are. Can you do that, sir?"

Amanda got the distinct impression that even if he could tell them who he was—which, of course, he couldn't—John's hackles were up, and he'd withhold the information out of sheer spite and stubbornness. He set his jaw, lifted his chin, crossed his arms, and stood as silent and grim as a palace guard.

The constable sighed and nodded at his young helper. "Well, then, there's only one thing left to do—"

Amanda squeezed her eyes shut and braced herself for a wrestling match between John and the constables. But an unfamiliar voice came from the direction of the doorway to pierce the strained silence.

"I can tell you who this man is."

Amanda's eyes flew open. Standing head and shoulders above Mr. Tebbs was a man with the sculpted beauty and grace of a Greek statue. He was fair-skinned and blond with startling pale blue eyes that were fixed on John. As Mr. Tebbs and the maids stepped aside with open-mouthed awe so the stranger could enter the room, John steadfastly returned the man's gaze. But he did not portray any emotions. His face was completely expressionless.

The stranger walked past Mr. Tebbs and the gap-

ing maids, and past the stunned constables without
sparing any one of them a single glance. Once inside
the room, as he stood a little removed from them
all and continued to stare at John, Amanda stared
at him.

From his snowy-white cravat and stiff collar to his
pale blue waistcoat with white stripes, his Bishop's
blue cutaway coat, white pantaloons and tall black
boots, he epitomized cool, patrician elegance. She, as
well as all the others in the room, waited breathlessly
for him to speak. Finally he did.

"This gentleman, whom you seem so eager to truss
up like a chicken and cart away to your offices, is
Jackson Thadeus Montgomery, Viscount Durham . . .
my brother."

Amanda was shocked. She glanced back and forth
between John—who apparently was a Jack—and the
stranger. They didn't look anything alike. Jack was
all darkness and fire, his brother was lightness and
ice. Jack was impulsive. His brother looked completely in control . . . although she did think she detected a particular brilliance in his eyes as he looked
at Jack that hinted at strong emotions held firmly
in check.

As Jack still had not moved or spoken, Amanda
caught his arm. "Do you recognize your brother,
John . . . er, that is . . . Jack?"

Jack stirred, throwing Amanda a furtive glance before locking eyes with the stranger again. "No, I
don't recognize him," he said coolly, then added in
what Amanda thought was a rather grudging tone,
"But there is a vague familiarity about him."

The stranger smiled wryly and took a step forward. "I should hope I look vaguely familiar, Jack.
What rig are you up to now, little brother?"

Amanda moved closer to Jack and held up a restraining hand. "Jack has had a memory lapse, sir,
due to an accident. It would be a wonderful thing if

indeed you *are* his brother, but since he has not yet recognized you, could you please introduce yourself and give us some proof as to your connection to him?"

The stranger stopped his approach, shrugged, and gave a slight, formal bow. "My name is Julian Fitzwilliam Montgomery, Marquess of Serling." Then he tucked two slim, elegant fingers into a waistcoat pocket and pulled out a chain and locket. In a leisurely manner, he pinched open the locket and moved closer, offering the jewelry for inspection.

"This locket belonged to our late mother. We were rather younger then, but as you can see, there can be no denying that these likenesses are of Jack and myself."

Jack and Amanda both looked at the tiny etchings. The evidence seemed irrefutable. Jack looked thoughtful and Amanda nodded, convinced. The marquess then offered the locket to the constables, who duly examined the article and returned it.

"Well, it looks like you won't have to come with us after all, your lordship," said the senior constable, giving his hat a straightening tug. "You're lucky your brother showed up just now."

"Yes, but how did you know to look *here* for your brother?" asked Amanda, turning toward the marquess.

"Mrs. Beane, the proprietress of the Three Nuns, gave me a clue as to which direction you were headed after leaving Horsham, and I've been on the lookout for you since I got to town yesterday afternoon. This particular inn escaped my notice when I made what I thought was a thorough search of places you might stay the night." He raised a brow, much in the same manner as Jack sometimes did. "But this one is rather off the beaten track, isn't it?"

Amanda blushed, all too aware that the inn had been chosen for just that reason.

The marquess continued. "I was making another round of the town before leaving and traveling westward when I spied these constables marching purposefully down the street as if on official business. I followed them on a hunch."

"You ought to have contacted us the minute you came to town," said the constable. "We are trained to handle such situations, my lord."

The marquess gave a soft, beleaguered sigh and removed a speck of lint off his otherwise spotless lapel. "I abhor a public to-do when I feel fairly confident in being able to handle things myself. Now if you don't mind," he continued, effectively taking charge, "I would like some time alone with my brother so that we might get reacquainted. Landlord, bring another setting, won't you? I haven't had breakfast."

Summarily dismissed, everyone scrambled out of the room except for Amanda. Jack had caught her hand and was holding fast. "Miss Darlington will stay, of course," he said.

The marquess looked at Amanda and bowed. "Of course," he agreed, smiling. If he did not like her presence in the room, he hid it well behind a polite facade.

They sat down at the table, and plateware for the marquess was immediately brought in. Mr. Tebbs hovered and served for a few minutes, but reacted promptly to a pointed look from Lord Serling and left the room.

"So, Jack," said the marquess, ignoring the food and leaning forward with his arms folded on the table. "Your memory is quite gone, is it? You remember nothing of your former life?"

"I remember nothing," he answered calmly. Amanda thought Jack was acting very cautious and reserved. But if he didn't recognize this dignified marquess as his brother, it would be rather daunting to suddenly find out they were so closely related.

"How dashed inconvenient," said the marquess, with a faint smile Amanda suspected was a little insincere. But why would Lord Serling make mocking comments at such a serious moment? "However, I am a wealth of information at your fingertips. Don't you want to ask me a few questions?"

Jack chewed consideringly on a piece of toast. "The truth?"

Lord Serling spread his hands wide. "But of course."

"Actually I'm not terribly interested in knowing particulars about myself just now."

"Jack!" exclaimed Amanda. "I should think you'd be dying of curiosity!"

"It is enough that my brother has found me and can help me return home when the time comes."

Lord Serling raised his brows. "When the time comes?"

"I have business to finish here first," Jack answered obliquely. Amanda had a bad feeling she knew exactly what that "business" was. She was going to have to make it perfectly clear to Jack that she would not allow him to escort her to Thorney Island. She was about to tell him so when the marquess spoke up.

"But you have friends and loved ones worried about you ... waiting for you," Lord Serling told him.

Jack sliced a piece of bacon. "Do I have a wife?"

Amanda held her breath. She had been wondering the same thing, agonizing over the possibility that she may have made love to another woman's husband.

The marquess sat back in his chair and watched Jack with a penetrating gaze. "No," he said at last.

Amanda released her held breath with a shudder of relief.

"Therefore I must conclude that I have no children ... at least none that I can acknowledge. Do I have parents still living?"

"No," said the marquess.

"Siblings?"

"Just me."

"So, if you are my closest living relative and you already know I'm safe and sound, I see no reason to rush home. Do you?"

Lord Serling cast a flickering glance Amanda's way and said, "You have responsibilities, Jack. Places to go, my dear brother, and ... promises to keep."

Jack dabbed his mouth with a napkin, then caught and held the marquess's gaze. "Any promises I've made *will* be honored ... have no fears about that. They must simply wait an additional day or two for my attention. In the meantime, perhaps you would be so good as to send word by messenger to my ... er ... friends and let them know I am safe and will see them within the week. Does that satisfy you?"

The two brothers stared at each other as if communicating in some unspoken language. Presently, the marquess stirred and said matter-of-factly, "I suppose it must satisfy me for now." He lifted his fork and began to eat.

"But there's no need for a delay of any kind," Amanda protested, unable to hold her tongue any longer. "Jack has some harebrained idea he must escort me to Thorney Island to pick up my nephew. But I can assure you that there is no need for his escort or assistance at all!"

"Is that the unfinished business you referred to, Jack?" the marquess inquired mildly.

"It is. But Amanda ... *Miss Darlington* ... is not telling the truth about her trip to Thorney Island."

"What?" Amanda exclaimed, laughing nervously.

"Are you calling me a liar, Jack...er...*Lord Durham?*"

"You might as well empty your budget, m'dear," said Jack, pushing back from the table with a huff of exasperation. "And we might as well call each other by our Christian names, particularly since you now know my *real* name, Amanda!"

Jack turned to the marquess. "Julian, Amanda and I have become very good friends over the course of the last three days. After I wandered, dead drunk, into the path of her coach-and-four and hit my head on a rock in a clumsy attempt to get out of the way, Amanda went to considerable trouble and effort to nurse me through a fever and undertake sundry other unpleasant tasks to restore my health. If not for her, I might be dead."

"Ah. You're as beholden to her, then, as you are to Robert, eh?"

"Yes." Jack looked confused, then said, "I mean... that is ... *who* is Robert?"

Julian watched Jack closely. "He claims to be your best friend. He saved your life in Oporto."

"Ah, I see. Not very good of me to forget something like that, eh?" He chuckled uncertainly. "Well, as I was saying, I feel I owe Amanda a debt of gratitude. And as she is so shatter-brained as to have undertaken a journey from Surrey to remote Thorney Island entirely without escort and with only three servants in attendance, none of whom are female, she has already placed herself in unspeakable danger."

Amanda felt the color rise in her cheeks as the marquess bent his keen gaze on her. "Yes, indeed," he answered, frowning thoughtfully.

"Add to that the fact that Amanda is *not* going to Thorney Island to pick up her nephew, as she told me, but ... forgive me, Amanda, for speaking plainly ... to find an illegitimate child somehow related to her."

Amanda sprang to her feet. "Jack! How did you ever get such an idea! I've never been so—"

"Settle down, m'dear," Jack said soothingly, grabbing her wrist and pulling her to her seat again. "Theo told me. Only he didn't tell me who the child belongs to. He just said Mr. and Mrs. Darlington would not allow the child on the premises at Edenbridge, but since their death you have taken a notion to restore the child to its rightful heritage. Am I correct so far?"

Feeling defeated, Amanda sighed and said, "Yes. So far you are absolutely correct."

Jack looked satisfied. "So why don't you tell me the rest, m'dear?"

Amanda searched Jack's face. "You thought the child was mine, didn't you?"

Jack looked chagrined. He bent near her and whispered. "I did, until—"

"Oh," said Amanda, growing flustered and confused as she understood his meaning. Last night he'd discovered that she was a virgin when they'd made love, and virgins weren't likely to have illegitimate children stashed away on remote islands. She hoped the marquess wasn't reading between the lines. Darting a quick, embarrassed glance his way, she could not imagine such a regal, masterful gentleman giving in to passion. He'd probably never understand why *she* had done so and would immediately label her a loose woman if he knew how wantonly she'd behaved last night in his brother's arms.

Despite all the judgmental opinions Amanda was attributing to the marquess, he did not appear disgusted or even particularly interested when he prompted, "If the child's not yours, Miss Darlington, whose is it?"

Amanda bit her lip and averted her gaze. "The child belongs to my father." She gathered her composure and turned back to Jack and Lord Serling. She found herself directing her conversation to Jack, in whose dark eyes she could detect some sympathy. Not pity, thank goodness. Just honestly felt and offered sympathy.

"Although my parents both died in a carriage accident months ago," she continued, "I didn't find out about this sibling of mine till three days ago, the very day I nearly ran down Jack with my coach."

She explained how the letter had been misfiled, the substance of it, and her concern for the child's well-being after several months had passed without the usual funds being sent to the caretaker.

Jack took Amanda's hand. "This is worse than I thought, Amanda! You don't have the slightest idea what you'll find when you get to Thornfield Cottage. You don't even know the sex or age of the child! My dear, you haven't the slightest notion what a responsibility you've undertaken!"

"Jack, how could I in good conscience do anything other than what I'm doing? I can't bear to think that my brother or sister has been so neglected when I've had every material comfort. I know what it's like to want for affection, too, and I'm determined to give this child everything it needs in the way of financial and emotional support. I want to make things right!"

"You are a very brave, right-thinking . . . and a very *foolish* young woman," Lord Serling said sternly: "Jack is right. You need an escort to Thorney Island and, particularly in view of the fact that you'll have a child with you, you should be escorted home, as well. Where *is* your home, Miss Darlington?"

"It's in Surrey, my lord. But I can't allow Jack to keep his friends in suspense any longer. He needs to return to *his* home!"

"He does indeed," the marquess said with grim determination. "And he will . . . after we have assisted you in locating your sibling and then returned you and your party safely to Surrey."

Amanda's eyes grew wide. "You mean you and Jack are *both* going with me?"

Jack frowned. "Julian, shouldn't you go back to London and tell the others that you've found me?"

Lord Serling gave Jack a bland look and rose to his feet. "As you suggested yourself, Jack, I will send word of your safety by messenger. Surely two escorts for Miss Darlington are even better than one?"

Amanda laughed sadly and shook her head. "But you are *just* the sort of fashionable people I had hoped to keep my family secret from. I wanted my little brother or sister to grow up without the stigma of illegitimacy!"

"You don't imagine, Miss Darlington," the marquess began in an aloof tone, "that either Jack or I would divulge any information about your family you did not wish to have divulged, do you?"

Mortified, Amanda was about to apologize for having offended him, when she discerned a gleam of understanding in the marquess's eyes. Instead she softly said, "Thank you, Lord Serling." She turned to Jack, who was still holding her hand and said, softer still, "And thank *you*, Jack."

She wasn't just thanking him for helping her or for understanding her need to go to Thorney Island. She was thanking him for last night ... for all the love and warmth and memories he'd given her ... memories that would help her get through the rest of her life without him.

Julian arranged for one of his servants to ride directly on horseback to London with a letter for Charlotte. Then he gave orders for his remaining servants to await him at the Charleston Arms, and to stable his horses and coach there, while he rode with Jack and Miss Darlington in her carriage to Thorney Island. The trip was hampered by heavy rain showers and took the better part of the day, therefore Julian had more than sufficient time to think and come to some interesting conclusions.

There were two facts about which he was quite convinced. The first was that Jack knew perfectly well who he was. There had a been a spark of awareness in those gypsy eyes of his when they first fell on Julian as he entered the parlor at the Angel Inn. Yes, it was obvious that Jack recognized him and was relieved to see him ... which wasn't surprising considering what a pickle he'd got himself into. After all, Miss Darlington had been ready to give him over to the authorities! Julian could only guess her motivation in doing so, but he suspected that she was trying to protect the child on Thorney Island, and she was trying to protect herself as well.

That brought Julian to the second fact he was so very sure of. He was sure Jack was in love with Miss Darlington. This would not be such a bad thing under other circumstances because, from what he'd gathered during the course of the day's conversation, Miss Darlington was a respectable female from good Surrey stock. And as he fleshed out the sketchy details he'd been given earlier about the accident and Miss Darlington's nursing endeavors in Jack's behalf, Julian was convinced that she had saved his ramshackle brother's life.

The question was, had Jack repaid this kindness by compromising the young lady? Their behavior toward each other hinted at intimacies. There was a tender consciousness between them. Jack behaved very properly toward her, and she didn't in the least flirt or play the coquette, but an aura of sheer erotic sensibility hung in the air. It was enough to make Julian want to loosen his necktie, for Christ's sake!

But regardless of what *may* have happened between Jack and Miss Darlington, the fact remained that his brother had made a commitment to Charlotte Batsford. Obviously Miss Darlington could know nothing of Jack's betrothal, so did she expect Jack to make an honest woman of her ... so to speak ... if in fact he *had* compromised her?

And did she love him as he appeared to love her? To unfamiliar eyes, Jack might not act like he was in love, but Julian knew his brother, and he could read the emotions behind the charming, devil-may-care facade. But could anyone truly form a lasting attachment for another after just three days together?

Julian sighed. Leave it to Jack to find just the right sort of circumstances and just the right kind of girl to fall in love with in three days ... but at the absolute worst possible time! Jack was engaged. He was promised to another. And there was no honorable way around it.

So when had Jack got his memory back? Or had he ever really lost it at all? Was he pretending amnesia now to stay with Amanda and ensure her safety ... or had he decided that marriage was not for him and therefore avoiding Charlotte?

Despite all these natural speculations, Julian couldn't help but give his brother the benefit of the doubt. He believed that Jack had indeed been afflicted with amnesia as a result of the head injury and the fever. And while he was keeping his recovery to himself, Julian believed Jack was doing it for the sake of staying with Miss Darlington and not as a way of avoiding Charlotte. Julian believed Jack had every intention of returning to London to marry Charlotte, but at what cost to him ... and to Miss Darlington?

Julian frowned. And, ultimately, at what cost to Charlotte?

Julian knew Jack was not in love with Charlotte, that he had *never* been in love with Charlotte. But then Jack had never been truly in love with anyone. Julian had been happy enough to discern a certain fondness Jack had for Charlotte; he was not so romantic and naive to expect more from his jaded brother. But Charlotte was too good a girl to be married to a man who was actually head over heels in love with someone else.

Better she should marry *him*, Julian thought grimly. Better to be married to someone who had never been in love in his life. The only passion Julian was familiar with was the physical kind he enjoyed in the discreet and elegant confines of his current mistress's abode in town.

He thought of Pauline and grimaced, an unwilling reaction that came frequently these days whenever he thought of his mistress. He'd leased the house for her for a year, and after six months he was already tired of her. She was so artificial, so practiced. He longed for innocence, naturalness.

Julian studied Miss Darlington and realized that she possessed the qualities of innocence and naturalness, and those qualities had helped capture Jack's affections.

Julian scowled at his boots. Charlotte had the same qualities. And Jack was going to have to forget Miss Darlington and pledge himself for life to another. It was that simple.

He wished he could discuss all these concerns with Jack, ask all the questions that nagged at him and be sure of a straight answer, but Jack was being skittish. He made sure he and Julian were never alone, never in a position to enjoy a private conversation. Obviously Jack wasn't ready to confide in him. Although his patience was sorely tried, Julian was resigned to waiting till his brother was prepared to talk.

Chapter 14

It was late afternoon by the time they reached the turnoff to Thorney Island, which was actually a small pouch-shaped peninsula of land jutting out into a large natural harbor. From the north it appeared heavily wooded and very secluded from the mainland.

The sense of privacy about the place was abetted by the rocky, rutted roads that led into what looked like a labyrinth of trees. The rain had finally ceased and the ceiling of dark clouds had broken up somewhat, but with dusk coming on and the fog creeping in, the prospect of venturing into such a dark maze of vegetation was still not altogether agreeable to Amanda.

They had made inquiries at the Bull and Bush Inn at Prinstead, the last village before the Thorney Island exit from the main road. The innkeep told them that the entire island was private property belonging to an absentee landlord. He also told them that he only knew of one structure on the land called Thornfield Cottage, which was lived in by an old woman by the name of Grimshaw.

Amanda was already aware of these facts, of course, but she was hoping the innkeeper knew something more. However, when she inquired if Mrs. Grimshaw lived alone on the island, the innkeeper declared that he'd never known Mrs. Grimshaw to keep company with anyone. She was a loner, an odd 'un, as the locals called her.

"She must come to town periodically for supplies," Jack suggested.

"Aye," said the innkeeper, nodding his head. "Every few weeks or so she comes out in her rickety gig pulled by that old piebald nag of hers and stocks up." He paused and scratched his head. "Can't say I've seen her for quite some time, though. You folks goin' up to the cottage, then?" he inquired as they were about to leave.

"Yes," said Jack. "Why? Is there some reason we shouldn't?"

"Does Mrs. Grimshaw know you're coming?" he inquired with his brows drawn together in a concerned frown.

"Not exactly," Jack admitted warily.

"Then be careful," the innkeep advised. "People who have ventured onto the island despite the signs declaring it to be private property have occasionally been shot at."

At Amanda's exclamation of surprise, he added, "Never hit, mind you, just shot at. But Mrs. Grimshaw don't like trespassers. And watch out for the dogs, too. They're mean devils." He grinned a little nervously. "The young folk hereabouts say Grimshaw's a witch."

These bits of offered advice and rural bogeyman philosophy did not reassure Amanda about the conditions in which her sibling had been living. What a dreadful atmosphere for a child! Seclusion ... and a *witch* for a caregiver! It was all perfectly horrible!

Jack warned Theo, Harley, and Joe about possible gunfire, which information understandably put all three of them in a bit of a fret. Then she and Jack and Lord Serling reboarded the carriage and headed into the wilderness that would take them to Thornfield Cottage. They lighted the lantern inside the coach and bumped along through the dark at a snail's pace.

By the rather forbidding expression on Lord Serling's face during moments when there was no conversation, Amanda was afraid he was regretting his generous offer to stand as one of her two gallant escorts. But she realized he was probably only putting himself to so much trouble for his brother's sake . . . simply to keep his eye on Jack. Though there had been no embraces when Lord Serling found his brother, it was obvious to Amanda that he was deeply devoted to and very fond of Jack.

But who could not be fond of Jack? thought Amanda, staring longingly at his strong profile as he looked out the carriage window. She had never imagined she'd have this extra time with him, but she suspected it was only going to make it harder on her when she finally had to say good-bye to him for good. Still, it was wonderful of him to be so concerned for her safety and to want to lend her emotional support during this trying period.

She was very glad, too, and immensely relieved to discover that Jack had a brother and friends that would help to restore his memory. And even though she'd felt all along that Jack wasn't married, she was still surprised that such an eligible fellow hadn't been snapped up by now. Of course, he didn't appear to *want* to be married, which was a very good reason for Amanda not to get her hopes up even though he was apparently still available.

After what seemed like an eternity, the deplorably bumpy road ended at an open stretch of beach. There had been no shots fired at them, but everyone's nerves were frayed just the same. It wasn't hard to get jittery when you imagined bullets zinging past your ears. Theo hollered "whoa," and the horses stopped.

Jack assisted Amanda as she eagerly climbed out of the carriage and looked around. It felt good to be free of the claustrophobic wilderness of beech trees and poplars they'd just passed through and to be standing on open land. The tide was in, which made the beach seem rather narrow. In the rays of the setting sun, the sand appeared pale butter-yellow, and the small, frothy waves that lapped at the shore were limned with gold.

At the horizon, the deep orange orb of the sun was sinking into the sea, leaving behind a sky full of spun-sugar clouds in colors from fiery red to palest pink. Seagulls cawed and flapped through the cool, humid air.

"Why, it's absolutely beautiful here!" exclaimed Amanda, taking in a pivotal view of the place. "But where is the cottage?" She could just imagine how lovely it would look, a snug, white-washed bungalow with creepers on its walls and arbors of roses, and with a little fence enclosing a tidy garden.

Amanda saw Julian touch Jack's elbow, and they glanced grimly at each other. They were looking past the carriage and farther inland. Amanda followed the direction of their gazes and saw that there was a gradual rise of land that finally amounted to a small hill. Unlike much of the landscape, the hill was not entirely overgrown by trees but was dotted here and there by an occasional poplar. And at the top of the hill was a house—an absolutely wretched, run-down pile of rotting wood with a sun-blistered door and a sunken roof.

Amanda clamped her hand over her mouth to keep from exclaiming aloud. Oh, it was dreadful, *too* dreadful to imagine her brother or sister living in that terrible place! And worse still, it appeared to be presently uninhabited.

Yes, even worse than *living* in such abject poverty was the possibility that her sibling had been thrust out into the cruel world to fend for himself. But no candlelight spilled through the forlorn cracks of the building, nor was there smoke coming from the crumbling chimney to give Amanda hope that someone still resided there. The place looked utterly desolate.

"Don't despair, m'dear," came Jack's consoling voice near her ear. He wrapped one arm around her waist and pressed her against his side. "We'll go up and investigate. Though it appears abandoned, there may be something inside that can give us a clue as to where its usual occupants have gone off to. Possibly they aren't gone for good. Maybe they're just somewhere else on the island."

But where? Amanda thought morosely. It was dusk, time for children to be inside having a hot supper before being tucked into a warm bed. But with no smoke coming from the chimney, how could there be a hot supper? And she would wager her farm and every shilling she owned that there was no warm bed waiting, either.

Lord Serling remained silent and carried a lantern ahead of them as Jack steadied Amanda with an arm around her shoulder as he walked her up the muddy path to the house.

Jumpy and suspicious and with his blunderbuss at the ready, Theo took Joe with him and scouted the beach. Harley stayed with the horses.

Amanda tried to compose herself but couldn't help the tears that trailed slowly down her cheeks. "I'm too late, Jack," she told him bleakly. "The child is already gone!"

"We don't know that for sure, Amanda darling. Don't cry." He gave her a reassuring squeeze, but Amanda couldn't be comforted. Who knew what had become of her brother or sister? If Mrs. Grimshaw had abandoned her charge, the child could be dead. Or sold to the slave trade. Or made to work as a chimney sweep!

Amanda's vivid imagination tortured her as they walked toward the sagging steps of the old cottage.

But before they'd gained their objective, Amanda heard a deep snarl. Frightened, she looked up and saw yellow eyes and sharp canine teeth reflected in the light from the lantern. A huge, black, short-haired dog was barring their path.

Then another growl was heard behind them. Aware of the danger of sudden movement, Amanda turned her head slowly and saw the menacing shape of another large black dog, crouched for attack.

"Don't move, little brother," Lord Serling said in a fierce undertone. "They'll go for our throats."

"I'm not a Johnny Raw, big brother. Did you think I was going to kick up my heels doing the Scottish fling?" Jack replied through gritted teeth.

Amanda was shaking from head to toe. "What ... what are we ... we going to do, Jack?"

"Where's that damned Theo when you need him? He's always nosing about when he's not wanted, but when real danger rears its ugly head, he's off parading up and down the beach and collecting seashells!"

"What would you do if they were Frenchies, Jack?" Lord Serling asked. "You're the soldier."

"But I was fending off swords and bullets, Julian! I never let the Frenchies get close enough to *bite* me!"

"There's a hefty stick on the ground yonder," said Lord Serling, holding himself ramrod straight and speaking out of the side of his mouth. "Maybe I'll lunge for it and use it to scare them off."

"If anyone's going to 'lunge,' Julian, it had better be me," said Jack. "I'm faster than you."

"But *I'm* more precise."

The dogs were inching closer, and Amanda could see the drool slathering off their tongues and drip-

ping out of the corners of their mouths. "Oh, don't
do anything, please!" she implored them. "They're
just waiting for you to move so they can attack!"

"We can't stay frozen like this forever, m'dear,"
said Jack. "Don't worry. Just do—"

A strange-sounding "meow" was heard coming
from the direction of the carriage. Surprised, they
carefully turned their heads to see what was making
the catlike noise and saw Harley inside the carriage,
sticking his head through the window. Making absurd faces and yowling like a cat, he was taunting
the dogs to come after him so they'd leave Amanda
and the others alone.

The dogs seemed indecisive at first, turning their
heads toward the carriage with their small, pointed
ears pricked up, then turning back to Amanda, Jack,
and Lord Serling with flattened ears and gnashing
teeth. But Harley continued to yowl and had even
forced his rail-thin body halfway out the window
opening and was wildly waving his arms.

This was too tempting for the dogs. They could
not resist the lure of a moving target. They dashed
off toward the carriage, howling like the hounds of
hell.

"Harley!" cried Amanda.

"Don't worry about him," Jack said with a touch
of appreciative amusement as he watched the dogs
go loping down the hill. "Harley's smart enough to
pull his head inside when vicious dogs are snapping
at it. You ought to be more worried about the paint
on your carriage."

Amanda could see this was so. Harley had immediately disappeared inside the carriage and thrown
down the leather window flap. He was perfectly safe,
but the dogs were jumping up and down and
scraping the carriage with their sharp claws.

"Oh, dear. Theo will be livid," said Amanda.

"He's got more to worry about than the paint on

the carriage," said Lord Serling. "When the dogs
catch sight of him or Joe, they'll go after them with
a vengeance." He took a quick visual appraisal of
the area and said, "Ah, yes. That will do." Then he
turned back to Jack. "There's some sort of barn or
shack over there, Jack. We can lure the dogs inside
and barricade the door. Let's search the house and
see if there's some food to use for bait."

Moving quickly before the dogs got tired of snarl-
ing and snapping at the carriage, Lord Serling, Jack
and Amanda hurried through the unlocked door of
the dark cottage. Lord Serling set the lantern down
on a table just inside what appeared to be the kitchen
area and immediately began flinging open cup-
board doors.

Jack was busily searching for food, too, and it was
he who found a hard half loaf of bread. He sniffed
it. "It's quite stale, but those beasts won't notice a
little mold, I daresay."

"It appears to be the only thing edible in the
house," observed Lord Serling, closing the last cup-
board door.

"If you can call it edible," said Jack, wrinkling
his nose.

"It will have to do. Come, Jack."

Jack caught Amanda's arm as he moved to the
door. "You stay inside, Amanda. We'll be back in a
pig's whisper, just as soon as we've got those blood-
thirsty hounds locked up."

Amanda nodded, then moved to the window and
watched nervously. The dogs started running up the
hill as soon as Jack and Lord Serling came out of the
house. She clasped her hands tightly together and
prayed their plan would work. Jack and Lord Serling
held out the hunks of bread and waggled them allur-
ingly, all the while jogging backward toward the
shack. You could almost see the dogs' eyes narrow
and fasten on the food. Just as they got to the open

door of the shack, with the dogs fast behind them, Jack and Lord Serling threw the bread inside.

Naturally the dogs' first and most instinctual reflex was to go after the food. As soon as the second dog's tail disappeared inside the shack, Jack and Lord Serling closed the doors and pressed their backs against it. As there appeared to be no latch or lock of any kind to secure the door, Lord Serling held it shut while Jack pulled over two heavy bales of hay and pushed them against the door.

Amanda gave a sigh of relief. At least the dogs were taken care of. She suspected that as well as being trained as guard dogs, they were behaving especially aggressively because they were hungry.

Hungry. Like her little brother or sister might have been in the last few months after her father's money quit coming.

Amanda slowly turned around and looked at the house that had been home to her brother or sister.

Poverty. The sparse furnishings, threadbare curtains, bare floors, empty cupboards, and cold grate screamed of poverty. It was a small, cramped hovel of a place, and Amanda couldn't imagine a child flourishing in such a cheerless atmosphere. She would have thought that the amount of money her father sent would have supported them in better comfort than what she saw evidence of today. It made her suspicious as to exactly how Mrs. Grimshaw spent the ready.

Her eyes filled with tears as she began to walk slowly about the small room that combined a sort of parlor with the kitchen. She trailed her hand over the scarred top of a chest, expecting her fingers to be dirty from several months' worth of dust built up on the furniture. But to her surprise, though her fingers were dusty, they weren't *that* dusty. Dashing her tears away, she looked about her in a more alert and inquiring manner. If the house had been abandoned months ago, there would be more cobwebs in the corners and the dust would be thicker.

She turned quickly to inspect the fireplace. Though it was empty of wood and quite cold, the ashes looked undisturbed and were, therefore, probably only a few hours old. A hope began to blossom in Amanda's chest.

With her heart beating rapidly, she hurried to the only inside door in the small house and opened it. As she expected, it was a bedchamber. And the bed looked as though it had been recently slept in! A much-mended multicolored quilt was thrown rather haphazardly over some rumpled sheeting and a small pillow.

Amanda was much encouraged and hurried into the parlor when she heard Jack and Lord Serling re-enter the house.

"Jack!" she cried, rushing forward and grabbing hold of his hands. "I don't think they've gone for good. The bed looks recently slept in, and the ashes on the grate are new. Someone is still living here!"

Jack smiled uneasily and gave her hands a returning squeeze before letting go. "Yes, that's very encouraging, Amanda m'dear, but if someone's still living here, what the deuce are they eating? There's not a morsel in the house. And where's that piebald nag and the rig the innkeeper described?"

"Maybe Mrs. Grimshaw went into town to procure more food," Amanda suggested hopefully.

"We'd have ran smack into her," Jack said reasonably. "The innkeeper said that poor excuse of a road was the only way in and out of the place. And where's the child?"

"I don't know, Jack," Amanda said, unable to keep the desperation out of her voice, "but I can't just leave without knowing! I need to stay here till I know something for certain. I want to at least spend the night and see if someone shows up."

When Jack frowned and cast a disparaging glance about the room, Amanda squeezed his arm and said, "Oh, you *do* understand, don't you, Jack? You'd do the very same thing if you were in my shoes, I daresay!"

Jack was silent for a moment as he looked into Amanda's pleading eyes. Then his expression softened, and he said, "You can't stay here without food, Amanda. We'll have to send Theo back to town to procure something for all of us to eat."

"I'll go with him," Lord Serling said decisively. "I want to make inquiries about town . . . discreetly, of course. There may be people who know more about this Mrs. Grimshaw and her comings and goings than the innkeeper at the Bull and Bush seemed to know."

Amanda turned to the marquess. "You're so good to help me," she said feelingly. "I don't know what I would have done without both you and Jack along to help out." She laughed shakily. "I daresay those dogs would have had me for dinner and buried my bones by now."

"Speaking of dinner, I'd better go," said Lord Serling, moving to the door. "Theo won't be thrilled to undertake that wretched road again . . . nor will I. But I've no notion of going without my dinner, and I'm sure Theo hasn't either." He raised a brow and looked at Jack. "I'm sure you'll take care of things in our absence, little brother."

Then he was gone.

Suddenly finding herself alone with Jack for the first time since she'd summoned up all her willpower and crept out of his bed that morning, Amanda was overwhelmed by sudden shyness.

She moved to the window and pretended to be watching Lord Serling's departure. It was growing darker outside by the minute, with the last rays of the sun well below the distant horizon, and she could barely make out Lord Serling's tall, shadowy figure as he conversed with Theo, then climbed inside the carriage. But she was only half registering the scene, anyway. She was all too aware of Jack standing behind her. She could almost imagine she felt his heat radiating toward her ... drawing her closer.

As the shadows lengthened and the room darkened by the instant, the window became like a mirror. The carriage drove off, but Amanda hardly noticed it leaving because she was too transfixed by Jack's ghostly reflection in the black glass.

He was watching her. He was moving closer. He lifted his hands, and her eyes drifted shut as she anticipated his touch.

His hands fell lightly on her shoulders. He'd touched her before that day, but the little hand squeezes and shoulder hugs were supportive gestures. This was different. She knew it and he knew it.

Next she felt his chin press into her hair, then his warm breath as he dipped his head and skimmed his lips across the nape of her neck. Involuntarily she sighed and slumped against him, his hard chest a wonderful prop for her drooping shoulders.

"Amanda, darling," he murmured with his face buried in her hair and his hands sliding along her collarbone. "You've had a wretched day. Lean on me, sweetheart. Lean on me."

His words were a soothing balm to her shattered nerves, his strength so comforting. His arms around her were like another visit to the Angel Inn, which was Amanda's idea of heaven on earth. . . .

Then she remembered. The man whose charms she wanted desperately to give in to at the moment was Jackson Thadeus Montgomery, Viscount Durham, not the John she'd traveled with and fought with and nursed through the fever ... the John with no last name, no title, and no life beyond the present.

Maybe Jack didn't have a wife, but he had a past

and a future, a life back in London, and a high place in society. Jack's world—and indeed her world, too—was a different existence than the one they'd created in that small enchanted room at the Angel Inn. In the real world there were structure and rules and things one did and didn't do.

And one thing you didn't do if you were a respectable, unmarried female was make love with a man . . . particularly if that man had no desire to exchange his bachelorhood for matrimony.

And Amanda knew that the sooner she began playing by the rules of the real world, the easier it would be to let Jack go.

She pulled away.

Jack looked at Amanda, and by the distraught expression in her soft blue eyes, he knew she wasn't going to let him touch her again. "So, that's how it is, eh?" he said.

Amanda bit her lip and folded her arms around her waist in a poignantly protective gesture. It was all Jack could do to keep from grabbing her and clasping her against his chest. "That's how it has to be, Jack, from now on."

He threw her an aggrieved look. "Just because my brother shows up and I've suddenly got a name doesn't mean everything has to change." But he knew his words had a hollow ring.

"I expected you to be out of my life this morning, Jack. Last night we enjoyed a few wonderful, beautiful, stolen hours. But now we have to get back to our real lives, Jack. The longer we play at this . . . this fantasy affair between us, the harder it will be for me to accept it for the fairy tale it is and get on with reality."

"It wasn't fantasy, Amanda. It wasn't a fairy tale. The feelings between us are genuine. I know *mine* are."

Amanda's mouth curved in a sad, wise smile.

"Yes, I believe you. I do believe you care for me . . . a little. And you're right in another respect, too."

"How's that?"

"You insist that our night together was no fairy tale. I agree with that assessment wholeheartedly, Jack, because one of the hard and fast rules of a fairy tale is that it must have a happy ending. Our little story won't have a happy ending, will it, Jack?"

She didn't have to say the exact words. Jack knew what Amanda was asking him. He'd made it perfectly clear to her that he couldn't make her any promises, couldn't offer her anything binding or lasting in return for sharing her love with him last night. But now that his brother had showed up and he'd been given back his identity, Amanda was probably wondering if there was a chance Jack wanted to take back those cautionary words and perhaps embark on a real courtship with her.

The truth was, as far as Amanda was concerned Jack didn't know what he wanted. He knew he cared very much for her, that he desired her, respected her, and admired her more than any other woman. He knew he'd lay down his life for her if need be. But if Charlotte could miraculously disappear off the face of the earth and make Jack a free man once more . . . would he willingly turn right around and get himself betrothed again?

He didn't think so.

On the other hand, once he'd discovered that Amanda was a virgin, if he'd been free to do it, he would have proposed marriage. He *had* compromised her, and it was the honorable thing to do in such a case.

But all that was a moot point. The fact of the matter was, Jack was in a muddle. He would marry a woman he didn't love and hurt a woman he probably could love quite desperately . . . if things were different.

Amanda broke into Jack's brooding reverie with a soft sigh. "You don't have to answer, Jack," she said softly. "I know there won't be a happy ending, and I do understand."

Jack wanted to scream that she didn't understand. He wanted to tell her he'd offer her marriage if he was free to do so, but it was far too late now to confess that his memory had returned. If he confessed, he'd also have to admit that he was engaged to be married and had been well aware of that fact when he took her to bed. In other words, he'd compromised her knowing full well he could never do the honorable thing because he was already promised to another.

More than ever before, Jack felt himself desperately in the wrong. He was a first-class cad, and he must never touch Amanda again. He owed her that much. The best thing he could do would be to allow her to believe whatever she wanted to about him, then gradually . . . and hopefully sooner than later . . . forget his very existence. After all, the truth was worse than anything she could come up with to explain his reprehensible behavior.

"You must be exhausted, Amanda," said Jack, keeping his hands to himself but unable to keep the concern and affection out of his voice. "Why don't you go lie down on the bed till Julian returns with the food."

"Maybe I will," she said, chafing her arms.

"I'll build a fire and get the place warmed up in the meantime, all right?"

"All right," she said, sounding uncharacteristically tired and defeated. She walked to the door leading into the bedchamber and turned to look back. "You'll let me know if you see or hear anything, won't you?"

He smiled. "Of course."

She went into the bedchamber and shut the door. Jack sighed, called himself every kind of miserable name, then went outside and found enough wood to keep a fire going for the rest of the evening. He built it up to a substantial blaze, then lay down on the moth-eaten old sofa in the parlor and closed his eyes.

He didn't expect to hear anything or see anything that would make Amanda feel any less tired or defeated. He thought she was grasping at straws by believing that there was still a chance Grimshaw and the child would return. He was very much afraid that Amanda would never find anything out about her half-sibling and would have to go through her entire life never knowing what had become of the child.

He closed his eyes and listened to the beginning patter of returning rain. He dozed off, hoping the rain that would surely seep through the decrepit roof would not land on him.

Later, Jack awoke with the distinct sensation of cold water dripping on his head ... and cold, hard steel pressed against his throat.

We opened his eyes and found himself face-to-face with a dirty youth in a tattered riding cap, with two black dogs foaming at the mouth on either side of him. A rifle muzzle was pushed against Jack's Adam's apple.

"Who the deuce are you?" the skinny lad demanded. "And what th' bloody 'ell are ye doin' in my house?"

Chapter 15

Jack stared up into eyes that were exactly like Amanda's; almond-shaped, finely lashed, and a clear, true blue. Hair, more the color of a golden guinea than Amanda's pale blond, escaped the disreputable cap in the front in a riot of damp curls. The face was thinner, the features a little sharper than Amanda's, but he'd no doubt at all that this lad was the half-sibling she'd come to Thorney Island to fetch home.

The lad was certainly no child, but by his narrow shoulders, his only moderate height, and the obvious lack of muscle on his thin frame, Jack judged him to be barely in his teens.

"Did you hear me, mister?" said the youth, giving Jack's throat another jab. "Who the bloody 'ell, are you? Speak up or I'll blow you t' bits!"

"Here, here," said Jack, lifting his hands in a show of capitulation. "There's no need to shove that muzzle down my throat. I've no objection to telling you who I am, but it would be easier to do so without that quite unnecessary pressure on my tonsils!"

The lad sneered, but he pulled the gun back an inch. "All right then, empty yer budget. There's nothin' hurtin' your pretty throat now, is there?" he mocked. " 'Cept maybe that white-as-snow necktie what's stranglin' you."

Jack raised an imperious brow. "My name is Jackson Montgomery. And you are . . . ?"

"Makes no never mind who *I* am! *I'm* not trespassin'! What are you doin' 'ere?"

Jack dropped his hands and folded them over his chest. The boy watched his every move, his finger poised on the trigger. Jack didn't believe the lad was a killer, but there was no point in taking chances. He didn't want either of them getting hurt because Jack's impatience had egged him into an unwise move.

Besides, those dogs looked like they could easily finish what the boy couldn't, particularly as they might hold a grudge from earlier. Jack debated for as long as he dared on what to say, then decided fatalistically on the truth.

"I'm here because I escorted a young woman to these premises looking for her sister . . . or brother."

The lad's brows furrowed as uncertainty flickered in his eyes.

"What young woman?" He jerked his head around, trying to look behind and next to him without taking his eyes off Jack for more than half a second. "I don't see no woman."

"I believe she's sound asleep on your bed. Otherwise," he added wryly, "I'm quite sure she'd have leaped into the fray by now."

Jack could see the boy's chest rise and fall with rapid breathing. His head swiveled toward the door leading into the bedchamber, then back to Jack. He guessed the boy was at least as much afraid and excited as he was angry. "She's got no business sleepin' on my bed, no more than you got any business breakin' into my house and lockin' my dogs up in the barn!"

"They weren't behaving in a very friendly manner," Jack explained with a smile, briefly lifting his fingers off his chest in an apologetic gesture. "But you don't set them a very good example, so you? You ought to be grateful that—"

"Grateful!" the boy spat. "About what? I ain't never had nothin' and nobody t' be grateful fer in my whole stinkin' life!"

Jack could easily believe this to be true. "That's going to change, my boy. Your sister's come to fetch you home."

The astonishment on the boy's face was almost humorous. His mouth fell open and his eyes widened to the size of saucers. Without the scowl or the sneer, his face was quite handsome. Almost pretty. When he recovered, he gasped out, "I don't know what kind of gammon you're tryin' t' pitch, mister, but I'm no bufflehead. I ain't got no sister. All I've ever had was an old witch caretaker by the name o'—"

"Grimshaw," Jack finished for him.

Again the boy's reaction was of extreme astonishment. "How do you know her name? You've been talkin' to folks in town, 'aven't you?"

"I would be very happy to explain everything to you, young man, but I shouldn't like to carry on such a lengthy conversation at such a disadvantaged angle. May I sit up, please?"

The boy shook his head. "No," he said gruffly. "You just stay put. You're lying to me! I don't know why you're here. Lord knows I ain't got nothin' t' steal, but—"

"I told you why I'm here. I brought your sister to—"

He shook his head faster, more vehemently. "No! I'm a bastard. Grimshaw said I was a bastard with no family to care whether I lived or died! And now that Grimshaw's gone, I got nobody at all ... not that Grimshaw was anything worth cryin' over when she up and left in the summer. All she ever did was cry and complain into 'er cups o' gin."

So that was where the money went, Jack thought. The situation had been just as dreadful as Amanda feared. And the present situation was getting pretty bad, too. Jack could see tears collecting in the boy's eyes. He was getting more and more agitated. Living here alone for so long—and lately, without even Grimshaw for company—he probably didn't know how to deal with other people under ordinary situations, much less in emotion-charged situations like this one.

Jack's gaze flicked down to the lad's unsteady finger on the trigger. He might have to make a move if things didn't improve soon.

"If I got a sister," the boy demanded to know, "where's she been fer the last seventeen years?"

Jack was still trying to fathom the idea that the boy was actually seventeen years old when he heard Amanda's voice.

"I didn't know about you," she said.

The boy jerked around so fast, Jack was afraid his finger would involuntarily press the trigger. At such close range, Amanda would have a hole through her chest the size of a fist! Jack abruptly sat up, his hands clenched and propped behind him on the couch, ready to push to a standing position and only held back by the dogs who snarled and snapped and seemed ready for a full-fledged attack.

Amanda staggered back two steps as the gun swung in her direction, and the boy leaped backward several feet, too, his gun sweeping back and forth . . . first at Jack, then at Amanda, then back to Jack.

"I don't like bein' snuck up on," the boy said in a trembling voice.

"I didn't mean to startle you," Amanda said softly, her hands pressed against her skirts.

"Who are you and what do you want?" the boy again demanded.

"Jack was right. I'm your sister," Amanda told him

in the same calm, careful voice. "And I want to take you home with me."

The boy got an odd smile on his face and continued to shake his head disbelievingly. "You're lyin'."

"No, I'm not. Truly, you must believe me! My father and mother died six months ago and my father . . . who is also *your* father . . . left a letter explaining that he'd a child living on Thorney Island."

"Six months ago?" he repeated suspiciously.

"The letter was misfiled and I didn't get it till last Thursday," Amanda hastily explained. "The very instant I knew of your existence I decided to end this wretched arrangement and bring you home with me where you belong."

The boy's eyes raked Amanda's trim, immaculate form, then glanced down at his own grimy, shapeless garments. "I don't belong with you," he said belligerently. "You're a fine lady, and I'm nothin' but . . . but someone's bastard child, sent away so's the family wouldn't be shamed."

Amanda took a step forward and lifted her hands beseechingly. Jack got ready to lunge for the gun as the boy tensed up. "You are not to blame for your illegitimacy. And you shouldn't have to suffer for it." Amanda bit her lip and continued in a low, choked voice, "Dear God, you've already suffered enough, haven't you? I want to give you a home and a family. And an education." She gestured toward the bed-chamber. "I saw some books in there. I saw your name printed inside. It's Sam, isn't it? I think it's wonderful that you know how to read, Sam. I have a huge library at my house in Surrey that I know you'll love."

Jack thought he saw the boy's eyes brighten for an instant, then grow dull with a hopeless longing. "I'm happy for you, miss, that you got such a *grand* library with so many fine books, but I got no use fer you nor your books."

"But I could hire a tutor for you," Amanda continued to implore, talking quickly, urgently. "You could study whatever you wanted and someday distinguish yourself in the army or learn a trade and go into business. Whatever you wanted to do, I could help you accomplish. I want to help you ... can't you see that?"

The boy shook his head again. "This ain't nothin' but a trick," he said bitterly. "Or pity. I don't want your tricks nor your pity. I don't even believe you're my kin."

Amanda threw up her hands in exasperation. "Look at me. How can you say that? Except for the fact that you're a man and I'm a woman, we're like two peas in a pod. There's no denying it, Sam. You're my brother."

The boy looked. He must have seen the dead-on similarity between them the minute Amanda came into the room, but now, staring at her, it seemed to be sinking in. There was no denying it. They were definitely related.

Seeming to sense a slight relenting in the boy's anger, Amanda pressed her advantage. "He wasn't a bad man, our father. In fact he was generally very well respected and admired. But he made one terrible mistake ... a mistake that I can never forgive him for."

Sam stiffened. His jaw locked at a belligerent angle. "He had a bastard child and shamed you, right?"

"No. That's not the reason I can't forgive him. It's because he deserted you, Sam." Her words were nearly strangled by emotion. "But now you can come home." Amanda extended one hand toward Sam and smiled tenderly. Her eyes glistened with tears. "Won't you come home, Sam?"

Jack didn't know how anybody could not be deeply touched by Amanda's warm concern, as well as completely convinced of her sincerity. But Sam's isolated and impoverished upbringing had made him distrustful and bitter. Even when a rainbow showed up on his otherwise gloomy, stormy horizon, he was afraid to believe it was actually shining for him. He had gone too long without anyone caring about him. He couldn't fathom the fact that Amanda truly did care and was offering him everything he'd ever dreamed of having. A family. Hope for the future. Security and love.

In a blinding, intuitive moment, Jack saw himself in that shirking, frightened boy. Wasn't Jack afraid of the same things? Didn't he want a family, a future . . . love and security? But maybe, like Sam, he didn't have enough faith in his own lovability, so he shunned love when it was freely . . . and unconditionally . . . offered.

Jack had always felt he could never know if a woman wanted him for himself or for his title and fortune. Except in Amanda's case. With her, he'd been a nobody without a title, a fortune, or even a name.

But then she'd only wanted him for one night . . . hadn't she?

Suddenly there was a sound outside. The creak of a carriage and the dull thud of horses' hooves on the sand. Julian was back.

Sam heard the carriage, too . . . and panicked. Jack saw the boy's head rear up and heard the rasp of his frightened breath. Then Sam's finger convulsed on the trigger.

Jack lunged. He caught the muzzle of the gun just as the shot went off. He could feel the vibration of the ball as it traveled through the barrel and exploded into the air not six inches above Amanda's stunned face. He fell hard against the bare floor, every bone in his body jarred by the impact. Pain seared through his weak knee and his still tender head.

Then, before he could even turn over, the dogs were on him. Jack felt the hot breath of one dog at his neck as it ripped the collar of his jacket ... working down to the flesh, he thought rather desperately ... as he kicked off the other dog who was after his leg.

"Zeus! Neptune! Down, boys. *Down!*"

Miraculously, the dogs obeyed. Jack pushed up with his elbows and rolled over. Amanda had picked up a reed-backed chair and looked prepared to do battle with the dogs for Jack's hide but had been forestalled by Sam unexpectantly calling them to order. The panting beasts sat obediently at their master's feet, and Sam stood by the door looking horrified and frightened by what had happened ... and what had *almost* happened.

"I didn't mean to shoot!" cried Sam, wild-eyed with distress. "Truly, I didn't! I just twitched when I heard the carriage comin' and next thing I knew—!"

"I know you didn't mean to shoot," Amanda said soothingly, setting down the chair and advancing carefully. "And we do appreciate your calling off the dogs."

"Yes ... thank you, Sam," Jack said between ragged breaths.

But Sam, at the end of his emotional tether, apparently couldn't bear to be thanked. He burst into tears, threw the door open, and ran out into the darkness with the dogs in close pursuit.

"Oh, no! *No!*" cried Amanda. "Go after him, Jack. I'll never see him again if he gets away!"

Jack heaved quickly to his feet and, disregarding the shooting pain in his knee and the dizziness that came over him, raced through the door after Sam, nearly running down Julian in the process.

"Good *Gawd!*" Julian said succinctly as he clasped Jack's shoulders and steadied him. "I heard a shot. Is anyone hurt?"

Jack ripped out of his grasp. "No, no one's hurt.

But there's no time to explain, Julian. Amanda's brother, Sam, he—"

"He went *that* way, Jack." He pointed with one finger and twirled a dirty riding cap on another. "Lost his hat, too. When he saw me coming, he went round the house and up the hill ... due north, little brother. Go! I'll follow you."

Jack registered the irony of the fact that had Julian not headed him in the right direction, he'd have run himself ragged on a wild goose chase. As usual, Julian was more precise and knew exactly which way to go, but Jack—and Julian was fair enough to concede this point—was the quicker and the more enduring runner despite his weak knee.

The day's persistent rainfall made climbing the hill a rather slippery affair. And it was difficult to see. The half-moon was one moment shining full on the landscape below and the next moment dodging behind a cloud. When Jack could see, he strained his eyes and more than once caught the gleam of moonshine on golden curls. He was gaining on Sam.

At the crest of the hill, Sam stopped to turn back and see how closely Jack followed. He must have been alarmed to see Jack so hot on his trail because he cursed colorfully, then ran like an eligible bachelor being chased by a pack of debutantes. The dogs ran with Sam, seeming to enjoy the excitement and the exercise, their snouts raised to the sky as they barked and bayed at the moon.

Having reached the top of the hill, Jack could see that they were on a plateau of sorts that dropped off steeply on one side, making it a rather sheer fall to the rocky seashore below. The terrain was gorse and scrub and bracken, interspersed with patches of slippery mud and lichened stone that shimmered in the moonlight. In other words, it was damned difficult navigating his way through the natural booby traps of undergrowth and keeping up with Sam, who knew his way in these parts as well as Jack might know his way about his own darkened bedchamber.

He tripped several times and once came down with a shouted "damnation" on his bad knee, sinking inches deep in the mud. But somehow he still managed to keep up with Sam and actually gain on him. Sam, stopping more and more frequently to turn and observe Jack's progress, seemed to be tiring. This came as no surprise to Jack, since it had been obvious to him that the poor little whelp was half-starved to death! He didn't expect the chase to go on much longer.

But neither had he expected it to end the way it did. No more than ten feet ahead of him, sucking in huge gulps of air, Sam was peering over his shoulder at Jack when he stumbled and fell. As he went down, he slipped and rolled several feet in the mud as the land veered downward to the cliff's edge, stopping just short of actually sliding over the dark brink and out of his sister's life forever. He was holding on for dear life to a scraggly, half-drowned thatch of gorse, the weak roots of which could be easily pulled up from the saturated earth.

Without a moment's hesitation, Jack went down on his stomach, dug his boots into the mud and tufts of grass, and reached over the edge of the cliff to grasp Sam's wrists. With a gasp and an unintelligible exclamation, Sam let go of the small gorse bush and caught hold of Jack's forearms.

"Hold on, Sam!" Jack rasped, pulling with all his might. But Jack wasn't exactly sure what he thought Sam was gaining by holding on to *him*. He might have done better by keeping hold of the gorse bush. Gravity was definitely not on their side. Although Sam was light compared to Jack, with the lad's entire weight pulling them over the edge, Jack's foothold in the mud was virtually worthless. It appeared as though, unless a miracle occurred, they were both going to end up on the rocky shore, their bruised bodies washed out to sea with the tide.

Not for the first time since he'd wandered away from The Spotted Dog three days ago, it became apparent to Jack that he might ultimately avoid the dreaded marriage trap but by distinctly unpleasant means. It occurred to him again that death was rather too painful and permanent a solution to his problem.

It also occurred to Jack, as he slid ever closer to the edge, that he was going to miss Amanda quite desperately . . . and with no hopes of ever seeing her again in the hereafter. Upon his untimely death, he knew he'd be going south to a much warmer and arid climate than he was used to in misty, verdant England, and she'd be going north, to the pearly gates and into St. Peter's open arms. Damned if he didn't wish in that moment that he'd been a better man!

Then the miracle occurred. And a miracle it could be called even in earthly terms. The elegant, the fastidious, the immaculate Julian Fitzwilliam Montgomery, Marquess of Serling, had grabbed hold of Jack's filthy boots and was dragging him—and Sam—back across the brink to safety and another shot at repentance and mortality.

It was a slow and gruesome . . . not to say extremely dirty . . . process. But eventually Julian was on his rump in the mud, with Jack pulled half on top of him and Sam pulled half on top of Jack. It was in this interesting position, while they each caught their breath and allowed themselves to savor the realization that no one was going to be compelled to meet their maker today and receive their eternal comeuppance, that Jack made a most interesting discovery.

Sam's head and chest were resting against Jack's chest. And beneath the layers of Sam's clothes he could feel the boy's heart hammering with relief. He could also feel the boy's . . . *breasts*.

There was no mistaking it. Two distinct outlines of soft, rounded femininity were pressed against Jack's own flat masculine chest. Hiding beneath those ragtag clothes were curves decidedly female.

Sam was a girl.

Amanda had a sister.

Jack shook his head at the implications and couldn't help a wry smile. Lord, was Amanda ever going to have her hands full with this little hoyden!

Amanda was pacing the floor in front of the fire, doing her Aunt Prissy impersonation by distractedly wringing her hands. She felt absolutely helpless waiting behind like some delicate flower while Jack was out in the cold, wet night chasing down Sam. But in her long skirts, Amanda felt she'd have been more of a risk than a help in running after Sam. She'd have probably fallen and broken her neck or some such freakish thing and simply made matters worse.

Lord Serling was putting himself to a great deal of trouble, too. Amanda was wondering what she'd have done without the two Montgomery men today and was already anticipating and depending on their usefulness and comforting assistance during the journey home.

Theo and Harley and Joe had joined her in the cottage, and they were all keeping a sober and silent vigil. Waiting was sheer misery.

Amanda was still trying to absorb the fact that she had a seventeen-year-old brother. She had been expecting a child of perhaps three years old and now had to hurriedly rearrange her thinking and reconsider strategies.

It would be much harder undoing the damage of seventeen years of neglect than three. Sam was almost a grown man, and although he had somehow scrambled into a little education—he apparently was able to read and at least write his name—his manners and speech were extremely vulgar and crude. He'd definitely have to be taught to comport himself differently. Amanda could only thank the stars above that Sam wasn't a girl. A female raised so negligently would be impossible to redeem.

Amanda heard the dogs barking, the din growing ever closer. She hoped this meant Jack and Julian were returning with Sam in tow. She hurried to the door and flung it open. Coming up the steps were the three of them, arm in arm, Jack and Lord Serling on the outside holding up Sam. Immediately after they stepped over the threshold, Amanda quickly shut the door to exclude the dogs.

"Oh, Sam's not hurt, is he?" Amanda exclaimed, rushing forward.

"Just exhausted," Jack assured her. "As we all are," he added ruefully.

"Nothing a hot bath and a clean bed won't mend," Lord Serling remarked as he helped Jack deposit Sam's rag-doll form in a chair by the fire. He looked down at his soiled clothes and made a face of revulsion.

"Ye gods," he said. "I don't believe I've ever been so filthy in my life. Sorry, Theo, old man, but there's nothing for it but to return to Prinstead for the third time tonight and rent rooms. There's no longer any need to stay here ... thank God ... and that way we can all have baths and clean beds. You'll be happy to know, Jack, I brought some of your clothes along so you can change." He threw Jack a look that was both affectionate and disparaging. "Those togs look a trifle worse for wear."

Jack leaned against the mantle and raked his hands through his damp hair. "You think of everything, don't you, big brother?"

"I try," Julian said dryly, then turned to Amanda

and whispered, "I think Sam should have a bath before we go. A good way to warm up the undernourished little whelp, and, besides, I don't think Sam's had a bath in a fortnight . . . at least. Those clothes should be burned. In the meantime, Theo can set out the food and have it ready to feed the ragamuffin once all that grime's been scrubbed off."

"Look 'ere! Who's callin' who a ragamuffin?" Sam demanded to know. Till this outburst, Sam had been huddled miserably by the fire, his small hands extended toward the warm flames. Now he had turned and was glaring resentfully up at Julian, his belligerence apparently revived along with his body temperature.

"I'm calling you a ragamuffin," said Julian, staring down his aquiline nose at the boy. "And a dirty one at that."

"My lord! Don't scold him," said Amanda, rising to the defense of her pathetic charge. "He's not been raised properly. He doesn't know any better—"

"Don't make excuses fer me, missy," snarled the boy, taking Amanda by surprise. She looked down at her brother, with his golden mass of cropped curls skimming the edge of his coarse shirt, thinking he looked like one of heaven's cherubs that had fallen from some celestial perch and ended up in a pigsty. Though he scowled at her, she was determined to believe that underneath that dirt was an angel's apprentice.

"And don't talk to your sister that way, brat," Lord Serling ordered, "or Jack and I might regret that we saved your life tonight."

This information demanded further explanation, and Amanda turned to Jack, who briefly and diffidently described what had occurred on the cliffs.

"Then I must thank you yet again, Jack," Amanda said softly, stifling the urge to throw her arms around his neck and cover his dear face with kisses.

"Not only did you save my life when the gun went off accidentally, but you saved Sam's life, too. How will I ever thank you?"

Jack gave Amanda an eloquent look indicating that they both knew exactly how he'd like to be thanked. However, as they knew that such a gesture of gratitude also was impossible, Jack quickly averted his gaze and said modestly, "Sam and I'd both be over the cliff and washed out to sea by now if it weren't for Julian. He caught my heels and pulled us to safety."

Amanda turned to Lord Serling. "Then I have you to thank as well, my lord," she said, smiling warmly. "How can I show my gratitude?"

Lord Serling raised a haughty brow. "It will be quite simple to show your gratitude to me, Miss Darlington," he assured her. "All I ask is that you oversee the bathing of this troublesome sibling of yours so we can return to Prinstead as quickly as possible." His aristocratic nostrils flared as he flicked a distasteful glance Sam's way. "And remember to burn the clothes."

Amanda's brows knitted in a frown. "But what shall he wear, my lord? I saw no change of clothes in the bedchamber, and even if your or Jack's clothes were here, they'd be far too large for the boy. We can't very well bundle him up in sheeting and take him naked into Prinstead!"

"Sam's a mite smaller than you, but you females have a way of altering your clothes to fit with a stitch here and a stitch there, don't you?" Julian inquired.

"Now see 'ere!" bellowed Sam, "I'm not wearin' any fussy female finery!"

"Of course you aren't," Amanda agreed, staring at Lord Serling with a mixture of confusion and consternation. "I have no notion why his lordship is finding his amusement at your expense, Sam, but I'd appreciate an explanation from the gentleman."

"I can explain, Amanda," Jack offered with a sly grin as he pushed away from the mantel and stepped forward. "I thought I was the only one privy to Sam's little secret, but once again I haven't taken into account the acute perspicacity my brother's known for."

Amanda propped her fists on her hips and looked from one smug Montgomery brother to the other. "What are you babbling about?"

"Sam's a girl," Jack answered succinctly.

"What a bag of moonshine!" Amanda blurted. "I don't believe you!"

"Oh, but it's true," Lord Serling assured her with a convincingly careless shrug. "Strip the little baggage for a bath and you'll find definite proof beneath those flea-infested rags."

Amanda shook her head disbelievingly and stared at Sam. "Sam, is . . . is this *true*? Are you really my sister instead of my brother?"

Sam made a noise of disgust, shoved her hands in her pockets, and kicked at some invisible object on the floor. Then she screwed her face into a pugnacious scowl and scornfully replied, "Bah! Who in their right mind would want to be a *girl*. On the island, I could be whoever I wanted, and I wanted to be a *Sam*, not a *Samantha*!"

"Good lord," Amanda said faintly, sinking into a chair Jack scooted behind her just in time.

Sam watched her sister's reaction with a sullen fascination, then said sulkily, "Anyhow, Samantha's a name for some simpering little chit. And, believe me, you'll never make me into one of *those*!"

Chapter 16

Following orders, Theo, Harley, and Joe fetched water, heated it up, and poured it into a misshapen tin tub they found in a dusty corner of the kitchen, covered with cobwebs. As there was no soap in the house, Amanda borrowed a bar she carried in her portmanteau when she traveled. The none-too-clean sheeting from the bed would have to do for drying Sam off after the bath, as there appeared to be no huckaback in the house set aside for bathing purposes.

Once all the preparations were finished, the gentlemen went outside: Theo, Harley, and Joe to tend to the horses, and Jack and Lord Serling to linger for the required amount of time in a neglected wilderness at the back of the house that used to be a garden. Since the tub was set in front of the fireplace in order to keep the bather as warm as possible, there was really no place in the house the men could go ... except for the tiny bedchamber, which was obviously out of the question ... and still preserve Sam's modesty.

"There!" said Amanda with enthusiasm as soon as the door had closed behind the last male. "Now you can climb into that deliciously hot tub of water, Sa-

mantha. You'll feel much more the thing once you've
had a bath!''

But Sam, who had sat, silent and sullen, throughout the process of preparing the bath, looked suspiciously at the steaming water, turned up her nose,
and said disdainfully, ''You ain't gettin' me in *there*.''

Amanda had been afraid something like this
would happen. Obviously Sam wasn't used to bathing regularly, but considering the amount of dried
mud she was coated with ... on top of the dirt that
was already there ... she'd hoped Sam would be
cooperative.

''My dear, you can't go into town covered in muck.
Besides, you'll feel much more comfortable cleaned
up and wearing a proper garment.''

''If you mean that black dress you've draped yonder, I won't put it on. I ain't goin' to no funeral, and
I ain't puttin' on mournin' for a pa what deserted
me.'' She folded her thin arms across her chest and
lifted her pointed chin. ''Likewise, I ain't goin' to
town, and I ain't takin' a bath!''

''Samantha, don't you want to make a good impression on your first trip off the island?'' Amanda
reasoned.

''My name is Sam,'' Sam reminded her. ''And fer
your information, I been off the island plenty o'
times.''

''Indeed?'' Amanda replied patiently, glancing at
the tub and hoping the water wouldn't cool too
quickly. ''Where did you go?''

''I snuck round Prinstead. You know those books
in my room?'' She looked smug. ''I stole 'em. And
don't tell me it's a sin to steal. I already know that,
'cause Grimshaw used to read me all about sin from
the Bible every night.'' Her narrow chest puffed with
pride. ''That's how I learned to read. Grimshaw
would read out loud and I'd follow along without
her bein' any the wiser. She wouldn't teach me to

read, 'cause she said bastards don't need to know nothin'. She said I was only here on earth 'cause of sin . . . your pa and my ma's sin."

Amanda's heart expanded painfully. "Sam, don't talk that way. You aren't—"

"Grimshaw, she used to beat me fer stealin'," Sam continued matter-of-factly, "but I didn't care 'cause books was what helped me know there was a better place out there somewhere, and that maybe someday even *I* could have a better life, too."

She grew thoughtful, staring off into the middle distance and probably remembering the fantasy world she'd created to keep her sanity. "I used to think all the time about runnin' away, but I was afraid Grimshaw would find me and haul me back and make me sorry I'd ever left in the first place." She shivered, whether from the cold mud coating her or the remembered dread of Grimshaw, Amanda wasn't sure.

"I can understand your reasoning," Amanda agreed softly. "But, tell me, why did you stay after Grimshaw left?"

Sam didn't answer. She hung her head, set her jaw, and stared broodingly at her feet. But Amanda knew why she hadn't left. She was afraid. And who could blame her? She'd never known anything beyond the boundaries of Thorney Island, except for brief, furtive forays into town, hiding and stealing to get her precious books. She didn't know how to act around people, and she had no reason to expect them to be kind to her. Grimshaw certainly hadn't been kind, and Grimshaw was the only human being she'd ever known.

Sam had been repeatedly told for seventeen years that she was a bastard, the product of sin, unwanted and practically a nonperson, undeserving of anyone's love or even their passing interest. Of course, she'd be terrified to venture beyond the squalid safety of the only home she'd ever known.

While Grimshaw remained on the island, she'd been Sam's keeper, and Sam had probably developed a strange sort of dependency on the old crone. Then, after Grimshaw left, she'd been trapped on the island by her own fear, forced to hunt or steal for her food and scrounge for the most basic necessities.

It made Amanda sick at heart to consider how wretched Samantha's life had been as a result of a sanctimonious and cowardly decision made by their so-called respectable father all those years ago. She burned with indignation and an almost physically painful need to make things right, to undo the wrongs done to her sister.

But Sam had an innate pride and seemed to despise anything that remotely resembled pity. She was determined to refuse any help or accept any of the kindnesses Amanda was aching to shower her with.

But most importantly, and most essential to Sam's recovery from her dreadful upbringing, Amanda wanted Sam to realize that nothing that had happened to her was her fault. She wanted her to know that she was cared for, that she was no longer alone in the world, that she wouldn't have to just dream about a good life . . . she could live it.

"Samantha . . . er . . . *Sam*, I wish I knew the words to say that would convince you how very sorry I am about what our father did—"

Up came that stubborn chin again. "It don't matter whether you're sorry or not. It won't change things."

"But together we can change things . . . don't you see? If you come with me, we can—"

Sam stopped her with a look as frigid as a mountain stream in January. "Get this straight, Miss Priss. I ain't goin' nowhere with you: not tonight, not ever. And there's no way in bloody hell you're goin' to get me in that tub!"

Amanda was exhausted, hungry, and overwrought. She considered wrestling Sam into the tub, but she wasn't sure if she had the strength or the energy, and she wasn't sure it was the best way to start off their sisterly relationship. She refused to believe she was entirely defeated, however, and decided to seek advice on the matter.

And who did she immediately think to turn to for help? Why, Jack, of course.

"I'll be right back, Sam," said Amanda, moving to the door. Sam initially looked surprised, then shrugged and pretended not to be the least bit curious about Amanda's next strategy. She probably didn't think it would work, anyway.

As it was such a short distance, and all the lanterns were in use, Amanda walked around the cottage toward the back without bothering to carry a light. She was about to turn the last corner when her shoe got bogged down in the mud and slipped off her heel. She was standing on one leg, with one hand braced against the outside wall of the cottage as she gingerly pushed her shoe back on, when she heard Lord Serling say something that made her freeze in place.

"Well, Jack, you've told me the broad particulars of what happened to you after you stumbled out of The Spotted Dog to relieve yourself, but you haven't yet told me when you recovered your memory."

"It was when we were leaving Patching."

"So, you've been lying to Miss Darlington ever since you left Patching?"

Amanda felt sick. She'd been duped! Jack had been pretending to have amnesia since yesterday afternoon! She should have figured it out, but she'd been blind to so many clues! For example, the way Jack and Lord Serling talked to each other during the dog attack indicated that Jack remembered a great many things. She'd apparently been too preoccupied with other matters to take note. And she'd trusted Jack. Why would he do such a thing?

"I had to pretend I still needed her assistance, Julian, or she'd have booted me out the door."

"And your reasons for wanting to stay with Miss Darlington were entirely altruistic? You wanted to assist her in the recovery of her abandoned sibling?"

"Exactly."

"But I didn't think you understood her true reason for traveling to Thorney Island till this morning?"

"Well, er, it's true I didn't have an altogether *precise* idea of her reason till this morning, but I suspected"—he gave a self-derisive little chuckle— "actually, I suspected a great many things and was very far off the mark in one particular. . . ." His voice trailed off. "But there's no changing that now," he finished on a note of regret. Amanda wondered exactly what part of the last four-and-twenty hours he regretted.

There was a pause, then Lord Serling continued. "I concede wholeheartedly that Miss Darlington was very much in need of help in this little undertaking, and I shudder to think how she would have got on without your assistance, Jack, but are you being completely truthful when you say you had no other inducement for pretending amnesia? Could you possibly have been procrastinating your return to London because of the wedding?"

The wedding? Amanda knew she shouldn't be eavesdropping, but she couldn't help herself. Things were coming to light that she had every right to know. Apparently Jack had not only been lying to her but had also kept important facts a secret.

"As you know, my nonappearance at the wedding was not my fault. My initial loss of memory was very real. But once I recovered my memory, I saw no reason to *rush* back to London."

"No reason, eh?" Lord Serling's tone was sardonic.

"Your bride behaved stoically when she and her family found it necessary to send out five hundred notes of apology the night before the wedding."

His *bride*? Amanda couldn't believe what she was hearing!

"Her grace under fire was extremely commendable, Jack. Charlotte is a fine girl, and she was genuinely worried about you. Returning to London as soon as you got your memory back, or at least sending word that you were alive, would have saved Charlotte several hours of worry."

"Damn Charlotte! I wish I'd never met the girl, much less promised to marry her," he said with a bitterness that sent a chill down Amanda's spine. "Getting leg-shackled is the *last* thing on earth I want to do. Hell, I may never go back to London, Julian!"

Amanda had heard enough. With her trembling hand clamped over her mouth, she turned and stumbled away, no longer caring that her skirts dragged in the mud. She couldn't believe it! The night Jack made love to her he knew himself to be betrothed. He had betrayed both her *and* his bride-to-be. She was a woman that Lord Serling esteemed, but the poor thing had become just another casualty of Jack's lethal charm! And now it appeared that Jack regretted his proposal of marriage and was wishing . . . perhaps even planning . . . to disappoint and shame her again.

Jack was just like her father, Amanda fumed. He was unwilling, perhaps *unable* to meet his responsibilities. No wonder he'd insisted on remaining with her. Jack told Julian he'd stayed with her so he could help her, but Julian didn't know about their lovemaking at the Angel Inn. Perhaps Jack had seen Amanda's willingness to dally . . . with no strings attached . . . as an opportunity too golden to pass up.

She strode quickly past the house and headed for the beach, taking care to stay out of sight of Theo as he fussed about the horses. Her mind was in turmoil, and her throat ached from holding back a deluge of tears and emotion. She was hurt and angry and growing more furious by the minute.

Perhaps, she thought now, he'd been meaning to get her into bed all along. She was just his sort, wasn't she? The sort that asked for no commitments, just a single night of unbridled passion to keep as a memory for her dotage! His initial reluctance—on grounds of "pledged honor"—must have been pretense, just like his amnesia was a pretense.

Amanda shook her head. *How pathetic I must seem to him*, she thought, *but what perfect prey for a man like Jack, who shunned commitment like the plague!*

She should have seen it coming. Even when he had no memory, his aversion to marriage was frequently brought out in conversation. He talked intimately in his sleep of women. Even Theo had labeled him a rogue from day one. But Amanda had been too starved for affection, too beguiled by the man to be sensible. Oh, how she wished she'd never clapped eyes on Jackson Montgomery!

"You know I don't approve of such language when you're speaking of a lady, Jack," Julian said stiffly. "I find it particularly offensive when you use it in the same sentence with the name of Charlotte Batsford."

"Good God, Julian," said Jack, dragging both hands through his hair. "If you think so highly of her, why don't you wed the chit? That would settle things nicely for everyone!"

"I had a feeling you were regretting your betrothal, but I never once entertained the idea that you would try to weasel your way out of the wedding. I defended you to Lady Batsford when she insinuated as much."

"Thank you, brother," Jack said grimly. "But now

I suppose you're wondering if your gallant leap to my defense was precipitant."

Julian's silence spoke volumes.

Jack sighed with weary resignation. "No, blast it. I'm not going to jilt Charlotte. I'm very sorry I cursed just now while discussing her. I'm going to go directly back to London as soon as we've safely escorted Amanda and her sister to Surrey. I'll repeat my vows at the altar whenever Charlotte sets the date. I've never seriously considered any other course of action."

"I'm relieved, Jack," Julian admitted. "Normally I wouldn't doubt you in the least, but recently I had begun to wonder if your affection for another woman had fuddled your reasoning."

Jack didn't bother denying Julian's suggestive words. "I suppose you're speaking of Amanda?"

Julian shrugged. "But of course. Who else? You *are* in love with her, aren't you?"

Again Jack sighed. He stuffed his hands in his trouser pockets and threw back his head to stare at the sky. Bright stars pricked the velvet darkness and violet-gray wisps of clouds scudded across the moon. He turned and faced his brother. "Damnit, Julian. How did things get so complicated so fast?" he wondered desperately. "I've only known Amanda three days and—by God!—it's true what you say! I hadn't realized it till tonight, but I *am* in love with the baggage! What am I going to do?"

Julian stood still as a statue, his eyes black sockets in the dim moonlight, his posture straight and unyielding . . . like his words. "You have to do the honorable thing by Charlotte, Jack. There is no other alternative."

But what if Julian knew that he'd compromised Amanda? Jack wondered dismally. Then what would he advise? How could he do the honorable thing by *both* of them?

"Deuced bad timing, brother," Julian said sincerely, breaking into Jack's unhappy speculations.

"Isn't it, though?" Jack agreed gloomily.

There was a moment of commiserative silence broken by Julian gravely suggesting that it was time to go in. Jack nodded, and they walked slowly back to the front of the cottage.

Julian knocked on the door, and Sam's voice called, "Come in." But when they entered, expecting to see Sam clean and dressed in one of Amanda's black gowns, they saw nothing of the sort.

"Where's Amanda?" Jack demanded to know, instantly worried. "And why do you still look as though you've been wallowing in the mud?"

"I wouldn't talk if I were you," Sam retorted. "You don't look none too spiffy yourself."

"Answer the question, brat," Julian inquired in a deceptively mild tone. "Where's Miss Darlington?"

"I told her I wouldn't get in the tub no way, no how," Sam informed them with a triumphant sniff. "So's she left, saying she'd be right back. I don't know where she went and I don't care." She crossed her arms a little higher on her chest and shifted in the chair till her back was to them.

"Surely you have an idea which way she went?" Julian persisted in the same mild tone but taking a deliberate step forward. Jack was sure Sam noticed the threatening suggestion in Julian's manner. The subtle but undeniable authority in his voice, his daunting stature, and his haughty mien had made many a man tremble in his boots. Sam darted a nervous look at him and squirmed in her chair.

Julian took another step and Sam hastily capitulated. "I thought she'd gone round back," she said. "Then later I saw her goin' down to the water like her bloomers were afire and she had to put 'em out." Resentfully, she added, "But like I said, it don't matter to me where she went."

Jack exchanged a panicked glance with Julian. "You don't think she . . . ?"

"Heard us? Possibly. You'd better go after her, Jack. I'll take care of this one."

After Jack left, Sam watched with wide eyes as Julian removed his jacket and rolled up his sleeves. "Wh-what do you think you're doin', mister?" she inquired in a timorous voice.

Bland-faced, Julian replied, "You should have co-operated with your sister. Now you're going to have to bathe in water that is tepid at best. So, Sam, are you going to take off your clothes, or am I going to have to take them off for you?"

He advanced.

Jack scanned the beach and easily spied Amanda walking with her head down at the very edge of the surf. She wasn't wearing a shawl or a wrap of any kind, and the wind was rather chilly. He knew she was probably upset, though he didn't know for sure if she'd overhead him talking to Julian, so he'd have to tread carefully till she revealed the source of her troubles. She could simply be upset about Sam. Under the same circumstances, who wouldn't be?

As he approached, she looked up, then immediately looked down. Such a reaction did not bode well. She must have heard him talking to Julian, but how much had she heard? Had she heard *all* his confessions? Did she realize he was in love with her?

He fell into step beside her. "It's cold," he offered.

"I hadn't noticed," she answered crisply.

"Will you take my jacket?"

"No."

"Then can I put my arm around your shoulder to keep you warm while we walk?"

She shook her head vehemently. "Absolutely not."

"And why not?"

She stopped and faced him. The moonlight picked

out highlights in her hair, and her eyes shone an icy silver blue. "Because you are betrothed, Jack. I don't think your bride-to-be would appreciate your dallying with another woman, do you? And don't blame your involvement with me on your amnesia. We both know you've had your memory back for some time."

Jack dragged an open palm down his jaw. "You heard me and Julian talking."

Amanda averted her eyes. Staring out to sea, she said in a voice rendered dull and lifeless from shock, "I should be ashamed of eavesdropping, but I'm not. You should have told me. I had a right to know. I'd never have . . . have stayed with you last night if I'd known you were engaged."

Jack grabbed her upper arms, and in a fierce voice he said exactly what was in his heart. "Then I'm glad I didn't tell you."

She slapped his face.

Jack rubbed his jaw and grimaced. "I deserved that," he admitted.

She did not reply but started walking again, toward the house this time.

He followed, desperate for things to be right between them. "Amanda, I have to ask you one more thing before we join the others. I have to know. . . . How much did you hear?"

She turned on him. "What kind of question is that?" Her voice was full of exasperation and hurt. "Are there other things I should know . . . things you're afraid I'll find out that will make me even angrier? Maybe it's best we leave things the way they are, Jack."

"But I have to know—"

"What could I possibly tell you that would make any difference in the way things are?"

She was right. Even if she'd heard him tell Julian he was in love with her, even if she loved him back, what difference would it make? He was still honor-bound to marry Charlotte. And if he didn't do the honorable thing, Amanda would despise him anyway. She would consider him as irresponsible and cowardly as she considered her father.

He just wished he knew how she felt. . . . It was selfish of him, of course, but it would be the most wonderful memory to take to his dotage if she told him she loved him, too. But he couldn't just come out and ask her, so he said instead, "Amanda, naturally I'll marry Charlotte if she still wants me. But what if she doesn't want me? What if she won't marry me?"

Jack held his breath while he waited for Amanda's answer. Her pained expression as she searched his face was the most punishing feeling in the world, but her words stung him to the quick. "If she refuses you, once again you'll be a carefree bachelor, Jack. Therefore I can only suppose you'll be the happiest man on earth."

Then she turned without another word and walked away.

Jack had been absent from London less than a week, but he felt as though an entire lifetime had passed since he'd last tooled his shiny black phaeton down Great Stanhope Street toward the stately residence of Charlotte Batsford, his fiancée.

It was a gloomy afternoon and the leaden skies matched Jack's mood precisely. He had arrived very late at his own town house the night before, having driven up from Prinstead in Julian's carriage the morning after he and Amanda had walked on the beach at Thorney Island. The pain of that last parting was never far from his thoughts.

Leaving Julian to stand as escort and protector on Amanda's homeward journey had seemed the most sensible thing to do. To say the very least, there had developed an awkwardness between Jack and

Amanda since the moment she'd overheard his conversation with Julian behind the cottage. She could not forgive him for his deceptions, and Jack could not blame her for that. Besides, Jack was wanted in London as soon as possible.

In addition, Julian seemed to have a way with Amanda's sister, Sam. Ever since he'd bullied her into bathing, she considered Julian with something akin to religious awe. Julian would not say how he had accomplished the task of turning Sam from a grubby hoyden to a clean, quiet girl in a black dress that night, and no one seemed to want to know the particulars . . . not even Amanda. She simply seemed grateful for the transformation by whatever means Julian had resorted to.

Julian was also the one to convince Sam to return to Edenbridge with her sister. He'd made her some sort of confidential promise, which Sam sometimes coyly alluded to but didn't share with anyone. Jack wasn't surprised by Julian's influence with the child, but he was surprised and pleased that Julian took the time to help Amanda with her troublesome sibling.

However, once Sam was left alone at Darlington Hall with her sister, without Julian to intimidate and charm the little brat into behaving respectably, Jack knew Amanda would have a difficult time of it. Sam needed a firm hand to offset Amanda's soft heart. Now, if it were up to him . . .

Jack's hands tightened on the tethers, and he urged his matched grays to a brisker trot. He had to quit thinking about Amanda. He had to quit wishing he could involve himself in her life somehow. She wanted nothing to do with him, and even if she did it wouldn't matter anyway. He'd be married soon and off on his three-month honeymoon abroad.

He shook his head ruefully. He was on his way to his fiancée's house, and some complicated explanations and difficult apologies needed to be made, but he hadn't spared a thought for what he was going to say to Charlotte.

All he could think about was Amanda and how very desperately he missed her.

He stopped the phaeton in front of the Batsfords' mansion, jumped off the high perch, and tossed the tethers to his tiger. "Walk 'em, Reynolds," said Jack. "I may be a while."

"Righto, milord," said the diminutive Reynolds, immediately following orders.

Jack stood for a calming moment on the walkway in front of the house. He had dressed carefully for this interview with Charlotte. He wore a Clarence blue morning jacket with an ivory satin waistcoat and buff-colored pantaloons. His Hessians were polished to a reflective brilliance by his valet's personal mix of water and champagne and a great deal of elbow grease.

He'd had a steaming, scented bath, a manicure, a shampoo, and a very close shave. But despite all these pampering devices, he felt like hell and hoped Charlotte wouldn't notice the dark circles under his eyes from two sleepless nights. But if she did notice and comment, he'd blame his altered appearance on his recent ordeal and injury. Charlotte must never know it was taking all his force of mind and spirit to present himself as a willing groom. He had no choice, however. It was the honorable thing to do.

He used the door knocker and was not surprised when the Batsfords' barrel-chested majordomo, Phipps, instantly appeared. Jack was expected. He'd sent a note immediately upon waking that morning and had received a note in return suggesting three o'clock for tea and—Jack couldn't doubt—a great deal of questions. He only hoped Lady Batsford had calmed down somewhat from the initial shock of discovering her daughter's bridegroom to have disappeared on the very eve of the wedding.

"This way, milord," said Phipps in stentorian

tones, but Jack noticed a telltale gleam of excitement in the staid servant's usual vacuous gaze.

From what his valet had related to him that morning, Jack knew his disappearance had caused a great deal of gleeful gossip among the *ton*. His reputation for avoiding commitment had set the groundwork for some very uncharitable speculation. Jack took a malicious pleasure in knowing that he'd be disappointing their voracious greed for scandal by showing up with a perfectly valid reason for his untimely vanishing act.

Jack followed Phipps up the stairs to the drawing room, and they entered through the narrow double doors held open by a liveried footman. Just inside the formal chamber the butler intoned, "Lord Durham, miss," then bowed and left, closing the door behind him.

Jack wasn't sure what to expect, but he was surprised and relieved to find Charlotte entirely alone. As he hesitated by the entrance, his fiancée rose slowly from a red velvet sofa near the windows. Bathed in the lambency of bright afternoon sunshine, she looked quite lovely in a midnight blue gown trimmed with white ribbons and lace. Her auburn hair was artfully arranged with soft ringlets framing her oval face.

But as Charlotte came closer with slow and measured steps, Jack realized how pale her usually blooming cheeks were. He'd never seen her so sober and drawn, and a pang of guilt reminded him that he was the culprit responsible for her distress. It was a reprimand far more effective than a blistering scold.

Reacting with instinctive sympathy, he opened his arms and she walked into them, laying her cheek against his chest. "Jack," she said in a soft, choked voice. "Thank God you're safe."

As he comforted Charlotte with awkward little pats on her back, Jack was aware of a great many thoughts and feelings ... most of them self-condemnatory. Regardless of how little he deserved it, it appeared he was forgiven. He'd still make his explanations and apologies, but apparently he needn't worry overly much about whether or not Charlotte would accept them at face value. He could tell her he'd been visiting the moon and she'd believe him. How did a bounder like him attract such trusting females?

Amanda ... she'd trusted him, too. It had been her decision to make love with him, but if he'd known she was a virgin he'd have somehow found the strength of will to gently refuse her beguiling advances. And now he'd have memories of her to torment him for the rest of his life.

Her pale hair scattered on the pillow. Her sweet, warm body eagerly responding to his. The prim way she'd reprimand him, with her hands perched on her slim hips and her aristocratic nose in the air. Her eyes gleaming with excitement as they'd danced. Her gentle hands as she'd bathed his brow and nursed him through the fever. Her wit and intelligence. Her compassion and her loyalty to her sister.

There was no one like Amanda. No one who would quite fit in his arms like she did. No one who could plumb the depths of his heart and still leave him feeling whole and alive and peaceful.

"Jack?"

Jack blinked and looked down into Charlotte's face. He'd been a million miles away. "Yes, Charlotte?"

She moved out of his arms and two steps back. She studied his face. "We need to talk, Jack."

"Yes," he agreed, forcing a smile and trying to look playfully rueful. "I've got a lot of explaining to do, I know. But hopefully I won't be so long about it that I delay the wedding ceremony again."

Charlotte smiled sadly and lifted a hand to tenderly stroke his cheek, her fingers lingering on the scar. "There's no rush, Jack. There's not going to be a wedding. Not for us."

Chapter 17

Robert Hamilton had been walking up and down Great Stanhope Street, trying to look inconspicuous, for nearly an hour. "How the devil long does it take to cry off from a betrothal?" he grumbled to himself, glaring up at the forward-facing windows of the Batsfords' first-floor drawing room. "Charlotte was determined to tell Jack she's not going to marry 'im, so what's the delay?"

Rob was impatient. Charlotte had to be free before he could ask her to marry him, and he was desperate to know the outcome of her little reunion with Jack. He pulled a handkerchief from his waistcoat pocket and mopped his brow. It was a humid day and unusually hot for October, but his damp forehead was probably more the result of worry and stress than uncomfortable weather. He'd laid some careful groundwork in the past week while Jack was missing, and the result of today's interview between the affianced couple would determine whether or not he'd wasted precious time.

After blotting the beads of sweat and tucking away his handkerchief, Rob began again to walk slowly toward the Batsford mansion. As the minutes ticked slowly by, he wondered if Jack's lethal charm had swayed Charlotte's decision to break off the engagement. He did not suppose he'd overestimated Charlotte's growing regard for him over the past week, but one ingratiating gesture or word on Jack's part might very well undo all Rob's hard work. He could just picture Jack settled in a sofa with his arm around Charlotte's waist, her face reflecting her besotted condition. The picture made Rob clench his fists with fury.

Jack's effect on women galled Rob to the core. He'd seen them melt at a mere glance from the charming Viscount Durham time and time again. From scullery wenches to duchesses, from French divorcées to American heiresses. Many just wanted to share his bed for a few hours, but most of them wanted him till death did they part.

That Jack could have a rich wife at the flick of his wrist was the most galling point of all to Rob, because Jack didn't need a rich wife. But Rob did, and he was determined to get one ... in Charlotte. And the dire nature of his predicament was growing more pronounced by the day. He was as deep in dun territory as a man could be. Soon he'd be run out of town on a rail ... or worse.

If he didn't come up with money to placate his bankers and the break-a-leg-if-you-don't-pay moneylenders at the Two Sevens, a gaming hell on St. James Street, where he'd bartered his very soul to the tune of five thousand pounds, he was going to have to do what the Beau Brummell had done just last May ... flee his creditors by leaving the country.

Damn it, but gaming was in his blood. What was a wager-loving bloke to do?

Then there was that other matter.... It had been over a month since he'd sent any money to that hovel in Spitalfields, and even longer since he'd paid a visit. But Sophie would have to wait. He had to save his own skin before he would even consider sending a bit of financial relief to Sophie and the baby.

Damn her for getting pregnant! he thought for the umpteenth time. The pregnancy had ruined her figure, and now they'd another mouth to feed. As well, Sophie was unable to earn even a pittance on her own with the babe to care for. She should have done as he'd advised at the outset and taken a potion to rid herself of the child before it was born. But such an irritating and trivial problem did not bear thinking of at the moment. He had much more important fish to fry.

Rob hesitated at the bottom of the steps leading up to Charlotte's front door. He'd climbed these steps too many times to count in the last week. In fact, he'd practically lived with the Batsfords, playing Jack's concerned friend and selflessly pouring out support and consolation to Jack's fiancée.

All along, of course, he'd dropped hints for Charlotte to pick up and ponder. Hints that Jack was not exactly ecstatic about the marriage. Hints that his disappearance might reflect a definite reluctance on the groom's part to buckle himself to a bride. And Charlotte, trusting little goose that she was, had listened.

Of course, there was a great deal of truth in what he'd said, Rob rationalized. After all, Jack was entering the wedded state out of a sense of family responsibility. But since he had made the initial plunge by proposing, he'd never cry off and leave both him and Charlotte shamefaced and socially *de trop*. He'd go through with the wedding no matter what.

But if Charlotte, who actually imagined herself in love with Jack, knew of his reluctance, and if Rob exaggerated that reluctance, she'd feel duty-bound to grant him his freedom.

Then Rob would waltz in and nab the vulnerable and heartbroken bride for himself. Such was the plan, and it was a good one in Rob's opinion.

Jack could be useful sometimes, as he'd been useful since their return from the peninsula in serving as Rob's entre into *le beau monde*, the highest echelon of society, the members of which wouldn't have considered accepting him under any other circumstances. Jack's brother, Lord Serling, for example, was just such a nob who wouldn't countenance him if it weren't for Jack's sponsorship. Yes, Julian—damn those preternaturally pale and eerie eyes—seemed to suspect him of being a hanger-on, a mushroom, a user. Rob couldn't care less what Julian thought of him, but the man gave him the jitters.

Jack was easier to fool because he had a trusting and open spirit. And Jack felt an obligation and a deep desire to trust and like Rob because Rob, an enlisted man serving under Jack's captaincy, had had the great good luck of saving Jack's life one fateful day. Thus Rob had secured Jack's blind friendship and loyalty ever since.

But Julian Montgomery was an entirely different bag of tricks. He didn't like Rob, and he only tolerated him because he'd saved Jack's life. He had a shrewd, suspicious nature and was ruthless when crossed or whenever a member of his family was threatened in any way. Rob knew he had a foe and not a friend in the imperious Marquess of Serling. Wisely, he steered clear as best he could.

Rob was standing on the porch now and was about to make use of the knocker when the door suddenly opened and Jack came out. Rob was hopeful that his friend's dazed expression meant his scheme had been successful. In a moment he'd know for sure, but first he'd a role to play....

"Jack! Jack, you old sod!" He clutched Jack to his chest and gave him several hearty thumps on the back. "Heard you was back! Coming round to see you tonight, but thought I'd best check in on Charlotte first. Been a Trojan, she has. Kept the stiff lip and all that. How the deuce are you, old man?"

"Hello, Rob," Jack replied, once he'd been released from Rob's affectionate stranglehold. He straightened his cravat and smiled wryly. "So you're glad to see me, eh?"

"Thought you'd turned up your toes, Jack. Was worried sick about you. 'Twas devilish queer the way you disappeared outside The Spotted Dog. Was sure you'd been murdered."

Jack walked down the steps and Rob followed. "As you can see, I'm in fine fettle except for another scar to add to my collection." He stopped, turned in the street, and pointed at his forehead where a narrow bandage an inch and a half long was secured.

Rob inwardly seethed. Another scar that females would find interesting. The scar on Jack's cheek had won him a great deal of feminine sympathy in the form of bedchamber romps, and this one would only add to his allure. They didn't seem to detract from his basic good looks, either. Actually, they gave him a dangerous air and saved him from being too pretty. Damn the man.

"How'd you get it?" Rob inquired, falling into step with Jack as he walked toward his approaching phaeton and horses.

"How much do you know about what happened to me, Rob?" Jack asked.

"Only as much as Charlotte was told in the note from your brother. That you were injured and that you'd temporarily lost your memory."

"Well, that's enough for now. You'll have to come visit me to get the details. Only don't come tonight. I've got a lot to do. I'm driving to Surrey on the morrow, and I'm not sure when I'll be back."

"Why the deuce are you going to Surrey all of a sudden? What's there? And why aren't you staying in town to prepare for your wedding?"

"You ask too many questions, Rob. Besides, I thought you were on your way to see Charlotte?"

Rob peered closely at Jack's face. He couldn't gauge his mood. "Why don't *you* tell me how she is?"

Jack shrugged and smiled sheepishly. "She's in excellent form. I've never given her enough credit before, I daresay, but I think her an extremely wise young woman. She's refused to marry me, Rob. Seems she's had second thoughts. Don't blame her, mind you. In fact, I applaud her. Now, if you don't mind, I'm in a bit of a hurry." The phaeton had pulled up alongside the walkway, and Jack easily swung himself up several feet into the high seat.

"What the deuce are you talking about, Jack?" said Rob, feigning astonishment. "Don't tell me the wedding's been called off for good this time?"

Jack took the ribbons from his tiger and held them aloft. He bent a serious gaze on Rob. "That's exactly what I'm saying, Rob. Charlotte says you've been a staunch friend to her while I was gone. Go and keep her company, will you? She says she's fine, and I think she's much better off without me, but just in case she's feeling a little blue-deviled—calling off the wedding and all, and having to put up with that dragon of a mother—why don't you see what you can do to cheer her up? There's a good fellow." Then he flicked the ear of his leader and was off.

Rob watched Jack tool his phaeton down the road and envied him the kind of wealth that could afford such a spanking equipage and the means to stable horses in town. It was a monumental expense. But Rob's surly expression turned into a smile as he contemplated his own plans for acquiring a tidy fortune. He didn't know the details of Jack's weeklong adventure, and he thought his friend extremely preoccupied and uncommunicative. But none of that mattered any more. Once he was Charlotte's husband, he'd be nearly as flush in the pocket as Jack.

Rob turned and walked back toward the Batsford town house. He was a bit worried that the Batsfords would think it indelicate to press his suit so soon after Charlotte and Jack had broken up. But Rob hadn't the time to consider delicacies. Besides, on the other hand, the Batsfords might be relieved and delighted to be able to puff off to the papers news of Charlotte's most recent engagement. They might even use her attachment to Rob as a reason for her breaking things off with Jack, a way . . . as it were . . . of saving face.

Rob's chest swelled like a preening toad's as he imagined the latest *on dit* about town: Charlotte Batsford jilts Jackson Montgomery, Viscount Durham, for the mere Honorable Robert Hamilton. What tittletattle it would cause in every drawing room among the exalted ranks of the upper ten thousand. And wouldn't haughty Lord Serling be flummoxed!

With supreme self-confidence, Rob gave the door a hearty whacking with the knocker. Smiling smugly to himself, he waited for Phipps to open the portal to golden opportunity. Rob could almost hear the extra coins jingling in his pocket already. . . .

"Samantha's been sulking ever since he left, you know," said Prissy, wringing her hands.

"Yes, and she absolutely refuses to cooperate with the dressmaker," Nan added fretfully. "If Lord Serling . . . the dear man . . . had only stayed another day, she might have stood still long enough to be fitted for a few day dresses, at least. What are we going to do with the child, Amanda Jane?"

Amanda sighed and stroked imagined creases out of her own jonquil-colored morning gown with a worried expression on her face. The noonday sun was shining in through the downstairs sitting room windows as the three ladies sat in chintz-covered chairs around an oak worktable. A vase of yellow chrysanthemums graced the unoccupied end of the table and stitchery boxes and balls of yarn littered the end where the ladies were sitting and knitting socks for the orphanage in nearby Crowhurst.

"Lord Serling was anxious to return to London," Amanda said. "Besides, I've presumed on his kindness quite enough already and wouldn't dare ask him to stay another minute. Sam will get used to us—and to her new home, I daresay—and in time she won't miss Lord Serling at all."

Both aunts looked doubtful.

"He had such a way with her," Prissy couldn't help saying in a tone of lament. "He knew how to make her behave. Just a look from him, or a raised brow, made her absolutely docile!"

"I wouldn't go that far, Aunt Prissy," Amanda replied dryly. "Certainly Sam behaves much better for Lord Serling than for anybody else, but I've heard her talk back to the marquess, too."

"Nevertheless, his influence over the girl is considerable," Nan piped in. "And who would have guessed such a man would take the slightest interest in an ... er ... underprivileged child like Samantha? Most people would be amazed to know what a kind heart he has considering how ... er ... well—"

"Aloof he seems?" Amanda finished for her with a wry smile. "How toplofty? How high in the instep, dear aunt?"

"I will admit he frightened me quite speechless when he first arrived with you yesterday, Amanda," Nan confessed, her faded brown eyes wide and wondering. "My, such a grand man he seemed, and so excessively tall! But now I think him the dearest fellow."

"He said he'd call again in a few days, Amanda Jane," Prissy reminded her quite unnecessarily, "to see how we're getting on. If we're not succeeding with the child by then, hopefully he will advise us what to do."

Amanda picked up her knitting and trained her eyes to the job. "I don't think it would be wise to involve Lord Serling in our problems, Aunt Prissy," she said evenly. "And, quite frankly, I think you're underestimating our abilities. You talk as though we can't muddle along at all without a man to direct us."

Out of the corner of her eye Amanda caught the aunts exchanging meaningful glances. She braced herself for what she was sure was coming next.

Aunt Nan cleared her throat. "Well, Lord Serling and his brother certainly came in handy on your trip to Thorney Island," she asserted. "And *they're* men!"

"Yes, but—"

"I gather from the snippets I've heard from you and Sam that if not for their help you might have found yourself in quite a tangle, Amanda Jane," Prissy added emphatically. "I hope you're not being ungrateful, dearest."

"Certainly not," Amanda snapped, dropping her knitting in frustration. She gave her aunts a look of sheer exasperation. "I'm very grateful to Lord Serling for his help, but you don't know ... you can't even imagine how much trouble his *brother* was!"

Amanda broke off and picked up her knitting again as she felt her face flush with heat and color. She couldn't even allude to Jack without a strong emotional reaction. She tried not to think of him at all, but the aunts were curious, and she'd been quite vague and sparse with details when she'd explained her adventures of the last few days ... particularly when the explanations required mentioning Jack.

Prissy tsked-tsked at Amanda's outburst and said, "He couldn't help losing his memory, dear. You can't fault him for that. And he saved Samantha's life! I wish I could meet the dear man and thank him face-to-face. Maybe we should invite him and Lord Serling to dinner, Amanda Jane. 'Tis only a half-day's drive from London. Don't you think that would be the proper thing to do?"

Amanda threw down her yarn and needles and abruptly stood up. With clenched fists propped on the glossy tabletop Amanda glared down into her aunts' startled faces. "No, I don't think that would be proper, or the least bit wise. I never want to see that man again for as long as I live!"

"But why, Amanda Jane?" Prissy inquired in a quavering voice.

"Yes, why?" echoed Nan.

Amanda closed her eyes. "If you must know, aunts, Jack Montgomery's behavior on our trip was anything but prop—"

"Miss?"

Amanda opened her eyes and looked toward the sitting-room door, where Henchpenny stood at attention. She straightened up and endeavored to compose herself. "Yes, Henchpenny?"

"There's someone to see you, miss."

She took a deep breath. This would be the first caller since she'd returned home. Had Vicar Pleasely already heard about Amanda's strange houseguest? Or was it the nosy Bartholomew sisters, Mary and Martha? She'd rehearsed in her mind a hundred times how she would explain Samantha to her neighbors. She hoped she was ready to lie convincingly.

She took another deep breath and inquired, "Who is it, Henchpenny?"

But before Henchpenny could reply, one long, trousered leg slipped through the half-opened door, and then another. And then the entire elegant figure of Jackson Montgomery appeared. From the top of his fashionably tousled blue-black hair to the tips of his polished Hessians, he was as neat and glossy as a raven's feather. He held his hat in his hand and had a sheepish half-smile on his lips.

"It's me, Aman—Miss Darlington. May I come in?"

Amanda felt as if every bit of air had been squeezed from her lungs. She grabbed the table for support as she felt herself slightly swaying. His appearance was so unexpected, the shock was considerable. But even if she'd known he was coming, she'd have reacted just as violently to the sight of him.

The sight of him . . . was it possible that she'd forgotten how handsome he was? How his presence filled a room? How he made her heart pound and her pulse drum through her veins till she was as heady as a June bride?

Beyond her swimming senses, all of which seemed to be concentrated on the man standing at the door, Amanda was vaguely aware of her aunts' incredulous and curious stares. Their white heads swiveled back and forth from Amanda to Jack, back to Amanda, then . . . inevitably . . . back to Jack. And there their gazes remained fixed. The aunts were as mesmerized by Jack as Amanda was . . . as all women were. Apparently there was no age limitation on keen sexual awareness.

Frightened by her initial reaction, Amanda strived to remember why she was furious with Jack. She recalled every hurtful detail that would reinforce her against the onslaught of tender and passionate feelings flooding through her heart and soul. As the seconds ticked by, she was able to dredge up enough anger to save her from rushing headlong into the villain's strong arms. At the same moment, she found her voice.

"Henchpenny, you may go," she said evenly. The man inched away slowly, his lips pursed in disapproval. He had no doubt noticed the thick-as-pea-soup tension in the room.

"Come in, Lord Durham," Amanda said with regal formality. She made a split-second decision to behave with icy decorum instead of anger. He'd still get the message, and she wouldn't have to air her and Jack's dirty laundry in front of her aunts.

Jack frowned and moved forward. He'd been limping when she walked with him on the beach at Thorney Island, but now it appeared his limp was gone. All the better to walk down the aisle, she thought with caustic humor that only hurt herself. His eyes searched her face, but she forced herself to remain expressionless.

"Lord Durham, these are my aunts, Miss Priscilla and Miss Nancy Steeple. Aunts, this is Lord Serling's brother, Lord Durham."

Jack tore his troubled gaze away from Amanda and smiled down at the aunts. His lips parted to display straight white teeth that seemed to glint dazzlingly in the sunshine that bathed the room. He bowed elegantly and took each of their hands. "Your niece has told me a great deal about you. It's a pleasure to meet you at last."

The aunts blushed and stuttered. They were in awe. And they didn't have a clue what to say because they couldn't make the same polite comment in reply. Amanda had told them nothing about *him*!

"To what do we owe this visit, Lord Durham?" Amanda inquired without inviting him to sit down or offering him any refreshment after his long drive down from London. The aunts noted the rude omission and stared at their niece disbelievingly.

Jack dropped a caressing look down the length of her dress, then up again to her face and hair, seeming to take in every detail. "You've left off wearing black," he said. "You're lovely in yellow. It makes your hair look like sunshine . . ."

Amanda tried to control the rush of blood to her cheeks, but it was impossible. He still had the power to thrill her, to charm her, to crowd and confuse her senses with his smile, his words, his vital presence.

She briefly closed her eyes to compose herself. "Don't flatter me, Jack. Just state your business and be off."

Jack shook his head and dropped his hat on the table. He was dressed in a burgundy riding jacket, a waistcoat with a subdued paisley print, and buff-colored kerseymere trousers that clung to his shapely legs like a second skin. "I can see you're not going to make this easy for me, Amanda."

She raised her brows and moved so that the entire length of the oval table was between them. "I don't know what you're talking about."

"Could we speak privately?"

The aunts dear-deared and tut-tutted and began to scoot back their chairs.

"Don't go," Amanda ordered in a no-nonsense voice, and the aunts remained seated. She didn't take her eyes off Jack, but she could see her aunts' confused flutterings in her peripheral vision. "There's nothing Jack needs to say that he can't say in front of other people." She threw him a challenging look. "Is there, Jack?"

Jack's jaw tightened. He'd been patient and conciliatory so far, but now his eyes flashed with angry determination. A chill raced down Amanda's spine.

"Do you take pleasure in seeing your aunts squirm in their seats, Amanda?" he inquired with deceptive calmness. He placed his splayed hands on the table and leaned forward. His voice lowered seductively. "Or are you insisting that they remain because you're afraid to be alone with me?"

Amanda's chin tilted up. "Of . . . of course I'm not afraid to be alone with you," she lied.

He raised his black brows, implying disbelief.

Amanda sighed shakily and turned to look at her aunts. They indeed appeared as though they were feeling decidedly awkward and uncomfortable. "If you want to go, aunts, please feel free to leave the room, but if you'd rather stay, don't let Jack—"

But Amanda didn't bother to finish the sentence. Her aunts had already scurried out of the room and closed the door behind them. She was alone . . . with Jack. She forced herself to meet his unwavering gaze with assumed unconcern.

"Thank you, Amanda," Jack said gravely.

"Don't thank me," she snapped back. "Just tell me why you're here. By-the-by, does your bride-to-be know where you are this lovely afternoon, or does she think you're at Weston's being fitted for a wedding suit?"

Jack smiled wryly and slowly edged toward the curve of the table, trailing the fingers of his gloved right hand along the smooth, gleaming wood. Amanda's stomach clenched with longing. She could remember the feel of his hands on her skin. Gentle, urgent, thrilling. But she stood her ground.

"You really do think me a villain, don't you, Amanda? But do you honestly imagine I'd be here if I was supposed to be at Weston's being fitted for wedding togs?"

"When you left your house this morning you might have forgotten your destination, my lord," she answered tartly. "After all, you do have a lamentable memory."

He laughed and eased around the curve of the table, inching closer. "How's *your* memory, Amanda?"

"Perfect, as usual," she retorted. She glared at him, daring him to come closer. "But there are things . . . times . . . *people* . . . I'd as soon forget."

"Ah well," he conceded with a nonchalant wave of his hand. "Haven't we all been guilty some time or other of wishing for a selective memory loss?"

"Some of us have been more guilty than others," she answered dryly.

Jack took another step. He'd worked himself half-way around the table and was now almost close enough to reach out and touch her. The hairs on the back of Amanda's neck prickled with anticipation ... and fear. Fear of her own response should he dare to take her in his arms. Fear that he *wouldn't* take her in his arms ...

"If you are referring to me, m'dear—as I suspect you are—at least concede that I kept my recovery from amnesia a secret from you because I wanted to protect you."

"From whom did you wish to protect me, pray tell?" she said with a low, harsh laugh. "Not from you, as I recall."

"From yourself, you willful baggage," he ground out, taking two more hasty steps. Now they were separated by mere inches, but he made no attempt to touch her. "You'd have been in a pickle without my help on Thorney Island!"

Amanda could feel the heat of Jack's body.... She could sense the intensity of his feelings by the fiery expression in his eyes. "If—if you're here to be thanked again for saving Sam," she stuttered, desperate for him to back away and give her space to think, to breathe, "then—then—*thank you*! Thank you a million times over. Now please go!"

Jack grabbed her and pulled her against his chest. Amanda gasped. Her arms hung stiffly at her sides. She knew she mustn't touch him. She dared not make a move or she'd twine her arms around his neck and shamelessly offer her lips to be kissed, just as she'd offered them before. His breath hissed across her face as he said, "I don't want your gratitude, Amanda. I want—"

This time Jack didn't wait for an invitation. He lowered his head and captured Amanda's lips in a fierce kiss, his tongue plundering her mouth, his arms crushing her against him.

What do you want, Jack? Amanda silently screamed as she helplessly returned his kiss with equal fervor, her hands wending their way up his hard, muscled back and into his glorious hair. *Do you want me? Do you truly want me?*

Then, suddenly, Jack let her go and stepped back to a safer distance. Amanda's head was reeling, her heart was pounding. She was left feeling bereft, disappointed . . . and prickly as hell.

"Why *are* you here, Jack?" she demanded in a low, raspy voice, wrapping her arms around her aching breasts. "Surely not just to steal a last kiss?"

Jack rubbed the back of his neck, and a muscle ticked in his jaw. He stared at her with anguish in his eyes. His chest rose and fell with quick, uncontrolled breathing. What was he feeling? Was it only lust? What did he really want? Amanda wondered desperately. To hold her? To kiss her? To *kill* her?

"Do you remember at Thorney Island when I said I'd marry Charlotte if she still wanted me?" he said at last, his expression and voice carefully neutral.

"Yes." She swallowed hard. "So?"

His gaze raked her face, searched her eyes. "Well, she doesn't want me."

A thrill of excitement coursed through Amanda, but she ruthlessly suppressed it. He was lying. What woman wouldn't want Jack? Or worse, he was telling her the truth and had come to propose to her out of a sense of obligation. She refused to be an obligation, and she refused to be second choice! Her heart hammered away, trying to be heard above her pride and common sense, but she turned a deaf ear to it. She would not be duped twice, or hurt twice, by the same man!

"You're silent," he said.

"What do you expect me to say?"

"I don't know. I thought perhaps— that is, I'd hoped—"

Terrified what he might be leading up to, she quickly interrupted. "You should be happy, Jack. You're free again. Isn't that what you want?"

His dark eyes, amber in the sunlit room, gleamed like jewels. "No. That's not what I want. Not any more. Not since I met you. Now I *want* to be married . . . to you, Amanda."

Amanda laughed bitterly. "You insult me, Jack."

Jack flinched. "Do you think so poorly of me that you consider my proposal an insult, Amanda?" he inquired mildly, but with a dangerous glint in his eyes. "I may not be the greatest matrimonial *parti* on the isle of England, but I—" He stopped suddenly, seeming to catch himself before saying something he'd regret. She could see his mental wheels turning; decisions being made, options being weighed. Finally he said, "But I'll do everything in my power to make you happy."

"How can you expect me to believe you, Jack?" said Amanda, tears of disappointment stinging her eyelids. *If only he'd said he loved her!* "You've made no secret of your aversion to marriage. And you've lied to me before."

Harshly, he said, "And you'll never forgive me, I suppose."

"It's not a matter of forgiveness. It's a matter of trust. But that's not the reason I'm refusing your offer of marriage."

"Then why?" he inquired stiffly.

Because you don't love me, her heart screamed. "Because you're only offering out of a sense of obligation . . . because you think you've compromised me. You didn't compromise me, I assure you. What happened between us was as much my doing as yours. I'd rather die than shackle myself to an unwilling groom . . . to a man who doesn't—"

Jack, tell her you love her, you stupid jackass! Maybe that's what she wants to hear! And Jack wanted to tell

her that he loved her with all his heart . . . but he
couldn't.

Why was it so hard to say those three little words?
He'd admitted to his brother that he loved Amanda,
so why couldn't he tell her? Maybe he was afraid
that Amanda wouldn't say it back. Afraid that if she
did say it back, she'd be saying it for the wrong
reasons.

And she'd laughed. She'd laughed at his proposal.

"You're speechless, Lord Durham."

Amanda's coolly spoken words interrupted Jack's
agonized thoughts. He stared at her. She was lovely
but so unapproachable. Her delicate features seemed
carved in stone, her eyes shimmered a frosty silver-
blue. She had refused him, and it was absurd of him
to keep standing duncelike in her sittingroom as if
she'd suddenly change her mind. She wasn't going
to change her mind.

Jack forced a grim smile and bowed. "I can see
this is a fruitless endeavor," he said, icy and rigid. "It
was very good of you to receive me, Miss Darlington,
particularly as it is quite obvious that you'd have
rather not. As well, please accept my apologies for
intruding on your pleasant day with such a repellant
suggestion as to buckle yourself for life to the likes
of *me*! I assure you, it won't happen again. Good
afternoon . . . and God bless you."

Amanda watched him march out the door, his spine
as stiff as a northern breeze, the pained expression in
his eyes a sight that would replay itself over and over
in her mind and steal her sleep night after endless
night. Completely overcome, Amanda slumped into
her chair, cradled her head in her folded arms atop the
table, and wept bitterly.

Nan and Prissy came into the room, saw Amanda
sobbing at the table, and exchanged stricken glances.
They scurried to take up positions on each side of
Amanda's chair.

"There, there," said Prissy, stroking Amanda's bright head.

"Yes, dear, don't fret," soothed Nan, patting her niece's trembling shoulders. "All will be well."

But the look she gave Prissy belied her consoling words. She and Prissy had been listening at the door, and she very much feared that all would *not* be well till dear Amanda Jane got her Jack back.

Chapter 18

"Tha's one. Tha's two. Tha's—"

"Bloody hell, Jack. Why d'ya always hav'ta count your drinks? S'not important."

Jack stared bleary-eyed at his drinking companion across the table in a smoky corner of a small but notorious gaming hell in Covent Garden. It was not the usual haunt for nobs of Jack's aristocratic caliber, but that was exactly why he'd chosen it. He was avoiding all friends and acquaintances that might wish to question him about his broken betrothal or quiz him about his previous fit of amnesia and subsequent disappearance. Rob was simply hiding from the duns.

Yes, despite another generous loan from Jack just recently, Rob was as deep in debt as ever. No wonder he had as many empty tumblers in front of him as Jack did ... maybe more. His situation was desperate. Jack had given him thousands of pounds already and had extracted many promises from Rob to curtail his gaming habit, but the poor bastard just couldn't keep away from the green baize tables where great sums of money were won and lost. And Rob always seemed to lose.

Then there was that unfortunate incident he'd had

recently with Charlotte.... Jack completely sympathized, too. No man liked to be turned down when he humbly offered his hand in marriage.

"I like countin' the glasses, Rob," Jack said, finally picking up the conversation, as it were, where they'd left off. "Gives me somethin' t' do besides thinkin' 'bout that—" He paused, staring with unfocused deliberation into empty space. He conjured up Amanda's face. Not the way she'd looked two weeks ago when she'd refused his marriage proposal, but the way she'd looked that night at the Angel Inn when they'd made love. He smiled, his eyelids drooping drunkenly. "—'bout that *woman*," he finished, but in a much more tender and wistful tone than he'd originally intended.

Rob let go with a healthy belch and rubbed his bloated stomach. "*Women*," he said emphatically, the single word conveying a wealth of meaning. He raised his right arm and extended his index finger in an orator's pose. "A wise man once said—"

"What wise man?" Jack inquired sleepily.

"Aristoph—something or other," Rob mumbled. "What does it matter, Jack? Anyway, he once said, 'There's nothing in the world worse than woman ... save some other woman.' He couldn't have been more correct, the ol' Greek bugger." Rob took another long drink of gin.

Jack pulled thoughtfully on his chin. "Tha's a good one, Rob. Very much to the point, eh? But I like this one better." He cleared his throat and endeavored to keep his eyes open by raising his brows as high as they could possibly go. "An *anonymush* fellow once said, 'Woman is the chain by which man is attached to the chariot of"— he hiccuped—"folly.' "

Rob nodded gravely. "Too true, Jack. If not fer women, we'd be as happy as larks in a hedgerow, eh?"

Jack pursed his lips and squinted his eyes. "That

makes me think of another one, Rob. I believe it was that old woman-hater Tom Dekker who said, 'Were there no women, man might live like gods.' "

"Gods. There you go, Jack," said Rob, much impressed. He raised his tumbler high for a toast. "That says it perfectly. And that's just how we'll live now that we're rid of women for good . . . right?"

"Right!" Jack said, then lifted his own nearly empty tumbler and attempted to make contact with Rob's. After three tries, the tumblers connected and the chime of crystal rang through the room.

"Like the gods!" they chorused.

After downing the remaining contents of their glasses and ordering another round, Rob's head sunk to the table. Rolling his brow against the wood, he lamented, "Oh, *why* wouldn't Charlotte have me, Jack? I thought we were friends, she and I!"

Jack shrugged and sucked his teeth. "You pounced too soon, Rob. She wasn't over me yet, I daresay."

"You bloody sod," Rob grumbled, his words muffled by his mouth's proximity to the tabletop. "Don't know why women like *you* so much and *me* so little!"

Jack frowned and sighed. "Don't *all* of 'em like me. 'Manda don't like me above half. Won't marry me. And now I don't think I'll ever stick my tail in parson's mousetrap. Love 'er like mad . . . don't ya know. Bloody shame she don't love me back."

Full of self-pity, Jack lowered his own head to the table as well, his forehead hitting the wood with a dull thump at the end of his hopeless descent.

"Good *Gawd*!" drawled a familiar voice, and Jack peered up into the revolted face of his elder brother. Julian held his quizzing glass aloft and was staring down at him through it with obvious contempt. His pale, cold eye appeared enormous at the opposite side of the glass, and the effect was chilling.

"What are you doin' here, Julian?" Jack wondered aloud. "Ain't your sort of place at all."

A corner of Julian's upper lip lifted in a sneer as he took a swift and scathing appraisal of their surroundings. "Indeed not, little brother. Nor is it your sort of place, either." He reached down and took hold of Jack's arm just above the elbow. "Been looking for you all over town, you young jackanapes."

"What for, Julian?"

"We need to talk. You're coming home with me, where I can pour black coffee down your throat till you're sober enough to comprehend what I'm saying."

Jack wobbled to his feet. "Don't mind goin' home, Julian," he admitted, his head throbbing from the sudden change of altitude. He made a wide gesture toward the table. Rob's eyes were closed, and he was drooling. "But what about Rob? Think he's passed out, Julian. Can't leave 'im to the mercies of th' pickpockets and guttersnipes."

"No, I suppose not," Julian replied unenthusiastically, "though they'd get little enough for their trouble. Nevertheless, I'll have the postilions carry him out and put him in a hack. Don't worry. If I make myself known to the driver and pay him well enough, he'll get your ... *friend* home and into his lodgings without mishap."

Jack nodded and allowed himself to be partially supported as he stumbled out to Julian's shiny black-and-silver drag. The moment he got inside and settled himself against the plush gray squabs, he lost consciousness. The next thing he knew, he was waking up in Julian's dark panelled library on the leather couch.

Several cups of black, scalding coffee later, he was wide-eyed and sober, his head pounding from the after-effects of another night spent drowning his sorrows in cups of gin. Sitting opposite him in a wing chair by the fire, Julian watched Jack's gradual return to sobriety with a sapient eye.

Jack felt his hackles rising. "You look at me as though I've sprouted an extra nose."

"I wish you'd sprout another brain. The one you've got now doesn't seem to be working very well."

Jack frowned. "What's the matter, Julian? You've seen me drunk before."

"You used to get foxed now and then, just like every other reckless scapegrace about town, but lately you've made a bloody habit of it."

Jack shrugged and flashed a rakish grin, even though the effort made his head throb all the worse. "I've been celebrating my lucky escape from the nuptial knot, don't you know."

"You've been doing nothing of the sort," Julian replied repressively. "You're wallowing in drunkenness to numb your sensibilities, brother. You're trying to forget that Miss Darlington refused your offer of marriage."

Jack stiffened and set down his cup of coffee with a shaky hand. "How do you know about that?"

"Amanda's aunts told me. They tell me everything." He smiled ruefully. "They tell me some things I'd just as soon they'd keep to themselves."

"Got cozy with them all, have you? You take a lively interest in the welfare of that family," Jack growled, his jealousy stirred. "Tell the truth, Julian. . . . Are you after Amanda for yourself?" Every muscle in Jack's body tensed while he waited for Julian's reply.

Julian stared haughtily down his aristocratic nose. "Certainly not. Do you think I'd pursue a female my brother is passionately in love with? And a woman, moreover, with whom he's been . . . intimate?"

"Did the aunts tell you that, too?" Jack inquired truculently.

"Do you take me for a gull? I figured that one out for myself."

Jack's eyes narrowed warily. "I was intimate with

that opera dancer last spring, and that didn't stop you from dallying with *her!*"

"That was an entirely different matter altogether. We're talking about a lady, Jack. You've somehow managed to entangle yourself with respectable females lately. First Charlotte, then—"

"*Charlotte*, you say?" Jack raised his brows. "Are you on such familiar terms with my ex-fiancée that you—a stickler for proper social protocol—refer to her by her Christian name?"

Julian crossed his legs in a gesture of complete ease ... almost of indifference. He waved a dismissive hand. "I *have* been calling on her. I've made no secret of my admiration for Charlotte. If you remember, I was quite pleased you were going to marry the girl." He scowled. "But she's too damn good for the likes of Hamilton and his sort. Couldn't believe the impudence of the fellow to ask Charlotte to marry him ten minutes after she'd broken off with you. Even if she'd been inclined to accept his offer, her parents would never have allowed it. Can't think where the fellow gets his cheeky confidence!"

"By God, you *like* her! You really like her!" Jack exclaimed, amazed. "I never dreamed ... is this serious, Julian?"

"Possibly," Julian admitted coolly, his features returning to their usual regal placidity.

Jack grinned. "You mean you might actually take on the task of perpetuating the Montgomery dynasty? You're so deuced particular about females, etcetera, I always thought *that* undertaking would fall to my lot. Bloody hell!"

"I did not bring you here to speculate about my future, Jack. There's another matter I wish to discuss. As you know, I've been helping Miss Darlington with her sister, Samantha."

"Yes, you've been driving out to Surrey several times a week." Jack suppressed the pang of envy. He wished *he* were as welcome at Darlington Hall. "How is the little hellcat?"

"As impudent and obnoxious as ever," Julian drawled. "She's extremely bright, however, and has what I can only describe as a certain *spirit* about her that if properly guided—" He shook his head and frowned, stumped for words. "In short," he resumed, "if she would only cooperate and put a little effort into it, she could easily be turned from the proverbial sow's ear to a silk purse."

Interested, Jack nodded. "You don't say? But will she cooperate?"

"So far she's driven to distraction every tutor Miss Darlington has engaged to educate the ungrateful little baggage."

At another mention of Amanda, Jack couldn't resist asking, "Do they get along?" His voice unconsciously softened. "Sam and Amanda, I mean. Is Amanda happy she rescued the girl? It was so important to her to make amends to Sam for her father's neglect."

"They seem to have developed a measure of trust and do sometimes talk with a degree of amiability between them. However, Sam frequently does things for the sole purpose of annoying Miss Darlington."

Jack smiled, satisfied. "Sounds like siblings to me."

"But I'm apparently the only one that can get Samantha to apply to her studies, to concentrate on improving her language, her comportment, her social graces . . . as it were."

"And who better than you, Julian? You wield a double-edged sword. You are *the* arbiter of social graces in the *haut ton*, and—forgive me for saying so—you are as intimidating as the devil himself. You'd be the perfect instructor for the chit."

"Exactly. But I dislike traveling to Surrey so frequently. That's why I've induced Miss Darlington to take a house in London till Christmas."

"What?" If Jack wasn't completely sober before, he was now.

"I found her charming lodgings in Mayfair. Very respectable."

"But—"

"That way I can see Samantha regularly and terrify her into the silk purse we earlier used as an analogy. I've been bored lately, and the idea of performing such a miracle amuses me."

"Are you saying—?"

"At the same time, I've encouraged Miss Darlington to enjoy what's left of the little season. Naturally she'll pay outward respect to the passing of her parents by wearing the darker colors of half-mourning."

"As long as she doesn't drape herself in black again," Jack said gruffly.

"No, indeed," Julian agreed. "That won't be necessary. She won't dance, of course, but I dare say it will be perfectly acceptable if she attends other sorts of gatherings."

"But, Julian—" Jack tried to interrupt.

"As for Sam, she'll be kept out of sight till she's respectable. As she isn't 'out' yet, no one will think to inquire about a schoolroom miss. Excursions will be brief and controlled. She'll have to do without acquaintances beyond her family circle till her official coming-out in the spring. We'll introduce her as Amanda's orphaned cousin. Conveniently, Amanda had an aunt and uncle in Cumbria who died childless several years ago. He was a curate . . . poor as a mouse, but respectable, she tells me."

"Dash it, Julian, I want to know—"

"By the start of the season, I fully intend Sam to be worthy of presentation in the best drawing rooms in London. With the handsome dowry Amanda has generously set aside for her, and with *my* sponsorship, she should be able to make quite a respectable match."

Jack leaned forward, grabbed Julian's lapels, and said wonderingly, "Amanda is coming to London?"

Julian produced a lazy smile. "Haven't you been listening, little brother?"

"She told me her first and only season was a catastrophe." Jack leaned back, his brow furrowed. "Are you sure she means to go out in society?"

"I'm quite sure. She's much more confident now. Back then she was a green girl just out of the schoolroom. And I gather her parents raised her rather too priggishly. She's got past that, I think. I've arranged for Sally Jersey to send her a voucher for Almacks and have already secured her an invitation to the Cowpers' for a musical evening."

"Bloody hell," was Jack's only comment.

Julian stood up, crossed his arms, and peered down at Jack with a sardonic expression. "That means—just in case you've lost track of what day of the week it is—you've got exactly eight-and-forty hours to pull yourself together, brother."

Jack frowned up at Julian. "You don't really think I've got a chance at changing her mind about me, do you?"

"There's only one way to find out, Jack. If you make it your business to attend the same social functions she does, and you strive to be as charming as possible, maybe she'll unbend a little. I don't think she's an unfeeling girl. In fact, I think she's quite the opposite. I like her, Jack."

"That's praise indeed," Jack said with a dry chuckle, then sobered. "But I don't think charming her will have as much to do with winning Amanda's favor as proving she can trust me again."

"You know her better than I do, Jack. Use your own judgment." Julian hesitated, staring at the floor as he seemed to consider whether or not he should say more. Suddenly he looked up and said, "And follow your heart. Matches forged by genuine affection are extremely rare. Don't let true happiness slip away, little brother." Then, as if he were embarrassed to have expressed such sentimental views, he turned abruptly on his heel and exited the room.

Jack smiled and shook his head. Julian terrified most people. If they only knew how human he was beneath that jaded, imperious facade. But Julian didn't want anyone to know, and Jack was bound by an unspoken pact between brothers to keep his secret.

Filled with new resolution and hope, Jack stood up and braced himself with a hand against the back of the sofa till the room quit spinning. He smiled like a May Day fool. In two days he would see Amanda. How would she look? he wondered, and his heart replied, *like an angel. . . .*

"How do I look, Sam?" Amanda pirouetted in front of the cheval mirror in the bedchamber of her London town house. "Will I do?"

Sam sat in the middle of Amanda's canopied bed, engulfed from neck to toe in a demure white nightdress, her feet tucked beneath the flounced hem, her arms wrapped around her updrawn knees.

She cocked her head to the side, her shiny crop of golden curls tumbling over one eye. Clean and plumped up a bit after three weeks of regular meals, Sam looked decidedly more feminine than she'd appeared when Amanda first clapped eyes on her on Thorney Island.

Her figure was lithesome. She had a tiny waist, small pert breasts, delicate hands and feet, a slender, swanlike neck, and a gamine face. Except for her eyes, which were more gray than blue, her features were very similar to Amanda's. They looked like sisters and would pass very easily as cousins.

"Well, Sam?" prompted Amanda. "You aren't saying anything."

"Don't know what to say," Sam finally admitted. "I don't know what a fancy female should look like when she goes go to a musical evenin'."

She said "musical evenin'" as if it were a contagious disease, making Amanda laugh. "You've looked at several lady's magazines."

Sam grimaced. "Only 'cause you and that dressmaker lady made me."

"How does my gown compare to the other evening dresses you saw in *La Belle Assemblée*, for example?"

Sam considered for another long minute while Amanda nervously smoothed the skirt of her midnight-blue evening gown. The waist was very high, coming to just below her breasts. The heart-shaped neckline was demurely cut, showing the merest hint of cleavage. The sleeves were puffed and edged with black lace. The skirt flared at the bottom to touch the floor in an elegant sweep when she walked, and it, too, was decorated with several rows of black lace.

Her black gloves came to just above her elbows. She wore blue satin slippers that exactly matched the color of her gown. Her jewelry was simple, consisting of a sapphire pendant around her neck on a delicate gold chain, sapphire earrings, and a black velvet ribbon that wound through her hair, which was braided in the back and coaxed and crimped into ringlets at her temples and forehead.

Amanda felt like a butterfly emerging from a dark cocoon. She was eager and afraid and quivering inside, but she was determined to have another go at enjoying a London season, even if it were only the little season, which fewer people attended in the autumn, and even if her activities were limited. And no matter how many times she told herself Jack had nothing to do with the excitement that thrummed through her veins, she couldn't quit wondering if she'd see him tonight. If he'd approach her, talk to her . . .

She gave herself a stern mental shake and told herself that she had no business fantasizing about Jack. He'd done his duty by proposing marriage to her, and she'd rejected him. They'd parted on less than amiable terms. He'd probably completely dismissed her from his mind by now and was enjoying the favors of a new mistress.

If only she could forget *him* just as easily. . . . Even if something as miraculous as male admirers materialized during her stay in London, Jack had ruined her for anyone else. Not only was she no longer the virginal maid most men demanded of their proper brides, but she had this unshakable feeling that she actually belonged to Jack now. She couldn't imagine being intimate with another man.

"Why're you so dreamy-eyed all of a sudden? What are you thinkin' about?"

Amanda jerked out of her reverie and looked at Sam. Her sister's large eyes were fastened on her with a keen inquisitiveness that made Amanda decidedly uncomfortable. Sam might be lacking in education, but her mind was as sharp as a hatpin.

"I—I wasn't thinking of anything, really," Amanda lied with a smile. "I was just imagining how the evening will be, and . . . and waiting for your opinion on my appearance."

Sam raised her tawny brows disbelievingly but tactfully refrained from saying what was really on her mind. Where had the little ragamuffin learned *tact*? Amanda wondered. Or was it really cunning she was displaying? She could certainly believe Sam had learned to be a little devious while struggling to survive.

Sam cocked her head to the side again and surveyed her older sister from head to toe. "I think you look like what I always imagined an angel from the Bible would look like," she said at last in a matter-of-fact tone that Amanda was inclined to believe was sincere. After all, Sam had never tried to flatter her before. She felt her cheeks glow with gratification.

"But shouldn't angels be dressed in white?" she demurred modestly.

"You're an evenin' angel," Sam said consideringly. "Your gown's the color of dusk."

"Why, thank you, Sam," Amanda said earnestly and with a warm smile. "How kind of you to compare me to an angel."

Now it was Sam's turn to blush. She hated to be thanked or fussed over. And she didn't want anyone to think she had a kind bone in her body.

"Ah, don't make a to-do over it," she grumped, waving her hand. "What do I know, anyway?"

Wisely, Amanda did not pursue the subject but secretly savored her satisfaction as she collected her black beaded reticule and her ivory-handled blue fan with ostrich feathers, and moved to the door. Just as she was about to exit the room, her aunts bustled in.

"Hurry, Amanda Jane!" exclaimed Aunt Prissy, holding her dove-gray silk skirts high above her small feet as if she were about to make a sprint down Bond Street. "We're going to be late!"

"It's fashionable to be late," Nan admonished her sister. "Besides, Amanda *is* ready to go. If you'd quit twittering about, you'd see for yourself, Pris!" Then she smiled with pleasure as she took in Amanda's appearance. "And she looks lovely. Don't you think so, Samantha?"

Sam shrugged, not about to be caught being nice again. "What would I know?"

With a tiny, almost indiscernible shake of her head and a meaningful glance, Amanda dissuaded her aunts from giving Sam a lecture for being impolite. Miraculously they caught the hint and maneuvered themselves out the door and down the stairs without a single scolding word, Amanda following just behind.

At the bottom of the stairs, Amanda looked up at Sam, who was leaning over the railing with what appeared to be a rather wistful expression. Was it possible that Sam truly wanted to dress up and play the lady, and her recalcitrant act was only a front? Amanda wondered.

"You're going straight to bed, aren't you, Samantha?" Nan called up.

"S'pect I will," she said in a surly tone. "Ain't nothin' else to do."

"I'll tell you all about the party tomorrow morning at breakfast, Sam," Amanda promised her as the footman helped her with her winter wrap, a black velvet cloak trimmed at the hood and hem with swan's down.

Sam shrugged, ducked her head, and nonchalantly kicked her bare toes against the wooden banisters. "If you want to," she mumbled, then slid her eyes up and inquired, "Will there be dancin'?"

"None is planned," said Nan, pulling on her gloves. "And that's just as well, because Amanda Jane can't dance."

"Do you still dance . . . when there's dancin', Aunt Nan?" Sam wanted to know.

Nan tittered behind her hand. "Oh, dancing's not for old duennas like me and Pris. We watch the dancing and flirting and folderol from afar and play chaperon. Tonight Pris and I will be watching to make sure no young buck gets out of line with your sister."

"Aunt Nan!" exclaimed Amanda, laughing. "As if anyone would!"

"You underestimate yourself, my dear," Pris murmured dryly. "You may find that even two chaperons aren't enough to keep the scoundrels at bay."

Amanda simply shook her head and smiled.

"Does Julian dance, do ya think?" Sam asked, reverting to a subject that seemed uppermost in her mind.

"I'm sure he does, but only if he wants to," Amanda answered with a smile. "Why do you ask, dear?"

"Well, isn't Julian *old*?"

Pris gave a most unladylike whoop of laughter, then covered her mouth with her hand and said coyly, "He's not too old for dancing . . . or for a great many other things, I daresay. Such a well-looking man," she said with a giggle. "And Jack, too!"

Nan gave Pris a hard, repressive stare from under her bonnet. Then, while Amanda fumbled confusedly with the ribbons of her cloak and averted her blushing face, Nan smiled up at Sam and said, "Shall I tell Lord Serling you said hello, my dear?"

Again Sam assumed a careless attitude. "If you want to."

"I will, then," Nan assured her with a decided nod. "Good night, my dear."

"Yes, and sweet dreams!" Pris added.

Amanda recovered her wits, which had been scattered by the mere mention of Jack's name, and managed to say goodnight to Sam, too. But the minute she walked out of the house and boarded the carriage, her thoughts became focused on one thing and one thing only.

Would she see Jack tonight?

Sam ran to the window and watched the carriage drive away to Lady Cowper's musical evening. She braced her elbows on the window ledge and gazed dreamily at the foggy nimbus of light surrounding the street lamp directly in front of the house, listening to the clatter of horses and carriages going to and fro.

Sam wasn't sure if she liked London or not. It was quite noisy and very closed-in compared to the only two other places she'd lived in her seventeen years. She missed Thorney Island because of the sea and the endless beaches. The serenity and beauty of dusk there, with her and her dogs sitting by a fire as they watched the sunset, was something she frequently pined for. But she didn't miss the constant hunger and the loneliness.

Darlington Hall was nice. She'd rode a sweet horse at the Hall, a frisky mare named Hollyhock. She'd had her dogs there, too, and they'd run and run on the acres of ground that were part of her rich sister's vast estate. The food was plentiful and the servants were kind. For that matter, Amanda and her aunts were kind, too ... although she supposed Pris and Nan weren't really *her* aunts because they were sisters of Amanda's mother. But since they insisted on claiming her as an adopted niece, she had come to think of them as relatives, too.

She'd even grown rather fond of bathing and liked the fresh scent of her clean sheets when she tumbled into bed at night. All in all, she was getting accustomed to her new life but had a sinking sensation that the hard stuff was yet to come.

At Darlington Hall, she'd managed to frighten away the fuddy-duddy instructors Amanda had hired to help her become "an educated lady" by being as coarse and stupid in their company as she dared. She didn't want *them* to teach her. She wanted Julian and *only* Julian telling her what to do.

Sam smiled, her cheeks cradled in her hands and her bottom sticking up in the back as she continued to linger at the window. The very best thing about coming to London, the one thing that made it bearable to leave her precious dogs behind at the Hall for a few weeks, was the fact that she saw Julian almost every day!

Sam pushed away from the window and walked to the full-length cheval mirror Amanda had used to check her appearance. She stared at her reflection, and decided that in a voluminous nightgown that didn't show her figure to the least advantage she looked like a rather tall *child*. She frowned. Certainly that was the way Julian treated her ... like a child.

But was Julian really so much older than she? When she'd asked Aunt Prissy about Julian's age one day, she'd told her she supposed he was somewhere around five-and-thirty. In this modern day and age, Sam suspected that five-and-thirty was rather old. It certainly sounded old to her. But in the days of Methuselah, Julian would have just begun to live. And he'd have had several wives and a bevy of pretty concubines to keep him spry and happy.

Sam smoothed her hands down the front of her nightdress and cupped her breasts. Was *she* pretty? Was she enough of a woman to attract a man like Julian? Her arms dropped to her sides as she pondered these conundrums.

In the days of the Old Testament, she'd have been happy to be a concubine among tens of dozens of concubines, just to belong to Julian. But she'd much rather be his one and only. Nowadays men were permitted only one wife, and Sam was determined to be that one wife. She smiled demurely. Or his mistress.

But then she frowned. Where had such a thought come from? Of course she would never be anyone's mistress! Her mother had been a mistress, and she'd been a sinner. And Sam had paid for her mother's sin by being disowned and deserted, hidden away on an island for seventeen years.

Sam shook her head, attempting to dislodge the bad thoughts and feelings old Grimshaw had instilled in her every single day till the old witch took off and deserted her, too. Forcing herself to embrace lighter reflections, she took a handful of nightdress on each side and curtsied at the mirror.

"Yes, your lordship," she simpered, touching her index finger to the point of her chin. "I'd be ever so delighted to dance with you. But shouldn't you dance with the *princess* first?"

She batted her lashes and fluttered an imaginary fan. "Oh, la, Julian, don't flatter me so! It fair turns me head!"

Then she extended her arms in a graceful arc and began to make circles on the cabbage-rose carpet surrounding Amanda's bed, humming a discordant tune. But in Sam's imagination, it was the sweetest melody in the world.

Chapter 19

By the time Jack showed up at the Cowper soi-ree, the elegant chambers of the town house were filled with the *crème de la crème* of English society ... at least those who had not deserted town for more pastoral settings and activities. He stood at the door and adjusted his shirt cuffs as he searched the glittering crowd, looking for Amanda.

"I say, Jack, I don't know why you were in such a devilish hurry to get here tonight," Rob complained as he came up behind Jack, still out of breath from climbing the stairs. "I was hoping we could stop at Boodles and get a drink first. Bound to be a dreadful bore."

"You've already had plenty to drink, Rob," Jack said, eyeing his companion with disfavor. "You're starting to look as dissipated as the Prince Regent."

Rob ran a hand through his disheveled blond hair and peered through his bleary, bloodshot eyes. "You've done your share of drinking lately. I only look bad to you tonight because you happen to be sober. Besides, I can't help it. I'm worried about the money." He looked about the room, blinking against the glare of dozens of candles and the thousands of dollars' worth of jewelry that decorated the distinguished guests. "If I could only get my hands on that diamond choker Dorothea Lieven's got round her skinny neck, all my troubles'd be gone in a trice."

"Don't resort to thievery, Rob," Jack advised drily. "You know I've arranged to pay all your domestic expenses, so things aren't desperate, but I won't put out the ready to settle any more gaming vowels. You're going to have to wait for your quarterly allowance from your uncle in Yorkshire and work out a payment schedule with your debtors. In the meantime—"

"Yes, yes, I know!" Rob retorted testily. "I must quit gambling. It ain't that easy, Jack."

"I know. But right now, Rob, I don't want to argue with you about it." Jack had just spied a pale blond head in the middle of a knot of town bucks, and he had a sinking suspicion that the female getting all that attention was his sweet, *shy* Amanda.

"This does not bode well," Jack mumbled.

"What?" asked Rob, straining to see what Jack was staring at so gloomily. "Say, who's the new chit?" he inquired, immediately interested . . . like a wolf who'd caught the scent of a lamb who'd strayed from the herd.

"That's Amanda, Rob."

Rob's eyes bulged. "*Your* Amanda?"

"Miss Darlington to you."

"Fine-looking filly, Jack. Rich, too, I suppose?"

"So I've gathered."

"Thought you said she wouldn't have anything to do with you?"

"So she said." Jack advanced, his eyes never wavering from his intended objective. "But I'm going to give it another go."

"And you'll probably bloody well succeed," Rob grumbled, snatching a glass of champagne off a tray as a liveried porter walked past. Then he watched morosely as Jack politely shouldered his way through the crowd toward his Amanda.

Jack was glad Rob had stayed behind ... even if he did resort to downing champagne by the glassful. Lately Rob spent his entire waking hours either gaming or drinking. He was ruining his health and his appearance and making himself unacceptable as a guest to most of the noble hostesses. He'd not have been welcome tonight if he hadn't come with Jack. And Jack wasn't sure how long he could support Rob, financially and socially, if he didn't change his ways. But he was honor-bound to do as much as he could because Rob had saved his life. It was that simple.

Right now, however, Jack didn't want to think about Rob and Rob's problems. He had a big problem of his own. He had to extricate Amanda from a crush of admirers and somehow get her alone. He'd made a decision. In fact, he'd made a monumental decision. No matter what her feelings for him were or what she'd say in return, he was going to tell Amanda that he loved her. It was a big gamble, but there would be a huge payoff if things went his way.

Luckily, Jack had been able so far to work his way through the crowd without having to stop for more than a polite "how do y' do." Most people were flabbergasted to see him again after his self-induced exile from society. But word was getting round that Jackson Montgomery was showing his handsome face—with a new scar!—for the first time since his broken engagement and that absurd fairy tale about losing his memory, and a buzz of excitement rippled through the crowd.

Ten feet from his objective, Jack was suddenly besieged and surrounded. There were two men in the group, but the rest of those in the imprisoning circle were women. Trying to be polite, but wishing they'd all go to the devil, Jack looked frantically over the

head of one petite and gushing redhead to see if
Amanda was still within reasonable reach.

She was in reach, all right. In fact, her circle
seemed to have inched closer and had parted in the
middle so that she had a clear view of Jack and his
effusive companions. Their gazes met and held.
Jack's heart hammered in his chest, and his mouth
went dry as the Sahara.

God, but she looked beautiful! He'd been right to
expect her to look like an angel because that's exactly
the sort of celestial being she resembled. Only trouble
was, all those damned pinks of the *ton* were just as
enamored of her beauty as he was. The difference,
he thought fiercely, was that he knew her and loved
her for more than her beauty. She belonged to him
body and soul. Like a savage, he wanted to pounce
into the middle of Amanda's circle of admirers, scatter them like so many lesser beasts of the jungle,
throw Amanda over his shoulder, and haul her to a
cave to have his way with her.

Jack was very much afraid that the brutal posses-
siveness and wild need he felt were reflected in his
expression. Amanda's eyelids fluttered. She shivered
and he could almost see the gooseflesh rise on her
arms. For a dreaded instant, he thought she was
going to swoon. He'd either aroused her or frightened her senseless. He had to get to her. He had to
get *free*. . . . But people persisted in pressing him with
questions, and he was forced to tamp down his fero-
cious impulses and pretend to be civil.

Jack dragged his eyes away from Amanda and
made conversation for several minutes . . . precious
minutes he wanted to spend with Amanda. When he
was finally able to make his excuses, he looked up
eagerly, but she was gone.

Luckily Jack was tall. Evading more hangers-on,
he skimmed through the crowd looking over heads
for Amanda. Just when he was about to despair—

and strangle the nearest unsuspecting person just to vent his frustration—he saw a wisp of midnight blue disappear behind a potted palm, headed for the French doors leading to a first-floor balcony. He quickly followed, darting and dodging and trying to ensure that no one followed him.

The door Amanda had gone through stood slightly ajar. He silently opened it just enough to squeeze through, then just as silently closed it securely behind him. She was standing with her back to him, staring out over Lady Cowper's gardens and mews at the back of the house. The moon was nearly full and shone on her pale hair, making it gleam like silver, silken threads. He advanced.

Just as he reached her, she turned. Her mouth had formed a small circle of surprise. It was too damned inviting. He couldn't help himself. Gone was any pretext of subtlety. He took her by the arms, crushed her to his chest, and kissed her.

At first she struggled. Her hands curled into fists, and she beat them against his waistcoat. Then she melted. He felt her muscles relax under his fingertips, her skin turn warm and pliant. She pressed closer, and he wrapped his arms around her waist and shoulders.

Her hands slipped up his jacket lapels, around the nape of his neck, and into his hair. Her hands were eagerly, tenderly grasping. His own hands moved with the same desperate passion. He needed to touch her, hold her, possess her.

And the kiss deepened. Oh, so deep . . . so warm and wet and wanton. He delved and dipped into the velvet sleekness of her mouth, their tongues mating wildly. Jack was immediately aroused, as hard and hot as he'd ever been in his life.

Their lips parted, and they gasped for breath. She stared up at him, her eyes wide and dazed, her breasts heaving against his chest, her arms trembling. "Oh," she said faintly, sudden moisture welling in her eyes. "Oh, how I *hate* you, Jackson Montgomery!" Then she buried her face in his neck cloth and burst into tears.

Jack was stunned. He didn't know what to do, except hold her. She clung to him, which was a good sign he supposed, but did she really *hate* him? He forced himself to be patient while she cried herself out, tenderly patting her shoulders and trying to ignore the enormous ache in his groin. Eventually her crying subsided to sniffles, and she began to grope for a handkerchief. Jack pulled his own out of his waistcoat pocket and gave it to her.

Amanda stepped back as she dried her tears and gave a ladylike little noiseless blow into the handkerchief and wiped her nose. When she finally looked up at him, she said haltingly, "I suppose I ... I look a fright. Has my nose swelled up like a strawberry?"

Jack cupped her face and smiled down at her. "You look adorable." And the strange thing was, he was telling the truth. There was a slight pinkness at the tip of her nose, but it was barely noticeable and not unattractive. Her eyes glistened and her lashes were dark and heavy with the residue of tears, but that only made them lovelier. "You're more beautiful than ever, Amanda, darling."

"You're just saying that. You can't mean it," she demurred, glancing down at the handkerchief she'd crumpled into a ball.

He slid his hands down her neck and rested them lightly on her shoulders. She shivered again, and he began to hope that such a response was a positive one.

"Did you mean what you just said?" he inquired gently. "That you hate me?"

She sighed and laid her cheek against his chest. "No, but I wish—"

He bent his head to catch the muffled words. "What, Amanda? I can't hear you, darling."

She lifted her head and sniffed. "I said, no, I don't hate you. But I wish I did."

He chuckled. "Why?"

"Because you're a lady's man. Seeing you tonight with all those women flocked around you just made that fact even clearer to me."

"But you, my dear, were just as guilty tonight of attracting suitors. When I arrived, the crowd around you could have rivaled the Regent's royal entourage in Brighton when he takes his daily saunter down the pier. You're the belle of the ball, Amanda."

Amanda blushed prettily but did not argue with him. That made him smile. He squeezed her and heaved an exaggerated sigh. "Dear, sweet Amanda. I do wish you weren't so enamored with the idea of hating me."

She lifted questioning eyes to his, the wet, spiky lashes gleaming in the moonlight. "Why, Jack?"

"Because it makes it rather harder for me to tell you how I feel about *you*," he admitted with a lop-sided grin.

She bit her lip. "About . . . me?" she quavered.

Jack's grin fell away. Deadly serious, deeply stirred by the depth of his feelings, Jack reached up to cup Amanda's face. He lovingly, thoroughly examined every feature. By the time he met her dewy, wondering gaze again, she was trembling.

"For weeks now—possibly since the moment I first clapped eyes on you, Amanda Jane Darlington—I've loved you more than life itself."

"Oh, Jack . . ." Amanda's eyes welled with tears. He'd said them. He'd said the words she'd longed to hear. And the knowledge that he loved her made everything right . . . and anything possible. She was ready to forgive and forget. To trust. To even marry the man . . . if he'd only ask her again.

"I love you, too, Jack," she breathed, trembling harder than ever.

Jack's eyes shone like golden stars. "Does that mean you forgive me for lying to you, Amanda? Can you trust me again? I've missed you dreadfully and haven't been able to think of anyone or anything but you. Tell me we can start fresh, give me another chance to earn your trust, and you'll make me delirious with joy."

"Jack, I forgive you and I trust you with my life," she answered, lifting her hand to stroke his cheek. "Let's not spend any more time worrying about past misunderstandings. I think I understand why you did what you did, anyway. We're together now, and that's all that matters."

He smiled tenderly. "How wise you are, Miss Darlington," he teased. "After all, what's more precious than the present? I propose we spend every moment doing what makes us happiest." Then he bent and kissed her . . . reverently, lingeringly, and she clung to him, her heart bursting with happiness.

"Jack?" Startled, Jack and Amanda turned toward the sound of a mature female voice. There, sticking her head just around the corner of one of the French doors, was Lady Cowper herself. Amanda and Jack jumped apart like guilty children.

Lady Cowper laughed. She was a lovely woman, and though Amanda didn't know her beyond their brief introduction and conversation earlier in the evening, she knew she was rumored to be one of the most warmhearted and tolerant of the patronesses at Almacks. She waggled her finger at them.

"I don't know what your chaperons are about, Miss Darlington, to allow you to stray outside on this private balcony with a rake like Jack . . . or any man, for that matter. But if the tattle-tongues start wagging, Sally Jersey might decide to request a return of that voucher she sent you. I suggest you two come in at once, or Miss Darlington's reputation will be in tatters."

"Thank you, my lady, for the gentle reminder," Jack said with a charming grin that Amanda was sure no woman could resist. "I certainly don't want Miss Darlington's reputation to be tarnished . . . and for more reasons than you can guess."

"Indeed, Jack?" said Lady Cowper, raising her finely arched brows. "How very interesting."

Amanda wondered if she dared hope that Jack was hinting that he meant to make her his wife. If only Lady Cowper hadn't disturbed them at just that moment, perhaps Jack would have proposed to her again! Amanda sent a hopeful prayer winging toward heaven. He loved her . . . and that fact alone made her mad with happiness. Was she destined to be even happier? Was there a chance her dearest dreams would come true?

"There, you see, Nan. They're coming back into the room now. I'm sure Lady Cowper wasn't angry but was only cautioning them to be careful of Amanda's reputation."

Rob was standing in a deep window embrasure, behind a dropped red velvet curtain, when he heard the conversation between the two elderly females. He was completely hidden from view, which is just what he'd intended. As soon as he'd seen Jack follow his darling Amanda outside onto the balcony, he'd retired to this secluded spot to feel sorry for himself and finish off the flask of Irish whiskey he kept in the deep inside pocket of his jacket for just such emergencies.

He was beginning to truly hate Jack. It looked like the bloody sod was going to get the girl of his dreams after all. It just wasn't bloody fair. He was even wishing he could somehow prevent Jack from getting what *he* couldn't.

Then, as if an evil fairy godmother had heard his vengeful wish, he realized he was overhearing Miss

Darlington's two aunts discussing her. He listened carefully. As they were seated well away from the general hubbub and were unaware that they were being listened to, there was a chance they'd drop some little tidbit of information that Rob could use to make things unpleasant for Jack. He stood very still and strained to hear.

"Well, if it had been anyone but Jack, I shouldn't have allowed it at all, Pris," said Nan.

"Of course not," said Pris. "But we know Amanda's in love with Jack. Any little question about her respectability, should people choose to gossip— which, of course, they usually do—will be put to rest by their betrothal announcements in the papers. No one will care that she spent twenty minutes alone on a balcony with him."

"You think he'll propose again, do you?" Nan said in a worried voice.

"Of course he will," Pris replied comfortably. "Those two are *so* in love it makes me quite envious! I wish I were still young enough to be kissed by a dashing blade like Jack! He gives me the chills ... you know, the *good* kind of chills!"

"Pris!" admonished Nan with a girlish giggle. "You're such a naughty tabby, but I must confess that Jack gives me the chills, too, and in the most ticklish of places!" Now they both burst into giggles.

Rob grimaced and took a swig of whiskey. He was beginning to think eavesdropping on those two randy old crones wasn't going to get him anywhere. Just like every other woman he knew, Amanda's aunts were smitten with Jack, too.

Presently the aunts settled down again, and Nan said, "It looks like Amanda Jane's going to have a happy ending after all." She sighed. "I hope Samantha is just as fortunate, but she has so much more to overcome ... not the least of which is her illegitimacy."

Rob stiffened and pricked his ears. Who was Samantha? he wondered.

"Do you think Lord Serling's scheme to pass her off as Amanda's orphaned cousin will work?"

"I'm sure if Lord Serling tells polite society Samantha is Amanda Jane's cousin, polite society will believe it . . . particularly after he has tutored her in all that's proper and forced her to acquire the usual accomplishments. She can't perhaps aspire to wed into the first circles, as her obscure roots might be questioned by high-sticklers, but I daresay she'll make a respectable match."

"To be sure, she deserves as much," observed Pris. "Amanda Jane's father was an absolute villain to hide her away like he did. Imagine, Nan, Amanda Jane's half-sister living secretly on that dreadful island all those years and none of us having the least idea . . . !"

"Yes," Nan said soberly. "And it must remain a secret, known only within our small family circle. Otherwise, Samantha won't have a chance for happiness. She'll be hampered all her life by her past. It's extremely important to Amanda Jane to make sure Sam's future is secure."

"Yes," Pris agreed. "I know. *Dear* Amanda Jane! She'd do anything for Samantha!"

Anything? Rob wondered with an evil leer. Well, he'd test that theory first thing tomorrow morning.

The duns at the gaming houses were getting downright nasty lately about wanting their money, threatening him with physical harm and such. If he didn't want to be beaten to a pulp in some alley, he either had to pay off his debts or abscond to the continent to live out his days in squalid obscurity.

Rob wasn't ready to leave England, and he'd just been given a thread of hope that there might be an alternative. He knew blackmailing Amanda Darlington was risky business. If Jack—or Julian—found out, there'd be hell to pay and not much consolation for him even if he still managed to thwart their plans to launch Amanda's bastard sister into respectable society.

Rob knew he was taking an enormous gamble ... but he was a gambler by nature, wasn't he? And what the bloody hell did he have to lose?

Amanda was awake bright and early the next morning, filled with rapturous expectation. Jack had promised to come by at eleven. And by his manner of parting with her the night before at the Cowpers' musical event, she had good reason to hope he was coming expressly to propose.

Amanda was unable to keep from humming blithely as her abigail helped her into a very flattering morning dress of deep green jaconet muslin with a low round neckline that showed off Amanda's long neck. The gown had elbow-length sleeves trimmed with wide white lace and another more narrow trimming of lace at the hem. The gown was simply styled, but the color made Amanda's complexion glow. Or was that simply the result of her extreme happiness? she wondered, smiling into her mirror.

It was true that Jack had lied to her about his amnesia, but now she understood why he'd done it. Perhaps she'd understood it all along, but she'd needed to hear him tell her he loved her before she could drop the emotional barriers she'd constructed. It had been easier to tolerate being without Jack if she could stay angry with him. But now that sort of self-defensive behavior was unnecessary. He was a good man, a brave man who'd saved her sister from sure death and shown her the sort of tenderness she'd always dreamed of finding in a life's companion.

And he truly wanted her! If he proposed to her that morning, he wouldn't be doing it out of obligation; he'd be doing it because he loved her. And she'd say yes because she loved him, too. . . .

As Amanda went downstairs to the breakfast room, she passed through the entry hall and was astonished and delighted to find it filled with bouquets of hothouse flowers sent from various gentlemen she'd met the night before. It was gratifying to realize she was no longer the social failure she'd considered herself during her coming-out four years ago. She supposed Jack had been right all along. All she'd needed to do was relax and be herself.

She read some of the cards sent with the flowers, finding the tributes to her "charm and beauty" flattering for the most part but not forgetting for a minute that most of them were exaggerated or insincere and penned by men who would forget her the minute someone else caught their eye or someone else's reputed fortune caught their interest.

A small bouquet of bright blue forget-me-nots that was nearly lost in the profusion of roses and gardenias caught Amanda's eye just as she was about to leave the room. She picked up the pretty bouquet, wrapped in crackling vellum paper and tied with a white ribbon, and detached the card.

Darling Amanda,
Even if I lost my memory again—God forbid!—
I'd never forget how much I love you.

Jack

Clutching her bouquet to her chest, with happy tears in her eyes, Amanda floated into the breakfast room and discovered it quite empty. She found another note, this one from her Aunt Nan.

Prissy and I have taken Samantha with us to the
women's relief house in Spitalfields I told you about.

*I know we've been going nearly every day since we
arrived in London, but they are in desperate need
right now of willing volunteers to help out. Don't
worry about our safety, as usual we've got Theo,
Harley, and Joe to protect us. Samantha needs to
learn about charity work, and besides, we thought
you'd like the house to yourself today just in case
you get a special caller. . . . Don't expect us back
till dinnertime.*

Aunt Nan

Amanda pressed the card against her chin, smiling
like a cat in a cream pot. Her dear aunts! She'd said
nothing last night. She'd been afraid to jinx herself.
So, how did they know?

Amanda left off wondering and ate a solitary and
quite meager breakfast. She couldn't seem to concentrate on chewing. She was too eager for eleven
o'clock to come.

Settled in the small ground-level morning room at
ten-thirty, making an attempt at doing a little
stitching for Nan and Prissy's favorite new charity
house in Spitalfields, Amanda was interrupted by
Henchpenny.

"You've a visitor, miss," he informed her.

Amanda leaped to her feet, her heart racing. It had
to be Jack! He was early by an entire half-hour! She
hoped that meant he was just as eager to see her as
she was to see him.

Licking her dry lips and pressing her hands tightly
together at waist-level, Amanda tried to present a
composed front. "Show . . . show him in, Henchpenny," she instructed, not bothering to ask for the
caller's name.

Still frowning, Henchpenny flicked a dubious
glance about the empty room. "Are you sure you

wish to see the gentleman *alone*, miss?" he inquired. "He doesn't look exactly—"

"Oh, don't be a fusspot, Henchpenny," she admonished him with a giddy smile. "Just show him in." Amanda supposed Henchpenny was remembering Jack's visit to Darlington Hall and wasn't sure if she truly wanted to see him again.

"But, miss—"

"I've been expecting the gentleman, Henchpenny," Amanda assured him.

He raised a brow but withdrew, returning in half a minute with Robert Hamilton . . . a disheveled-looking Robert Hamilton with a swollen and bruised right eye.

Amanda was so stunned and disappointed, at first she could not command her tongue. She was speechless.

"Miss Darlington, you appear surprised to see me," he said smoothly, removing his hat. "Were you expecting . . . someone else?"

Amanda realized how foolish she'd been to assume any gentleman caller that came to the house would be Jack. Especially after her success at the Cowpers' last night, it wasn't inconceivable to expect several male callers in the course of the day.

But Robert Hamilton couldn't possibly be there to court her. He was Jack's particular friend. They'd been introduced last night and had exchanged a few words. She'd thought him rather morose and unkept, and possibly drunk, but this morning there was no doubt in Amanda's mind that, despite the early hour, he'd been imbibing alcohol freely.

He looked worse than ever. His clothes appeared clean but untidy, as if he'd thrown them on hastily or without care. He was pale and haggard and his good eye was as bloodshot as the bruised one. She could only conclude he'd been indulging in fisticuffs

in some local pub last night after he left the
Cowpers'.

But he was Jack's friend. He'd saved Jack's life during the war, and that made his welcome unqualified.

Amanda forced a smile and extended a hand. As
he caught her fingertips and made a wobbling bow
over them, Amanda gave Henchpenny a nod of dismissal. He left looking grave, but he shut the door
behind him.

"Will you sit down, Mr. Hamilton?" Amanda invited, gesturing toward the sofa. He sat down in a
rather sprawled position with one elbow propped on
the sofa arm and the other draped over his crossed
knee. Since the moment he'd walked through the
door he'd had a sort of perpetual smirk on his face.
She supposed he was simply making a polite morning call, but his drunken condition and his cavalier
attitude was quite disrespectful. She was confused
and offended, but she was resolved to get through a
civil visit with the fellow, then question Jack later
about his friend's strange behavior.

"It's kind of you to call on me this way," she ventured. "I'm a little out of touch with the ways of
London society, having rusticated in the country for
the past four years, but I suppose you've come to . . .
to welcome me to town."

Robert Hamilton leaned forward, uncrossed his
legs, twined his fingers together, and dangled his
hands between his knees. He leaned so close,
Amanda could smell his gin-laced breath. "My purpose in visiting you this morning, Miss Darlington,
has nothing whatsoever to do with welcoming you
to town."

Amanda felt a shiver creep up her spine as a
dreadful possibility presented itself to her vivid
imagination. "Then why are you here? Jack's not
hurt, is he? Were you both fighting?"

The smirk took on a contemptuous aspect. "There

was no fight, Miss Darlington. I got my black eye by . . . er . . . walking into a street lamp. And as far as I know, Jack's fine. Nothing permanently damaging ever happens to Jack, you know. He leads a charmed life. Even his misfortunes somehow turn to his advantage."

Amanda frowned. "You say that as though you wish it weren't true. I thought you were Jack's friend."

Rob leaned back and draped his arms on the sofa back. "I am Jack's friend, and that's why I'm doing him a very great favor today."

"Wh-what do you mean, Mr. Hamilton?"

"I'm going to save Jack from shackling himself to an unsuitable female."

Amanda's hands clenched in her lap. "I don't understand you, Mr. Hamilton," she said stiffly. Had Jack confided in this man that he was going to propose to her?

"You understand me well enough, miss," Robert sneered.

"You're drunk, Mr. Hamilton," Amanda pointed out.

"So?"

"It's making you rude . . . and reckless. I daresay you're about to utter something you'll regret."

"I'm only thinking of Jack," he insisted with a grin that made Amanda's skin crawl.

"I assume you are expecting Jack to make me an offer," she continued, eager to get to the point and finish this strange interview as soon as possible, "and you have come here this morning to express your disapproval. May I ask why you disapprove of me?"

Robert shrugged and lifted his hands as if to imply the answer was self-evident. "You present a respectable front, Miss Darlington, but we both know you are harboring a bastard sister in your midst, meaning to palm the girl off to the polite world as your orphaned cousin."

Amanda felt as if she'd been hit on the head by a falling brick. She was stunned and sick to her stomach. How had this man found out about Samantha? Surely not through Jack . . . ?

She hid her growing terror and fixed him with a cold eye. "I don't know what you're talking about."

"Yes, you do. Don't play the dolt with me, Miss Darlington. It won't fadge. Whether you admit the truth or not, it doesn't matter. Once I start the rumor about town, your sister, Samantha, will be known for exactly what she is."

Fear and frustration crowded Amanda's throat. Her voice came out in a raspy whisper as she said, "Jack won't allow you to do such a cruel thing. He'll, he'll—"

"What can Jack do to stop me, short of killing me? And he won't kill me because I saved his life during the war."

"Julian—"

"I'll make bloody sure the rumor is started before Julian can get his hands around my neck. He'd be happy to kill me, of that I'm quite certain. But the damage will have already been done."

"No one will believe you. The Montgomerys are well-respected, and they'll refute anything you say against my sister."

"The *ton* love gossip and are generally more likely to believe something injurious than something good about a person. They may claim to believe the Montgomerys, but they will still whisper and point and gleefully persist in believing the worst."

Amanda's eyes filled with angry tears. "Why are you intent on exposing my sister?"

"Normally I wouldn't concern myself with such trivial matters. She could fool the prince regent into believing she was the Queen of Sheba for all I care, but I've found a way to use the unfortunate circumstances of your sister's birth to good purpose. Your sister is simply the pawn in this game."

She swallowed hard. "You're blackmailing me, aren't you? You're threatening to expose Samantha if I marry Jack. And I suppose you want money, too?"

He smiled unpleasantly. "Besides being beautiful, you're sharp as a tack, Amanda. Of course I want money."

Amanda's brows furrowed. "I understand the money part. But I don't understand the stipulation about not marrying Jack. He knows about Sam. He understands. He does not seem to find the situation an impediment to marriage. If Jack does not object, why do you? Why don't you want me to marry Jack, Mr. Hamilton?"

"Because, my dear," he said with a malevolent smile, "I intend to marry you myself."

Amanda shook her head disbelievingly. She gave a strangled little laugh. "You're mad. Why would you want to marry me? You don't even know me."

"I know you're rich."

"But you intend to blackmail me anyway, so why—"

"My propensity to gamble won't be cured by paying off my debts. If I married you, Miss Darlington, I'd control your entire fortune."

"Ah, I see. Then you'd have the ready to pay off *future* gaming vowels."

"Quite right."

Amanda stared suspiciously at Rob's black eye. "Your duns are getting insistent about repayment, are they?"

Rob self-consciously touched his swollen eye and winced. "They're not very patient," he concurred bitterly. "In fact, they're getting rather more violent every day. As I said, Miss Darlington, I've really got nothing to lose."

·

Amanda felt the blood drain from her face. If Rob's life was at risk, that meant he was more dangerous than ever.

Rob leaned forward and slid an index finger along the curve of Amanda's jaw. Repelled and angry, she jerked her head away. He laughed. "Besides relieving me of my pressing financial problems, marrying you enables me to take something away from Jack... something he wants desperately. Just this once, I'll be able to show Jackson Montgomery how it feels to lose."

"And today, if he proposes?"

Robert grinned. "Why, you'll say no, of course."

Amanda recognized hate when she saw it. Rob, who had been posing as Jack's friend for so long, hated Jack. And she recognized desperation, too. Obviously, Rob was at the end of his tether or he'd not attempt such a harebrained scheme as to try to blackmail her into marriage. He was apparently willing to risk everything ... including his own life.

Trouble was, when a man was willing to risk his own life, he was willing to risk the lives of others, too.

Chapter 20

"I'm sorry, my lord," said Henchpenny with the blandest possible expression, "but Miss Darlington instructed me to inform you that it will be impossible to see you today."

Jack couldn't believe what he was hearing. He stood at Amanda's door in his finest togs, with a forget-me-not boutonniere in his lapel, a foolish smile spread from ear to ear on his fresh-shaven face, and a heart full of hope. Now the smile wavered and the hope faded.

"Are you sure, Henchpenny?" Jack urged.

"Quite sure, my lord."

A possible explanation came to him that offered a bit of hope mixed with alarm. "Miss Darlington's not ill, is she?"

"As far as I can presume to say, my lord, Miss Darlington seems healthy as usual."

Jack lowered his voice. "Has Samantha done something to throw the household into mayhem?"

"Not . . . er . . . *this* morning, my lord."

"Then why is Miss Darlington refusing visitors?"

"She hasn't refused . . . er . . . *everyone*, my lord."

Jack couldn't ignore the obvious any longer. Amanda was shutting him out. Did that mean she was shutting him out her life ... her heart ... for good? What had changed since last night? Had she finally succeeded in convincing herself that she hated him instead of loved him? Jack refused to accept that possibility.

"Very well," said Jack at last, lifting his chin in a determined pose. "You may *warn* Miss Darlington that I fully intend to return on the morrow."

"I will relay the message, my lord," said the expressionless butler. Then, just as Jack was about to turn to go, Henchpenny extended a sealed envelope toward him in an immaculate gloved hand.

"What's this?" asked Jack, his brows knitting worriedly. Sealed envelopes from females who refused to be visited were a bad sign. A very bad sign, indeed.

"Miss Darlington instructed me to give this to you, my lord," said the butler. Reluctantly, Jack took the envelope, and Henchpenny immediately withdrew and shut the door.

Jack stood for a minute at Amanda's threshold, eyeing the envelope with grave misgiving. Then he turned and slowly descended the steps to the walkway. He crossed the street and entered a small park through a wrought-iron gate. His boots crunched through a smattering of tinder-dry leaves as he walked to a marble bench under an oak tree that was rapidly losing its foliage to the advancing season. Mechanically, he broke the seal, unfolded the missive, and began to read.

Dear Jack,

Too late last night I realized that I may have misled you into believing that something more intimate than friendship is possible between us. While I treasure our times together and will always be grateful to you for the kind services you rendered me and my family, I hope you understand there can be nothing more between us. As well, coming to London has opened my imagination to many possibilities as to what my future might hold. If I have presumed too much, and you had no intention of declaring yourself this morning, forgive me. However, if I am correct in believing you meant to declare yourself to me this morning, again I say ... forgive me. Please don't try to see me. It will be better if we avoid one another for a while. If we chance to meet in public, pray treat me as a friend ... which is how I will always think of you. Dear friend, God bless you.

Amanda

Jack sat in a state of shock. Then, as he reread the letter twice over, he got angry.

"Her imagination has been opened to new possibilities, has it?" he snarled, glaring at the letter. "In other words, her pretty head was turned by all that attention last night, and she means to buckle herself to someone who can offer her more than I can!"

But Jack's heart and sense of fairness rebelled against the idea that Amanda could have mercenary ambitions. He knew her better than that. But maybe she was looking for someone she could trust and love without reservations. Jack had made a good many mistakes in his life and had given Amanda reason to doubt and distrust him more than once. His anger turned inward.

Jack stood up, crumpled the paper in his fist till it was no larger than a walnut, and threw it on the ground. "If I don't deserve Amanda, I may as well go to the devil," he muttered fiercely. He turned and looked at Amanda's town house. He saw a white face staring out of an upper window. It was her.

He stood stone-still for a moment, then pulled the forget-me-not boutonniere from his buttonhole, kissed it, extended it in the air in a tragic last toast and tribute to Amanda, then dropped it at his feet and crushed it with the heel of his boot. He turned away, headed for the darkest tavern and the foulest bottle of Blue Ruin he could find.

Tears streamed down Amanda's face as she watched Jack stride away, leaving the small park through an opposite gate without looking back. She had hurt him terribly, and her own heart was breaking in two. But she'd had no choice. Until she could think of a way to foil Robert's plan, she must keep Jack as far away from her as possible.

Every fiber of her being rebelled against giving in to Rob's demands, but she had no intention of confiding her troubles to Jack. He'd charge to her rescue like the gallant knight he was ... and possibly get himself killed. As she'd endured Robert Hamilton's loathsome company for the brief time he stayed, Amanda was easily able to see that Robert was insanely jealous of Jack. He wanted money, yes. But he wanted revenge, too. And he was desperate ... which made him extremely unpredictable and dangerous.

If Jack knew the truth, he'd challenge Robert to a duel. She could not bear the thought that Jack's life might be jeopardized in any way. She'd rather hurt him now by sending him away disappointed and heartbroken, and hope she could patch things up once she'd figured out what to do about Robert.

Besides, the rat had threatened to spread the rumor about Sam even if Jack or Julian came after him intent on killing him. Amanda couldn't stand the thought that Sam's chances for a respectable marriage and a shameless life could be ruined by Robert's cruel tongue. There had to be some way to stop the detestable man ... but how?

Amanda dashed away her tears, trying to block out the image of Jack in the park, grinding that for-

get-me-not boutonniere into the ground. It seemed
so unfair! She and Jack had just come to an understanding! But she refused to collapse under the strain
of it all and instead paced the floor continuously and
cudgeled her brain to come up with a solution to
her dilemma.

Dusk was nigh when Amanda finally realized that
she'd been shut up in her bedchamber for hours. The
room was cold and dark. She had instructed Henchpenny to refuse any visitors and told the servants
not to disturb her until she summoned them. She
hadn't eaten since breakfast, but she wasn't hungry.

She moved to the mirror over the mantel. She grimaced at her wan appearance. Despite her determination to bear her troubles with fortitude and to fight
back as best she could, she felt overpowered by an
unshakable gloom. She had to pull herself together
for the sake of Sam and Prissy and Nan.

Then she suddenly realized that it was far past the
hour she'd expected Sam and the aunts to return
from Spitalfields. She knitted her brows and glanced
at the clock, concern replacing the numbness paralyz-
ing her since morning. She hurriedly lit candles, piled
the fire with wood, and gave the bellpull a yank.

When her chambermaid arrived, she ordered tea
and toast, fortifying herself for the vigil of waiting.
Amanda refused to entertain thoughts of a dire nature. Fate could not be so cruel as to deliver two
devastating blows in one day.

A half hour later, it was with weak-kneed relief
that Amanda heard her carriage clatter to a halt out
front. She left her room and hurried down the stairs,
arriving in the entrance hall as the door swung open
and Aunt Prissy scrambled through with a look of
excited agitation.

"What is it, Aunt Prissy?" exclaimed Amanda,
rushing toward her aunt and clutching her cold
hands. "Has something happened?"

"Yes, indeed!" Pris gasped out, breathless. Then in a great rush, she gabbled, "We were driving home—going rather slow, you know, as the streets are narrow there and cluttered with debris and poor, dirty children running free like stray dogs—when he stumbled into the path of our carriage! We didn't hit him, mind you, but he fell to the ground! At first we thought he was only drunk, but I fear, Amanda Jane, he's lost his memory again! He's in a daze and doesn't seem to have a notion who he—!"

Amanda grasped her aunt's thin arms and gave her a shake. "You aren't telling me, Aunt Prissy—you're *not* saying—"

"Pardon, miss," came Theo's aggrieved voice from the porch just outside the door. "What do ye want us to do with 'is lordship? He's as heavy as ever, he is!"

Amanda turned and her greatest fear was realized. Theo had hold of an unconscious Jack at the shoulders, Harley had his feet, and Joe was supporting his middle parts. Nan and Sam stood behind them, their eyes wide and expectant.

"Hurry up and decide which room you want him in, dear," Nan prompted anxiously as Amanda stood with her mouth agape. "The dear boy needs to be put to bed!"

Collecting her scattered wits, Amanda darted a quick look outside to make sure no nosy busybody was observing the scene, then motioned them all inside. "Take him to my room," she ordered.

Four hours later, Amanda stood over her bed and stared down at the prone figure of Jackson Montgomery. After what had occurred that morning, she'd never in a million years have expected to see him in *her* bed, snuggled under *her* sheets, with his tousled head resting on *her* pillows. It was a stroke of cruel fate, that was certain, because he looked far too tempting for Amanda's already devastated peace of mind. But at least this time she hadn't been required to disrobe him; Henchpenny and a couple of footmen managed that particular task.

Sam had been ordered to retire an hour ago, but the aunts stood at the foot of the bed like two grandmotherly sentinels and shook their heads dolefully.

"I don't understand, Amanda Jane, why you wouldn't let us notify Julian," said Nan.

"And it certainly wouldn't have hurt to get a doctor's opinion on Jack's condition," Prissy added accusingly.

"He's not injured," said Amanda, "he's only drunk. He'll sleep it off. There's no need to alarm his brother or get a doctor in here poking about unnecessarily."

Amanda wasn't entirely sure Jack was only drunk, but she'd had a great deal of experience nursing him, and he did not appear to have any of the alarming symptoms he'd had during his initial head injury. His heart rate was slow and steady, his color was good, and his eyes weren't dilated.

As she glanced at her still doubtful aunts, she reached down and brushed a pitch-black lock of hair off Jack's forehead. "Anyway, he hates doctors," she said. She remembered the first time she'd touched him like this, so full of virginal awe. She was no longer a virgin, but Jack still affected her the same way. She adored him.

Under other circumstances, she'd have had a doctor in to be absolutely positive Jack was all right, but she didn't want to take the chance of Rob finding out Jack was in her house . . . in her bed.

"He's not just drunk. He's lost his memory again, Amanda Jane," Nan insisted.

"If that's true—which I doubt—it's probably just a temporary relapse. Once the liquor's out of his system, he'll remember everything . . . except, perhaps, how he got so drunk."

"But don't you think Julian should be told?"

Amanda straightened and looked sternly at her aunts. "I don't want anyone to know Jack's here. Tomorrow, after he's gone, I don't want anyone to know he's *been* here, either. It has to be kept a secret." If Robert Hamilton heard about this, he might consider it a breach of their agreement. She was supposed to avoid Jack and here he was . . . in her bed! Despite the danger of the situation, she felt a thrill go through her. In her *bed!*

"I don't understand, Amanda Jane," Nan persisted.

"I can't explain. You must trust me on this one, Aunt Nan, and . . . *please* . . . just do as I ask."

"Why was he drinking, do you think?" Pris ventured. "Was he . . . er . . . celebrating, Amanda Jane?"

Amanda sighed. "I know what you're trying to find out, and you might as well know now as later. . . . I refused to see Jack this morning."

The aunts exchanged horrified glances, then exclaimed in unison, "But he was going to *propose!*"

"Yes, I think so, too," Amanda admitted sadly. "That's why I couldn't see him."

Pris moved closer and laid her hand on Amanda's arm. "What's wrong with you, Amanda Jane? You're not acting yourself. If you'd only let me send for Julian—"

"Don't keep at me like this, Aunt Prissy!" Amanda snapped, closing her eyes in frustration. "I won't allow you to send for anyone, do you hear?"

Prissy jumped back and took up her former station by Nan. They both stared at Amanda as if she'd grown cloven hoofs and a forked tail. Ashamed, Amanda moved to the end of the bed and put her arms around them in a warm embrace. They hugged her back, and when she pulled free they looked at her with tender concern.

"I'm sorry, aunts," she said contritely. "I'm a bit on edge. Can we talk more in the morning?"

"Henchpenny said you had a visitor after breakfast, Amanda Jane," said Pris, her brows furrowed. "A man named Robert Hamilton. Nan and I were talking, and it occurred to us that we've heard that name before ... but we just can't remember where."

"Henchpenny said that after this man left you stayed locked in your room for hours, right up till we came home," said Nan, joining the interrogation. "Who is Robert Hamilton? What did he want? And why does his name sound so familiar to us?"

"He's Jack's friend, aunts," Amanda replied lightly. "I'm sure that's where you've heard his name."

"But why did you stay in your room all afternoon?"

"I had a headache, that's all," Amanda lied. "And I think it's coming back. I need to rest."

"Dear, dear," tsked Nan. "But where will you sleep, Amanda Jane?"

"I doubt I'll sleep at all tonight. I'll lie down on the chaise longue if I get tired. But I want to be near Jack in case he wakes and needs me."

The aunts seemed to readily understand these sentiments and were finally coaxed to go to their own bedchambers. Sound sleepers, once abed they'd not make another peep till morning.

As the door closed behind them, Amanda moved to stand at the end of the bed, just as she used to do at the Inn of the Three Nuns at Horsham when Jack was first laid up with a head injury and amnesia. She shook her head and smiled disbelievingly. *It was déjà vu all over again*, Amanda thought to herself, repeating Aunt Prissy's favorite redundancy.

The whole thing was uncanny. What were the odds of Jack stumbling in front of her carriage again? Thank goodness, this time he wasn't injured, he wasn't in a coma, and ... despite what the aunts thought ... she didn't think his memory had been affected. But once again here he was in need of watching over, and once again she was the reluctant nurse. Only this time, she was in love with him.

After another uneventful hour passed, Amanda observed that Jack still slept soundly, so she lay down on the chaise and closed her eyes. She dozed off but was soon stirred from sleep by someone calling her name. She sat up and blinked in the direction of the bed. The room was softly lit by a brace of candles on the mantel and a single slender taper on a bedside table. Jack was sitting up in bed and looking at her.

"Jack, you're awake," she said, swinging her legs to the floor and standing up. She moved toward the bed. He had pushed up against the plump pillows and, with his elbows locked, was leaning back on his hands. His hair was a sexy tumble, and his white shirt was unbuttoned to the middle of his chest, exposing a delicious peek of brown skin and a light matting of dark hair. She remembered how it felt touching him there. Sheer heaven. She swallowed hard. "How ... how do you feel?"

"Thirsty," he admitted in a raspy voice and with a lopsided grin. "Got a slight headache, too. Have I been drinking?"

Amanda handed him a glass of water. "Don't you remember?"

He frowned. "Details a bit fuzzy." He chuckled. "Daresay, if you'd not called me by name, I wouldn't even know I was a Jack!"

Amanda watched warily as Jack took a long drink of water, wiped his mouth with the back of his hand, then returned the glass with a rakish smile. "Thank you, darling. Coming to bed? I promise not to snore. Was that why you were sleeping on the chaise?"

"Jack, are you playing another farce with me?" she demanded suspiciously.

"Playing a farce?" he repeated, looking genuinely

perplexed. "Don't know what you're talking about, sweetheart. Too sleepy, though, to get into it tonight. Are you coming to bed or not?"

Amanda nervously licked her lips. "Shall I send for Julian?"

Jack grimaced and shifted in the bed till he was on his side, facing Amanda, with his jaw propped in his hand. "Who the devil is Julian? And why would I want you to send for whoever the fellow is at *this* hour?"

"Jack!" Amanda exclaimed, backing up a step. "Don't you know who Julian is?"

"Don't know and don't care," he replied glibly, grabbing her skirt with his free hand and tugging her closer. "The butcher? The baker? The candlestick maker?" he teased. "You can tell me in the morning, Amanda. Right now all I want is my wife to come to bed."

"Your *wife*?" Amanda nearly dropped the glass she was still holding.

Jack laughed and took the glass, placing it safely on the bedside table. "Don't tell me you've forgotten you're my wife, 'Manda, darling? My thinking's a bit fuzzy tonight, but if there's one thing I could never forget, it's my better half."

He paused and eyed her appreciatively, his gleaming gaze lingering on the swell of her bodice. "You look luscious in that color, my dear. Makes your skin glow like sweet cream." He smiled wickedly. "Come to bed and I'll play cat and do a little lapping."

Amanda broke out in gooseflesh all over. "I thought you were sleepy, Jack," she said weakly.

"Not anymore. Randy as a goat, sweetheart. Now, are you coming to bed, or am I going to have to wrestle you to the floor in order to have my wicked way with you?"

Amanda was faced with a dilemma. She wasn't sure if Jack had lost his memory again or not. She didn't think he'd dare fake amnesia again, not after she'd got so furious with him over the last time ... would he? If he *had* lost his memory, it was oddly selective. He certainly knew who *she* was ... except for one very important misconception. He thought she was his wife.

Either way, whether Jack had genuinely lost his memory or not, it was an opportunity for Amanda to steal one more precious night of lovemaking. With this mess with Rob, it might be a long time before things got back to normal. And even then, under the strictures of a "proper" courtship, they would have little opportunity to be alone like this.

"Amanda? What's the matter, sweetheart? Don't you love me anymore?"

Amanda was recalled to the here and now by Jack's teasing remark and sly wink. He had the most incredible eyelashes, too sinfully thick and black to belong to a man. But his other more than masculine assets made up for that apparent whim of nature. His firm, square jaw. The bold, sensuous curve of his lips. The dark stubble of beard that made her skin tingle on contact. The chiseled nose. The scar.

She reached forward and traced the scar on his cheek. It was proof of his reckless courage and his patriotism. It was just another reason to love him.

Jack raised a brow. "Sweetheart, you look so serious tonight. I think it's time for a little slap and tickle, don't you?" He grabbed her by the hips and pulled her down. With a squeal of surprise, Amanda tumbled onto the bed on top of Jack. His hard body beneath hers made her senses reel. It brought back all the memories, all the desire, all the desperate need to be possessed by the only man she'd ever love.

Their lips were inches apart. His lips were smiling; hers were trembling. Then he kissed her.

It was a warm, deep, thorough kiss. He kissed her as if he'd kissed her a thousand times before but would yet kiss her a thousand times more. It was a kiss like those between husbands and wives who still loved each other to distraction... familiar but steeped with excitement and pleasure.

As they kissed, his hands slid down the curve of her back to cup her buttocks. With the skill and confidence of a man sure of his wife's response, he caressed and fondled her, then pressed her against his erection, rubbing himself against her till she moaned into his mouth.

Amanda lifted her head and gazed dazedly into Jack's eyes. The expression there was still playful but with a brilliance that implied urgency.

His hands skimmed up her sides to cup her face. "Ah, Amanda," he said, smiling. "You minx! After all this time, after all the lovemaking we've done, you still take my breath away."

"You do the same to me, Jack," Amanda whispered, caught up in the fantasy. "Every day I want you more and more."

He traced her lips with his thumbs. "Then why, my love, are you still in your clothes, and your hair still up in that decorous little knot? You look fetching, but I still prefer you *au naturel*."

She smiled timorously and moved to climb off the bed. He caught her waist and grinned up at her. "No, darling. Don't go. Stay here where I can still feel you and touch you while you undress for me."

Amanda was sitting astride Jack. The idea of disrobing with such a close observer made her cheeks bloom with warmth.

"You're blushing!" he exclaimed, his dark-amber eyes bright with loving amusement. "Are you still shy with me, Amanda?"

She bit her lip and ducked her head. "Not with you, Jack," she said quietly. "Never with you."

Then, suddenly, Amanda became what she most wanted to be. Jack saw her as his wife, so she'd be his wife. She'd thrill and pleasure her husband to the best of her ability. She'd show him, in every possible way, how much she loved him.

Amanda looked at Jack through eyes filled with desire. She lifted her arms and pulled her hairpins out slowly, allowing them to drop haphazardly over the bedclothes. He watched with sleepy pleasure in his eyes, a bemused half-smile on his lips. When the last pin was out, her hair cascaded down her shoulders, drifting to her waist. A tress fell across Jack's chest, the pale gold looking startlingly erotic against his bronzed skin and the silky mat of dark hair.

As she began to undo the buttons and ribbons of her gown, she could feel his erection growing harder and hotter under the bedclothes that pressed against her woman's core. She parted her lips and touched them with the tip of her tongue, her breath quicker and more shallow. She saw how his jaw tensed with longing, and felt a surge of womanly power. He wanted her as much as she wanted him.

She pulled her bodice and shift down and her breasts seemed to spring eagerly out of their bindings, her nipples turgid and erect and rosy. He stared at her and lifted his hips as if he were practicing or making provocative promises. . . .

Layer by layer she pulled off her clothes till she was completely naked except for a squat little bustle that perched on the dip of her fanny. Her hands went to her waist to undo the ties that secured the bustle, but Jack stopped her.

"Leave it on for a while, Amanda. It's kind of . . . er . . . interesting. If it gets in the way, we'll take it off later."

Amanda raised her brows. "You're a devil, Jack," she taunted him.

"And you love it," he taunted back, reaching up to take both breasts in hand. Amanda gasped, and her eyes drifted shut. His hands on her body were the closest thing to heaven she could imagine. He kneaded and squeezed softly, luxuriously, then caught her taut nipples between thumb and forefinger and rolled them gently.

When she gave a soft cry, he encircled her waist with his large hands and lifted her, guiding her to his mouth. She balanced on her knees as he took each nipple in turn and suckled it. Spears of pleasure shot through her, making her womb weep with longing.

He kicked away the covers, then lowered her again. Her splayed thighs came down around his bare flanks, his erection pressed against her stomach. She pushed herself to a sitting position with her hands on his chest and stared down at him, softly panting.

She held his hot gaze as she undid what buttons remained fastened of his shirt, then parted the white material. Now she looked down. His torso was magnificent . . . fluid with muscle. She explored the length of him from chest to belly, her fingers tracing the fine, silky hair down the cleft of his abdomen to where it spread out coarsely. Then she wrapped her fingers around his erection. He was so hot, so firm. They both groaned together.

"I think it's time, Amanda."

She nodded eagerly.

He grinned. "Do you want to ride me, love?"

"R-ride you, Jack?"

"For the whole race, sweetheart. Over every stone fence and bubbling brook, right down the home stretch to the finish line."

Amanda finally understood that Jack was making an analogy. . . . So, if she was the rider and he was the horse— Her eyes opened wide as she caught the vision.

"Yes, Jack," she said, hoping she wouldn't expose her ignorance. "Let's . . . let's race."

He laughed and pulled her down for a quick, hard

kiss. Sitting upright again, Amanda hoped Jack would show her what to do, how to mount, so to speak, because she didn't have a clue how it was done.

"Lift up a little, love," he said, and she obeyed. He positioned himself, then ordered, "Now, Amanda. Easy does it. . . ."

As Amanda lowered herself, she watched Jack's face. His jaw tensed and his eyes fluttered shut as he slid slowly into her. Then she, too, closed her eyes and savored the bliss of their joining.

At first her movements were tentative and awkward, but soon she caught the right rhythm, found the right angle. Jack let her set the pace, and the ride was long and filled with building intensity. The urgency in Amanda's womb increased with each thrust, and she braced her splayed hands on his hard chest and pressed her thighs tightly against his hips.

She whispered his name over and over again as they soared higher and higher on a crest of pure pleasure. He, too, chanted her name like a benediction.

Then came the explosion of senses Amanda remembered from before. She tensed and arched. Jack curved forward, caught her in his arms, and heart to fiercely beating heart, they found their release.

Later, curled together in the bed, they held each other tenderly. No words were spoken. The love between them was understood and deeply felt. Sated, they sank into sweet, dreamless sleep.

Chapter 21

When Jack woke up, he thought at first he must still be asleep and dreaming. He was lying on his side, completely naked, his arms wrapped around the ribs of a sleeping female who was also naked. His nose was buried in her fragrant hair. Her smooth white back was flush against his chest, and her curvaceous derriere was snuggled against his groin. But the best part, the most surprising and dreamlike aspect of this delightful scene, was the fact that the female was . . . Amanda!

Without disturbing her, he lifted his head and peered into the dim light that filtered around the edges of the closed curtains to take a quick perusal of the room. He felt fairly certain he'd never been in this particular chamber before. The plush and tasteful furnishings were immediate proof that it was no public inn but a private residence, and the feminine folderol scattered here and there indicated that it was a bedchamber belonging to a woman.

The truth hit him like a runaway gig. He was in Amanda's house . . . Amanda's bedchamber . . . Amanda's own bed! But how on earth had he got there?

He craned his neck and made a few more discoveries. While his clothes were neatly folded and hanging over a nearby chair, Amanda's clothes were in a rumpled puddle on the floor by the side of the bed. All the evidence pointed to the astonishing conclusion that he and Amanda had made love right there in her own bedchamber under the respectable auspices of her two resident aunts. But how was that possible? Maybe he'd climbed in through the window, he speculated wildly. Or perhaps Amanda had sneaked him into the house after the aunts were abed.

Jack concentrated hard. The last thing he remembered was sitting in some squalid pub in the seamy side of town getting drunk. He cudgeled his brain for more information, then recalled with painful vividness the reason for his drinking spree. When he'd come to offer his heart and hand in marriage to Amanda yesterday morning, she'd turned him away at the door! Or rather, she'd had Henchpenny turn him away. But if, as he recollected from her letter, she wanted nothing more to do with him, why was he in her bed?

Jack frowned. This appalling gap in his memory was worrisome. He'd thought his amnesia due to the accident was a thing of the past. But perhaps he'd had a setback, brought on by booze and emotional distress. Before getting himself engaged to the *wrong* woman and falling in love with the *right* woman, he'd hardly ever got more than mildly tipsy. He was going to have to find some other way to drown his sorrows besides getting cup-shot.

But did he have any sorrows left to drown? he wondered, settling into the pillows again and tightening his arms around Amanda. From where he stood ... lay? ... things didn't look half bad. The worst part of this whole strange incident, of course, was the fact that he couldn't remember making love to Amanda last night. He'd regret that lapse of memory till his dying day.

She stirred in his arms and gave a soft sigh. The slight movement of her body against his immediately aroused him. He began to contemplate the agreeable prospect of making new memories . . . .

No such luck. Jack heard voices and approaching footfalls outside the bedchamber door. It sounded like the nervous, high-pitched tones of Amanda's Aunt Prissy and the lower, more reserved accents of her Aunt Nan.

Panicked, he considered making a mad dash for his clothes. Then he realized that he didn't have time to get more than one leg in his trousers. He mentally pictured himself frozen in such an embarrassing position—balanced flamingolike on one bare leg with the Montgomery family jewels on full display—and he decided it was best to stay under the covers. He scooted to a sitting position and pulled the blankets over his chest, tucking them securely under both arms. Blissfully unaware, Amanda slept on.

The door opened, and three figures entered the room. Miss Priscilla, Miss Nancy, and . . . Julian. Prissy had been whispering something to Julian as they entered, but her words trailed into oblivion as her cataract-clouded eyes adjusted to the dim light and she surveyed the scene before her.

Shock appeared to have turned them all into statues . . . except for their heads, which swiveled in unison as they looked first at Jack, then at Amanda, then at the telltale pile of wantonly discarded clothes at the bedside, then back to Jack.

Finally the aunts reacted with startled wheezes and by pressing their hands, one on top of the other, to their bosoms. Julian took out his quizzing glass, attached it to his eye, and lifted his chin, staring down at Jack with quelling hauteur.

"Good *Gawd*, Jack," Julian said, finally breaking the silence. "Is this how you repay Miss Priscilla and

Miss Nancy for rescuing you from the gutters of Spitalfields, by compromising their niece . . . *again*?"

Jack shrugged and grinned sheepishly. "Would it make some little restitution if I told you I don't even remember doing the compromising?"

Amanda sighed and rolled over, nearly baring her breasts in the process. Jack hurriedly pulled the blankets up to her chin and said, "Wake up, Amanda. We've got company."

Amanda blinked her eyes open, smiled up at Jack, and reached for him. Tactfully prying her arms from around his neck, Jack rolled his eyes toward the door. "Didn't you hear me, sweetheart? I said *we've got company.*"

Amanda looked dazedly in the direction he indicated, then screamed and scrambled to a sitting position, clutching the bedclothes to her chest.

"Wh-what are you doing in here?" she stammered, her eyes as big as plum puddings, her pale hair in charming disarray about her shoulders.

"We might ask you the same thing," Nan primly replied, clasping her hands together and holding them at waist level. She bent forward and asked in the tone of a reprimanding governess who'd caught her naughty charge with her fingers in the sugar bowl, "What are *you* doing in here, Amanda Jane?"

"I should say that's perfectly obvious, Nan," said Prissy. She sucked in her cheeks and tried to look stern and sour, but Jack could see how her eyes sparked with humor. She waggled a gnarled finger. "And, as we all know, this isn't the first time for you two!"

"Nor the last, I'll wager," Julian observed dryly. He'd turned his back out of respect for Amanda's modesty and was standing with his arms crossed, looking at the wall. "When's the wedding to be, Jack?"

"Oh, but—" Amanda began.

"I've always fancied a Christmas wedding," said Nan.

"Wouldn't Amanda Jane look lovely all in white and holding a poinsettia bouquet?" Pris added dreamily.

The two aunts nodded at each other like a couple of hens.

"Christmas sounds perfect to me," said Jack, throwing his arm around Amanda's shoulders. "What do you think, sweetheart?"

Amanda turned stricken eyes to Jack. "But I can't be your wife, Jack!" she choked out.

"What nonsense is this?" demanded Nan, scowling. "We know you love him. You can't just bed the man indefinitely. You might conceive a child, for heaven's sake!" She paused, scowling harder. "You *do* love him, don't you?"

"Yes, of course I do," sniffed Amanda, crushing the edge of the sheeting and dabbing her teary eyes. "But I *can't* marry him. Not yet!"

Jack caught Amanda's shoulders and turned her toward him. Reluctantly, she raised her eyes to his. "You love me, Amanda, and I love you. And you definitely show no aversion to sharing my bed—"

"No, indeed"! Pris corroborated.

"—so would you mind telling me *why* you won't marry me?"

Everyone stood stock still, waiting, as Amanda's pained gaze drifted from one face to the other.

"Because Robert Hamilton thinks I'm going to marry *him*!" she finally blurted out. Then the rest came in a babble. "He's . . . he's blackmailing me, Jack!"

"What?" Jack was incredulous. "Rob's blackmailing you? Why?"

"Jack's friend is blackmailing Amanda Jane?" Pris repeated incredulously, turning a confused gaze toward Nan.

"If he's a blackmailer, maybe we heard his name at the relief house in Spitalfields," Nan speculated.

Julian turned. His pale eyes blazed silver-bright with anger. "Do you really have to ask why he's blackmailing her, Jack? The little fiend needs the money. More to the point, *how* is he blackmailing you, Amanda?"

"He somehow found out about Sam, and he's threatened to tell everyone she's illegitimate! I couldn't allow that, Jack. I couldn't let him ruin her life once and for all. I had no choice but to promise to marry him, although I never intended—"

"The bloody bastard!" Forgetting he was naked, forgetting everything but his growing rage, Jack flung back the covers and stood up.

The aunts squealed and turned away, and Julian exclaimed, "Good *Gawd*, Jack! Show some decorum!"

"I beg your pardon, ladies ... but to hell with decorum, Julian!" Jack spat, shoving his feet into his trousers. "How dare Rob threaten and coerce Amanda? You always said he was corrupt, but I never believed you. Now I have to kill the little sod!"

"Oh, this was just what I was afraid of!" cried Amanda, wrapping herself in a sheet and scooting to the edge of the bed. "This is why I didn't tell you sooner! I was hoping I could keep things from getting violent. Oh, please, Jack, don't do anything foolish! I couldn't bear it if something happened to you!"

Jack buttoned his pants, then searched for his shirt. "Where the bloody hell—" He finally spied it wadded up on the rumpled bedclothes, grabbed it, and thrust his arms into the sleeves. He threw Amanda a furtive and tender glance. "You don't understand, Amanda," he told her. "What Rob has done is detestable. He has to answer for it. Not only has he tried to harm you and Sam, but he's made a mockery out of our friendship."

"Are you going to call him out?" Amanda asked faintly.

Jack sat down on the side of the bed and tugged on his boots. "Twenty paces at dawn," he affirmed grimly. He peered up at Julian who stood near the door, silently watching. "Will you be my second, Julian?"

"Of course," Julian promptly replied.

Amanda rebuked him with her eyes. "Must you encourage him, Lord Serling?"

"A man must always defend his honor and the honor of his loved ones, Miss Darlington," Julian replied coolly. "It is a rule that cannot be broken."

"Honor!" wailed Amanda. "What's it worth if you're *dead*?"

"What's life worth without it?" Julian countered.

Jack stood up and slipped into his jacket. He bent down and gave Amanda a hard kiss, then cupped her chin and forced her to look at him. "Have you no faith in me, my love? Don't fret. Sam's future is safe, *our* future is safe. I'm *not* going to die."

Then he turned on his heel and left the room, Julian following closely behind, the two of them nearly running down Henchpenny in the hall.

Startled to see Jack rushing from the premises half-dressed, Henchpenny exclaimed, "Er ... my lords! I don't think you want to go downstairs just now."

Jack and Julian paused at the top of the stairs. Jack scowled and demanded, "Why not, Henchpenny?"

Henchpenny stood stiff and formal, but his eyes widened significantly. "Because Miss Darlington has a visitor waiting downstairs."

"What?" exclaimed Jack. "This early? Who is it?"

"It's the same gentleman Miss Darlington received yesterday morning, my lord. A Mr. Robert Hamilton, I believe."

Then, to Henchpenny's utter amazement, instead of waiting till the visitor was gone or leaving through the backdoor in the servants' quarters to preserve Miss Darlington's reputation, Jack flew down the stairs two at a time with Lord Serling fast on his heels.

To add to his shock, Henchpenny was privy to the astonishing sight of Miss Darlington herself emerging from the open door of her bedchamber, her face as white as the sheeting she'd wrapped around her otherwise naked form, rushing down the stairs exclaiming, "Jack! Please, Jack, don't do anything foolish!"

When Miss Priscilla and Miss Nancy scurried from the bedchamber, as well, with their palms flattened against their withered cheeks and their eyes bright with agitation, Henchpenny decided to join them as they followed Miss Darlington down the stairs. Mischief and mayhem were loose in his ordered household, and it was Henchpenny's duty to keep abreast of the situation. Besides, he wouldn't miss witnessing the outcome of this to-do for all the tea in China. Miss Darlington's life had certainly got more exciting since that fateful trip to Thorney Island. . . .

When Amanda burst into the parlor, not thirty seconds behind Jack and Julian, Jack had already picked Rob up by the lapels and pushed him against the wall with his feet dangling inches from the floor. Robert's arms were forced into a stiff, painful position by the bunching of the jacket, making him look as though he were about to take flight. His face was bright red with anger and mortification and the collosol effort it took to breathe. Julian stood back and watched with his arms crossed and his face schooled to passivity, as if to say, "This is your fight, Jack. I won't interfere unless absolutely necessary."

"How dare you try to blackmail Amanda!" Jack ground out between clenched teeth. "You dirty bastard, I ought to kill you right here and now!"

"Can't . . . do . . . it, Jack," Robert panted out with

a sneer. "You owe ... me. I saved your ... life, you bloody sod!"

"I've more than paid you back for that, Rob. I've hauled your worthless arse out of dun territory more than I care to count. If not for me, you wouldn't have a friend in the world. And this is how you repay me, by God!"

Robert gasped and twisted, trying to grab hold of Jack's arms, but his sleeves bound him too tightly. "A hell ... of a lot of good your ... friendship has done me, Jack. All the women went for ... *you*." His eyes bulged and rolled in his head till he focused on Amanda. "See you got ... this one in bed, too. The little whore!"

Amanda heard a sharp intake of breath behind her, turned, and saw not only the horrified faces of the aunts and Henchpenny but Sam, too. She'd apparently wandered into the parlor from the breakfast room when she heard the commotion and was now standing with her mouth agape, a piece of toast hanging from her limp fingers.

"Now you've done it, Rob," Jack said with ominous calm. "No one calls the future Lady Durham a whore. Apologize and I won't hit you quite so hard."

Robert stretched his neck and sneered down at Jack, apparently not about to apologize. Jack seemed pleased. He smiled unpleasantly and slowly lowered Robert till his feet made contact with the floor. He waited for Robert to catch his breath and shake some life into his arms; then he pulled back his fist and hit Robert square on the jaw.

Robert's head snapped back, and he slid to the floor. Bloody drool oozed from one side of his mouth.

"Get up and fight me, Rob," Jack invited with his fists clenched at his sides. "Come on, you swine. I'll give you the next shot free and clear."

Robert remained seated, his legs sprawled in front

of him. He glared up at Jack, rubbing his chin, working the hinge of his jaw. "You'd beat me to a pulp and you know it. Things'd be a lot more equal if we faced off with guns instead of fisticuffs."

Jack crossed his arms and raised an imperious brow. "I agree with you completely. Where would you like to meet?"

Robert pulled out his handkerchief and dabbed at his mouth, grimacing as he studied the bright red blood that had soaked through the white linen. "Don't know. Need to find me a second first, then he'll send word. Is that all right with you, *my lord*?" he added sarcastically.

"Perfectly," Jack said coolly. "Just as long as we get this business over with tomorrow at cock's crow. I can't wait any longer than that to give you exactly what you deserve."

Robert smirked. "You can't kill me, Jack. You owe me."

"So you keep saying," Jack replied in a bored voice.

Robert laughed. "No, you won't kill me. And winging me in the arm won't stop me from talking. I have every intention of telling the world about Miss Darlington's bastard sister. The only way you'll ever silence me is by sending me to my grave, and you have too many scruples for that, Jack."

"Get out, Robert."

Robert smirked again, braced his shoulder against the wall, and slid to his feet, then staggered across the room. Everyone parted the way, and he walked with his head down till he got to the parlor door. Sam was standing just inside, still motionless with shock. As Robert passed, he lifted his head and stretched his lips into an evil smile, the blood from his injured mouth coating his teeth and giving him a demonic look. Sam reached for her throat with both hands in a fearful, protective gesture.

No one moved till they heard the front door open and close behind Robert. Amanda threw herself into Jack's arms and he held her close, grabbing the sheet in the back as it threatened to unwrap from around her.

As if they all had the same idea at once, Julian, Nan, Prissy, Sam, and Henchpenny all withdrew from the room, leaving the two lovers alone for a few moments to comfort each other.

In the hall, Nan turned to Henchpenny. "As I'm sure you can deduce for yourself, Henchpenny, if there happen to be any visitors for Miss Darlington, tell them she's . . . er . . . temporarily indisposed. And do steer the servants away from the parlor for the next half hour."

"Yes, of course, Miss Nancy."

"If there's talk at the servants' table about this, as I'm sure one or more of the maids saw Miss Darlington racing down the stairs in a sheet, threaten them with dismissal if they dare repeat a word of it to anyone."

"Yes, Miss Nancy. You can be sure I shall squelch any attempts at gossip within the house as well."

Nan smiled weakly and nodded, and Henchpenny strode purposefully and with great dignity down the hall to the kitchen.

"What's going to happen?" said Sam, her eyes wide and frightened. "Will that man tell everyone I'm—"

Julian slid his hand around the nape of Sam's neck in a comforting gesture. "Don't worry about that man," he said. "Neither Jack nor I will allow him to hurt you in any way."

"Why was he so hateful, Julian? Why does he want to hurt me? Is Jack really going to fight a duel? And why was Amanda in a *sheet*?"

"Come, child," said Prissy, slipping her arm in Sam's. "I'll explain everything to you upstairs."

Sam balked. "But I want Julian to explain things to me."

"I need to speak to Lord Serling alone, Samantha," said Nan. "Now do be a dear and go upstairs with your Aunt Prissy."

"But—"

Julian gave Sam's neck a squeeze and bent down to look into her unhappy face. "Do it, brat. I'll come by later and see how your Roman history is coming along." He smiled encouragingly.

Sam looked up through her thick lashes and gave a grudging smile. "If you promise."

"I promise."

"Oh, all right."

Prissy pulled Sam up the stairs before she could change her mind, and Nan invited Julian into the morning room. Curious as to what she was up to, Jack stood and waited in the center of the room while Nan closed the double doors securely behind her.

"So, Nan, what is it you wanted to talk to me about?" Julian thought it rather odd how he'd got on such friendly terms so quickly with Amanda's aunts. He'd developed a sincere respect and affection for them and was interested in anything they had to say. But then they'd certainly lived long enough to have attained a little wisdom and knowledge of the world.

"Do you mind if we sit down, my lord?" Nan said, peering up at him. "If I have to look up so far for the entire conversation, I'll get a crick in my neck for certain."

Julian chuckled and took her elbow, guiding her to a sofa and sitting down beside her. "Is that better?"

"Much." She leaned close and lay her hand on his, saying seriously, "Besides defending Jack's honor, etcetera, this duel isn't going to settle things with that Robert Hamilton fellow, is it?"

"Not unless Jack shoots to kill," Julian admitted with a sigh.

"Do you think he will?"

"I don't know. I hope not. I hope it won't be necessary."

Nan breathed a sigh of relief. "I'm glad we think alike on that, my lord. Jack is furious with his friend, as well he should be, but he'd have a hard time living with himself if he actually killed Robert Hamilton ... even though the little beast deserves it! No, I don't mean that! I'm a Christian woman, and I don't believe in violence of any kind, but—"

"I know what you mean, Nan. I've disliked and distrusted Robert for the past two years, and now I despise him. He's taken advantage of Jack's trusting and loyal nature for too long. But now that Jack's eyes have been opened, I can finally take steps to get rid of the little ... er ... swine for good."

Nan's eyes grew wide. "You don't mean to say—"

"No, I don't plan to murder him, either, however much I may be tempted," Julian said wryly. "But whatever is done must be done before the duel tomorrow. I don't want Jack living with a guilty conscience for the rest of his life."

"What will you do?"

"I haven't figured that out yet, but I've got several hours to come up with something. I need damaging information about him, something we could use to counter his blackmail against Amanda. Something that could force him out of town for good. His gaming debts and profligate ways aren't scandalous enough; half the young bucks in London are nearly as deep in debt as Rob."

Julian looked up and saw Nan gazing into the middle distance, her eyes narrowed, her lips pursed. "What's that look for, Nan?" said Julian. "Do you think you can help me?"

Nan's eyes met Julian's with a canny expression. "I think I just might, my lord. When Pris and I got home last night from the relief house in Spitalfields we regularly visit, we heard from Henchpenny that Amanda had had a visitor by the name of Robert Hamilton. We thought we'd heard the name before, but we weren't sure where." She shrugged and smiled. "Sometimes we old tabbies forget things. Anyway, Amanda told us we must have heard it in connection with Jack. But now that we've seen the scoundrel in the flesh, we know exactly where we've heard the name ... *and* seen the face."

Amanda was snuggled up to Jack on the sofa, the sheet she wore tucked around her updrawn feet. Her head rested on his chest, her arms were wrapped around his waist, and his arm was wrapped around her shoulders. They stared into the fire, their expressions sober and thoughtful. Troubled.

"We've certainly had a unique courtship, haven't we, Amanda darling?" Jack said at last, giving her a squeeze.

"Very unique, indeed," Amanda agreed.

He turned to look at her and brushed a lock of her disheveled hair off her forehead. "Do you know when I first realized I loved you?" He smiled tenderly.

She smiled back. "Tell me."

"I first *admitted* it to myself—and to Julian—that night on Thorney Island. By the way, did you hear that part of the conversation?"

"No." She chuckled. "I daresay if I had, we might have come to an understanding sooner!"

"Yes. Well, anyway, that's when I admitted to myself that I was head over heels in love with you, but I think I first *knew* it when you blushed so delightfully that time I teased you about my war wound."

She shook her head. "You were such a devil! You had me blushing constantly!"

"When did you first fall in love with me, Amanda?"

She raised a brow. "I dare not tell you. You'll become a conceited coxcomb."

"Aren't I already? Tell me, sweetheart."

"You weren't even conscious yet!"

"Just tell me!"

She shrugged her bare shoulders. "I think it was when you mumbled something in your sleep on the way to the Three Nuns. It was provocative—"

He grinned. "Of course."

"—and you called whomever you were dreaming about a *minx*! I found myself wishing you'd call *me* a minx and say provocative things to *me*! And I didn't even know you."

"You got your wish, eh? I'm sure I've called you a minx and said provocative things on several occasions."

"Yes, I got my wish. But I'm a selfish being, Jack, and now I want the happy ending." She scooted up, braced her hands on his chest, and gazed into his face. "I want to marry you, Jack, have babies with you, and grow old with you. I want the fairy tale."

"You'll get it, Amanda. I promise."

"But what about the duel?" She bit her lip and searched his face. "I'm afraid, Jack."

He rubbed his hand along her bare arm. "Don't be afraid, Amanda. I've waited a long time to be this happy. I'm not going to let Rob ruin it for me."

"He's jealous of you."

Jack smiled, his loving gaze roving over her face. "Now that I have you in my life, I can understand why he'd be jealous."

"Promise me, Jack—"

"I already have."

"But—"

He pressed a finger against her lips. "Trust me, Amanda."

She kissed his finger, then caught his hand and cradled her cheek in his warm palm.

"Yes, Jack. With all my heart."

Chapter 22

J ulian walked alone down Abingdon Street toward Rob's apartment. The sky was overcast and the fog was thick. Despite the occasional street lamp, visibility in some places was reduced to as little as ten or twelve feet. Young bucks staggering home from their evening's entertainment, as well as other assorted anonymous figures in greatcoats, loomed out of the darkness unexpectedly. In the distance, Julian heard the watchman chant the time. Two o'clock.

Despite Rob's profligate ways, Julian expected to find the villain home by this relatively early hour. A man would have to be daft not to catch a little sleep, or at least a little rest, before participating in a duel. Rob's second, Percy Mingay, a hell-born babe with a reputation as foul as Rob's, had paid Julian a visit that afternoon to set the time and place for the duel and to state Rob's preference of weapons.

They were to meet at St. James's Park at five-thirty. And it came as no surprise to Julian that Rob chose to duel with pistols instead of swords. He'd never best Jack at anything that demanded stamina or athletic ability, and he knew it.

Once again it was borne home to Julian that it was truly amazing that Rob had ever saved Jack's life in the first place. The story told was that Rob had bodily thrown himself onto Jack and toppled him to the ground, thereby removing him from the path of on-coming gunfire shot by an enemy at close range. Julian thought it more likely that Rob was trying to save his own skin and Jack had simply got in the way and been plowed down. Of course, the scoun-drel would be only too happy to take credit for being brave and quick-witted rather than cowardly and clumsy.

No one could ever prove the truth one way or the other, and Julian had been forced for two years to give the little bugger the benefit of the doubt. Never-theless, whether by accident or on purpose, Rob had saved Jack from potentially fatal wounds. But even so, Rob's actions that fateful day on the peninsula certainly didn't give him license to ruin innocent peo-ple's lives. And Julian wasn't just talking about Sam and Amanda and what Rob had tried to do to them. Information he'd grubbed up, with the help of Amanda's observant aunts, proved that Rob had been busily ruining other people's lives, too.

Julian found the address he was looking for, went through the unlocked outside door, and walked up the dimly lit narrow flight of stairs to the first floor. The place had little security, but it was in a fairly quiet neighborhood filled with houses just like this one with apartments to let to single gentleman. It was not a fashionable address, but it was respectable and cheap. However, despite the moderate expense of living there, Julian strongly suspected that Jack was paying Rob's rent.

At Rob's door, Julian rapped sharply on the peel-ing wood several times. When there was no immedi-ate answer, he knocked again and persisted till the door finally opened. Rob's manservant, a do-it-all chap of the sort that single men hired to keep their small lodgings tidy and prepare occasional refreshment as well as oversee all the usual duties of a valet, answered the door. He was still dressed in his day clothes, but they were wrinkled and his person unkept. He looked and acted as though he'd been drinking. His bald pate was gleaming with sweat, and his nose was as red as a radish.

"I'm here to see Mr. Hamilton," Julian informed him briskly.

The unsteady manservant peered up at Julian with eyes that looked painfully bloodshot. "T' master is sleepin'," he said.

"Wake him up," was Julian's uncompromising response.

The servant blinked confusedly, his bleary gaze traveling slowly up and down Julian's tall, impeccable figure. "But it's the wee hours," he argued. "What's a fine gent like you doin' 'ere at this time o' night, anyway? I kin tell ye fer a fact he ain't got no money. Owes *me* wages fer four months."

"That's regrettable, my good man. I advise you to sober up and find another position as quickly as possible. But I'm here for reasons that have nothing to do with extracting money from your master. A fruitless endeavor, I should think." He stepped past the servant and into the tiny parlor.

"You goin' t' kill 'im?" the servant inquired.

Julian smiled ruefully. "You're the second person to ask me that in the last few hours. I'm tempted, but ... no ... I'm not going to kill him." He dipped into his coat pocket and came up with several shillings, handing them to the surprised servant. "These ought to secure you lodgings and food till you can find new employment. Don't spend it on gin, because you probably won't get such another chance to change your luck in a million years. Now, show me where Hamilton sleeps, then leave us alone."

Startled into soberness, the servant obeyed, gesturing toward a door at the end of a short hall to indicate Rob's bedroom. Then he hurried to his own minuscule chamber to gather and pack his few belongings in an old hatbox. Within five minutes, he had thanked Julian for the tenth time, said good-bye, and was gone.

Julian picked up a brace of candles off the mantel in the parlor, walked down the hall to Rob's chamber, and opened the door. As Julian held the candles aloft, light spilled over a narrow bed that shared very cramped quarters with a tallboy and a small wardrobe closet. Rob was sprawled on the bed, fully clothed. On the floor next to the bed was a half-empty bottle of whiskey. He was sleeping off his latest drinking spree.

Julian lifted his leg and none-too-gently jabbed Rob's ribs with his boot. Rob startled, drew up one knee, and shielded his eyes from the light with a splayed hand. "Lord, Percy," he croaked sluggishly, "that you? Can't be time already. . . ."

"No, it's not time, and I'm not Percy Mingay, come to coddle and coax you to relative sobriety so you can take careful aim at my brother. Get up, you distasteful little worm."

Rob scooted over the rumpled bedclothes, propping himself against the headboard. His hand was still up, trying to buffer his weak eyes from the candlelight. He blinked and squinted and peered around and through his fingers. "Serling," he said at last, his tone incredulous . . . frightened. Then, trying to cover his initial fear, he lowered his hand and demanded, "What are you doing here?"

Julian set the brace of candles on the tallboy. "Aren't you going to ask me if I'm going to kill you? That seems to be the question uppermost in people's minds today."

Rob made a sneering smile, trying to appear confident and unconcerned. "You won't kill me. Not here. It's not your style."

"How right you are," Julian observed, removing his snuffbox from his jacket pocket, flipping it open, and taking a sniff. "But Jack will certainly kill you this morning at St. James's Park ... if you go."

Uncertainty flickered across Rob's face before his bravado returned. "Of course I'm going. Why wouldn't I? For some reason you think your brother will shoot to kill, but while he may want to, he won't. Too honorable, that one."

"Honor isn't something you're overly encumbered with, is it, Rob? Even women and children are fair game to you when it comes to getting what you want. You don't care a fig how they suffer, do you?"

Rob slid forward till his feet met the floor. He reached down, picked up the bottle of whiskey, and took a long swig, at the same time keeping a close account of Julian's every move ... or nonmovement, in this case. Julian knew that remaining calm and as still as a nun at prayer would unnerve Rob. He would feel as though he were being watched by a coiled snake about to strike. It was an apt metaphor because Julian was only biding his time before delivering his own brand of poison.

"So what if I got desperate and tried to blackmail Amanda? Does that make me a complete villain? And I wouldn't call that sister of hers a *child*." He leered. "She looks pretty mature to me."

Julian suppressed the urge to grab Rob about the Adam's apple and squeeze his scrawny neck till his eyes popped. For some reason, his lecherous insinuation about Sam made him furious ... more furious than the situation warranted. He should expect Rob to be vulgar and disrespectful, but—perhaps like an older brother—Julian had developed strong protective feelings for Sam.

"At the moment, I'm not speaking of Amanda and Sam." He paused, stretching the tension. "I'm referring to your shameful abandonment of your wife and child and your intent to commit bigamy."

Julian had the supreme pleasure of watching Rob turn white as a corpse. "Wh-what are you talking about? I don't—"

"Don't bother denying it," Julian interrupted in a bored drawl. "You'd be wasting my time, and you've wasted far too much of it already."

Rob sat with his hands braced on the edge of the bed, hunched forward as if he had a huge knot in his stomach. His eyes were wide and anxious; his arms trembled. "You're mad. I don't know what nitwit story you've made up about me, but—"

Julian sighed and pulled a sheet of paper from his waistcoat pocket. He unfolded it and offered it to Rob. "Here. Read this if you want proof. Don't bother tearing it up because I've got another copy in a safe place. The vicar at St. Mary's obligingly searched his books and found your name and the name of a Miss Sophia Lansdown entered in the section for recorded marriages. The date of the ceremony—attended by only you and your bride—was June fifth, eighteen-thirteen, prior to your stint in the army."

Rob stared at the paper in Julian's outstretched hand but said nothing and made no move to take it. His trembling increased. Julian raised a brow. "What? You don't want to see the vicar's confirmation of your marriage, Rob? But then why should you? I suspect you remember that glorious day as clear as a bell." He folded the paper and returned it to his pocket.

"How . . . how—?"

"Amanda's aunts gave me the first clue which led me on today's appalling journey of discovery. The hovel your wife and child live in is squalid and unsafe. Mrs. Hamilton—who is sadly naive and pitifully loyal to you despite everything you've done—finally broke down after your recent prolonged absence and applied to a relief house for help. Amanda's aunts have taken a special interest in that particular charity since they've been residing in London, and got to know your wife rather well. The poor thing thinks you're working from dusk to dawn at some clerk's job to get them out of Spitalfields, and thusly justifies to herself your constant absence and the fine clothes you wear when you pay her and the child a rare visit."

"This is all an absurd lie!" Rob spluttered. "You've paid that woman to testify falsely against me. As for Amanda's aunts . . . why they're nothing but a couple of senile old crones!"

"You're quite wrong. Miss Nancy and Miss Priscilla are very sharp and spry. They'd heard your name from Sophia but didn't make the connection immediately. They had also seen you once or twice in Spitalfields, talking to your wife . . . most recently, yesterday. Imagine their surprise when they likewise saw you at Miss Darlington's and understood you to be a suitor for their niece's hand in marriage! And, as I recall from what the ladies told me, you actually gave your wife a guinea and promised more. Were you expecting to come into some money, Rob? Perhaps enough to support your *first* wife and child and keep them hidden away and secret from the public while you took another woman to the altar under false pretenses?"

"I never—"

"And all this after spending the quarterly allowance grudgingly sent by her invalid father from Yorkshire . . . your supposed 'uncle.' Lucky for you he was conscientious enough to send the money—to your Abingdon Street address, of course—but too angry with his daughter for eloping with the likes of you to allow for her to confide in him and seek his further assistance. He thought he was helping her, but he was only plumping your pockets and helping support your bachelor ways and gaming habits."

"I made a mistake in my youth," Rob defended himself petulantly. "I should never have married her. She's beneath my touch."

"In other words, she isn't rich enough and you think you can do better? The allowance isn't enough to support yourself—never mind a wife and child—in the manner to which you aspire?"

"She's nothing but a country squire's youngest daughter! Rough and uneducated. Her Yorkshire accent is as broad as a horse's arse!"

"And you imagine her beneath your touch for those reasons?" Julian shook his head and smiled derisively. "On the contrary, she is as far above you as the moon and the stars. You are nothing but a self-serving opportunist with no morals, no natural feelings, and no honor." His aristocratic nostrils flared. "You disgust me. I've had to watch you take advantage of Jack's good-natured decency for two years. It thrills me to the core to know that after this last interview I'll never clap eyes on you again."

Rob sat up straighter and thrust his chin forward, seeming to try for a last show of defiance. "What makes you so sure of that?"

Julian crossed his arms and peered down at Rob with chilling contempt. Rob's chin tucked back in. "If you are so foolish as to remain in England, I will make sure the truth about you is known in every household of my acquaintance," Julian informed him in a tone that left no doubt of his absolute sincerely. "Your reputation will follow you wherever you go. You will be shunned by everyone. You will be known for what you are: a deserter, a would-be bigamist, and a blackmailer. As Jack's friend your debts were tolerated. But without Jack's support, the duns will fall on you like a pack of ravening wolves."

Julian paused, letting his words sink in. "A boat

is scheduled to cross the channel this morning at four-thirty. I suggest you purchase passage on it and climb aboard."

Rob dragged his hands down his face, the clenched fingers leaving red streaks in their wake. "But I haven't got a groat to my name! I'll starve, I'll be forced to—"

"Live like your wife and child? No, I would not wish that on a dog." Julian pulled a pouch full of coins out of his pocket and threw it at Rob. Rob caught the pouch and stared dazedly at it. "That should keep you going till you find employment of some kind.

"Oh, and I know how worried you must be about leaving behind your wife and child," he mocked scornfully. "Let your mind be at ease. Once they've been properly fed and clothed, I plan to restore the young woman to her family in Yorkshire. I'm sure she can reconcile with her father when she tells him you're dead."

"Dead?" Rob gulped.

"Yes," said Julian. "And murdered in the most gruesome manner."

Rob's head darted up. His anxiety was palpable.

Julian smiled. "Your throat slit in a dark alley."

"But . . . but that's a lie!" Rob quavered, wild-eyed. "I won't be dead. I'll be—"

"As good as dead," Julian finished for him. "Because if you ever set foot in England again, I'll bloody well make sure the reports of your death aren't the least exaggerated. And the same fate will befall you if the tiniest bit of scandalous gossip makes its way across the channel casting doubt on Samantha Darlington's antecedents. No matter where you've hidden, I'll track you down like an animal and kill you. Do I make myself clear, Rob?"

The two men locked gazes. Julian's expression was grimly earnest; Rob's was filled with terror. Julian meant every word he'd said, and Rob knew he meant it.

"Well, Rob?" Julian prompted. He tsk-tsked sarcastically. "What *will* you do?"

At twenty-five minutes past the hour of five in the morning, St. James's Park was deserted. The sunrise was a diffused gleam of gold on an otherwise gray horizon, and fog swirled thickly through the trees that dotted the dew-drenched grass. The damp cold crept into Jack's blood, mixing with his aversion to the task before him. To protect Amanda and Sam, he was going to have to kill Rob.

He sighed. He wasn't killing Rob as punishment; judgment belonged to the courts and God, and Jack would never presume to sentence a man to death for his crimes. He was killing Rob as a precaution against injustices the bastard was planning against innocent people. Jack compared it in his mind to killing one's enemies at war. On the battlefield you were protecting what was near and dear to you: your country. And—even ranking above sweet England— there was nothing more near and dear to Jack than Amanda.

Jack frowned. It was easy to rationalize. He was convinced he was doing the right thing. So, why did he feel so wretched? He kept remembering what Rob had said: *You owe me.* Yes, he owed Rob for saving his life, but he couldn't let that fact stop him from doing what he had to do. He'd have years to feel guilty about it as penance. For now he must set aside those doubts and regrets and simply do what he considered his duty.

Jack felt Julian's hand on his shoulder. "How are you, brother?"

Jack looked up into Julian's sober countenance and forced a smile. "Ready and impatiently waiting."

"How was Amanda when you left her last night?"

"Resigned, I think. Anxious, I know."

"I'm surprised she didn't insist on coming this morning. She's a strong-willed baggage, eh?"

Jack smiled ... this time genuinely. "That she is. I didn't tell her where or when we were meeting. She was miffed, of course, but I didn't want her watching when I ..."

Jack's words trailed off. Any vestige of a smile entirely disappeared. Julian squeezed Jack's shoulder, then let go. He understood Jack's dilemma and sympathized; it was unnecessary to put his feelings into words.

Presently a black gig pulled up several yards away under a canopy of trees. It was the doctor. As was frequently the custom, a medical man was present when a duel had potential for serious injuries.

"Did you send for the old sawbones?" Jack asked his brother.

"No," Julian replied. "Must have been Mingay's idea."

"Well, that either means Rob intends to mortally wound *me*," he observed dryly, "or they think I intend to mortally wound *Rob*."

Julian did not comment, and growing more restless by the moment, Jack plucked his watch from his greatcoat pocket and squinted in the inadequate light at the roman numerals on its face. "Where *is* the bastard, anyway? It's five-thirty-two! However late he shows up for everything else, you'd think he'd be on time for a duel!"

Julian shrugged. "Maybe he's changed his mind."

"He has," came a voice from behind them. They turned and observed Percy Mingay walking toward them through the fog. When he reached them, Jack could see the irritation and exasperation on Percy's face. "I don't even like the little sod, but I got up at four-thirty this morning so I could roust him out of bed and stand as second for him at this hellish hour, and he had the gall to cry craven and leave the country! Can you believe it?"

Jack was astounded. "No, I can't believe it. What proof do you have?"

"When I got to his apartment this morning, he was gone. But he left a note behind saying—" Percy had been in the process of extracting an envelope from his coat pocket when he seemed to spy something over Jack's shoulder. He froze and stared. "Unless, by God, that's him coming now on horseback at full gallop. What's he up to now?"

Jack turned and tensed. He could feel Julian's tension, too. Just as Percy had indicated, there was a man on horseback approaching at a fast speed. He was small in stature like Rob and shrouded in a billowing great coat. In the dim light it was impossible to see whether or not the rider had a weapon ... such as a gun aimed directly at Jack's heart. Or even at Julian's heart ... God forbid.

It had to be Rob. Who else would be out at this hour? Who else knew of the duel except those directly involved? But why was Rob on horseback, and why was he charging toward them hell-bent for leather? Jack was afraid he knew.

"Hand me the pistol, Julian," he said quietly, careful not to make a quick movement and alert the rider to his intentions too soon. Julian handed him the loaded gun, and Jack dropped it to his side, his finger resting lightly on the trigger. He wouldn't shoot—he wouldn't even prepare to aim—till he had proof there was sufficient reason, like the glint of steel from an upraised pistol or rifle.

"Don't do this, Rob," Jack pleaded under his breath. "Don't let things end like this."

As the rider got closer, Percy swore vehemently and darted behind a nearby tree, peeking out from behind the thick trunk like a frightened child. But, as Jack knew he would, Julian stood stalwartly beside

him. Jack clenched his jaw and held his breath ...
then suddenly let it out in a hiss of profound surprise
and relief.

"*Amanda?*"

The horse slowed to canter, then a walk. Amanda
pulled on the reigns, and the sweating horse pranced
to a stop. Julian took the tethers and grabbed the
horse's bit, while Jack set the pistol carefully down,
caught Amanda by the waist, and helped her
dismount.

"Jack! Jack!" she exclaimed, throwing her arms
around his neck. "Thank goodness you're all right!
Is it over?"

Jack let her cling for a minute, then pulled free,
grasped her by the shoulders, and looked her over.
She was dressed from head to toe like a man, with
her long hair tucked inside an old hat Jack thought
he recognized as one he'd seen Harley wearing on
their trip to Thorney Island.

"What's the meaning of this, Amanda?" Jack demanded to know. "Why are you dressed like this
and why are you riding about London alone at this
hour?" Relief and surprise had given way to anger.
"Don't you realize the danger involved in such
foolishness?"

"Oh, Jack, don't be angry!" she pleaded, tilting her
beautiful face to look up at him beseechingly. "I was
worried sick about you. I couldn't just sit at home
sniffing salts and dabbing away tears while I waited
for word!"

Jack was already softening. Amanda was a winsome lass, hard to stay angry with for long. But he
deliberately hardened his voice when he asked,
"How did you know where to find us?"

Amanda bit her lip, the unconscious gesture making his heart romp and skitter like a frisky pup. "I
didn't know," she admitted meekly. "I guessed
you'd come here because this park is smaller and

more remote than the others. And I was right! But I'm late because even this park is large enough to get lost in! I was so afraid I'd be *too* late!''

Jack shook his head with a beleaguered sigh and gave her a slight shake. "You goose! I asked you to trust me, and you said you did! What happened to all that trust, Amanda?''

"I do trust *you*, Jack. But I don't trust Robert Hamilton. If he'd ... he'd *hurt* you, I was going to kill the little sod!'' She stepped back a pace, pulled a pistol out of her greatcoat pocket, and waved it in the air.

Jack was so shocked and surprised by her use of vulgar language and her brazen brandishing of a firearm, he laughed out loud. "Amanda! Do you even know what a 'sod' is, sweetheart? But before you answer, give me that gun just in case it accidentally goes off.''

She shrugged and relinquished the pistol without argument. Jack laid it on the grass with the other weapon. "I don't know exactly what sod means, Jack,'' she admitted. "All I know is it's something quite despicable. Robert *is* a sod, isn't he, Jack?''

"And a coward into the bargain,'' Percy Mingay said, stepping forward. "Is anyone interested in hearing what Rob wrote in the note?''

"What note?'' exclaimed Amanda. "Didn't he show up?''

"No, and I don't expect any of us will ever see him again,'' Percy remarked with unfeigned satisfaction. "The note reads, 'Got an offer I couldn't refuse. Crossing the channel at four-thirty. Won't be back. Sorry for the inconvenience, Percy. Rob.' ''

"An offer he couldn't refuse?'' Jack repeated, frowning and turning to face Julian. "That's odd. . . . Do you think someone threatened him? The moneylenders from the gaming hells, perhaps?''

"Why would they try to force him out of the country, Jack, if he still owed them money?" Amanda wondered.

"You can't get blood out of a turnip, Miss Darlington," Julian observed coolly.

"Who knows what happened to him, and who cares?" said Percy, tossing the note over his shoulder. "He has more enemies than I do! He's gone, that's all. And good riddance, I say. Only wish he'd let me know his plans last night. I could have slept to my usual hour this morning instead of rising with the bloody chickens."

"Watch your language around my fiancée, Percy," Jack growled.

Percy raised his brows. "Sorry. Forgot she was female in those clothes and . . . er . . . with her colorful vocabulary and all. Apologize sincerely," he added for good measure. He bowed low, then turned to go, apparently eager to flee before he found himself replacing Rob as Jack's duelling opponent.

"Send the doctor away," Julian called after Percy as he strode away through the diminishing fog, then muttered, *"Rattle."*

Jack turned back to Amanda and slipped his arms around her waist. "And a blind rattle at that. I don't know how he could ever forget *you're* female, Amanda," Jack said, eying her slim thighs and deliciously rounded derriere encased in tight buckskin breeches. "Especially in those togs. Makes me want to—"

"Good *Gawd,*" Julian interrupted, managing to look bored and offended at the same time. "I have no desire to see the two of you coo and kiss. What you do in private is your concern, but please spare me from being privy to your 'sweet nothings.' Take her home in the carriage, Jack. I'll ride the horse. You don't want anyone to see her dressed like that. If she's to be your wife, you might want to maintain a *modicum* of respectability."

Jack grinned. "You're right brother, as you so frequently are. I envy you your wisdom and perspicacity ... not to mention your splendid sense of style. In fact, I'd say you were the luckiest man alive if"—he stopped abruptly and turned back to Amanda, his grin softening to a tender smile—"if I didn't already hold that distinction. Even with all my faults, *I'm* the luckiest man alive."

Jack looked into Amanda's beautiful blue eyes. They glowed with love. Long moments passed while they basked in the warmth of their hard-won happiness.

"Don't you agree, Julian?" Jack asked at last, turning for his brother's corroboration. But Julian had vanished.

"He moves like a cat," Jack said with grudging respect. "And he has impeccable timing."

Amanda smiled impishly and blushed. "Your timing's not so bad, either."

"You minx," he murmured, growing painfully aroused. "Just wait till I get you alone."

He bent to kiss her, but she pressed her fingertips against his lips and drew back. "Aren't you forgetting something, Jack?"

He raised a brow. "My memory *has* had some recent lapses," he admitted slyly. "What am I forgetting now, Amanda?"

She toyed with his neck cloth, stroking the smooth linen with absentminded sensuality. "I haven't yet received a proper proposal of marriage from you, Lord Durham," she told him coyly. "That being the case, all this cooing and kissing—as Lord Serling so aptly phrased it—is quite improper."

Jack grabbed her hips and pulled her flush against him. Her playfulness and the look of her in breeches was making him as randy as a rooster. But he loved her ... oh so much! And he'd give her exactly what she wanted ... which was exactly what he wanted, too.

"Amanda, darling, will you marry me? Will you stay with me and love me even when I'm toothless and gray, when I repeat myself constantly and forget where I've put my slippers even when they're on my feet?"

Amanda looped her arms around his neck and stared up into Jack's mesmerizing amber-brown eyes. "Yes, I'll marry you," she said with quiet intensity and a dazzling smile. "And, yes, I'll stay with you and love you even when you're a decrepit old man. But promise me something, Jack—"

"Anything, Amanda."

"Promise me that no matter what else you forget"—she paused, pouted, and poked him in the chest with her finger to underscore each word—"never"—poke—"forget"—poke—"you love me!" Poke, poke, poke.

He threw back his head and laughed; then he sobered fast and dipped his head till their lips were nearly touching. He looked into her eyes and said, "That's an easy promise to make and keep, Amanda, darling, because you are my love"—he kissed her forehead—"my life"—he kissed the tip of her nose—"and you are quite simply ... *unforgettable*."

His breath spilled warm against her lips, and Amanda's eyes fluttered shut in anticipation. They kissed, forgetting everything and everyone but each other.

Riding past on Amanda's horse, Julian saw the happy couple embracing. He smiled. He was glad for Jack, but he envied him, too. How would it be to find true love?

He leaned back in the saddle and considered pretty, auburn-haired Charlotte Batsford. So serene, so controlled, so well-educated. Was it possible to stir up that sweet girl's passions like Jack had stirred up Amanda's? Could he make himself fall in love with her ... and she with him ... or did true love just ... *happen?*

It was an interesting thought, deserving of much rumination. But in the meantime, Julian had a far more pressing challenge at hand. Sam, that hoydenish, kittenish, noisy, and charmingly mobcapped child must be made into a silk purse by spring. He'd turn her into a diamond of the first water if it killed him, then foist the little brat onto some unsuspecting man blinded by her glitter.

Oh course, he'd make sure the man was kind to her and loving. He wouldn't want her to be unhappy. But even so, thought Julian with a rueful grin, he pitied—and halfway envied—the man who got himself shackled to Sam. The poor devil would certainly never be *bored*, now, would he?